The

UNDERTAKER'S
ASSISTANT

Books by Amanda Skenandore

BETWEEN EARTH AND SKY

THE UNDERTAKER'S ASSISTANT

THE SECOND LIFE OF MIRIELLE WEST

THE NURSE'S SECRET

Published by Kensington Publishing Corp.

The

UNDERTAKER'S ASSISTANT

AMANDA SKENANDORE

KENSINGTON
PUBLISHING CORP.

www.kensingtonbooks.com

*For my beloved sisters
Jennifer and Kasandra*

CHAPTER 1

1875

Geo. whitmark, undertaker, read the weather-bleached shingle above the door. Below, in ragged knife-carved lettering: scalawag.

Effie shuddered, but knocked nonetheless. No answer. She turned the knob. Locked. A crack snaked across the storefront window. She wiped the dusty glass with her hankie and peered inside. An hour past noon and already the interior lamps were dampened. Several caskets stood on display in the shadows. Older models, bare of adornment.

A few paces beyond the front entry, she found the gate to the carriageway ajar and slipped inside. It led to a back courtyard and outbuildings. She ducked beneath a limp, green-tinged clothesline and laid down her luggage. "Colonel Whitmark?"

A rustling sounded from the residence above the shop and she called out again.

"Put the delivery in the storeroom and be gone with you," a voice hollered from the upstairs gallery.

"I've not come with a delivery, I . . ." She stepped beyond the canopy of an overgrown fig tree and looked up. A man with an untrimmed mustache and bloodshot eyes leaned over the balustrade. "Colonel Whitmark?"

"Who are you?"

"Euphemia Jones, sir. I've come to offer my services as—"

"No, thank you. I'm not looking for a maid."

Effie pursed her lips. The dirt-crusted pavers, untamed garden, and grimy windows spoke otherwise. "I'm not a maid. I—"

"How'd you get in?"

"The gate was open, sir. I believe you were waiting for a delivery."

"Was I?" He shook his head and swilled from a brown bottle. "Close it on your way out, won't you?" He pushed off from the balustrade and stumbled backward out of sight.

Effie glanced down the shadowy carriageway. She'd come directly from the steamboat, fighting the tide of buggies and wagons, her trunk and embalming cabinet in tow. Would that she might find work elsewhere. But who else in New Orleans would hire her—a Yankee, a woman, a Negro? The thin stash of bills hidden in her petticoat pocket couldn't buy a steamboat ticket back to Indiana. Not that she'd return. Not for all the bank notes in the South.

"I believe"—she hesitated, hating to mention the connection—"you knew my former employer. During the War. Captain Kinyon."

The clatter above went silent. "Kinyon did you say?" More silence. "John Kinyon, of Indiana?"

"Yes, sir. I worked as his assistant going on nine years."

He peeked his head back over the balustrade, looked at her, and chuckled. "By assistant you mean maid?"

Effie slipped a hand into her skirt pocket and clenched the cool brass button tucked within. "No, sir. As an embalmer. I even mix my own preserving fluid, and to far better effect than that premade slop you have stacked in your storeroom."

"Ha! And that there's an alligator." He jutted his chin in the direction of a small green lizard scurrying up the stucco outbuilding.

"No, sir. That's a lizard. *Anolis carolinensis,* I believe."

"It's an expression, Miss . . ."

"Jones."

"It means . . . never mind." He took another swig from his bottle. Even from a dozen feet below, Effie smelled the sharp fumes. "What makes you think I'm in need of an assistant any more than I am a maid?"

She squeezed the button again, then let it roll back into the corner of her pocket. "Colonel Whitmark—"

"No one calls me colonel anymore," he said, an edge rising in his voice. "It's Mister. Or better yet, nothing at all."

A cold breeze stirred the air, agitating the leaves. Effie glanced at her battered trunk. Thirteen hundred and fifty miles she'd traveled, and for what? To be turned out like a beggar?

"Col—Mr. Whitmark, your showpieces are outmoded and dusty. Your desk is cluttered with invoices. You've got feathers and crepe heaped about as if you run a junk shop, not a funerary establishment— and that's just what I could see through the front window." She stamped across the courtyard and flung wide the storeroom door. An acrid smell stung her nose. "These empty fluid jars are in sore need of rinsing. As are your instruments, which you haven't bothered to pack away. And when was the last time you oiled the hinges of your cooling table or laundered the canopy?" She turned back to the gallery. "Whatever your objections to my employment, Mr. Whitmark, it's clear you're in want of an assistant."

The colonel's lips flattened and his nostrils flared, but Effie paid no mind. She'd not leave without saying her peace. "If it's my sex that offends, I can assure you my skill with the syringe matches that of any man. If it's my color, I can only wonder to what end you fought if not the freedom and advancement of my kind."

For a long while, he was silent. Across the street, a shoe-shiner hollered out to customers. A cat mewled from a nearby yard. Unlatched shutters knocked about in the breeze. When at last Mr. Whitmark spoke, his voice was flat, tired. "I fought for the preservation of the Union, Miss Jones. Nothing more, nothing less."

"I see." She held his gaze until he looked away and gulped again from his bottle. With a slow step, she crossed the courtyard, tucked her embalming cabinet beneath her arm, and reached for her trunk.

"John really taught you how to elevate an artery and inject preserving fluid?"

Effie turned. "I can embalm any body you lay before me, Mr. Whitmark. Start to finish."

His gray eyes glinted. "This I have a mind to see."

Winter's chill followed them from the shop to the morgue. Inside, overhead kerosene lamps cast a fickle glow on the rows of bodies laid out for recognition. Wooden blocks were wedged beneath their necks, keeping their faces upturned and visible. Their death-day shirts and hats and petticoats hung limp from nearby hooks.

Despite the dank air, Effie removed her coat. Neither Colonel Whitmark nor the bespectacled coroner offered to take it for her. Foolish to expect such consideration coming South. She hung her coat apart from the others on a rusty nail jutting from the plaster wall and followed the men across the morgue. They stopped before a body at the far end. Its purple-tinged arm lolled over the edge of the examination table. A grimy sheet covered its bulbous legs.

"Have you an apron?" she asked.

The coroner gaped a moment, then fetched her a balled-up wad of checkered linen. Stained, but seemingly laundered. Effie flapped open the apron, sending a whiplike snap echoing through the room. Gooseflesh prickled her skin. But surely, that was just the cold.

She tied the apron around her waist and rolled up her dress sleeves. A sweet, fetid odor rose from the body, overwhelming the burning kerosene and stench of corn juice bleeding from Colonel Whitmark's pores.

Not Colonel. Mister.

His bloodshot eyes followed her, steady, even as his body swayed. Undoubtedly, he was waiting for her to faint or fall into hysterics. Then he might dismiss her and return home to his bottle.

Such scrutiny seldom bothered her. She'd spent enough time in bedrooms and parlors crowded with the living—bereft widows, curious children, nosey in-laws—that ignoring them was second nature. Once they realized she didn't mean to slice open the body but only make a tiny cut to lift the artery, they'd leave her in peace. But *Mr.* Whitmark remained intent. Hands twitching. Watching. Waiting.

She plucked a few strands of slimy foliage from the body's auburn hair and probed the skin. Two days dead, maybe more depending on the temperature of the water. "He drowned."

It was not a question, but both Mr. Whitmark and the coroner nodded.

"Did you drain the water from the lungs and stomach?" she asked.

"*Bien sûr,*" the coroner said. "Of course."

Taking care to keep the head elevated, she turned the body on its side and pressed her knee just below the sternum. Dark water bubbled from its lips onto the cracked tile floor, splattering her boots and the hem of her skirt.

Mr. Whitmark chuckled. "Looks like you missed some, Lafitte."

She pulled over a rickety side table and wiped away the flecks of dried blood before opening her instrument case. A bulb syringe and long rubber tubing lay neatly coiled in the bed of the case beside a spool of silk thread. Her other tools—tweezers, scissors, trocar, needles, catheters, and scalpel—were fastened with elastic loops to the underside of the lid. The long journey had left the scissors and one of the catheters askew. She realigned them with the others, then withdrew the long metal trocar. "First, I'll tap the abdomen to draw off the gas. Then the injection. Four pints should be sufficient."

Mr. Whitmark's gray eyes narrowed. Hitherto he'd regarded her with that jovial indifference common to drunkards, as if she were merely an amusing, though somewhat tedious, apparition.

"You do want that I should continue?" she asked.

He ran an unsteady hand over his flushed cheeks, whiskers rasping against his palm. "I'll get the jars of fluid from the wagon."

He shambled off and the coroner with him, leaving her at last alone to work.

She found a pail of clean water and a few strips of linen on a cluttered workbench nearby. Her hands trembled as she dunked the linen and wrung it out. Careful not to damage the fragile, discolored skin, she set about wiping the mud from the body. Soon her hands steadied. This was what she was good at—her work among the dead.

She lit another lamp for better light and pierced the body's bloated abdomen, just above the navel. Gas whistled through the trocar and the body began to deflate. Effie didn't flinch at the foul odor. Mr. Whitmark returned with the embalming fluid, setting the jars beside her before slumping onto a stool in the corner. She did her best to ignore him, even as he began to snore.

Her hands worked almost by rote, her mind drifting from the mechanics of the task, from the well-known map of arteries and organs beneath the skin, to the man dead before her.

Had he jumped into the river, well aware of the swift tides and swirling eddies beneath the water's surface? Had he slipped or fallen? Had someone pushed him in and watched as he drowned?

Surely he had a wife at home wondering at his absence. A mother or uncle or cousin awaiting his return. Yet here he lay, unclaimed.

Perhaps he too was alone. An orphan, a vagabond. Nameless and faceless in this overcrowded city. She drew her scalpel over the neck, revealing the carotid artery, and readied her catheter and syringe pump. Better that way, alone. No one to mourn you in death meant no one to hurt you in life.

After completing the injection and soaking the skin with embalming fluid–saturated rags, the body's purple hue had all but vanished. For a man two days' drowned, the corpse looked downright handsome.

Mr. Whitmark startled awake and staggered over when she announced that she was finished. He probed the body's now-hardened flesh. Sniffed the soap-scented air. Peered at her impeccable sutures. Effie waited, shoulders back, chin high, fingers clasped around her brass button.

"I'd be mad as a March hare to take on a carpetbagger Negress as my assistant," Mr. Whitmark said, shaking his head. He poked a few more times at the body, then glanced at her. The set of his stubbled jaw softened. "Come by the shop tomorrow."

CHAPTER 2

———◆———

Dusk had just begun to settle on the city when Effie reached the shop. The smell of roasting duck perfumed the cool air. Firecrackers popped in the distance, and tin whistles crooned from the streets. In Indiana, Christmas Eve had been a staider affair. The festivities here in New Orleans, chief among them the noise, unnerved her.

In the three weeks since Mr. Whitmark had hired her on, she'd come to know the American Sector well. Newspaper Row on Camp Street. The Cotton District, still fledgling after the War and recent recession. The tiny Chinatown to the northwest, just beyond the commercial bustle.

Immigrants crowded around the business district—Irishmen, Germans, Italians—living in rundown cottages or subdivided town-homes once occupied by Americans who'd since fled to the subur-ban reaches of the city. Her kind, the freedmen, lived back-of-town, where the city petered out to swampland.

The French Quarter was different. Creoles of every color lived side by side. But Mr. Whitmark had few clients in that part of the city, and Effie had ventured past Canal Street only once to procure embalming chemicals from a pharmacist there.

Work had been inconstant, a dribble of clients some days, none others. The first body they'd been called to, Mr. Whitmark embalmed entirely himself, lecturing her as he worked, as if she'd never seen a syringe pump or mixed a quart of preservative. His technique was solid, if a bit outdated, but his execution sloppy. He cut too large an incision, and his sutures ran uneven. His hand tottered as he worked. No doubt from the liquor.

The next call—a man dead of apoplexy—began the same. Mr. Whitmark bid her stand aside and watch as he demonstrated how to puncture the heart. He'd been called away by the family before retrieving his trocar from the case, though. When he returned, Effie had already drained the right ventricle, injected fluid into the cavity, and cannulated the brachial artery. Thereafter, he'd left the embalming to her.

Days when they hadn't a case, he didn't wake till noon and retired before the bells of nearby St. Patrick's tolled six. Sooner if he found his bottle empty. While he slept, she dusted and polished and swept. She oiled the squeaky hinges about the shop, organized the storeroom, and righted his account books. She repainted the sign and sanded away the word *Scalawag.* She sent for new catalogs from the casket makers. After airing out the wrinkled, moth-eaten skirts from the storeroom, she fastened them around the showpieces in the shop so they didn't look so naked through the newly scrubbed windows.

If Mr. Whitmark noticed these things, he didn't say. But he paid her a dollar at the end of each day and said she might as well come back tomorrow. A man of her skill would earn more than twice that sum. Yet with her position so tenuous, she dared not squabble. Besides, it was more than she'd ever made. Captain Kinyon hadn't paid her at all. Theirs was a family business. At the time, Effie hadn't minded. It allowed her the delusion she was more to the captain than an apprentice or assistant.

Now, with the overgrown foliage and high courtyard walls buffering the Christmas Eve din, she laid down her equipment, shook out her weary arms, and set about cleaning. She scrubbed and polished her tools. Flushed the rubber tubing. Plunged her smock and the dirtied floor sheet into the washbasin.

Christmas carols sounded from an open window a few buildings down, the accompanying piano slightly out of tune. The carolers seemed not to mind and sang on gaily, punctuating each song with laughter and applause. She raked the fabric over the washboard until her fingers were numb and every stain vanished, then cranked it through the ringer and draped it over the line.

"That you, Effie?" Mr. Whitmark appeared on the gallery dressed in only his shirtsleeves and wrinkled trousers. "It's Christmas Eve. What are you still doing here?"

She frowned. Wasn't that obvious? "I'm attending to the supplies."

He shambled down the stairs. "This can wait. Go home. Celebrate."

Home seemed too sentimental an appellation for the boardinghouse where she lodged. The roof was sound, the floorboards solid, the bed free of fleas, and the food palatable. She wasn't in want of much else. Certainly not celebration.

She heaved the sudsy water into the gutter flowing to the street. "I'm nearly done."

"If you insist on finishing up, at least have a drink with me." Mr. Whitmark shuffled to the kitchen and rummaged through the cupboards.

"I don't drink," she called, but he paid her no mind, returning with a bottle of brandy and tin cup.

He handed her the cup, filled it halfway, then clanked it against the bottle in a toast. "Merry Christmas, Effie."

She took a cautious sip. It tasted like horse piss—or what she imagined horse piss to taste like—and she spat it out onto the stone pavers.

Mr. Whitmark laughed and drank a long swill. "I gather John and the missus didn't drink."

"Teetotalers," she said. Never mind the whiskey the captain kept tucked away in his study.

"That doesn't surprise me."

A firecracker popped from a neighboring courtyard. Mr. Whitmark flinched. "Blasted toys."

"The captain hated them too."

"You called him that? Captain? " He plopped into a creaky rocker. "Even as his ward?"

Effie paused, then set to packing up the instruments she'd laid out to dry. "What else should I have called him?"

"I don't know . . . papa, father. You were just a girl, weren't you, when he took you in?"

Effie didn't know how old she'd been. Seven? Eight? Too young to remember much of what came before. And though he'd been the closest thing to a father she'd known, he'd never said she might call him papa. "I called him sir sometimes."

Whitmark chuckled again. "He was a bit of a fussy fellow. So serious all the time. What'd he do to send you running?"

Her stomach clenched. "Nothing, I—"

"Most Negroes with any money and a lick of sense are pulling up stakes these days and heading North."

"I just . . ." She took another sip of brandy, regretting it the moment the rancid liquor hit her tongue. "Wanted to see the land where I was born."

More than that, she'd wanted to find a place where she could blend in. Disappear. Belong. Where people, well-meaning or not, wouldn't regard her as a specimen.

But Mr. Whitmark seemed satisfied with her answer, for he leaned back in his chair and nodded. The wicker groaned beneath his weight, as if it had been decades since someone had last sat and rocked in it. "This is where he found you?"

"Nearby, I believe."

"What of your own folk?"

Effie looked down at the amber liquid in her cup. She hadn't any folk, any kin, any true family. None she could name or remember. "I haven't much recollection before the War, sir."

"Don't you go calling me sir now too." He took another drink from his bottle and stood, swaying a moment before finding his balance. "I have something for you." He fished in his trouser pocket and tossed her a small paperboard box. "Merry Christmas."

Effie held the box in her palm and examined it. It was light, almost weightless. One corner mashed and rounded, the string tying it shut fashioned in a sloppy bow. She glanced back at him. His hooded eyes glinted with a kindness she'd hitherto overlooked. "I . . . thank you."

He flapped a hand, his cheeks flushing beyond their usual ruddiness. "It's only a trifle."

She set aside her cup and untied the bow. Inside was a large brass button with an embossed eagle in the center. In one talon, it clutched three sharpened arrows. In the other, an olive branch.

"I've seen the other buttons you keep tucked in your pocket and thought . . . well, you might like this one too."

"You didn't take this from your uniform, did you?"

"Ain't doing nothing but gathering dust. Hell, I was surprised I still had the damn thing."

Effie turned the button over in her hand. Angled it toward the light. The years had tarnished it some, but otherwise it was unblemished. She closed her fingers around it and cradled it in her palm. "It's beautiful."

"Like I said, it's nothing to me now." He drained half of the remaining brandy in his bottle with one guzzle.

She winced, recalling all the bloated, jaundiced bodies she'd attended over the years. "You ought to read Dr. Benner's report on diseases of the liver. He contends that hot climates and excessive consumption of spirits are chief among—"

"I know what causes cirrhosis, Effie."

"Then why do you drink so much?"

He sighed and smiled at her. "We all do things that aren't in our best interest."

"That's illogical."

"Maybe, but it's the only damned thing that separates us from the rest of the beasts of the world."

She frowned. "Mr. Darwin has posited we differ from animals in ways of degree not kind. In—"

Mr. Whitmark threw up his arms, the remaining liquor sloshing against the sides of his bottle. "I yield, I yield! Off with you. Surely you've better things to do on your Christmas Eve than debate naturalism with a surly old man like me."

To the contrary, she quite liked the topic and hadn't anyplace more pressing to be. But she ventured not to say so. She stowed the button back in its box, closed the latches on her embalming cabinet, and grabbed her coat from the storeroom. "Day after tomorrow, then?"

He nodded. "You're an odd fish, Miss Jones, but a damn fine worker. Whatever your reasons for coming here, John was a fool to let you go."

"Merry Christmas," she said, glad he didn't pry further. "Happy tidings to you and . . ." *Yours,* so went the saying. But he hadn't a wife or children or family of any kind, as best she could tell.

"Same to you."

She left through the carriageway and rambled down Carondelet

Street in the opposite direction of her boardinghouse. The carolers from down the way had ceased their crooning, but an occasional peel of laughter still rang from the window. A group of young boys blaring their horns and whistles dashed past.

An odd fish. Would she ever escape such a stigma? Life had laid the course. She simply followed and made the best of it. In the War years, helping in Captain Kinyon's surgery tent had saved her from the cotton fields and contraband camps. Her deft little fingers and quick step proved useful to a man already middle-aged and suffering from rheumatism. That, and she didn't recoil at the sight of blood. Only natural that when he took her North with him after the War she'd continued as his assistant, even as he traded his surgeon's saw for an embalmer's syringe.

Perhaps she was odd. But at least she had another day's promise of work.

Most of the shops and businesses had closed early. Garlands of holly and evergreen decorated their darkened windows. The smell of baking bread and turtle soup set to simmer until after midnight mass made her stomach grumble, but she had little desire to turn around. The other lodgers at her boardinghouse—all maids in the big houses that lined St. Charles Street—would undoubtedly be in, chewing over the trivialities of their days.

Her housemates' incessant conversation baffled Effie as much as the Christmas noise. As with most things, the Kinyons had been sparing with their words, leaving her unschooled in the art of chatter. The dead afforded no practice either.

She wandered down Gravier Street toward the river. Carriages rolled past at frequent intervals, and small groups of revelers loped along the sidewalks. No, not sidewalks. Banquettes, they called them here. Ahead in the distance a train whistle blared. She walked, and daylight retreated. Fewer people passed by. The air turned smoky from the bonfires alight on the levee, welcoming Père Noël.

Effie relished this sliver of time, when night had wrestled all but a few smudges of light from the sky, when families were home around their supper tables and street urchins had returned to their dens, when no one yet thought to don their opera coat or leave the saloon. When the streets were entirely hers. She enjoyed the rhythmic clack of her boot heels upon the pavers, the cool air in her lungs, the scent of honeysuckle or wintersweet wafting from courtyards. In Indiana, spring alone hoarded such pleasures.

She turned up Common Street to wend her way to the boarding-house. This part of the city was unfamiliar to her. The lamplight-ers had yet to make their pass, leaving her to navigate by the pallid moonlight. Some ways on, a narrow, two-story building flanked by a high brick wall caught her eye. Her feet faltered. The air no longer smelled of honeysuckle or smoke, but of dust and excrement. Her heart sped until she felt it like a paddle wheel against her breastbone. Curiosity propelled her from the banquette and across the street toward the building, even as her muscles tensed in protest.

A cry rang out from behind the tall wall, high-pitched and plain-tive. Had a woman made that noise? It came again and Effie nearly retched. She stumbled forward and braced herself against the wall. The rough brick with its crumbling mortar felt . . . familiar. Not fa-miliar in the abstract. These bricks and this smell and that frightful sound—she'd been here before. A dark, crowded enclosure flashed in her mind. A short, bone-thin finger following the lines of mortar as if it were a maze. She felt the sensation of sweat trickling along her hairline, but when she brought her hand to her forehead it was cool and dry. The stench of human shit and . . . frying bacon filled her nose. A new sound came—grunting—and when she closed her eyes shadowy figures shambled across the black backdrop of her lids.

She pulled her hand away from the brick and tried to steady her breath. A few yards down the wall gave way to a short stretch of rotting picket fence, offering her a glimpse into what lay behind the high wall.

Effie stepped forward, rallied her courage, and took another step. The grunts and squeals grew louder. A shiver pricked its way across her skin. Ghosts didn't exist. She'd sat with death enough to know. But as she neared the opening and peeked into the blackness, cer-tainty abandoned her.

The smell rose even stronger here and again her stomach heaved. Shapes took form in the darkness. She shuffled back from the pen and blinked.

Pigs.

Only pigs.

Effie forced a laugh and turned back the way she'd come, her quick step and clammy palms betraying the calm she strived to muster. Ghosts, monsters—how foolish! She pulled her coat tightly closed and headed home, keeping to well-lit and familiar streets.

Her heart had not yet stilled by the time she reached the board-inghouse. She hesitated a moment on the porch, leaning against one of the colonnades and drawing in a succession of slow breaths. A residue of terror remained in her bones.

Ridiculous, she told herself. Irrational. What harm could there possibly be in a dirty old pig yard? She pinned back her shoulders and went inside.

A cacophony of chatter and music and clanking glassware struck her upon entry. Roasting mirlitons perfumed the air, but Effie didn't trust her stomach. She tiptoed past the parlor, where the other boarders had gathered. One woman—Effie couldn't remember her name, only that her voice had the shrill quality of a parrot—sat before the rickety piano plucking out the melody line of a Christmas hymn. The others sang along, giggling when they missed a note or forgot the words.

Effie shimmied around the loose floorboard at the base of the stairs and skipped over the creaky third step. She'd almost made it to the landing when she heard her name. She winced and turned around.

Another boarder, Meg, stood grinning at the base of the stairs. "Come join us. Mrs. Neale's done cooked up some eggnog."

When Effie had first arrived at the house, the landlady, Mrs. Neale, bid Meg show Effie around. Meg took hostage her arm and—before they'd even made it out of the foyer—had told Effie her name, Margaret Louise Talbot; that she'd grown up in Livingston Parish; that she worked for the Clarksons down on Fourth Street; and that her favorite color was blue . . . or maybe purple. By that point, Effie had stopped listening.

"No," Effie said now, and then as an afterthought, "thank you."

"You don't have to drink no eggnog. Just come sing with us. We's—"

"I don't sing."

"You ain't need to have a perdy voice." She glanced over her shoulder, then whispered, "Maybelle sho don't."

"No, I don't partake in singing."

Meg gave a confused look and patted down her fluffy bangs. "Oh . . . Well, we's heading to midnight mass later if you wanna come."

"I'm not a Catholic."

"Oh . . ."

Effie turned and finished up the stairs. To think, only hours before she'd pitied Mr. Whitmark his solitude.

"Happy Christmas Eve!" Meg called after her.

She hesitated on the landing but did not turn around. "Good night."

CHAPTER 3

Gray clouds muted the afternoon sun. Winter's chill hung in the air. Talk about town was of tomorrow's Twelfth Night parade and ball. Effie had made the mistake of asking Meg about this peculiar celebration and suffered a quarter hour's explanation that meandered from the feast of the Epiphany to something about a golden bean and the beginning of Carnival. Had she not cut Meg off mid-sentence and walked away, Effie suspected she'd still be trapped in the parlor listening to an endless history of every krewe in the city.

Now, she hurried toward the business district. She'd not had a day off in well over a week, and her list of errands was tiresomely long. While others had filled the Christmas and New Year's holidays with social calls and parties, Effie had traipsed from one end of the city to the other with her cooling table and embalming tools.

Death knows no respite, Captain Kinyon had said to her some years back in Indiana, and she found the same to be true here in the South. Lockjaw, consumption, childbed fever, grippe—so many cases they blurred together in her mind. More lasting were the sideways stares and all-too-audible whispers: Negress assistant, darkie, wench. Not that she hadn't heard those words in Indiana; not that she wasn't—what had Mr. Whitmark called her?—an odd fish there too. Another reason she preferred the dead: their silence.

Still, she was grateful for the uptick in business. She crossed the street and cut through Tivoli Circle. Despite the gray day and cold breeze off the river, the circle teemed with people. Effie navigated around them—the Italians tossing their weighted balls across the lawn, the toothless Creole woman peddling toadflax and pansies, the children trundling their hoops—and decided it best to avoid the circle in the future. Near the St. Charles Avenue exit the movement of the crowd slowed and eddied. Effie shimmied and shouldered through until a voice, low and resonate, snagged in her ear. She stopped. The voice rose above the din of the crowd like music, and though she couldn't make out the exact words, the timbre and cadence seemed to vibrate inside her, stirring some memory just beyond her reach. She pushed in toward the sound.

"Republican rubbish," an older white man said, shoving past her toward St. Charles. Two women, shielding their fair skin with parasols despite the sunless day, looked toward the center of the crowd with puckered expressions and shuffled away. Everyone else, however, stood transfixed. Most of those gathered were Negroes, and of those, most were men. They nodded their heads and murmured the occasional "yes, sir" and "don't the good Lord know it." Over their slouch hats and derbies, Effie caught glimpses of the speaker—a black man in his shirtsleeves and a brocade vest, standing on a low platform. She caught snatches of his words now too: progress, equality, opportunity.

Effie squeezed in closer until she could fully hear.

"Our brothers in Mississippi have already lost those rights promised them in the fourteenth and fifteenth amendments to our great Constitution, rights we paid for with our blood. Blood drawn first with the lash and then the sword, as our Great Emancipator said."

His voice crescendoed and tapered like a well-written score, each word perfectly articulated, each pause allowing the weight of what he'd said to settle.

Effie had never cared overmuch for politics. Moving to New Orleans had not changed that. Her clients whispered and stared. Men who doffed their hats for white women brushed past her without thought on the streets. The steamboat she'd arrived on permitted coloreds to dine only after all the white folk had been served. Effie noticed these slights, recognized the injustice, but then, as she'd always done, tucked such notions away and focused on her work. Embalming took patience and care and attention to detail that left little room for thoughts as frivolous as politics.

Now, however, she stood inexplicably mired. The liveliness in the man's voice, his conviction, his passion made her lean in and nod along with the others. A young boy came up beside her and thrust a handbill into her palm. He smiled, revealing a checkerboard of missing teeth, and moved on to the next bystander. Effie looked down at the flyer.

Ward Two Republicans Club

Weekly Meetings Tuesdays 7 p.m.,

1010 Constance Street

All Welcome

"Wait," she called after the boy. "I don't want this." But he continued through the crowd, hoisting his flyer into unexpecting hands, and didn't look back.

The man's voice reclaimed her attention. He was speaking now of public accommodations, the right of any man to a seat at the theater, or racetrack, or restaurant, or—should he be thirsty and wish to imbibe—a stool at the saloon. The crowd chuckled.

"Hear, hear," someone hollered. Another rapped his cane atop the walkway.

Effie caught herself smiling and quickly righted her expression. What was she doing here? Already she'd tarried too long. The shops would be closing soon, and she mightn't have the chance to come back for days. She'd whittled her soap down to a sliver and used the last of her shoe polish yesterday. She needed tooth powder, new stockings, a length of twine to—

The gentleman in front of her stepped aside to say something to his companion, and for the first time, the orator stood before Effie in clear view.

Years of embalming had well acquainted her with variations of the human form—fat, thin, aged, youthful, muscled, wasted, crooked, straight. But she'd never seen a more perfect example, living or dead, than this man. His confident air suggested a man in his forties, but his dark, luminous skin—free as yet of lines or furrows—hinted at one much younger. Thirty perhaps, or younger still. He moved with graceful purpose as he spoke, turning to address each segment of the crowd, raising an arm, brandishing a loosely closed fist. His words no longer registered. It was the gentle slope of his wide-set shoulders that claimed her attention now, the outline of his deltoid and bicep muscles beneath his cotton shirt.

The bells of St. Patrick's tolled the hour, startling Effie back to her senses. The sun, no more than a smudge of white behind the clouds, lolled closer to the far horizon. The Italian men had finished their game and quit the circle. The bustling crowd had thinned from the banquettes.

What foolery to linger as she'd done, listening to this political babble when more pressing needs abounded. At this hour, she had little hope of finishing her errands before the shops closed. If she left now, she might at least make it to the apothecary and hosier.

Then the speaker turned and looked in Effie's direction. His heavily lashed eyes locked with hers. She forgot the soap and stockings and shoe polish. She forgot even to breathe. His earnest gaze penetrated her, singling her out as if she were the most enthralling person in the crowd. As if she were the only person in the crowd. His dark irises, the same glowing brown as his skin, held her there, affixed to the stone walkway as surely as iron nails.

"And you, miss? I see you are not blind to the ills of this fair city that so sorely try our souls. What issue would you bring forward for consideration?"

Effie glanced around her. Surely his question was meant for someone else. But no other women stood within a dozen paces of her. "Umm . . . er . . . the overcrowding of the cemeteries."

Several in the crowd snickered, but the man silenced them with a wave of his hand. "No, the lady's right." He paused, and for the first time during his stumping seemed to grope for something to say. "We've not done enough at the statehouse to address the unsanitary conditions of the city, it's true. And plots in the new cemetery in Metairie are a mighty high cost, such that the workingman is all but excluded. Yet another way they try to push the Negro and the immigrant out . . ."

He spoke on about injustices done the poor, the colored, the infirm. True enough, but not what Effie had meant. She really ought to attend to her errands, but she couldn't leave such a misunderstanding uncorrected.

"All must rise," he said now. "All must fight to ensure our collective advancement, to ensure that the rights granted us, not by man but by God Almighty, are realized by all."

Effie waited for him to pause long enough that she might interject and explain herself. But his words continued unbroken, and his gaze slipped away. Likely he didn't understand the gravity of the issue, for he said nothing more about the cemeteries. Effie tried to squeeze forward, to sidestep and shimmy through the horde. She made little progress. She stood on her tiptoes and waved her hand until those behind her complained they couldn't see.

If she could just correct the man on her point of overcrowding, then she could be gone and to her errands. But his stubborn eyes avoided her, sweeping the crowd, resting here and there, glancing in her general direction without settling upon her as they had before.

Sometime later—Effie couldn't tell if it had been ten minutes or fifty—applause sounded. The man stepped down from the banana box he'd used as a platform during his speech. Dozens of men circled around him, vying for a chance to shake his hand and offer their praise. Effie pressed in too, unladylike as it was, but found herself waiting just the same.

Slowly, the crowd dispersed. In its place, crept the cold. A few men yet tarried around the speaker, jabbering on about this or that. The young boy she'd seen earlier skipped about the circle, picking up abandoned handbills from the ground. He whistled as he went, the thin, shrill sound almost painful after listening to the man's richly toned voice. Her feet ached from standing so long on the hard stone, and her stomach grumbled for supper. She craned her neck to see St. Patrick's clock tower above the bald treetops. Already she regretted the afternoon's dalliance and knew she'd rue it even more tomorrow when she ran out of soap.

When she faced forward again, the man was standing right in front of her.

"You stumped me a moment," he said. The timbre of his voice was just as distracting up close, making molasses of her wits. Rosemary and perspiration wafted from his skin. "I thought for sure you'd say something about schooling or the recent spike in the cost of flour."

"You mistook my point," she managed at last.

"Oh?"

"What are we to do in an epidemic when we haven't enough plots and gravediggers? When yellow fever struck in fifty-three they resorted to dumping bodies in ditches only to have them wash up later when it rained."

He cocked his head and cleared this throat. "I . . . hadn't thought of that. A good point."

Effie bristled. He was just placating her now. "When you ask a woman her opinion, you shouldn't assume she'll make some dithering comment about domestic affairs."

"Indeed not, I see."

"And to your point about the unsanitary conditions of the city—"

He held up his hand and gave a tired smile. His teeth were large and white, nearly straight save for a narrow gap between his top incisors. "Come to our meeting and we can discuss the issue further then."

"What meeting?"

He nodded to the forgotten flyer in her hand.

"Oh . . . no. I'm not politically inclined."

"You seem rather so to me. And we could always use a spirited young woman like you."

"Why should I concern myself with politics? My vote doesn't count."

The man smiled again, one side of his lips pulling slightly higher than the other. "The enfranchisement of our race goes far beyond the ballot box. Consider the integration of schools, or right to purchase a first-class rail ticket."

"I could hardly afford a first-class ticket," she said. His easy answers combined with the distracting line of his mouth irked her further.

"That's another issue we fight for, fair wages."

Effie shook her head, as much to clear her addled mind as to dissent.

"Think on it," he said, nodding again to the flyer. And before she could say she most certainly would not think on it, he bowed and turned back toward his worn banana box.

A new group circled around him. The boy with his flyers. A stately woman perhaps twice Effie's age. A crutch-wielding man whose lower leg was missing. The orator's posture relaxed and he flashed them a smile more brilliant than any he'd shared with the audience. The woman offered him her hankie. He blotted his sweat-dappled forehead. The crippled man bent down with surprising agility and picked up the banana box. The young boy said something and they all laughed. Then the irksome man crouched down for the boy to clamber onto his shoulders.

Effie watched them leave, not turning from where she stood until the fading light and growing distance conspired to conceal them.

CHAPTER 4

Mrs. Neale called to her from the parlor before Effie could sneak past to her room.

"You home awfully late, Miss Effie."

The landlady sat in her usual chair beside the fireplace, her graying hair tied up in a silk scarf and a worn book of psalms open on her lap. The gas lamp on the far wall burned dimly and the fire had dwindled.

Effie squatted beside the hearth. She jostled the embers with the poker to bring down the ash, then added more coal. The lumps smoked and crackled. "I know."

"Third time this week you done missed curfew."

Effie started to speak, but the old woman flapped her hand. "I know, death don't follow no schedule. What was it this time?"

"Consumption."

Mrs. Neale shook her head and whispered a quick prayer. "How'd a girl like you get caught up in work like this anyhow?"

"The War," Effie said. "I was a runaway."

"They didn't toss you back into the fields?"

She shook her head.

Most of the officers had wanted to. What use was so small a child? But Captain Kinyon refused. She could still hear the rattling fervor in his voice. It was one of her earliest memories that didn't come in fits and snatches, and the only memory at all of the captain lit with such passion. "An army surgeon took me on. Brought me North with him after the War."

"What put him in mind to do that?" Her lips puckered. "A white man bringing a black girl North. Gracious me, you couldn't have been a day over ten."

"It was nothing like that." She stared into the gathering flames. "He'd had a daughter himself."

When they'd arrived North, Mrs. Kinyon had led her into the house and upstairs. "I expect Mr. Kinyon means for you to sleep here in Annabelle's room." She released Effie's hand but hesitated before opening the door. Stale, musty air rushed out.

Effie stepped into the room, but Mrs. Kinyon tarried at the threshold, as if a hex prevented her entry. "I'll heat some water for your bath."

For several moments, Effie stood in the center of the room, afraid to touch anything. A bed with a blue and red checkered quilt sat at one end. Beside it, a dresser and matching washstand. A wicker bottom chair. She set down her knapsack and unrolled her blanket along the opposite wall. Cobwebs fluttered in the corners. Two moths lay dead on the windowsill. She unpacked her spare shift and box of buttons, setting them neatly alongside her bedroll.

"Don't just throw your things on the floor like that, Euphemia," Mrs. Kinyon said when she returned.

"Where shall I sleep, ma'am?"

"In the bed, of course."

"But where will Miss Annabelle sleep?"

Mrs. Kinyon winced. "Our daughter is dead, Euphemia."

Effie blinked and looked away from the mesmerizing coals. "They were reformers, the surgeon and his wife," she said to Mrs. Neale. "Abolitionist before the War."

"Thought to make you their little charity case, then?"

"No, I was their . . ." Ward, that was what Mrs. Kinyon had said. A word Effie had to look up in the captain's leather-bound dictionary. *A minor or person under the care of a guardian.* Ward, not daughter. Guardian, not parent. How had Effie ever confused the two? "I was the captain's assistant."

"Hmm." Mrs. Neale's eyes narrowed a moment before softening. "Well, leastwise you back South and home now." She glanced at the mantel clock. "Suppose I can make an exception for you now and again with this curfew business. You've enough wit not to get into any trouble. Don't be lettin' on to any of the other ladies, you hear?"

"Yes, ma'am." Effie set the poker back in its stand and stood. Her thighs ached from crouching so long beside the fire. "Shall I read to you some?"

"Nah, you head along. I'm about set for bed myself. There's a plate of food for you in the kitchen."

The stove fire had burned to ash, but the small kitchen was yet warm. Effie poured herself a glass of buttermilk and uncovered the hoecakes, greens, and boiled ham Mrs. Neale had left out for her. All day she'd kept a tight rein on her thoughts, distracting herself with whatever busywork she could find. That morning while working her syringe pump, she mentally conjugated every Latin verb she knew. Later, she balanced the shop's account book, even though she'd double-checked the numbers the day before.

Now, as she nibbled at the cold food, her defenses slackened. She tried to focus on the silky texture of the greens, the way the buttermilk coated her tongue, but in a matter of bites, she was back standing in Tivoli Circle. The lingering smell of fried hoecakes and ham gave way to that of dried grass and horse manure. Din filled the silence and above the din, his voice.

Sometimes, it was just the raw quality of his rich, resonant baritone. Sometimes, like tonight, her mind replayed specific words and phrases. *Though the long night of slavery has ended, our work toward equality has just begun,* he'd said, in that Southern flavored way that reminded her just how far from Indiana she'd come.

The number of dialects in New Orleans was dizzying—the drawl of the Americans, the soft *h* and peppering of French common to the Creoles, the nasal brogue of the Irish, the backward *v*'s and *w*'s of the Germans, the *dems* and *dey* and *dis* of the freedmen. Effie had little patience for any of them. Conversation ought to be short and to the point. Cutting through someone's accent to decipher their meaning only belabored the exchange.

His way of speaking didn't bother her, though. His soft, drawn-out vowels, the errant *dem* or *jes* that crept back from his plantation days—all this only added to the songlike quality of his voice. It was more than that, though. The sound of it stirred something inside her.

She'd spoken that way once, hadn't she? But in those first few months after she'd escaped to the Union line, Captain Kinyon had righted her crooked speech the same way he reset a bone—sharp, quick, painful, but straight thereafter. What remnants of her former life, her life before the Great War, had been lost to the endeavor? She spoke like a damned Yankee now, and an uppity one at that—or so she heard daily from shopkeepers and streetcar drivers.

She ate another bite of ham and crumbled the last of her hoecake into the glass of buttermilk. How long had she stood there in Tivoli Circle and listened? An hour? Longer? Such a terrible waste. She'd only stayed to correct him on her point about the cemeteries. Not because of him. Certainly not because she gave a drat about politics.

Yet somehow, she couldn't scrub this dalliance from her mind. His words, his expressions, his fiery gestures. *All must rise, all must fight . . .*

Effie shook her head and stood, the legs of her chair scraping over the floor. What was wrong with her? She took her cup and plate to the dishpan and scrubbed until her fingers were numb. Every day had been like this—one wayward thought leading to another until five minutes, ten minutes, half an hour had been wasted.

He was clever, she had to give him that. The way he simultaneously acknowledged what she'd said and redirected it to some other point that served his purpose. Injustice, poverty, that silly club meeting. And he'd been kind to shush the crowd when they laughed at her remark about the cemeteries. It was that simple gesture, as much as his voice, that stirred her, recalling another time, another man, another kindness. Her true father perhaps? A brother? She pressed at the margins of her memory. Nothing.

Regardless of his wit and the small courtesy he'd paid her, this man from Tivoli Circle hadn't any right to harry her thoughts this way. She didn't need his vexing repartee. His crooked smile and beguiling voice.

Perhaps some sickness had infected her brain. She laid the back of her hand on her forehead. No fever. She probed beneath her jaw and down her neck. No swollen lymphatic glands. No headache, chills, or muscle pains. Subclinical, then. Prodromal. Tomorrow, she'd consult her textbooks. Tonight, she'd sleep and hope he didn't pester her in her dreams.

* * *

The next evening Effie made a point of returning before curfew only to realize as she mounted the steps to her room that it was Saturday and she needn't have bothered. Now she had an entire evening to whittle away alone with her thoughts. Her books could stand rearranging; her shoes polishing. She'd spied a copy of *The Louisianian* in the sitting room. If she read every word, including the advertisements and lottery schedule, she might enjoy an hour free from thoughts of him.

Meg and three other boarders flitted past her. They wore their Sunday dresses and a dusting of rouge across their cheeks. At the bottom of the stairs, their footfalls stalled. "No, don't ask her," one of them whispered. "She's a downright fuddy-duddy."

A few chirps of laughter sounded before Meg hushed them. "Effie, we's agoin' out. Wanna come?"

No readied on her lips. Whatever dancing or drinking or lollygagging they were getting up to, she wanted no part in. But then, mightn't an evening out prove more distracting than reading and polishing? She turned around. "Where are you going?"

Meg peeked over her shoulder into the parlor, where Mrs. Neale sat with her book of psalms. She climbed a few steps and whispered, "A séance."

"Séance?"

"Shh." Meg flapped her hand through the air, looking again to the parlor. The others shook their heads and snickered. "It's kinda like a party, only there's a medium who uses her powers to call up the dead."

"I know what a séance"—Effie lowered her voice after another flap of Meg's hand—"a séance is. I mean, why ever are you going to one?"

"For fun."

"There've been numerous scientific inquiries into—" Effie stopped. She'd happily pass the evening outlining all the ways extracorporeal communication and clairvoyance conflicted with the current scientific thinking. But judging from her already listless expression, Meg didn't care. And Effie needed distraction, however senseless. "I'll come."

Streetlamps lit their way downriver along St. Charles. Soon the old part of the city, with its dingy iron-railed balconies and moss-covered roofs, became visible beyond Canal Street.

"How far away is this place?" Effie asked, her feet going numb inside her too-small boots.

The leader of their little ensemble—Harriet, wasn't that her name?—stopped and turned. "Madame Desâmes does not leave the Quarter." Her shrill, parrotlike voice made Effie's arm hair stand on end.

"American spirits don't make good party guests?"

Effie marveled that she'd made a joke, but Harriet didn't laugh. Neither did the others. Meg flashed a smile, but flattened her lips when Harriet glanced her way.

They continued in silence until Meg asked, "How'd you meet Madame Desâmes?"

"Through a friend," Harriet said. She walked a step ahead of the others, her chin high, not bothering to look back as she spoke. "She hosts regular sittings for Madame Desâmes. Known her ever since Madame unhexed her sister."

A few of the women gasped.

"A witch planted a serpent in her sister's leg, see? It twisted round her knee and pained her somethin' good."

"Rheumatic gout is a more plausible explanation," Effie said.

Harriet stopped walking and turned again, this time with a scowl. She was shorter than Effie, her skin an even-toned sepia like one who hadn't labored away her childhood in the sun. "Is you telling this story, or is I?"

Effie gritted her teeth.

"One day, the pain got so bad—"

"Likely because the weather turned or she'd eaten too many sardines."

"Hush," Meg said, but not unkindly, taking Effie's arm and looping in her own, the way one might with an unruly child. Effie, never overly fond of such contact, fought the urge to pull away.

Harriet continued. "The pain got so bad she couldn't walk or stand or nothin'. Word got round to Madame Desâmes and she worked up a Voodoo potion for the poor gal."

Effie snorted, but managed to cover the sound with a cough. A serpent wound about someone's knee? Voodoo potions? Could the story get any more preposterous?

During the War, though she'd barely been tall enough to peek over the surgery table, Effie had seen legs bloodied by minié balls, sliced by bayonets, shredded by shrapnel. She'd seen shattered knee-caps, severed arteries, pulverized muscles. But never once a snake or serpent. Unless you counted the maggots.

Effie caught her tongue before sharing this, though. Over the years, she'd learned that few people had the stomach for such things. Perhaps that accounted for the stories—curses, spells, possession. To Effie, reality was plenty grim without such tales.

Next Harriet spun a tale about a different friend who'd attended one of Madame Desâmes's séances and communed with her de-ceased brother for over an hour. "The table they sat at left the floor and done float midair!"

Meg's hands flew to her mouth and Effie used the opportunity to disentangle her arm. She continued on beside the women, though, clenching her jaw every time she had the urge to speak. However silly their stories, she'd hardly thought of the man from Tivoli Circle.

She recognized the obsessive quality of her sickness over him and had endured such afflictions before.

In wartime, it had been buttons—the gilt brass or pewter buttons embossed with eagles, stars, and letters that decorated the soldier's uniforms. She never took them from the dead, or the living for that matter, but kept a lookout on the dusty, wagon-rutted roads and aban-doned battlefields for ones that had fallen. A shiny glint of metal winking in the sunlight. She had little in those days. A single set of clothes. A rag to cover her hair. A blanket. An out-of-date physi-cian's manual Captain Kinyon gave her to study her letters. And her buttons.

She kept them in an empty tobacco box cushioned with tufts of cotton. Each night when the camp was quiet, and especially those nights when it was not, when stray bullets whistled through the air, when rats scratched at the canvas, when the moans of the sick and dying resounded until dawn, Effie would take out her buttons one by one, fingering their raised designs, rearranging them by size, weight, and color. Eventually, sleep would come.

During her girlhood in Indiana, as Captain Kinyon began teach-ing her in earnest the art of embalming, anatomy became her obses-sion. She could recite the names of every bone and muscle in the human form and reassemble a skeleton in a matter of minutes. Later, she experimented with injection fluid, obsessing over which admixture and ratio of chemicals produced the least offensive fumes while maximizing preservation.

This latest obsession was different, however. Not an object she could collect, a diagram she could memorize, a formulation she could tinker with, but a man. A nettlesome one at that. There seemed no rationale or benefit, only a nagging preoccupation and a dull ache arising inside her. Indigestion, she'd thought at first, and vowed to steer clear of Mrs. Neale's gumbo. Then she ascribed it to a hysterical affliction, but her monthly courses were yet many days away. Winter fever, pleurisy, colic—no diagnosis fit. Distraction was her only remedy.

They crossed Canal Street and wound through the French Quarter. Passersby strolled more than walked here, chatting in an easy mixture of French, English, and Creole patois. Despite the cold, footfalls rattled on the balconies overhead. Tobacco smoke and laughter wafted down.

Harriet's friend greeted them from the doorway of a single-story cottage squeezed in a row of similar houses, each with cracked adobe walls and weed-grown tile roofs. Rust wept down the siding from the mental windbreak above. Even in its disrepair, the house had a stately quality, one mirrored in the erect, almost haughty posture of its mistress. She held out her hand as they entered, and each woman pressed a silver coin into her palm.

Meg turned and glanced at Effie. "Er, I forgot to mention, there's a fifty-cent fee."

"Honorarium," Harriet's friend corrected. "For *l'artiste.*"

Effie frowned. "Artist?"

"*Oui,* the spirit artist, Madame Desâmes."

A laugh pressed at Effie's lips. What nonsense she'd engaged in! Nevertheless, she untied her purse strings and plucked out a coin. It pained her to hand it over. Fifty cents could buy two pounds of coffee, a month's worth of detergent, a new blade for her scalpel. But relief from her thoughts, however temporary, was worth it.

Inside, must tickled Effie's nose. Their host led them through the front parlor into an adjoining dining room crammed with a large table and several mismatched chairs. The gaslight chandelier had been damped to an anemic glow, its flame fitful and sputtering.

At the far end of the table sat the most beautiful woman Effie had ever seen. With her fair skin, sharp cheekbones, and aquiline nose, Effie first mistook her for a white woman. But her eyes were dark, as was the sleek hair that peeked from beneath her tignon. The purple silk of her dress caught the flickering light, making her appear almost iridescent.

She stood with patrician grace and spread wide her dainty arms. *"Enchanté!* Welcome. Sit, please. Sit."

Effie, like the others, shuffled to the nearest chair and sat. For the first time that evening, she noticed her own cottonade dress. Dark blue and simply cut, it served her well during the long hours of embalming. But the thick fibers that kept her warm against the damp air now scratched against her skin. Perhaps she ought to have changed into her Sunday dress too. Not that it was any more—what did the Creoles say?—*à la mode.* God may have rested on Sunday, but death did not. And neither did she.

Madame Desâmes seated herself, taking great care to smooth and arrange her skirts. She smiled then, in an almost theatrical way, and looked over each of the sitters. "We mustn't admit anyone with too magnetic a temperament, lest they dampen the power of the spirits."

Once satisfied that none among them would scare away the spirits, the medium bid them hold hands and delivered a short prayer, calling upon the dead and offering herself as a conduit through which they might congress with the living. She closed her eyes as she spoke, and the other ladies did likewise.

All but Effie. It was bad enough to hold their hands—Harriet to her right, whose grip was limp and fingers cold; Meg to her left, squeezing every time Madame Desâmes said the word *spirit* or *dead* or *ghostly.* The other sitters leaned in, their faces screwed as if the moment demanded intense concentration. Strange that here in this shabby dining room with its feeble, trembling light they found talk of the dead palatable, titillating even. Effie need only mention her work as an embalmer and they grimaced and glanced away, avoiding her altogether when possible.

She looked from their intent faces back to the medium and found Madame Desâmes staring directly at her as she uttered her final words of supplication. For the flash of a moment, Effie felt the same way she had years ago when Captain Kinyon realized she was a girl.

A day or two after her arrival he'd handed her several trinkets from a dead soldier's pocket and watched intently as she set them aside on a nearby table, carefully folding the man's silk hankie into a square and resting the other objects on top.

"You're a girl," he'd said. Not a question, but a statement. Somehow, she didn't feel afraid that he might turn her out at this. She felt visible. Seen.

Now, as then, Effie found herself holding her breath until Madame Desâmes's sharp gaze released her.

"*Ma foi!* I sense the spirits circling around us now," she said. "Can feel you them?"

"*Oui,*" their hostess said.

Meg clamped down ever harder around Effie's hand. "Yes! Me too." The others echoed her response.

Effie said nothing. She'd spent her life around the dead and never felt a phantom touch, never heard ethereal whispers, never sensed an unearthly presence. She'd stared into the dead's eyes, sometimes just minutes after death, before the cornea clouded over. She'd stared into their wide and fixed pupils and seen nothing. No evidence of God or a soul. Only blackness.

"What about you?"

Effie startled. "Me?"

"*Oui,*" the medium said. "Is there some family member you wish to connect with? A grandmother? A sibling died in infancy? Perhaps they are here waiting."

A strange rapping noise rang through the room. Several of the girls around the table gasped.

A pricking sensation skittered down Effie's neck, but not on account of the rapping. "No."

Madame Desâmes's gaze narrowed. "*Non?*"

"I do," Meg said. "I do!"

She regarded Effie a moment more, her full, painted lips synched closed, her right eyebrow twitching ever so slightly. After a deep breath, she turned to Meg, all smiles again. "Very well. *Dites-moi* this person's name."

"Betsy-lou."

Madame Desâmes straightened and said to the room, "Betsy-lou, are you among us?"

Three loud knocks, just like the noise Effie heard before, sounded in quick succession. "She's here!" the medium said. "She has rapped upon our table."

She coaxed Meg into asking a series of simple yes or no questions to verify the spirit's identity. One rap in reply meant *no*. Three meant *yes*. The acoustics of the room muddled the source of the sound. A sleight of hand perhaps? But Madame Desâmes never let go of those beside her. Her feet? No. Those seated nearby would notice something so conspicuous. A pole hidden beneath her skirts? How would she operate such a thing? The more Effie listened, the more familiar the noise became. Sure as the dead, she'd heard it before.

The others seemed entirely convinced it was the spirits. They fed on one another's excitement until near hysteria gripped the room.

"Ask Betsy-lou if she's seen Big Joe up there," Meg said, her voice high and squeaky.

A single rapping sound.

"No, suppose not. The devil always did seem to have a hand in his ways." Meg shook her head and then said to the air, "'Member that time he done pulled Willie's arm clear from its socket?"

Of course! That was the sound. Effie turned her ear toward the medium, the next round of knocks confirming her suspicion. Madame Desâmes was popping her knee joint to emit the noise. Effie had reset enough limbs into their sockets to be sure. How clever and yet . . . deceitful.

Talk of the devil had dampened the women's elation. Their rickety chairs whined as they squirmed and shifted.

A well-played gasp and Madame Desâmes had them leaning in again. "Another spirit's come to our table," she said. "A man . . . so young and handsome to be among those who've crossed over. *L'amour* has led him here."

"Silas!" Harriet shouted, letting go of Effie's hand and reaching into the air. "It must be him."

"Pitiful spirit, is your name Silas?"

Silence.

Then three loud clicks.

Tears burst from Harriet's eyes. Even though Effie didn't care overmuch for the woman, rage flamed like fever over her skin. Long-gone family members were one thing, but this . . . this was cruel.

"The Klan done got him after the War." Harriet wiped her cheeks. "We was meant to marry that summer."

Not for the first time, Madame Desâmes's gaze flickered up to the chandelier. The flames blinked and struggled, starved for gas.

"I'm sensing . . . I'm sensing he wants to give you something. A token of his lasting affection."

Just then the lights died. Blackness shrouded the room. A chorus of gasps and cries erupted around her. Effie strained to see through the darkness, but with the pocket doors drawn and windows shuttered, not a sliver of light reached them. A sharp floral scent suffused the air. The gaslights blinked back aflame.

After but a breath of silence, a new commotion arose. A shock of pansies lay strewn across the table.

"*Mon Dieu!*" said their host.

"Sweet Mary and Joseph," Meg echoed. "It's a miracle!"

Harriet scooped up the flowers, the fledgling light glinting off her tears.

Effie wrenched her hand free from Meg and stood. How could these women be so gullible? "It's not a miracle. She's a fraud."

"What?" said their host. "Impossible. You heard the rapping."

"She's disarticulating her knee joint."

Madame Desâmes laughed weakly. "*C'est ridicule.*"

"What about the flowers?" Meg asked.

"Isn't it obvious? She was hiding them in her skirts, waiting for the lights to go out."

As a collective, their eyes turned to Madame Desâmes, who straightened her shoulders and smiled. "What of the scent? If I'd hidden them in my skirts as you say, surely you would have noticed their fragrance when first we met."

Their eyes swung back to Effie.

"Yeah, what about the scent?" Harriet said.

"Perfume." Effie waited for the truth to dawn on their faces. Instead, their expressions hardened with contempt. "Can't you smell the alcohol?"

"I told you she'd ruin the night," Harriet whispered loud enough for all to hear.

The fire that but a moment before had burned her to speak vanished, leaving Effie's skin cold and her chest empty. Why were the women's narrowed eyes and pursed lips turned on her? She hadn't ruined their night, Madame Desâmes—or whatever her real name was—had. Effie tugged on the wispy coils of hair at the nape of her neck and turned to Meg.

Meg looked down. "I'm sorry, Effie. I think you should leave."

Though she hadn't wanted to come, had hated linking hands, and had barely endured their hysteria, the thought of being cast out pained Effie like the cut of a scalpel. Madame Desâmes's smug gaze stung like chemical salts to the wound.

The dining room door squealed as Effie opened it and then again as she drew it closed. Any moment she expected the women to come to their senses, to see what, to Effie, was plain as buttermilk. Instead, her final glimpse of the room showed them turning back toward the table and clasping hands.

"Pay her no mind," Madame Desâmes said. "She's only jealous. *Une femme* like her wouldn't know love if it dropped on her head from heaven."

Their laughter followed Effie, haunting her lonely walk home.

CHAPTER 5

Rain dribbled down from the heavy gray clouds settled atop the city. It pinged against Effie's umbrella and dripped down onto her skirts, soaking through to her stockings. Paving blocks had given way to mud several streets back. It clung to her boots like a leprous skin, adding weight to every step.

She stopped before a long, narrow house that matched the number Mr. Whitmark had given her. In the shelter of the eave, Effie closed her umbrella and cleaned her boots on the iron scraper beside the door. Thankfully, the mourning badge tucked inside her dressing case had remained dry. She fastened the rosette to the brass knocker at the center of the door, adjusting the folds of black crepe and ribbon until they lay just so, then picked up her embalming cabinet and slipped inside.

Mr. Whitmark had already laid the body on the cooling table in the small sitting room just beyond the door and sat with the deceased's husband at a small dining table in the adjoining room.

"This is my helper, Miss Jones," Mr. Whitmark said.

Though she knew he meant no offense, Effie bristled. *Helper.* As if all she did was fetch supplies like some pickaninny. At least Mr. Whitmark could favor her with the word *assistant.* It set the client at ease, though, smoothing the furrowed brow and pinched lips he'd donned on her arrival. *Helper.* Yes, that made sense to the old man. Like a maid or errand boy.

She'd been a novelty in the North. A curiosity. Here she could pass almost invisible, as long as she kept to her place. Hadn't that been what she'd wanted? To disappear?

She nodded to the deceased's husband—a slight gentleman, with hunched shoulders and drooping skin—then closed the door between the rooms to begin her work.

In the five weeks since her arrival, she and Mr. Whitmark had fallen into a routine. He met with the families, moving the body to whatever room they preferred for the wake, and discussing casket and funeral details. She embalmed the body.

He'd managed a clean shave on himself today and wore one of the collars she'd had cleaned for him. His eyes were clear, and she'd smelled boiling coffee that morning at the shop instead of spirituous bitters. Perhaps he'd read Dr. Benner's report on diseased livers after all.

She turned to the body. A ribbon bound the jaw, and nickels covered the eyes to ensure they stayed closed as rigor mortis set it. She removed the cotton nightshirt that lay rumpled and stained about the body and bathed the fragile skin with cool, soapy water.

As Effie worked, she thought back to her solitary walk home from the French Quarter the night before. She'd heard Meg, Harriet, and the other women arrive several hours later, their voices high with delight. Effie's small room had grown cavernous in that moment—dark and empty, save for the distorted echo of their chatter.

Only jealous, Madame Desâmes had said in her raspy Creole-accented voice. *Wouldn't know love if it dropped on her head from heaven.*

Effie tucked her hands under her armpits, shivering in her wet dress. Love! What greater culprit was there in the abandonment of reason? Harriet's willingness to believe a dead man had conjured flowers for her a natural and scientific impossibility—further proved this fact. Effie was not jealous. That too would be illogical. Why wish for something that obscured one's judgment and caused such grief?

She rubbed her hands together, blew a few warm breaths over her stiff fingers, and picked up her scalpel. Through the sitting room door, she could hear the husband's choked voice as he responded to

Mr. Whitmark's questions about death announcements and casket options. Grief. She bent down over the woman's arm and made a straight, clean cut just above the inside of the elbow.

Grief called often during the War. The same brave men who charged toward bullets and artillery fire openly wept beside their dead friends, brothers, and sons. Later, when the captain brought her to Indiana and established his embalming business, Effie met grief with even more regularity. Wives now. Husbands. Mothers—whose grief seemed to surpass even what the greatest poets put to pen.

"She's like a corpse herself," a girl from church had whispered of Effie once. "She don't feel anything."

But that wasn't true. She did feel. Those who mourned beside the bodies she embalmed mirrored something inside her. She'd sensed it stronger as a girl, watching the soldiers wring their caps and clutch the pale, limp hands of their dead. It stirred recollections so raw she'd no choice but to shutter them away, to ball them up into a tiny black lump and bury them in the deepest cavity of her viscera.

Time had muted that echo of grief. The black lump inside her hardly stirred.

Until coming to New Orleans. Even now as she gazed over this woman's wasted limbs and sagging, aged skin, as she listened to her husband's shaky voice, Effie could feel it waking inside her. But the corresponding memories were gone. She'd excised from her brain whatever tragedy those soldiers' grief had recalled and with it nearly every other memory from her days before the War.

She attached one end of the syringe pump's rubber tubing to a jar of embalming fluid and the other to a cannula jutting out from the brachial artery she'd raised from the woman's arm. Effie pulled over a stool and sat down to begin pumping in the preservative.

As she worked, a soft humming played through her mind. A few tremulous notes. Her mother's voice. Somehow Effie was sure. Most of the melody was lost, though. Buried. Once, as a very young girl, she'd stopped dead in the street upon hearing the tune. Inclined her ear to listen. Heedless of the oncoming carts and wagons. But no. The song, the voice wasn't the same.

The rain pattering against the house's clapboard siding drowned out the humming in her head. Mr. Whitmark had gone, and the adjoining room was silent. Perhaps the husband had taken to bed. Twilight peeked around the drawn window curtains, and the smell of frying fish and simmering rice wafted from the nearby houses. She'd be home past curfew again. All the better. She hadn't wanted to run into Meg or Harriet anyway.

As she thought about the plate of cold food awaiting her later in Mrs. Neale's dimly lit kitchen, she couldn't help but compare herself to this woman's frail husband. He'd be eating alone tonight too. Probably for the first time in half a century.

An ill comparison, Effie decided. She was alone by choice. But as she disconnected her tubing and threaded her needle to close the incision, she found her hands trembling once again. No amount of rubbing or hot breath stilled them.

"We're stewards of the dead, Euphemia," Captain Kinyon had said to her once, not long after the War, when they'd been called upon to embalm the body of old Mrs. Allister. "A noble profession, but one that demands . . . distance."

While most townsfolk had greeted Effie's arrival with pursed lips and sidelong stares, Mrs. Allister had smiled. She waved to Effie from her front porch stoop and winked at her in church. She even gave Effie a few toffees once—sweet and sticky. Better than anything Effie had tasted.

Her fondness for the old woman must have shown—a wavering hand when she passed Captain Kinyon the scalpel perhaps, one too many tries at threading the suture needle—for he cleared his throat. "Distance, Euphemia. You must ever keep your distance. From the living and dead."

"What about Annabelle?" Effie oft spied him staring at her tintype atop the mantel.

His hand stilled. Eyelids twitched. He cleared his throat again. "Would that I was as wise then as I am now."

Effie nodded. She never said her name again.

Keep your distance. Over the years, she'd held as tightly to those words as she did her brass buttons. But today they rang empty.

Back at the shop, a light burned in the kitchen. Mr. Whitmark sat asleep on a low stool, his head cradled in his arms atop the table. A half-empty bottle rested beside him and a candle burnt down to a nub. Wax had overflowed the drip pan and pooled on the tabletop. So much for the morning's progress.

Effie used the meager flame to light a lamp, and rummaged through the kitchen for something to swap for the bottle. At least he'd stayed sober longer today than yesterday. A lone tin of coffee sat on the counter. The larder was empty save for a wedge of molded cheese; the dried goods cupboard likewise bare. Dust blanketed the shelves, and cobwebs dangled from the corners. Not in need of a maid indeed!

She corked the bottle and tucked it away behind a stack of rusted pots, then headed to the nearby shops for some food. The rain had stopped, but clouds yet curtained the darkening sky. Murky water sloshed in the gutters.

A stray dog barked from down the road. Effie flinched, her feet skidding on the wet pavers.

Captain Kinyon had owned such a dog. Otis, he'd called him, as if the dog were a person, not an animal. Effie's heart had hammered when he first came near. But she let his wet nose sniff and nudge her, hoping the captain would see how brave she was. He'd reached out, the captain, she thought to pat her shoulder. Instead, he'd patted Otis, ruffling his wiry fur.

Effie rattled her head. The stray had wandered off. She continued on to the shops, watchful lest the dog return.

After procuring bread from the baker and butter from the dairy peddler, she hurried back to the shop. Mr. Whitmark woke just as she began to grind the coffee. He blinked several times, then stumbled to the washbasin to retch.

"Have you eaten at all today?" she asked when he'd finished.

He shook his head.

"I thought not."

"Coffee smells good."

"That's not for you, it's for me. Here, drink this." She handed him a cup of water. His hand shook as he drank.

She cut a slice of bread, slathered it with butter, and passed it to him.

"Thanks."

"You need a maid." She turned back to the grinder and continued over the din. "While you're at it, another assistant too. Someone to mind the shop when we're out, help set up chairs for services, drive the hearse. I've gone over the account books and we've enough clientele now to—"

"Effie, why are you doing this?"

She paused and glanced at him. "I'm thirsty and have a good walk home yet."

"Not the coffee. This." He gestured vaguely about the room.

"I've a vested interest in keeping you alive and sober, sir."

"How sentimental." He laughed weakly and propped up his feet on a nearby stool. "Give me another slice of bread, will you?"

She cut more bread and mixed the coffee grounds with boiling water from the kettle. One sip and she wished she'd bought some cream along with the butter. "How old are these beans?"

He shrugged. "A year maybe? Tasted fine to me this morning."

Mr. Whitmark didn't offer her a chair, and Effie didn't presume to sit, but stood by the stove, hoping the small fire she'd lit to heat the kettle would dry her skirts. She managed a few more swallows of coffee before laying the cup aside. "I'll add new beans to your list for the grocer."

"Ain't you cheeky tonight," he said with a grin. "Puts me in mind of my sister . . . pestered me to high hell, she did."

"Sister?"

"I've got a whole heap of family here. They just don't see fit to call . . ." He smoothed his hand over the tabletop, his fingers tracing the grain of the wood. "Where's my whiskey?"

Effie refilled his water. "When'd you last speak with her?"

"January of sixty-one." He continued to paw at the table. "How long ago is that now? Twelve, thirteen—"

"Fifteen years last month."

"Humph." He wagged his head. "My brother comes around every once in a while. Can't figure if he means well or just likes to preen over his success." His hand stalled, and his fingers set to drumming. He craned his neck to see around her, his eyes wandering the stovetop and shelves.

"More bread?"

"I've got another bottle upstairs, you know."

"Suit yourself."

He stood, wobbled, and sat back down. "I'm not over thirsty anyway."

She set the water jug and lamp within easy of reach of him. "Don't fall asleep and burn down the kitchen."

"Yes, ma'am." He gave her a sloppy salute.

"Good night, Mr. Whitmark."

"Night," he said without looking at her, his gaze lost in the flickering lamp flame. As she brushed past him on her way toward the door, he reached out and captured her wrist. His skin was clammy, his grasp tight. "Thank you, Effie."

The mantel clock downstairs in the parlor chimed a single, lonely toll. Effie rolled onto her side and pulled back the thin drape shrouding her bedside window. Outside, darkened palm fronds and magnolia boughs undulated in the fitful breeze. The street beyond lay quiet and empty.

Insomnia—the newest symptom of her unexplained illness.

She let go the drape and groped for her matches. After lighting the charred wick of her candle, she watched the flame build and flare before it settled into a steady glow. Several more seconds she watched, her resistance softening as surely as the wax. Her hand slipped beneath the pillow and pulled out a worn slip of paper.

The handbill's lettering had begun to fade, and fold lines crisscrossed the page. Effie smoothed a hand over the print and held it to the light. Not that she needed to read it. The simple block text, the machine-cut edges, the smudge of ink at the bottom right—every detail had long since imprinted on her brain.

Think on it, he'd said.

She held the handbill closer to the flame. Her dalliance in Tivoli Circle had caused nothing but trouble. Daytime found her moody and distractible; nighttime bothered and listless. And over what precisely? The man's words had stirred her, yes, but that was the whole point of stump speaking. Rhetoric, intonation, and gestures—a skilled orator used these tools the same way a painter wielded his brush, a farmer his hoe . . . a charlatan her manipulation and misdirection.

Was Effie so different from Mr. Whitmark? As much a slave to this obsession as he was to his bottle?

She thrust the paper into the flame. What relief to watch it burn. For a moment, the entirety of her small room was illuminated. The chair and writing desk, dresser and washstand all cast trembling shadows upon walls. Black smoke climbed and twisted toward the ceiling. Heat singed her fingers, but she held on until only a scrap of paper remained.

There. No more reason to think on it. Obsess on it. On him. Besides, she'd read the papers. Even the *Lafayette Gazette* had covered the contested election here in seventy-two, the attempted coup against the Republican government September before last. Why just last week she'd seen the White Leaguers drilling with rifles up and down Camp Street. One would have to be crazy to attend a political club meeting in times like these.

CHAPTER 6

Effie stood outside the clubhouse on Constance Street, her fingers laced so tightly their tips had begun to tingle. What was she doing here? The building's cracked-brick facade and chipped-slate roof hardly bolstered her resolve. The shingle hanging above the door—WARD TWO REPUBLICANS' CLUB—had three bullet holes bored through the wood.

"That didn't happen when anyone was around."

Effie jumped at the voice.

A man with rich black skin and a shock of tight curls flattened beneath a wool cap stood beside her. "Still," he said, raising his cane and tapping on the sign. "We've been meaning to change it out for a new one."

She wondered at his cane. He looked neither aged nor of that foppish sort who preen about with such ornamentation, but as he ascended the steps to the clubhouse door the reason became clear. The lower part of his right leg was gone and, in its place, a crude peg.

"You know they make prosthetic legs," she said. "I read about them in the *Boston Medical and Surgical Journal*. They're fashioned from wood and leather, just like your peg, but anatomically speaking—"

He turned and looked quizzically down at her from the landing. "I know. I've applied with the Maimed Soldier's Relief Fund."

"Excellent." Effie scaled the three short steps to join him on the landing, her hands no longer locked and tense. "Was your amputation done above the knee joint or below? The hinge mechanism they've invented to allow for more lifelike flexion and extension is meant to be—"

"What's your name?"

She hesitated, realizing her questioning had perhaps been—how had Mrs. Kinyon always put it?—indelicate. She looked down at her feet, but then, worrying the man might mistake her for gaping further at his peg, whipped her chin up and faced him.

To her relief, he was smiling. "I'm Tom Button."

"Euphemia Jones."

"Pleasure to meet you, Miss Jones. And to answer your question: below."

"I'm sorry?"

"My amputation—it was done a few inches below my knee. And don't expect to see me jaunting about with a wooden leg anytime soon. They've got thousands of Yanks to outfit. Then I reckon they'll move on to the Rebs. We Negroes are at the very bottom of the list. Anything else you'd like to know about my leg?"

Yes, many things, but Effie shook her head.

"Well then"—he opened the door and held it wide—"after you, Miss Jones."

A rush of warm air fluttered the brim of her bonnet. Voices chattered from within. Effie found her hands knotting together again.

"Thank you, Mr. Button," she said, and shuffled one foot in front of the other until she made it inside.

"Call me Tom. We ain't formal round here."

The clubhouse looked more like an abandoned storeroom than a meeting hall. Roughly hewn beams buttressed the tall, vaulted ceiling. A tarnished gasolier lit the room, its feeble light aided by several oil lamps set about on tabletops and upturned crates.

At least fifty people filled the room. Negroes mostly, though Effie picked out at least half a dozen white men too. The women in attendance, all black, numbered around eight. Everyone sat on stools, benches, or mismatched chairs facing an older gentleman at the far end of the room. He cleared his throat, bowed his head, and the room went silent.

Tom shut the door behind them and removed his cap, just as the older gentleman began to pray. His voice started out small and swelled to fill the room. While he spoke, Effie searched the crowd. One man near the front caught her eye—but no, his ears were far too big. Another, three rows from the back, had the same lustrous brown skin, but when he raised his head after the prayer she could see the cut of his chin was wrong. Too old, too young, too fat, too slight, too dark of complexion, too light, too much hair or far too little—the man was not here.

She rose onto her tiptoes and craned her neck, taming her rising frenzy, forcing her eyes to move systematically down the rows. Had she misremembered his features? Memorized the flyer incorrectly and stumbled upon a different club meeting?

Impossible. She never made such mistakes.

Tom touched her lightly on the back. "Here, let me fetch you a seat. I'll introduce you round after they's done spouting."

He pulled another stool in line with the back row and dusted off the seat with his cap. Effie sat to give her tired feet a moment's rest before departing. She'd only come to see the man from Tivoli Circle again. To prove to herself that there was nothing special or godlike about him, that something else had agitated her that day, stirred up and befuddled her emotions. Maybe she'd eaten spoiled ham at breakfast. It had tasted a bit off. Or maybe so many straight days of work had overly taxed her brain, leaving her susceptible to the crowd's fervor. Whatever the true cause, knowing it was not this man would free her of this irrational obsession and return normalcy to her life. No more sleepless nights. No more spirit circles or other such foolery in the name of distraction. Certainly no more political club meetings.

The man at the front of the room, not the one who'd delivered the opening prayer, but a lighter-skinned Negro of maybe forty, called the meeting to order and discussed the night's agenda. Effie looked over her shoulder and eyed the door. What a waste of time to come out tonight. Not only had she disrupted her routine—Tuesday nights she darned her stockings and polished her instruments, tasks she'd now have to squeeze into some other night's schedule—but the latest edition of *The Casket* had arrived. She could be alone in her room at this very moment reading about new techniques for thoracic injection. Worse still, she remained infected by the memory of this man without hope of remedy.

Tom had taken a seat beside her and was keeping minutes in a leather-bound notebook. He wrote with a nub of a pencil, his letters neat and lines straight. She could see from previous entries that later he would go back and overlay it all in ink. His spelling was imperfect—*deligate* instead of *delegate, benedicion* instead of *benediction*—but easy enough to comprehend. He toggled his gaze between the front of the room and his notebook, his pencil moving across the page without pause. Despite his concentration, Effie doubted she could slip out unnoticed. She weighed her options of leaving now and causing a scene, or waiting for the speaker to cough or pause for a sip of water wherein she might whisper some excuse to Tom and leave unmolested. She opted to wait.

The speaker—the club's president, she guessed—droned on about the unlikelihood of President Grant seeking a third term in light of some newly passed resolution brought forth by congressional Democrats. The resolution, which the club president suffered them to read aloud, maintained a third term would be "unwise, unpatriotic, and fraught with peril to our free institutions." Grumbles rose amid the crowd. Several hollered objections.

This was Effie's chance. She leaned closer to Tom. He smelled of lye soap, machine grease, and newsprint—a strange, but not altogether unpleasant combination. "I just remembered I have—"

The door at the back of the room swung open and banged against the far wall.

"Sorry I'm late."

The voice struck her with the same force as it had in Tivoli Circle. While everyone around her turned and stared at the newcomer, Effie sat immobile, her lips parted and skin tingling.

"You didn't get down to the good stuff yet, did ya? Surely not without me."

Many in the room laughed. Tom smiled and shook his head. *Representative Greene—tardy, but present,* he wrote in the minutes.

Representative? The man was a legislator? Effie straightened and smoothed the hairs at the nape of her neck, only to have them spring back defiantly.

His boots clapped atop the floorboards as he made his way to the front of the room. Her eyes strained to the far edge of her sockets, eager to catch sight of him the minute he strode into view.

Her memory had not done him justice, had not captured the straight-backed confidence of his walk, or the easy exuberance of his smile. Even in the poorly lit room, he seemed to shine, as striking in the shadows as he was in the dancing light.

Effie jogged her head. This was a ridiculous assessment. Humans lacked the bioluminescent abilities of, say, a lightning bug. More likely he had this appearance *because* of the dim lighting, not in spite of it. Or perhaps she needed eyeglasses.

"You was saying, Ms. Jones?"

"Hmm?"

"That you'd just remembered something."

"Oh . . . er . . . yes." She wrestled her gaze from the front of the room, where the man—Representative Greene—now stood, shrugging off his woolen overcoat. "Yes, I just remembered how . . . fond I am of President Grant. What a shame about this . . ."

"Resolution."

"Yes, this deplorable resolution."

"Deplorable, I like that word." He jotted it down in the margin of the journal.

"*a*-b-l-e, not i."

He scratched it out and rewrote it with the correct spelling. "Ya know, you talk like a—"

"Uppity carpetbagger? Yes, I get that rather a lot."

Tom chuckled. "I was gonna say poet."

"Oh." She looked down at her interlaced hands, then back at his dark eyes. "Thank you."

The club president began speaking again and she returned her attention forward. He wasted little time introducing Mr. Greene, though it seemed from the smiling faces and ready handshakes that had greeted his arrival, Effie was the only one who didn't know the legislator personally. Mr. Greene spoke briefly about the latest happenings at the statehouse. Effie had passed the building several times on her way to the pharmacy without thought to the goings-on inside. Now, however, she listened as if nothing in the world held more interest.

His demeanor was more casual tonight than it had been that afternoon in the circle. But the timbre of his voice was just as pleasing, his expressions just as earnest. He could have been selling gutter water and she'd have bought it then and there without compunction. She scooted to the edge of her stool so that it balanced on a single leg, aware of her precarious perch, aware of her irrational rapture, yet helpless to pull back.

Too soon his legislative update ended. He sat down in the front row in a chair made vacant for him. Effie could barely see his closely cropped hair and sloping forehead above the dozens of heads in between them. The club president spoke again, then one of the white men who held some important position or other at the Custom House. A small, austere woman updated the group on an ongoing campaign to provide blankets for the Negro wing at Charity Hospital, followed by more words from the president. Effie tried to listen, to prove she still held command of her senses, but caught at best one sentence in ten. Several people stood and were stretching their backs and donning their coats before she realized the meeting had concluded.

"Here," Tom said, offering her a hand. "I'll introduce you to everyone."

Effie stood without taking his hand. She'd not heard St. Patrick's bell toll, but it must be getting on past curfew. A smart woman would head home. Instead, she followed him to a nearby group of people, hoping they'd eventually wind about to the front of the room, where Mr. Greene stood, shaking yet more hands. Of course, he wouldn't remember her from that afternoon at Tivoli Circle. How could he? Hers was not a face that stood out amid a crowd. But—

Effie brought her attention to heel, though several seconds passed before she remembered to smile and say "How do you do?" to the small cluster of people Tom had just introduced. Two were younger men, hardly old enough to vote, another in his middle years, and a gray-haired couple. Effie hadn't caught any of their names.

The woman who'd spoken about the hospital approached them, carrying a bundle of cloth. She was petite in every way save for her comportment. The assuredness of her step and set of her shoulders aggrandized her small stature to match that of any man's in the room.

"Euphemia Jones, may I present Mrs. Carrière," Tom said.

The woman nodded at Effie, "*Bienvenue.*" Then she turned to the others and unfurled a large banner of alternating green and purple squares. DEFEND THE BALLOT BOX was overlain in large black letters. "Voilà. What do you think?"

"Right lovely," Tom said.

The gray-haired woman let go of her husband's arm and took hold of one end. "Stitchin' ain't done, Marie."

"I know. Just here at the edges. I thought we might finish tonight." Mrs. Carrière turned to a small boy who squatted nearby playing with jacks. "Jonah, fetch me *mon étui, s'il te plaît.*"

Effie recognized Jonah as the same boy who'd handed her the flyer in Tivoli Circle. He loped to the front corner of the room and returned with a small wooden sewing box.

"*Merci,*" Mrs. Carrière said, and pulled over a chair. The older woman sat beside her. They both looked at Effie.

She shuffled back a step and glanced around for Tom. He'd moved off a pace and taken up conversation with another group of men. So much for further introductions.

Effie worked the strings of her purse over in her hands, recalling Mrs. Kinyon's quilting bees she'd so hated as a girl. All tedium and chatter. She glanced sideways at the door. Thirty paces and she'd be free. Her gaze swung to the front of the room. Mr. Greene, in his beige suit and burgundy necktie, still impossibly radiant in the dim, remained engaged in conversation. She'd wanted to write him off as a braggart. The confidence with which he spoke, the swagger with which he walked surely justified such an opinion. Except now he wasn't talking but listening. She remembered the intensity of his dark brown eyes and envied the speaker this attention.

"Surely you sew, Miss . . . Jones, was it?" Mrs. Carrière said.

"Yes—er—no. I don't sew, that is." But she sat down anyway, no longer sure of her feet to bear her anywhere.

"Course you do, dearie," the older woman said. "Ain't have to be perfect."

Mrs. Carrière handed her a needle and a length of thread. Her ochre-colored skin was smooth and bright as a newly minted penny. Only a few shallow furrows about her mouth and eyes hinted at her age. "Just hem that edge with a simple catch stitch."

Catch stitch? Effie was sure she'd learned this technique at one time or another from Mrs. Kinyon but had long since forgotten. Still, how hard could it be? She took up one edge and, after observing Mrs. Carrière for a minute, did her best to copy her technique. Happily, the two women took up conversation about the hospital, leaving Effie's thoughts and eyes free to wander.

"Your stitches are remarkably even, Miss Jones," Mrs. Carrière said after several minutes. "For one who doesn't sew."

"I'm more accustomed to the turgor and thickness of skin, but—" Effie's addled mind caught up with her mouth and she stopped. Experience had taught her it best not to bring up her work in casual conversation. No getting around it now, though. "I'm an undertaker's assistant. I embalm the dead."

"I'll be!" the older woman said. "That's where they drain the blood from the bodies and fill 'em back up with chemicals so they don't stink and rot, right?"

"Sort of."

"It's more than that," Mrs. Carrière said to the other woman, her tone even more solemn than before. "When you embalm someone it gives the family time"—her voice wavered—"time to bring them home, time to say goodbye before the burial."

Effie noticed the black trim of her dress and the thick band of crepe around her hat.

Mrs. Carrière's hands remained fast and steady at her stitching, even as her eyes glistened. "A noble profession. Though a bit peculiar, I must say. However did you come to such work?"

Effie shifted in her chair. Gasping and fainting over her profession she was prepared for; earnest questions she was not.

Jonah, who'd found a spot on the floor nearby and returned to his jacks, saved her the trouble of an answer. "You a Yank?"

"For shame, Jonah," Mrs. Carrière said. "Where are your manners?"

He shrugged. "She talks funny."

"I was educated in the North," Effie said. "But I was born here in the South."

"Whereabouts?" he asked.

Mrs. Carrière shot him a stern look. "Where about, *Miss Euphemia.*"

"Effie's fine," she said, though she rather wished they'd never ventured from talk of the hospital or her stitches. "Louisiana, someplace."

"You don't right know?" he said, and then, after another stern look from Mrs. Carrière, added, "Miss Effie."

"No."

"What about your kin?" Jonah asked. He bounced his rubber ball and grabbed at the rusty jacks scattered across the floor. One jack, two jacks, three . . . he got to eight before missing the ball after its bounce. He tried again, this time missing one of the eight jacks and sending another skittering across the floor to Effie's feet. "*Merde.*"

"Jonah!" Mrs. Carrière said.

"Sorry."

Effie set down her needle and thread and picked up the jack. She squatted down beside him. "Here, let me show you a trick."

He handed her the rubber ball and watched as she cast the jacks across the floor. Several pale scars stood out against the dark skin of his little hands. His palms were calloused, but his nails trimmed and clean.

"Best plan your strategy before you bounce your ball. Which jacks do you think will be the hardest to grab?"

He pointed to three jacks scattered far from the others.

"Good," she said. "Start there. Get the most difficult ones first and the rest come easily." She bounced the rubber ball and swept her hand over the dusty floor, scooping up the three outliers before snatching the rest and catching the ball. "You try."

He scattered the jacks and readied the ball. "I'm an orphan too." He managed eight, then nine, and cast the jacks out for ten. "Didn't mind the streets none. Expect when it rained." He missed and tried again. "But Mrs. Carrière ain't got no children, so I keep her company now."

"Mighty good of you," Effie said.

He snatched up all ten jacks and smiled at her with his mouth full of missing teeth. "Bet she'd let you come on for company too."

Effie glanced over at Mrs. Carrière, seated straight and prim as a sarcophagus, then back at Jonah. She'd always found children loud and squirmy and, often as not, smelly. But at least they spoke straight. They laughed when they were happy and cried when they were in pain. You never had to second-guess their motives or scrutinize their expressions.

"Penny to your nickel I can beat you to ten," he said.

"I'm supposed to be stitching."

He scrunched his face and fished a penny from his pocket.

"You turning our club into a gambling den, Jonah?"

Effie startled at the voice, teetering where she crouched as her balance faltered. She reached out to steady herself and planted a hand square atop a jack, its metal spike jabbing into her palm. A yelp built in her throat, but she strangled it back.

Mr. Greene knelt beside her and took hold of her arm. "Apologies, miss. I didn't mean to cause you fright."

Effie stared at his hand about her arm—his long fingers, his square knuckles, the swell of veins beneath his skin—then dared a glance at his face. He'd said something, hadn't he?

"Best watch out for Jonah, here. He's a regular blackleg." Mr. Greene helped her to her feet and released his grip.

"The odds seemed fair enough to me," she managed to say.

He laughed, a rich, deep sound like that of a drum. "I'm Samson Greene."

"Euph—Effie Jones."

He took her hand and, for the span of a moment, she thought he might kiss it. Instead he squeezed and gave it a quick shake. "Pleasure, Miss Jones. Glad you decided to come by."

"Me too," she said, her hand hanging stupidly in the air where he had released it.

"You had some concerns about the cemeteries, I believe."

She dropped her arm to her side. The rush of blood brought with it a dull throbbing where the jack had stabbed her palm. "I hadn't realized you were a state legislator, I might have spoke differently."

"But not about anything so dithering as education or the cost of grain."

"This is a serious matter, Mr. Greene."

"I have no doubt." But his crooked smile said otherwise.

"Most of the cemeteries in the city are privately owned and beyond the statehouse's control anyhow."

"You underestimate the power of the statehouse."

"Perhaps you overestimate it."

His rich laugh came again. "I like your spirit, Miss Jones. You'll be joining us at the parade, I hope."

"Parade?"

"We're meeting two blocks up from the Henry Clay statue."

"Oh, yes, Mardi Gras." She should have listened better during the meeting. "I'll . . . think on it."

"Good." He smiled, then turned to Mrs. Carrière. "An exceedingly fine banner, Marie."

"*Merci.*"

To Jonah, he said, "Don't let Miss Jones here take your penny." He winked at Effie, then fished through his pocket, tossed the boy a new rubber ball, and walked away.

Effie watched him go, her muscles overcome with rigor. The evening had not gone to plan at all, the calm and satisfaction she'd so hoped to obtain all the more elusive.

She snatched up her coat and purse, nodding to Mrs. Carrière and the others in lieu of a goodbye.

Why hadn't she said no when he'd asked about Mardi Gras? Why hadn't her lungs remembered to breathe when she'd looked into his face? Why had she come at all?

The bells of St. Patrick's tolled the hour, echoed in the distance by those of St. Louis. Her feet had taken her down Julia Street to the levee. Once the repartee of chimes died down she could hear the gentle ripple of the river.

Whatever was wrong with her? A Creole couple passed by her on their way downriver. Their patois mutterings reminded her of Madame Desâmes and all the foolery she'd undertaken to relieve herself of . . . whatever this awful feeling was.

Effie stopped suddenly. *Une femme like her wouldn't know love if it dropped on her head from heaven.*

She staggered from the walkway to the river's edge and splashed the silty water onto her cheeks, heedless of soiling her gloves and collar. The river's earthy rotten odor assaulted her like smelling salts. Despite the jolt to her senses, Effie couldn't rid herself of Madame Desâmes's words.

CHAPTER 7

Love. That was the purview of second-rate poetry and dime novels. Of silly young girls with nothing else to fill their heads. No, Effie was not in love.

Yet as she gripped the banister on her way to bed, her hand trembled worse than Mr. Whitmark's. Love or not, she couldn't carry on like this. Even though calls at the shop had doubled since her arrival, the mixing and the cleaning and the cutting and the stitching no longer proved sufficient distraction. Thoughts of Samson—his rousing voice, his handsome face, his gentle hand—swarmed in like maggots to a festering wound.

Today her blade had slipped, and she'd cut clear through the artery and down to the bone. Yesterday she'd miscounted their inventory of chemicals and purchased more muriatic acid instead of bichloride of mercury, necessitating a second slog across town to the pharmacy. The blisters from her ill-fitting boots still pained her.

She mounted the steps one by one, each contraction of muscle, each flexion of her knee a conscious effort. The mistakes bothered her more than the blisters. Effie didn't make errors. Not like this. Not before.

When she reached her room, she realized she'd not brought up water for her washbasin, and lumbered downstairs to the backyard cistern. The damp night air turned her skin to gooseflesh. Moonlight filtered down through a thin film of clouds. Had it been a mistake to come here? If she'd stayed in Indiana, she'd not have to endure her fellow boarders' prattle, nor the incessant humidity and the fetid smell off the river. Certainly not this vexing sensation called love.

But no. She could not have stayed. She turned the rusty spigot and filled her pail. Water plinked against the metal, sending a spray of icy droplets onto her hand. Even if things had ended differently and she could go back, Effie knew she wouldn't. Indiana had never been home. Maybe there wasn't such a place for her anywhere.

Climbing the stairs, she met Meg, already in her nightshirt, returning an empty teacup.

"You look a fright, Effie. You sick? Half the folks on the streetcar today were a coughin' and a . . ." It was the first time Meg had spoken to her since the séance, but now she chattered on like she'd saved each word.

"I'm fine." But instead of brushing past her to her room, Effie slumped against the banister, letting the weight of her body drag her down to the steps.

Meg sat beside her. "You upset about the séance?"

"No . . . yes . . . not in the fashion you think." She hugged the pail to her chest and hung her head. Her reflection in the trembling water was haggard and wan.

"You ought apologize to Madame Desâmes."

"I ought to go and get my fifty cents back, is what I ought do."

"You's too serious, Effie. There's plenty in life that can't be explained by all that science business."

Effie didn't have the energy to disagree.

"Maybe she could help with what's been ailin' you."

"I greatly doubt that."

Meg tucked an errant strand of her crimpy hair beneath her headscarf. Her skin, dark as the heart of a calla lily, had a bright underglow in the dim light. "Won't know till you try. Think of that gal with the serpent wound about her knee."

"Gout."

"Gout, a hex, don't matter. Whatever Madame Desâmes gave her worked."

"For some the mere suggestion of medicine is enough to cure them."

"See!"

"I'm not some superstitious girl with delusions of a snake inside my leg."

Meg stood and shrugged. "Real or imagined, she was cured."

Back in her room, Effie undressed and washed the day's stickiness from her skin. She dampened her lamp and lit her reading candle, but the words slipped around the page, jumping like a frog from one stanza to the next.

If only there were a pill she could take that could deaden her feelings. Some poultice to lay across her forehead that would draw out all these unwanted thoughts. Of course, there were such medicaments, ones smoked in darkened saloons in Chinatown or mixed with sugar water at the pharmacy. But opium or laudanum would dull her wits as sure as her emotions.

She blew out the flame and rolled onto her side. Perhaps Meg was right. Perhaps there was something curative in these charms and potions, even if only imagined. A British physician she'd read once had argued in favor of such phenomena. What harm was there in putting Meg's theory to the test, if only to prove her wrong? Better that than laudanum. And perhaps she could wrangle back her fifty cents too.

Effie double-checked the black and yellow street sign against the address she'd set to memory. Rue de Toulouse. She remembered it clearly from the municipal roll book at the clerk's office. Heading away from the river, she tracked the ascending house numbers painted on small iron plaques above the doors. Whoever had enumerated the city's plats must have done so while inebriated. Numbers varied block to block, so Effie had to reorient herself with each turn. She'd already had to double back twice in search of the right street.

The farther she walked, the more her cramped toes throbbed. The new boots she'd ordered just after New Year's had yet to be assembled, despite the cobbler's hardy assurances each time she visited his shop that he needed but a day or two more. Sunlight shone down from the cloudless sky, and savory aromas wafted from the restaurants and boulangeries tucked amid the shops and houses. Women of every skin color strolled by shading themselves with lace-trimmed parasols. Men rambled to and fro from the banks, businesses, and saloons. Not for the first time, she thought to turn around and return to the blissful solitude of her rented room.

When at last she found her destination, Effie couldn't help but laugh out loud. Someone in the long chain of those she'd interviewed to uncover that Madame Desâmes, medium extraordinaire, was really Adeline Mercier of 827 Toulouse Street must have gotten a detail or two wrong.

The house at 827 rose three stories above the street. A wrought-iron balcony stretched the length of the house, casting a filigree of shade upon the banquette beneath. Blue shutters framed the multi-tude of French doors that checkered the stucco facade. The grifting woman Effie had met at the séance could not possibly live here.

Effie loitered in the balcony's shade. Likely a white family lived here. How would she explain her unsolicited intrusion upon their afternoon? She squatted and loosened her bootlaces. The skin on her heels had surely worn to fresh blisters.

How much time had she wasted obtaining this address? Wasted in finding this house among the Quarter's assemblage of ill-marked cottages and townhouses, businesses and warehouses, saloons and cafés. How much more time would she waste before finally succeed-ing in purging her nettlesome affliction?

A sudden chill took her. She stepped from the shaded banquette to the street. What if she never succeeded? Already a glint of madness fluttered inside her. She thought of the gaunt lunatics with matted hair and dead eyes at the Lafayette asylum. She and Captain Kinyon had embalmed the body of a young woman there once, the daughter of a wealthy Indianapolis banker sent to "convalesce" after a severe bout of hysteria. It had taken Effie hours to clean the dirt and feces from the crevices of her cold skin, to detangle her lice-infested hair.

With no further heed to the consequences, Effie knocked on the lacquered door. A minute passed. Two. She knocked again. Waited.

Just as she was about to turn and leave the door opened and in the narrow breach stood Madame Desâmes.

"*Oui?*"

"Madame—er—Miss Mercier?"

"Yes?"

"My name is Euphemia Jones, we met—"

"I'm sorry, ma'amselle. We're not in need of any help." She started to shut the door. "Try the house two doors down."

Effie stuck her foot into the jam. "Wait."

Miss Mercier raised a delicate hand to her brow to shade her eyes from the sun. "Ma'amselle, really I—" Her eyes narrowed. "I remember you." She glanced over her shoulder and lowered her voice. "You're that Yankee *coquin* who caused all that fuss at my séance."

"I merely pointed out your ruse. Obvious to anyone with half a wit. But that's not why I'm here. I—"

"That cost me a heap of business." She opened the door wide and stepped so close the hem of her dress brushed Effie's. "Not one of those silly girls requested another sitting."

The heavy scent of vetiver wafted from her light brown skin. It drowned out the commingled smells of the street—dried horse manure, roasting peanuts, tobacco, rotting food scraps. Effie preferred the latter. She remembered the way the women at the séance had glared at her, Madame Desâmes's smug smile, and refused to back away. "They seemed duly stupefied to me."

"I provide an important service, a way for—"

"Service?" Effie laughed. "You swindle simpletons of their money."

"I—"

Footsteps clapped past them on the banquette. Miss Mercier straightened and flashed a smile over Effie's shoulder. "*Bonjou, Monsieur Tredoux.*"

"*Bonjou. Ça va?*"

"*Bien,*" she said, her wide, straight-toothed smile persisting until the man jaunted off.

"Another spirit-seeker you bamboozled?"

"Hush," she said, her eyes sweeping up and down the street. "He's a neighbor."

"I'm sure he has memories of some dead beloved you can exploit."

"Is that why you came? To harangue me?" Miss Mercier said. "How did you even find me?"

"It wasn't easy. You ought to employ the same care with your tricks as you do concealing your identity."

Miss Mercier turned back into the house.

"Wait, wait . . . I'm sorry." The words sat heavy and strange on Effie's tongue. She'd not taken the time to probe the wound cut that night at the séance. Now, upon actual inspection, she found it deep and festering. Still, she ought to be more conciliatory if she wanted this woman's help. "I'm . . . I'm too frank sometimes."

"I'll say."

"I heard . . ." Effie clasped her hands and looked down at the dusty pavers. "I heard you can make Voodoo medicines."

Miss Mercier's laughter drew her gaze upward again.

"*Ma foi!* Are you kidding?"

"You don't, then?"

A raspy voice sounded from inside the house. "Adeline, *qui est à la porte?*"

"*Personne,* Mamm," Miss Mercier shouted over her shoulder, then in a whisper to Effie, "You have to go."

She started to close the door, but again Effie wedged herself into the jam. "Please, I can pay you."

Miss Mercier hesitated. "Fine. But keep quiet."

She let Effie in and hurried her through a lavish parlor replete with Oriental rugs, a marble fireplace, and a lacquered piano. Decorative molding crowned the walls and edged the doublewide entryways. In the dining room, a gilded chandelier hung above the long table.

Yet for all its gilt and marble, something about this home struck her as different from the fancy homes she'd visited to attend to the dead. For one, she'd never known a Negro to possess such wealth. Meg talked of the *Gens du Couleur Libres,* who'd lived here free before the War. Several of the men at the Republican clubhouse were likely of this set. Effie had gathered from the bits of conversation she couldn't tune out that, as with the city's whites, strata existed among these Negroes based on income, family name, *lingua franca,* the lightness of one's skin. Miss Mercier seemed to possess the right admixture of these attributes.

Even this could not quite explain what stuck out to Effie about these sumptuous rooms. But Miss Mercier bustled onward, leaving Effie little time to consider. They passed through a sunlit loggia with a curving staircase at one end and into a stone-tiled courtyard. Overgrown camellia bushes and shaggy palms skirted the yard. An orange tree, heavy with fruit, lolled in one corner; a large crepe myrtle roosted in another. Crabgrass pushed up between the tiles at her feet. At the courtyard's center stood a dry fountain topped with a moss-covered cherub. One of its wings had broken off, leaving a craggy stub of feather-etched stone.

"*Allez-y,*" Miss Mercier said when Effie dawdled by the fountain. "This way."

A single-story outbuilding sat at the back of the courtyard, containing a kitchen and empty servants' quarters. They entered the kitchen and Miss Mercier pointed to a wooden stool, then opened a large cupboard. "What kind of gris-gris are you looking for?"

Effie sat. Dusty jars filled with an assortment of powders, liquids, feathers, bones, and even matted wool crowded the bottom shelf. Dried leaves, flowers, and tendrils of lichen hung from the shelf above. This had been a bad idea. Entirely irrational. An inert medicine only worked on a believing subject. Yet without hesitation she said, "I fear I've fallen in love."

"A *charm de l'amour,* then. Let me see." She rummaged through the jars. "Melon seed with boiled fowl's gizzard can make a man positively besotted."

"That's not what I meant. I don't want to cast a spell or a charm or hex on anyone. I want you to cure me."

"Cure you?"

"Of these feelings."

Miss Mercier continued to search through the cupboard. "He's married, then?"

Effie thought a moment. "I don't believe so."

"Engaged, then. A minor impediment."

"Not that I know of."

"You're married and afraid your husband will find out. I have a charm for that too. A little snakeroot—"

"What? No, I just want . . . don't you have something to, to . . . dampen one's emotions?"

Miss Mercier turned around and regarded her with a nonplussed expression. "The Chinaman down on Liberty Street sells—"

"Not opium. That's not what I'm looking for."

"Who is this man?"

"His name is Samson Greene." This too she said without hesitation, considering only after that she still hadn't any good reason to trust Miss Mercier and numerous reasons not to. Yet finally speaking his name aloud was freeing. "He's a legislator in the statehouse."

"A Creole?"

Effie shook her head. "A freedman, I think."

"You don't know for sure where he's from, you don't know for sure whether he's engaged or married—what makes you so sure you're in love with him?"

Effie shrugged, recalling Miss Mercier's words from the night of the séance, that a girl like her wouldn't know love if it dropped on her head. "All I do is think about him. That and try to devise ways not to think of him."

Miss Mercier leaned forward and rested her elbows on the waist-high table beside which Effie sat. "What's this fellow got that's so special? Legislator or not, if he's a freedman likely he hasn't much money."

It wasn't about the money. Effie could make her own money, after all. But what, then? She'd rolled this question round and round in her brain till it made her dizzy and still had no answer. "I don't know."

"Well, he must be handsome."

"He is."

"And kind."

"He seems so."

"And intelligent?"

Effie leaned forward too. They were close enough she could again smell Miss Mercier's vetiver perfume. "Most assuredly."

"But that's not why you love him?"

"His voice . . . it reminds me of someone."

"Who?"

"I don't know."

Miss Mercier stood and waved a hand in Effie's direction. "*Tu ne sais rien.*"

Again with the French. But her exasperation needed no translation. That Effie knew so little on such an important point exasperated her too. "And when he looks at me it's like . . . like he really sees me. Like I'm the only person in the world."

"Maybe he's sweet on you too."

"No." She'd analyzed their interactions at length. "His interest is of a professional nature. He's misguided on some points, I have to say, and overmuch confident, but—"

"Why not just seduce him?"

"Seduce him?"

"You know, make him fall in love with you."

She spoke as if that were easy as pie. "How?"

"With your feminine charms, *bien sûr*."

Effie stood. This was hopeless. An utter waste of time. She hadn't such skills. Never before had she been in want of them. *Keep your distance,* Mr. Kinyon had said. *From the living and the dead.* And she did.

"I'm not the charming type."

Miss Mercier's eyes roved from the top of Effie's bonnet to her ill-fitting shoes. "True. But surely your maman taught you something of the art of love."

A shiver worked down Effie's neck. Without a lit stove, the kitchen was cold. She buttoned her overcoat and reached for the purse she'd set upon the bare table. No, not entirely bare—a half-eaten loaf of bread sat at the far corner, a ceramic dish of marmalade, a bowl of eggs. "Where's your cook?"

"Pardon?"

"Why hasn't she started on dinner?"

Miss Mercier wrapped her arms around her waist and her gaze retreated to the floor. "It's . . . er . . . her day off."

But more than a day's worth of dust covered the stovetop. Of the various pots and pans stored hither and thither about the room, only the kettle appeared recently used.

When Effie had first seen Madame Desâmes, she assumed the fancy dress and flowery manners were part of the ruse. Arriving here had proved her wrong, yet why would a woman of such means grift about as a medium? Curiosity? Boredom? Pure maleficence?

It suddenly all made sense. There'd been an emptiness to the house, not enough furniture to fill the big rooms. Of course, all the requisite pieces where there—dining table and chairs, settee and armchair, sideboard and tea table —but no writing desk or card table, no ornate pedestals crowned with porcelain urns or marble statues. Bright patches in the otherwise faded paper suggested walls once replete with decoration, where now only a few scattered paintings hung.

"You haven't any money."

Miss Mercier dropped her arms to her side and raised her chin. "You don't know what you're talking about."

"That's why you go about performing séances and selling charms. That's why you let me in."

"*C'est ridicule!* Look at my dress—it's French silk. Our house, it's one of the largest on the entire Rue de Toulouse. We have our own box at *l'opéra.*"

"Then why the Madame Desâmes routine? You find swindling countrified folk entertaining?"

Miss Mercier snickered. "You talk like you're not one of them."

"I know enough to see through your two-bit ruse."

Miss Mercier grabbed Effie's upper arm and towed her from the kitchen. "I never should have let *un coquin* like you in."

Effie shrugged free and stamped across the courtyard with Miss Mercier following close as a shadow. "To think, I almost bought one of your trifling elixirs."

"It wouldn't have worked anyway. *Une vilaine négresse comme toi.* Nobody's ever going to love you."

Effie's toe caught in a crack in the stone tile and she tripped forward, catching hold of the loggia's arched jamb just before falling. Stucco flecked off onto her gloves. Suddenly she was small again, before the War, shelling beans on a splintery porch stoop. A sharp pinch stung the back of her arm.

"*Vilaine négresse!*" a sallow-faced white woman said, yanking Effie from the stoop toward a dilapidated outbuilding. Beans from her upturned bowl skittered across the dusty ground. "To the shed with you. You're likely as diseased as *ta mamm.*"

Effie clutched the jamb and tried to steady her breath. She stared at the tiled patio and creeping crabgrass, wrestling herself free from the memory.

"You clumsy—" Miss Mercier stopped. "Are you all right?"

"Fine," Effie said, straightening and brushing off her gloves. But her legs wobbled, as if the tendons connecting muscle to bone had snapped.

"I didn't mean—"

"I've been called worse by worse people."

"You really ought to get better shoes. One of these days—"

"Adeline?"

It was the same thin voice Effie had heard when she first arrived, only much closer now.

"*Fi donc*," Adeline said under her breath, pushing past her into the loggia. "You shouldn't be out of bed, Mamm."

At the base of the curving staircase stood a small-framed woman with the same light skin and dainty nose as Adeline. Black hair with only the errant strand of gray showed beneath her sagging tignon. Her lace-trimmed nightshirt clung sweaty to her spindly trunk and limbs. She sagged against the banister as if her meager weight were too much for her legs to bear. Even so, her posture had a royal air.

"*Qui est avec toi? Un homme?*"

Adeline sighed. "*Non,* Mamm. Not a man. This is . . . er . . ." She glanced sidelong at Effie.

"My name is Effie, ma'am."

"See, Mamm. Effie. *Une femme,* not a man. And an American. She doesn't speak French."

"*Une Américaine?*" the woman said this with some distaste. "Effie, come here. Let me get a closer look at you. Adeline lets hardly any friends call these days."

Mrs. Mercier's Creole accent clouded her words far more strongly than her daughter's, making it difficult to pluck out the Latin roots and mentally translate them into English. She glanced at Adeline, who pursed her lips but waved her onward to the stairs, where her mother waited.

Afternoon sunlight slanted in through the loggia's archways. Effie's heart still beat off-kilter from the apparition she'd had in the courtyard. Her toes had gone numb and the blisters on her heels cried out with each step. Even here in the sunlight, she was cold. Nothing seemed more luxurious at that moment than her tiny room and moss-filled mattress back at the boardinghouse. But an unmistakable authority buttressed Mrs. Mercier's weak, raspy voice, compelling Effie to stay.

When she reached the stairs, Effie bobbed with a quick, stiff curtsy. Though Mrs. Mercier stood a step above her, their eyes met squarely.

"*Bon Dieu,* you're a giant." She took Effie's chin between two bony fingers and moved her head side to side. "And so dark."

"That's not true, Mamm," Adeline said, joining them at the steps. Then, to Effie, "She doesn't see well anymore. Mamm, Effie's own father could be white."

"With such hair? I don't think so. What's your family name, *demoiselle?*"

"Jones," she said, pulling her chin free of Mrs. Mercier's grasp and smoothing her flyaway curls.

"*Américaine,* indeed. Who are your parents?"

Effie patted her pinned-back hair. "I . . ."

"This isn't an inquisition, Mamm," Adeline said. "Besides, Effie was just leaving."

"*Quelle absurdité.* It's nearly time for dinner. Effie, you must stay and join us."

"That's—um—very kind, ma'am, but I really—"

"It's settled. Why, I can smell Dorothée about in the kitchen already." Mrs. Mercier breathed deeply through her nose and smiled. "Oyster stuffed pheasant." She inhaled again. "Wax beans au beurre, *tarte aux poires.* Delicious, *non?*"

Effie glanced back at the empty kitchen. "Yes . . . er . . . it smells delicious. I'd be delighted to stay."

Adeline flashed her a smile. The fading afternoon light twinkled off her glassy eyes. "Dinner will be a while, Mamm. Dorothée's only just started the roux. You should rest." She wrapped an arm around her mother's waist and helped her up the stairs.

Effie watched them ascend, a strange, unsettling feeling overtaking her. She wanted to break one of the glass windows overlooking the dining room and use its shards to peel away her own skin and slip into Adeline's.

Instead, Effie hurried from the house the moment the two left her view.

Once outside, Effie could breathe again. She slowed to a hobble and drifted down Toulouse Street. Everything about the day had been a disaster. Had she really believed she'd walk away cured? If anything, she felt more broken. Was it this city that made her so foolhardy? Had she been too rash in leaving Indiana? Things had been familiar there, predictable. At least until the end.

She turned down Chartres toward Canal Street. A pack of children dashed past with their schoolbooks, nearly knocking her off the banquette in their gay parade. The whining breaks of the streetcar made her arm hairs steeple. On every corner, street vendors accosted her with their wares—mud-streaked turnips, squirming crawfish, drooping flower buds, ink-smeared copies of *L'Abeille de Nouvelle Orléans*.

Above the din, Effie heard her name. She turned and saw Adeline a block behind her. Effie half thought to turn around and pretend she'd not heard. She hadn't the energy for more sparring. But her curiosity won out and she waited.

Adeline reached her ruddy-faced and panting. She clutched her side and held her hand up until she caught her breath. "*Ma foi,* I thought I'd never catch you."

"What do you want?"

She pulled Effie away from the bustle and into the shade of an open carriageway. "You won't tell anyone, will you?"

"Tell whom what?"

"You know, your friends, from the séance. My real name. That I'm . . . well . . ."

"A charlatan after their money? I thought I'd already ruined that for you, that you'd given up on their repeat business."

She glared at Effie. "You did, and I have. But if word got around to others, those of a different set, it could ruin my reputation."

"Madame Desâmes's?"

"No, you ninny. My own." A few strands of glossy black hair had fallen free from her green and gold tignon. She tucked them back into place. The redness had drained from her face, leaving only the apples of her cheeks and her full, symmetrical lips flushed with color.

What must it feel like to be that beautiful? The time it must take her to layer on all her adornments, to fix her hair and tie her head wrap just so. She'd probably not run as she just had in ages for fear of staining her dress with perspiration. It seemed as much a burden as a gift. And yet, if Effie were more beautiful, not so tall and curly haired, Samson would remember her for more than just her pert comments about overcrowded cemeteries.

"What you said before, about feminine charms, is that something you could teach me?"

"*Moi?*"

"Yes." In the short time they'd been standing together, Effie had noticed several men casting slow, sidelong glances in Adeline's direction. "Whatever these charms, you seem to possess an overabundance of them."

Adeline smiled and ran a finger along her neck beneath her pearls. "*Je suis comme il faut,* it's true. But you, I . . . er . . . let's just say it would be quite an undertaking."

"Good." Effie walked back into the crowd and Adeline followed. "When do we start?"

"*Non,* you misunderstand me. I wasn't agreeing to teach you. Where would one even begin?"

Effie turned to face her. Passersby streamed around them. "I know you don't like me. And I don't like you. I know that I'm coarse, blunt, and unfriendly. But it shouldn't be any greater challenge than I must abide with your unscrupulous character and insufferable vanity." Effie continued, despite Adeline's scandalized expression. "I need your help and you need my silence. So when do we start?"

"Coarse doesn't even begin to describe you. Even your silence isn't worth that much." She turned around and stamped away.

Effie watched her go. She could always find someone else, couldn't she? Someone less detestable. Someone less . . . "Wait." She hurried after her, grimacing at what she was about to say. Damn herself for being so weak and susceptible to this infatuation. "I can help you with your spirit act. Improve your tricks."

Adeline stopped but didn't turn around. "How? Are you claiming to be a sensitive now too?"

"Of course not. With science and mechanics."

The last sliver of sun sank behind the buildings lining the Rue de Chartres. For a moment, fiery light crowned the rooftops. Then shadow overtook them.

"Fine. *Après-demain.* Bring me proof of this science magic. If it's any good, I'll help you."

CHAPTER 8

After cleaning the day's worth of grime from her equipment, washing and hanging her apron, and measuring out the right amounts of mercury, arsenic, and zinc chloride for the next batch of embalming fluid, Effie hurried from Mr. Whitmark's shop to the cobbler's. She arrived to find the shop door locked, but a gas lantern still aglow within. She rapped and waited.

The day had been a busy one with two bodies to embalm—a child taken by scarlet fever and a man kicked in the head by his horse. Business had continued to grow, thanks in no small part to the hours she'd spent cleaning and scrubbing and bookkeeping. Mr. Whitmark's fledgling sobriety helped too. He'd even taken her advice and hired on another assistant, an Irishman named Colm. A bruiser of a man, Colm was only a few years older than Effie, and—in her estimation—good for lugging supplies, hitching the wagon, and not much else. Had she known this was the sort Mr. Whitmark would hire, she'd not have suggested another assistant at all.

Today, as was quickly seeming to become his habit, Colm had managed to nettle her. She hadn't needed his help with the child—the boy was small enough to move on her own—and she'd asked Colm to ready the cooling table at the next house. He scowled at the request, reminded her she weren't his boss, then sauntered off to do as bidden, leaving Effie to the boy.

He was a beautiful child with hair the color of dried clay and freckles stamped across his nose. His small artery had been limp and fragile from dehydration, but she'd managed to secure her cannula and he took the fluid quickly. His mother had finished bathing him just as Effie arrived, and stayed in the room while she worked, her face turned away, her gaze locked upon the worn wool rug, her hand resting on the mattress beside his little feet.

In cases like these—children—Effie's hand never slipped, her mind never wandered. With enough focus, she could drown out even the loudest sobs and most deafening silences.

But today, after she left, thoughts of the boy's mother stayed with her, harrying her nerves, unsettling her calm. Her next case, though complicated in the careful reconstruction she'd had to do on the man's skull, did not prove sufficient distraction. She thought of Adeline and her mother, and the ache that watching them together had inflicted. She thought of the sallow-faced woman, freshly exhumed from among her forgotten memories, and what she'd said about Effie's own mother. Diseased. Besides a few hummed notes, this new fragment of recollection—of beans scattering and the woman yanking her toward that shed—was all she knew of *ta mamm,* her mother.

The cobbler emerged from the back of his shop. He carried the gas lamp to the door and, after shining it upon her face, smiled and let her in.

"Are they done?"

"Yes, yes, have a seat." He waved her toward a stool and headed back into the bowels of his workshop. "I had to use a man's mold, but I narrowed it some and tapered the toe." He reappeared with a pair of women's boots larger than any on display.

Effie ran her fingers along the smooth black leather and careful stitching, then knocked on the soles—thick and sturdy, each nail flush and evenly spaced. "They're beautiful."

"Try them on before you fall in love now."

Effie unlaced her old boots and yanked them off. Her scrunched toes unfurled. She wiggled them to bring back feeling, then slipped her feet into the new boots. The leather hugged the long, wide plane of her feet like a second skin—not too tight, but not so loose they'd slip and rub while she walked. Her toes spread and straightened without constraint, no longer crammed one atop the other like string beans in a jar. "I ain't never—I've never had a pair of shoes made just for me before. They're . . . perfect."

He smiled again. "Well, I saved the mold, so it ought not take so long next time you be needing a new pair."

"Thank you."

"Here, let me wrap them up for you."

"No," she said, scooping up her old boots. "I'm never putting these on again."

He laughed. "They're well-worn, that's for sure, but I'll take them to the poorhouse if you won't be wearing them."

Effie handed them over and he tossed them into a nearby crate filled with other cast-offs. The heels clapped together as they landed atop the heap, calling to mind Madame Desâmes's fabricated spirit knocking. Effie still had no idea what she was going to bring to Adeline to aid her act. Why had she offered to help in the first place? The whole idea of deception for profit repulsed her. Still, if it were going to be done, it could be done much better.

She pulled several bills from her purse, handed them to the cobbler, then turned to leave, glancing one last time at her wretched old boots. "How difficult would it be to make a hollow boot heel?"

"Not so hard, I'd think. But it'd have to be made of something pretty sturdy to bear someone's weight."

"Hmm . . . like steel?"

He shrugged, flipping through his keys and unlocking the bolt. "That ought to work. Little paint and you probably couldn't tell the difference." He opened the door. "Careful walking home now, don't scuff your boots on your first stroll about."

She smiled, only half hearing him, her mind roused with the possibilities.

"A hollow boot heel? That's your brilliant idea?"

Effie watched as Adeline rummaged through a basket of yarn, stuffing a few skeins into her carpetbag and tossing the rest haphazardly back into the basket. "All we have to do is fashion a lever and hammer mechanism inside. Depress it with your heel and you've got a veritable sound box. No more joint popping."

"It's worked fine so far."

"It took me two minutes to figure out you were manipulating your knee joint in and out of its socket. And you're likely to do permanent damage to your ligaments."

Adeline gave her a look that suggested both confusion and disinterest.

"The sinew that holds your bones together. You might lose your ability to tolerate long bouts of standing or repetitive squatting movements."

"Why ever would that matter?"

"Suppose you're taking the streetcar across town and all the seats are occupied."

"*Chère,* a gentleman always yields his seat."

Not in Effie's experience. "You mightn't stand dancing long either."

At this, Adeline stopped her rummaging and looked at her. "*Vraiment?* Tell me more about this hollow boot heel."

Effie further explained the contraption—how they might make it with soldered scraps of steel from the rail yard and a small, spring-loaded hammer with a rubber head—but Adeline waved her through the details.

"Are you sure it will be loud enough?"

"It will take some experimentation, but once we have all the dimensions and proportions right, the acoustics of the box will amplify the sound."

Adeline shouldered her bag and returned the basket of yarn to its place beside the settee. "*Bien.* When will it be finished?"

Did she think Effie just wiled away her hours like a fatted house cat? "I'll look for parts when I can, but I do have more pressing obligations."

"Ah, *oui,* I forgot. The encumbrances of employment. What are you? A teacher? One of those reformers come down from the North to educate the ignorant freedman and his children?"

Adeline's comment didn't surprise Effie—many people assumed she was a teacher—but her blithe, almost disdainful tone did. Light as her skin was, Adeline was still a Negro. Didn't she care for the advancement of her race? "Historically, societies who educate their citizenry fare better than those—"

"Yes, yes. No need to raise sand about it. I'm sure you—" The porcelain mantel clock chimed three. "*Fi donc!* We're late."

"For what?"

"Your first lesson. That's the deal, isn't it?"

The deal yes; the plan no. She had her clothes to press and new boots to polish back at the boardinghouse. She had errands to run on Canal Street. She hadn't brought pad and pencil to take notes. She hadn't even decided for sure a deal like this with a woman like Adeline was worth making, however much these feelings for Samson troubled her.

But she hadn't time to argue. Adeline had already quit the parlor and donned her shawl.

They walked in silence for several minutes, turning up this street and down the next. Not arm in arm as other women did. Not even side by side—for Effie still had no idea of their destination and lagged a step behind—but as two strangers strolling in a common direction. Adeline seemed to know everyone in the Quarter, bobbing her head to shopkeepers and coachmen, newsboys and Sunday promenaders, echoing their *bonjou.*

When they arrived at a large two-story home, more American in style with colonnades and clapboard siding, Adeline stopped. Her long, manicured fingers knotted around the straps of her bag and she eyed Effie from head to toe. "This is your Sunday dress?"

"Yes."

Adeline's lips screwed into a frown. "Is everything you own so dark and . . . plain?"

Effie smoothed a hand down her dress. Perhaps the navy-blue muslin wasn't as fine as Adeline's silk. Fewer ruffles, a smaller bustle. But the fabric was good—soft and durable. The color was, well, serviceable. Death, after all, could call at any time.

"*Nenpòrt,*" Adeline said. "Never mind. We'll work on your fashion sensibilities later. Today just try . . . not to speak. Listen and learn."

Effie's stomach quivered as she mounted the short flight of steps to the porch. What had she gotten herself into? Good thing she'd opted for only bread and butter for breakfast. She took a deep breath to settle her digestion and straightened her shoulders. Lesson one— how hard could it be? But when their hostess opened the door—a young woman of Adeline's ilk with a fine satin dress, light brown skin, and dark sleek hair—Effie's resolve wavered. She could see over the woman's shoulder to a large parlor, where several similarly styled women sat, their hands busy with needles, yarn, and other implements of domestic torture.

"*Ma chérie!*" the woman said, kissing Adeline on either cheek. "*Enfin. Nous avons pensé que tu as oublié.*" She turned to Effie and her ebullient smile sagged. "*Qui est ton . . . amie?*"

"*Ma cousine,*" Adeline said, and then, in a whisper, "*du nord,*" as if being from the North bordered on indecency. "*Elle s'appelle* Effie."

Effie didn't bother to point out she'd been born in the South or that she was not Adeline's cousin.

"*Bienvenue,* Effie," the hostess said, leaning in and kissing her too while Effie tried not to grimace. "*Je m'appelle* Odette."

Inside, Effie endured a bevy of kisses and names, of sidelong glances and pinned-on smiles, before the gaggle of women settled. Adeline sat on a damask sofa and tugged Effie down beside her. She pulled two sets of knitting needles and two skeins of yarn from her bag and handed one to Effie. The other women resumed their knitting, the clink of needles underscoring their chatter. Effie listened intently at first, deciphering the Latin roots of their creolized French, but the rumored affair between the young star of the visiting theater troupe and her tailor, or the relative advantages of the new tournure petticoat over the crinolette held little interest for her.

She looked down at the yarn in her lap as they jabbered on, and strove to remember how to use the dratted needles. Mrs. Kinyon had tried to teach her the full gamut of domestic skills, from cooking to crochet, but Effie preferred her books and color plate drawings of human anatomy. She watched Adeline from the corner of her eye and did her best to copy the twist and looping motions. It jogged her memory enough that she was able to lay the first row in what—if she were to mimic the others—was to be a child-sized hat.

Her hands did not take to the motion with the speed or grace the other women's did. She found herself hunching over or bringing her work needles-to-nose that she might scrutinize a stitch, while the others hardly gave their work a glance. By the time she'd managed another row—with more than a few dropped stitches—Adeline was already binding off the final row of a bright yellow cap.

But surely, this—knitting—was not what she'd come to learn.

The women's discussion meandered to the social calendar, busy now that Carnival had begun, and which fête or masked dance they most anticipated. As the others' voices grew sharp and animated, Adeline quieted. Her smile thinned and even faltered when the others' eyes looked away. When probed about which events she planned to attend, she demurred. "Oh, but you must come!" someone would say—as best Effie could translate—and then extol all the wonderments prepared for the occasion. Ice cream and orchestras, tableaux and dancing.

Effie didn't much like ice cream, the way it coated your tongue and numbed your throat. She abhorred dancing. Sweaty palms, clumsy feet, barbecue-scented breath inches from her nose. Worst of all had been the feeling that everyone was watching her, the lone black girl amid a sea of whiteness, the charity case every boy must take a turn with before claiming a second or third dance with another.

But Adeline didn't seem to share her distaste for such things. She sighed and reminded them of her mother's frail health. Her other difficulties—the impossible expense of new gowns and slippers and hired coaches—Adeline did not share.

Did these women not know of her money troubles? Not that Effie knew more than what she'd observed and deduced. Whatever the extent of Adeline's financial shortcomings, she hid it well.

And yet, these women were her friends. They'd kissed her cheeks and called her *chérie*. They must know, or at least suspect, but they preened and prattled on just the same.

"Effie, *qu'est-ce que vous faites comme occupation?*" one of the women said when the conversation lagged.

Effie looked up from her knitting and found the entire group of women staring at her. She hid her loose jumble of stitches in the folds of her skirt and replayed what the woman had said.

"*Pardonne,*" Adeline said. "*Ma cousine* does not speak French."

Several of the women gasped, dainty and affected. *Quel dommage! Excusez-moi! Non, vraiment?* they muttered, one on top of the other.

"I'm an embalmer."

Her declaration met with silence.

"I believe you asked about my livelihood. *Mon occupation.* I work as an embalmer."

"*Qu'est-ce que c'est* an embalmer?" a woman in green silk and a yellow tignon asked between giggles.

"Embalming comes from the Latin word *balsamum,* balm. It's the art of preserving dead bodies from decay by means of aromatics, antiseptics, or desiccation."

The giggling stopped. Knitting needles stilled. Several of the women crossed themselves.

"The Ancient Egyptians practiced embalming and—"

"*Bon Dieu,* Effie, that's enough," Adeline hissed at her. Then, with a tight smile, she said to the others, "The things *une femme* must do today to survive." They all nodded solemnly. "I, for one, feel quite blessed to be spared such necessity."

More nodding. The women returned to their knitting. Odette, speaking again in French, mentioned something about the weather and the others rushed to comment, talking over one another with forced lightness.

Effie took up her paltry hat and cast another stitch. She glared sidelong at Adeline, who returned the look with matching venom. *Spared such necessity*—ha! What would these women, her friends, think of Madame Desâmes? Effie clenched her jaw lest the temptation to reveal Adeline's secret burn any hotter.

She thought to leave—what had she learned of value to her situation with Mr. Greene, anyway?—but the women's trivial discussion of the weather had waned. They bound off their little hats, laid them in a communal basket, and stowed their needles. Effie hurried through her last stitches. The hat she'd made was misshapen and had several noticeable holes, but she cast it into the basket with the others. Whatever their intended use, hers would have to suit.

Adeline stood, donned her shawl and bag, and nestled the basket of hats in the crook of her arm. "*Qui vient avec moi?*"

The women busied themselves with their gloves and handbags and sewing boxes, muttering excuses why they couldn't come along. At the door, Odette embraced Adeline, but didn't suffer Effie any more kisses. She insisted again that Adeline must make a showing at the upcoming Carnival fêtes, mentioning the name Monsieur Chauvet. Adeline danced her fingers down the line of her carotid and looked away.

No sooner had the front door closed behind them than she seized Effie's arm. "*Tonnerre!* I told you to keep quiet." She pulled Effie down the porch steps and into the street. "The things they must be saying right now."

Effie shrugged free. "They brought it up."

"Lesson one—when someone asks you what you do, lie."

"Is that why you brought me here? To learn about deceit from the masters?"

"*Mes amies* and I—"

"Those women are not your friends."

"What do you know about friends? Even the women who brought you to my séance can't abide your company."

Effie looked down. Pounded shell paved the narrow way. She bore the toe of her boot into the jagged white shards, despite the grit it left on the new leather. "I don't claim them to be friends." She met Adeline's eye. "And I'd rather have no friends at all than those as counterfeit as yours."

Adeline opened her mouth but closed it again. Voices and laughter rang from within the house. She patted her shiny silk tignon. "They're just a little jealous is all."

Effie smirked. That was Adeline's answer to everything. The afternoon sun had dipped below the surrounding buildings, casting the street in shadow. A wagon rumbled past, chasing them to the banquette to avoid the spray dust. "Why bring me along if my very presence is an embarrassment to you?"

"We have a deal, remember. Besides, I rather like a challenge."

"I'm not the simpleton you think I am. I know I don't fit in. I don't need you parading me around your *chères amies* just to prove it."

"Clearly, you missed the point."

Effie gritted her teeth. Could she have brokered a deal with a more odious woman? "So enlighten me."

"When are you seeing this Mr. Greene again?"

"Tuesday next."

"*Parfait.* A Mardi Gras fête."

"The Republican Club is meeting at the parade."

Adeline gave a puckered expression. "Hardly the most romantic circumstance, *mais nenpòrt.* The principles still apply." She set to walking and Effie begrudgingly followed. "Now, wherever you are you must learn to read the social environment. Think of it like the opera. You've been to the opera, *oui*?"

"No."

Her expression soured again. "Well, in each company you have the lead, the prima donna. She's the one with the power, the one everyone else is trying to please. Then you have the mezzo. In an opera, she usually plays the role of the friend or caretaker. Think of her as the prima donna's second. You have the chorus—that's everyone else, really. Those people who follow along in the prima donna's shadow. Oh, and the soubrette. Be careful of the soubrette."

"Who's she?"

"She plays the role of the ingénue or comedienne. But she's got her sights set on being the prima donna someday and will claw through whomever to get there."

Effie's feet slowed as she worked through what Adeline had said. *Prima donna, mezzo, soubrette* . . . perhaps she was now ready to sit through a performance of *Faust* or *Fidelio,* but how did this help her fit in or win Mr. Greene's affections? "I still don't see the point."

"Like I said, you've got be able to read the social strata of those around you. If you want to gain entry into a group, you can't go up to the prima donna and expect her to give two fiddles about you. Or the mezzo for that matter. Start with someone in the chorus—befriend her and work your way up."

"Up to what? Is Mr. Greene the prima donna in this scenario?"

Adeline laughed. "Primo uomo. And no, of course not. Men are an entirely different matter."

They stopped at the intersection of Canal and Rampart to let the streetcar pass. The horse's flanks were slick with sweat despite the evening's chill.

"You'll never catch the eye of Mr. Greene, or that of any man, if you can't get along with the women around him," Adeline said as they continued on. "His mother, his sisters, his friends. You must find these women, figure who's who and how you can gain ingress. If you can't do that, you'll never have your Mr. Greene."

It still seemed a silly analogy, but Effie nodded.

"A new dress wouldn't hurt either. A different color, a more flattering décolleté." She tugged at Effie's straight-cut sleeve, but Effie batted her hand away.

"So, Odette is the prima donna in your group."

"What? *Non, c'est moi.*"

Of course.

"Odette . . . she's the mezzo. Béatrice, the one who asked about your livelihood—an impertinent question to begin with—she's the soubrette."

They stopped at a multistoried building with gable roofs. Leafless treetops peeked over the surrounding brick wall. CHARITY HOSPITAL read the bronze plaque beside the gate.

Passing through a dark foyer and up several flights of stairs, they arrived at the Negro ward. A row of beds lined both walls of the long hall. Feeble light drifted in through the grimy windows. They crossed to the far end, their boot heels clapping atop the scuffed wood floor. Effie kept her head down, eyes sweeping from one occupied bed to the next. The hacking, the shivering, the frailty—it made her skin itch beneath her chemise. Death she could stand; sickness was something else entirely.

Adeline stopped and handed Effie a stack of hats. The patients at this end of the hall were smaller, skiffs in a sea of stained white sheets. Children. She looked from the beds back to Adeline and shook her head.

"Don't be a ninny," Adeline said.

Effie clutched the stack of hats and watched as Adeline moved from bedside to bedside with her radiant smile. The children bloomed in her presence, their small hands grasping, eager for their gift. She spoke to them in quiet tones, and they replied with weak but exuberant voices. When they coughed, sneezed, retched, Adeline didn't flinch, but wiped their noses with her hankie and rubbed their spiny backs. Was this yet another ruse?

At a tug on her skirt, Effie looked down. A young boy had crawled to the foot of his bed and reached out to her. She knelt on shaky legs and held out the bundle of hats for him to choose from. He sifted through them, stroking the soft fabric of each. His tiny hands were all bone. A green tinge played beneath his black skin. How did Adeline do this? How did she look down at these children and smile? He selected a royal blue hat—Effie's hat, all misshapen and holey. She tried to offer him another, but he shook his head and tugged the blue hat over his closely cropped hair. It flopped down over his eyes.

She cuffed it twice until it fit snuggly about his ears. "Not so bad," she said aloud. His cracked lips parted, and his white baby teeth showed in full. Effie found herself smiling too.

CHAPTER 9

The streets teemed with maskers headed toward the intersection of St. Charles and Canal streets, where the Henry Clay statue signaled the start of the parade. Horns and rattles sounded from amid the throngs. Somewhere near off a snare drum nattered out a halting rhythm, while its brass accompaniment danced through scales and squeaked into tune.

Effie hurried home from the shop, passing gypsies, Arabs, and clowns. Men dressed as ladies and ladies dressed as witches. Harlequins and devils. At last, she reached Mrs. Neale's. Upstairs, she unbuttoned her bodice and shimmied out of her skirt. She splashed some water on her face and under her arms. From beneath her bed, she pulled out a large box tied with string. Inside lay her newest treasure—a gown of fine muslin. It had cost extra to have the hem let down and the sleeves lengthened for a total sum of three-and-a-half weeks' wages. An irrational expenditure and one that set Effie's heart trilling. As a girl, she'd worn the cast-offs of other children—most in good repair and only a few seasons behind in fashion—but nothing she'd chosen for herself or tailored for her large frame.

The skirt settled smoothly over her petticoat. Several flounces enlarged the bustle. At the shop, though she'd been tempted to select plain brown and black calico, she'd thought of Adeline's words and chosen lavender instead. The bodice buttoned snug over her corset and the sleeves, for once, neither bunched nor constricted. She refastened her bonnet and rushed down the stairs.

In the foyer, she grabbed her shawl from the peg and caught sight of herself in the small oval mirror hung over the settee. A thin film clouded the glass, giving her reflection a strange pallor. Who was this woman hurrying out—new dress, new boots—into the crowds and chaos. The Effie she knew would never brave such a thing. No, perhaps brave was not the right word. Foolery was more apt. Whatever it was—bravery or lunacy—Effie decided she didn't care. It was Mardi Gras after all.

The closer she got to Canal Street, the more packed the walkways became. The slanting afternoon sunlight, clipped and bullied by the surrounding buildings, cast the maskers in an ominous glow. Up close she could smell the sweat bled into their costumes and alcohol suffusing their breath. Young boys scampered like animals on all fours around her ankles, pressing to get closer to the parade route. They hung from the streetlamps and perched on windowsills, blowing on noisemakers and brandishing flags.

She wound her way toward Dryades Street, where the club had agreed to meet, but the growing crowd slowed her progress. Soon she was floating with the tide of bodies more than walking, trapped in its haphazard ebb and flow. Gone was any pretense of manners. No *pardons,* or *excusez-moi*'s. Someone elbowed passed her, jabbing her hard enough to leave a bruise. Another hissed "out of my way" as he pushed her to the side.

She bobbed like a piece of flotsam cast about on storm-riled waves. She gulped down several breaths, but still hungered for air. The chatter and laughter and horn tooting muddled in her ears. Here a black mask, there a Mephisto, a jester, a monkey. Her feet found the paving stones and she backed out of the crowd, fighting the current with each step.

A sliver of space existed at the fringe of the crowd between the fluid mass of bodies and the unyielding buildings. Here at least she could breathe. She leaned against the cool brick and tried to quiet her nerves.

Soon the thud of her pulse settled. Pleasant smells—roasting peanuts, simmering gumbo, cooling pralines—fought off the stench of the crowd. Farther up the street a brass band played.

She reveled a moment in the melody, then searched out a street sign. Once oriented, she skirted the crowd, her bustle pressed flat against the brick and stucco buildings behind her, toward the club's rendezvous. Green, gold, and purple banners festooned the galleries above her, fluttering like the wings of exotic birds in the gentle breeze off the river.

Rex approached, seated on a bedazzled white stead, at the head of the parade. The crowd pressed toward the street, widening the narrow passage Effie navigated. The band, some distance behind Rex, had switched tunes. A lively number now played, heavy on the trumpet and drum line, and her feet fell in step with the beat. Her eyes, searching the crowd for faces from the ward meeting, strayed to the approaching parade. Flanking Rex, but a pace behind, rode several more men dressed in medieval finery. Their shiny bangles and silver-trimmed coats glinted in the sunlight.

The music tapered, and the band began a new set. Through the cheers of the crowd, she heard her name.

"Miss Jones."

She pried her gaze from the parade and rose onto her tiptoes, scanning the crowd. Not twenty feet on stood Tom, waving and smiling, his shaggy hair capped with a slouch hat. Mrs. Carrière stood beside him.

Effie waved back and ventured into the crowd toward them. She'd not taken but a few steps when three large men stepped in front of her. They wore plain cambric shirts with an assortment of poorly dyed rags thrown over their shoulders. Cheap masks perched on their noses, the dull black paint covering the papier-mâché a sharp contrast to their white skin.

"Where's your costume?" one said to her.

Effie didn't answer but tried to move around them. They sidestepped to block her path. The other revelers formed a solid wall behind her, lost in their hurrahs and applause.

"He asked you a question, you uppity wench," another of the three men said. He grabbed hold of her upper arm, his dirt-stained fingers digging into her flesh.

"I . . . I don't have a costume."

The shortest of the men stepped forward. His upper left cuspid was missing and several of the teeth around it chipped. He slid a meaty hand down the bodice of her new dress. "Here and I thought you was dressed as a she-ape."

"I got a better one for you," the first man said, reaching into a pouch about his waist. He pulled out a handful of brownish-white powder and threw it at her face. "Now you's white."

Effie closed her eyes, but not before the powder struck her. The backs of her eyelids burned, and her tear ducts gushed. She coughed with such force she doubled over and nearly toppled.

The hand around her arm slackened. When she managed to open her eyes, the men were gone. She coughed and sneezed several more times. Her tongue burned with the same fire as her eyes. She tasted flour and dirt and something else chalky and bitter. Around her, the crowd continued to cheer on the parade. Music played. Horses whinnied and stamped the paving stones. Shape and color bled together.

Another hand encircled her arm. Effie tensed and tried to bat it away.

"It's all right. I've got you."

Though she could only make out the bleary shape of a man, she recognized Tom's voice.

Another hand and familiar voice. Mrs. Carrière. "To the alleyway there. Jonah, fetch some water."

Effie followed where they led until the roar of the parade had softened and cool shade enveloped her.

Tom thrust a hankie into her hand.

She blotted her eyes and wiped the powder from her mouth and lips. "Thank you."

"Miscreants," Mrs. Carrière muttered. She'd taken out her own handkerchief and dusted off Effie's cheeks and bonnet.

Embarrassment took hold beside the pain, and she prayed, for once, that Mr. Greene was not around. "I'm fine, really. Don't miss the parade."

"Hush," Mrs. Carrière said. Jonah returned with a bucket of water and held it up for her.

She splashed her face and eyes. The cold water stung her skin. It dribbled down onto her dirtied dress.

Tom held up his cane like a club. "Did you get a good look at them? See which way they went?"

"No, they were masked," Effie said, then turned to Mrs. Carrière. "What was that?"

"An old Mardi Gras jinx." She dabbed a bit more at Effie's collar and then put away her hankie. "It's meant to be just flour, but *mon Dieu,* judging by how red your eyes are, I'd say they mixed in dirt and lime."

Jonah tugged at Mrs. Carrière's skirt. "Come on, we'll miss the floats."

"Are you all right?" Mrs. Carrière asked her.

Her hands trembled at her side. Her eyes, her mouth, her lungs all still burned. Her new dress was soiled. "Yes, fine. Thank you. I'll join you presently."

The three of them left the alley and joined the crowd, casting backward glances at her over their shoulders. Tom's gaze lingered the longest. He smoothed a hand over his trimmed sideburn and down the slope of his jaw, as if contemplating returning to her. She mustered a wobbly smile to reassure him, then leaned against a nearby wall and closed her watery eyes, wishing she could disappear into the cold stucco.

The way that man had touched her, slid his calloused hand over her breast and stomach like she was a piece of furniture, brought bile to her mouth.

Images buzzed at the periphery of her consciousness. Fuzzy at first. Specters taking shape in the self-imposed darkness. Voices blurring with the clamor of the street.

"Lift your dress up, girlie," a man with a gravelly voice said in the sharpening memory. When she tarried, he slapped her about the head.

Another man dressed in a shiny suit coat with soft, manicured hands pinched her still-flat breasts. "She's younger than you say."

"Hard to know their age with certainty. But look, strong for a girl." The gravelly voiced man squeezed her bicep. "And healthy." He pried open her mouth.

The other man peered over her. He stank of musk and spices. He tugged on her front teeth. One wiggled in its socket. "She's too young to carry more than a few canes."

"Aye, but think of her potential." He grabbed his crotch and jostled whatever lay beneath his trousers.

The taste of bile again. The din of the parade a distant murmur behind the unfurling memory. She grasped at the sounds—music and laughter, flapping banners and trotting horses. But not until she heard his sonorous voice did she find purchase on the present.

"Miss Jones, are you all right? Tom told me what happened."

She opened her eyes. Mr. Greene stood before her, resplendent in the same brown suit he'd worn in Tivoli Circle. His cheeks were smooth from a recent pass with the razor and his hair glossy with oil. He'd asked her something, but she couldn't remember what.

"If you're not well, I can walk you home." He reached out and brushed her cheekbone. The rawness of her throat and lungs, the tingling of her gums, the sting in her eyes retreated, and she felt only the electric contact of their skin.

Her fingers retraced the path of his touch. Flour and dirt remained speckled on her skin. What a fright she must look! She swatted at her cheeks and the yoke of her dress, stirring a cloud of dirt-riddled flour and lime. Both she and Mr. Greene coughed.

"Sorry," she said, wishing with renewed vigor that she might indeed disappear.

"Think nothing of it." He took her hand and settled it in the crook of his arm.

The sudden clamor of her heart beat out even the street-side bedlam.

"Where do you live?"

"No, I needn't go home, Mr. Greene."

"Are you sure?"

"It's my first Mardi Gras," she heard herself say. "It'd be a pity to end on such a note."

He studied her. His eyes were dark and rich, like cypress bark after a storm. A thin scar followed his hairline just above his right temple. The delicious scent of his shaving soap—rosemary and bitter orange—hung in the air between them.

"To the parade, then. If you're sure."

She nodded.

"And call me Samson."

They twisted and sidestepped their way through the crowd. This time Effie hardly noticed the press of bodies and waft of sweat. She'd never taken a man's arm before, enjoyed the gentle clasp of bicep and forearm. Her fingers, chilled from the water she'd used to wash out her eyes, now tingled with warmth.

When they reached the others, who'd managed to secure a perch at the very front of the crowd, Samson squeezed her hand before letting it go. Effie let her arm dangle at her side, her fingertips cooling in the open air. She looked ahead at the marching drummers, trumpeters, and banjoists, but her mind's eye saw only her hand—gangly fingers, flat nail beds, twin scars from her experiments with embalming chemicals—as it had been, tucked in the bend of Samson's arm.

"Do you play an instrument, Miss Jones?" he asked, leaning so close his warm breath swept along her neck.

To anyone else, her response would simply have been no. Such a straightforward question necessitated no explanation or embellishment. Yet she found herself searching for something to say that might entreat another question and prolong the conversation. "I studied piano briefly under the tutelage of my warden's wife. My hands are of suitable size—I can span a tenth with ease—but she said I lacked the emotional breadth necessary and so we stopped."

Samson's eyebrows pulled together, creating a ripple of skin between them. "Emotional breadth, what the deuce does that mean?"

"I play with the vigor of a corpse." When the furrow between his brows deepened, she added, "Her analogy, not mine. But an apt one, I suppose, looking back on it."

"That's a monstrous thing to say to one's ward."

Perhaps it was. Effie had not considered that a kinder woman—Mrs. Neale or Mrs. Carrière, for example—might have come at the issue more obliquely. But to what end? Effie would likely have not caught her meaning and continued practicing though she lacked a fundamental skill necessary for excellence. At last, she shrugged. "I had other interests."

"Oh?" His brows had relaxed back into symmetrical arches above his thickly lashed eyes and he smiled. "Dolls and tea parties?"

"Human anatomy."

"I see . . . how interesting."

He straightened and returned his gaze to the parade. Effie did likewise. Clearly, that had been the wrong thing to say. If only Adeline were here to coach her.

The last of the king's court rode by, costumes a-shimmer. Behind them came a wonder unlike anything Effie had seen before: the famous floats.

At forefront of this lumbering display strode two men dressed in long black cloaks and beak-like masks. They carried a banner with great scrolling letters that read, MARCH OF AGES.

The first float, a chassis with steel-rimmed wheels pulled by a single horse, bore a man in a Roman toga. He stood still as a statue with white-feathered wings fashioned to his costume. In one hand he held a scythe; in the other an hourglass. Father Time, Effie guessed.

The next floats portrayed scenes from the past—crepe-festooned wagons with tableaux of Caesar, Charlemagne, and Washington. Behind the costumed figures rose papier-mâché backdrops of temples, castles, and clouds, each expertly painted and embellished with gold and silver leaf. They swayed and trembled with the movement of the wagons while the crowd gasped and applauded.

Effie marveled at the care and engineering. The time it must have taken to design and construct each one. Her gaze toggled between the floats and Samson, who himself stood in awe.

But the mood of the floats changed as they progressed to the present. One float carried a herculean man dressed in a shabby, ill-fitting suit and wearing blackface. He stood before a long cannon, lanyard in hand, ready to fire. But instead of facing outward, the muzzle pointed directly at him, as if he were too dim-witted to know at which end of the cannon to stand.

Other floats bore men completely ensconced in papier-mâché animal costumes with human-like faces and dress. So precise were the faces drawn, it took little imagination for Effie to make the link between animal and man. The tobacco grub was meant to be President Grant. The rattlesnake, Governor Kellogg. The snail, the leech, the gorilla, members of the state legislature.

The smile Samson had worn vanished. His jaw clenched, and his easy posture grew stiff. Effie too felt her muscles tighten, as if bracing against the spectacle, while those around them laughed and cheered.

The final float, the future, depicted the goddess Minerva in command of a disorderly band of Amazons. The revelers in the tableau, men dressed as women, stood in a sloppy show of arms, in mockery of the suffragists.

Effie felt undressed by the spectacle. Naked and shamed. The crowd's laughter was like lashes against her exposed skin. The measure of gaiety she'd mustered since the flour and lime incident stole away as sure as the breath from her lungs.

The men who'd dreamed up these floats had never looked upon the insides of a man. Never seen the heart, lungs, spleen, liver all laid out in the same grand order regardless of race or sex.

The last float had passed and now a throng of maskers, both on foot and in carts, danced and shuffled before them—knights, friars, jesters, Indians. A man and woman lurched theatrically under the weight of an enormous carpetbag they bore between them. Men, styled as Yankees with glossy top hats and exaggerated coattails, tossed wooden coins at the crowd. Others, dressed in shabby clothes and unraveling straw hats, their faces blackened with shoe polish, bounded from foot to foot like lumbering gorillas.

Effie started to turn away, but Mrs. Carrière clasped her arm. "This is why we're here." She handed Effie one corner of the banner they'd stitched that night at the club meeting and moved away several paces until the cloth stretched tight between them. Several of the Negroes watching the parade from the opposite sidewalk raised their fists and cheered.

With her dainty shoulders squared and chin aloft, Mrs. Carrière stepped into the throngs of maskers marching at the tail end of the parade. So too did Samson and Tom and even little Jonah. They each took hold of a section of the banner, moving into a solid line, and Effie was swept down from the banquette and into the street with them.

Boos and jeering now out-sounded the cries of support. Effie's fingers held strong to the fabric even as they trembled. An orange peel struck her cheek. A wad of paper bounced off her back. A youth in a devil costume shoved her with such force, she nearly toppled. Tom reached out and steadied her. Mrs. Carrière nodded her onward. Samson flashed his brilliant smile. Though her entire rib cage rattled with the thud of her heart, Effie marched on beside them.

CHAPTER 10

⟫⟫·◇·⟪⟪

The next morning, Effie arrived at the shop to find Colm waiting for her just inside the carriageway gate. A cross-shaped smudge of soot marked his forehead. He leaned against the iron fence with their equipment spread haphazardly at his feet. The ash from his cigarette drifted down, landing only a few inches from the crate of embalming fluid.

She pushed the crate away with her foot. It slid across the worn pavers with the sound of a blunt razor scraping over a bewhiskered chin. "I've told you before, the fluid's flammable."

Colm shrugged, took a long drag, and exhaled the smoke into her face.

She itched to pluck the cigarette from his fingers and grind it to dust beneath her boot heel. But Mr. Whitmark would deplore such a rumpus. So instead, she waved away the smoke and picked up the embalming cabinet and dressing case. "Where to?"

He took another drag, then snuffed out the cigarette on the sole of his shoe and tucked the half-spent fag into his shirt pocket. "Third and Prytania."

Though she'd not been upriver to the Garden District, Effie knew well who lived there: the crème de la crème of the city's rich Americans. A few were Northerners who'd made homes there after the War, but most of the mansions belonged to Confederate Seceshes. "Are you sure?"

To this, he only grunted and scooped up the crate in his meaty arms. Jars clanked and fluid sloshed. With his free hand, he grabbed the folded cooling table. "Let's go already," he said, as if she'd been the one dawdling.

Effie followed a pace behind him, not out of deference, but to avoid further conversation. Once they cleared the bustle of the city center, she allowed her mind to wander, leafing through yesterday's events like pages in a book. All in all, not a very good book or an especially happy one. It had taken her nearly two hours to comb the flour, dirt, and lime from her hair and brush it from her clothes. Tobacco juice and cooking grease streaked her lovely new dress from the refuse hurled at her during the club's short-lived march with the parade. They'd made it all of three blocks before two police officers corralled them aside with their billy clubs and asked for their papers.

"This is Mardi Gras! We don't need permission to march," Samson had said. But apparently, that didn't matter. They were escorted off the street and warned with threat of arrest should they try again. The officers, one of whom had the light brown skin of a *gens de couleur,* seemed almost apologetic as he spoke. These were Rex's rules, after all, not Governor Kellogg's. But the group agreed it best not to chance a run-in with less sympathetic officers, or worse— members of the White League. Besides, they'd made their point. So with a nodding of heads and a flashing of tired smiles, the group dispersed—Jonah and Mrs. Carrière to the fairgrounds, Tom and Samson to a nearby groggery, and Effie, at her own instance, alone to her boardinghouse.

When she'd spied her frazzled hair, ravaged dress, and red-rimmed eyes in the foyer mirror, her jaw slackened. A dusting of flour still clung to her neck and the insides of her ears. This was the face Samson had gazed at all afternoon? Still, she couldn't forget the way he'd taken her hand and held it in the crook of his arm. How soft the wool of his jacket, how warm the heat circulating through his limbs, how firm his sinews and muscle.

He'd taken her hand only out of politeness. She knew that. Yet it was enough to carry her through all the combing and brushing and cleaning that followed and write a happy ending to the day.

Even now, her arms beginning to ache from the weight of her supplies, elation stirred inside her at the thought of his touch. *Miss Jones,* he'd said in the alley. Did that mean he'd remembered her name? More likely he'd heard one of the other club members mention it before he'd gone to check on her, but what if—

Colm's voice intruded on her reverie. "Hurry up."

She glared at the greasy brown hair peeking out from beneath the back of his flannel cap. "The dead can't get any deader."

He laughed at this, a single sharp chuckle that shook his barreled chest, though she'd not intended it as a joke. His pace slowed until, despite Effie's best efforts, they were walking side by side. Tall oak trees lined the street. Modest townhomes and shotgun houses had given way to great boxy affairs of brick or freshly painted stucco with wide galleries and stately columns. Lush gardens penned in by scrolling iron fences buffered the houses from the street.

"Saw you at the parade yesterday," Colm said.

For a moment her feet forgot their purpose and entangled themselves in her petticoat, causing her to stumble and nearly fall. Had he been among the masked men who'd thrown that flour admixture in her face? No. Each one of the men had spoken and none with an Irish accent. And surely she'd have recognized his blotchy skin or the uneven slope of his shoulders. Still, the tone of his voice made her leery. "Oh? I didn't see you."

"Went in costume, I did."

"As Mephistopheles, I should expect," she said. But clearly, he'd not read Goethe, as he took no offense at the gibe.

"No."

"A leprechaun, then?"

At this, he frowned. "As a court jester, if you please. And you ought'a been in costume too for all that ruckus you caused, marching with them other darkies like that behind the parade. Mr. Whitmark would be none too pleased if he knew."

It had not occurred to Effie someone she knew might have seen her yesterday, holding the banner with the others. She'd thought of little else aside from her proximity to Samson. Six times their shoulders had brushed amid the jostle of the revelers. Then that first jeer rang out. An orange peel struck her cheek. Fear swelled inside her. Would the crowd mob them? But Samson had looked at her, as if he sensed the uptick of her pulse, and smiled bravely. She knew then there was nowhere in the world she'd rather be than there beside him. The clamor of onlookers beat against her eardrums, elbows jabbed at her back, wads of paper and peanut shells struck her skirts, but somehow she remembered the moment as a private one. Herself, Samson, the touch of his shoulder, the ease of his smile—the rest was just a blurry backdrop. Colm had no place in the memory.

"It was nothing."

"Nothing? Not two years ago there was an out and out battle—right there in front of the customs house—'cause of black leagues like yours."

"We're a Republican ward club, not some vigilante league."

"So you are part of them."

"No, I mean . . . not really."

"Why were you with them, then?"

It wouldn't do to explain that she'd fallen in love with one of the club's leaders. A brute like Colm would never understand. Besides, what she did with her precious few hours away from the shop and demands of the dead was none of his business.

"They're friends is all, and I'd thank you to keep out of my private life."

Friends. An ill-chosen word, perhaps. After all, she'd met the lot of them only twice. Surely that didn't fit Mr. Webster's definition. And yet, saying the word sent a strange thrill through her.

Colm snickered. "Maybe you ought'a find different friends then. Mr. Whitmark's got enough to do defending his name without one of his workers hanging out with the likes of radicals."

She took hold of both cases in one hand and shook out the tired fingers of the other. Was it so radical to want to walk down the street unmolested? To want to send your children to the same good schools white children attended? To want a seat at the theater, soda shop, or on the streetcar? It hardly seemed so radical to her. She switched cases to the other hand and gave her fingers a shake. Tiny pinpricks of pain spread across her hand with the return of blood. Besides, she wasn't *involved* with the ward club anyway. She'd attended one meeting and held the corner of a banner for the span of three blocks.

Still, she remembered the scratch marks on the shop's shingle the day she arrived. SCALAWAG. It couldn't be easy for Mr. Whitmark, a Unionist in a city of Seceshes. Would he mind her association with the club? Surely not. He was a Republican himself. Colm hadn't the slightest notion of Mr. Whitmark's true character.

"I dare say, he'd—" She paused and dropped behind him, skirting the edge of the sidewalk to make room for an approaching couple out on an early-morning promenade. The man wore a single-breasted frock coat of blue wool, the woman flounces of silk. Colm set down the cooling table and doffed his cap to them. The man touched the brim of this glossy top hat while his companion gave a languid nod in Colm's direction. Neither of them looked at Effie and proceeded on as if she'd not been there at all, even as the hem of the woman's skirt brushed Effie's in passing.

"I dare say he'd like even less knowing you steal sips from the flask of whiskey he keeps tucked away in the mahogany display casket," she finished.

Colm's neck turned scarlet. He glared at her but said nothing more.

Several minutes later, he stopped in front of a large house and opened the iron gate. Effie hesitated a moment before following him through. Sculpted hedges and well-tended flowerbeds perfumed the air. Leafing magnolia trees dappled the flagstone walkway in shade. A double-gallery colonnade with lacy iron railings rose above the yard.

"Who died here?" Effie asked, her voice just above a whisper.

"The son of some famous officer or other from the War."

"How old?"

"Twenty-three. I think that's what Mr. Whitmark said."

The beauty of the house disquieted her—its lush surroundings, its symmetrical facade, its vibrant blue shutters closed out of respect for the dead. Perhaps that was it. No matter how grandly or wretchedly you lived, death, in his time, would find you. She opened the dressing case and selected a door badge of black crepe with a white rosette and ribbon. She hung it over the knocker before following Colm around the house to the back entrance.

A young Negro maid greeted them in whispers and led them through a series of hallways before bidding them wait outside a set of closed parlor doors. Mr. Whitmark's voice sounded faintly through the wood—tense and thin.

The house still smelled of Mardi Gras, of cinnamon cakes and bourbon, of tobacco and day-old eau de cologne. But also of death.

That pungent sweetness of slowly rotting flesh. It was faint yet, and Effie doubted anyone else in the house sensed it. But if she didn't start her work soon, they would.

The maid tapped once and opened the door just wide enough for her slender frame to shimmy in. "Pardon me, sirs. The undertaker's assistants are here."

"Shall we begin, then?" Mr. Whitmark asked.

A long pause, then came a voice she recognized from several weeks back at the shop. Not a customer, but someone else who'd come just before suppertime, quarreled with Mr. Whitmark for several minutes, and then left. Effie, hanging laundry in the back courtyard, had heard only snippets—enough to gauge the man's anger and intimacy of their acquaintanceship.

Now the man's voice came calm and steady. "Think of your wife, Bill. You don't want her to see him like this."

Bill—whomever that was—did not answer.

"My brother's the best embalmer in the city. I'd stake my name on it."

Could this be the showy brother whom Mr. Whitmark had mentioned?

From inside the room, she heard a restless shifting and guessed it was the third man, this Bill, the famous officer Colm had spoken of, the father of the deceased, the only one hitherto silent.

"Fine," he said at last. "But I insist upon being present during the . . . procedure."

"I . . . er . . . don't recommend that. Best keep the memory of your son—" Mr. Whitmark stopped, silenced it seemed by some look or gesture. "Of course, Colonel Randolph. Lead the way."

The parlor door swung wide and an older man with broad shoulders and dark shadows beneath his eyes emerged. Despite the early hour, he wore full evening dress—coattails rumpled, white tie askew—and Effie guessed he'd not changed since yesterday. A look of unease played across his face, one that only deepened upon regard of Effie and her ash-marked companion.

"These are my assistants," Mr. Whitmark said, joining them in the hall. "Mr. McLeary and Miss—" But Colonel Randolph was already halfway down the hall.

Mr. Whitmark clenched his jaw and rubbed his knuckles the

way he did at the shop when he couldn't get the account books to add up or Colm left a mess in the storeroom. Rheum was crusted at the corners of his eyes, but he smelled sober. The man behind him, his brother—a few years younger by the look of him, and just as squarely built—clapped Mr. Whitmark quietly on the back and nodded for him to follow.

The body was laid out in a large bedroom on the second floor. Thick velvet curtains shrouded the windows. The smell was stronger here and not just that of putrefying tissue, but of shit and liquor and fifty-cent perfume, the kind the whores down by the levee wore. Colm flinched. The maid gasped and stopped in the doorway. The War had long ago rid the rest of them of such squeamishness. A strange fellowship, Effie thought. Officers of opposing sides and her, a runaway slave.

Colonel Randolph lit a silver-footed paraffin lamp atop the bedside table, then retreated to the far corner of the room, arms crossed, eyes flickering between them. The lamp cast a pool of yellow light over the body. Bruising covered the young man's face. His nose had been broken. She'd need makeup to hide the discoloration, extra cotton packing and perhaps even some wax to build back up the nose. But first the cleaning.

"A basin of warm water and another lamp," she whispered to the maid, who looked relieved to be sent away.

Colm began setting up the cooling table alongside the wall nearest the door.

"Not there," Effie said. "On the other side of the bed in case I need more light."

"Yes, yes," Mr. Whitmark said, talking over her, his voice unusually reedy. "Over here. I'll have better lighting closer to the lamp."

I'll have better lighting? He intended to embalm the body? If that was his plan, why was she here at all? Better if she'd stayed back to see to the shop. She almost voiced this, but his gray eyes fixed her with an intense look, obviously meant to telegraph something. Though she couldn't decipher his exact meaning, she stayed quiet.

When the maid returned with the water basin, Effie hesitated. Did he intend to wash the body too? But Mr. Whitmark nodded once, and she took that as permission to proceed. She stripped the body of its clothes, conscious of Colonel Randolph's eyes at her back. It felt like a giant furnace bellow had forced too much air into the room, belaboring her every exhale.

She handed the dead man's soiled clothes to the maid when she returned with another oil lamp, then set to work washing. The water was not as warm as Effie would have liked, and she struggled to get the soap to lather. The young man's bowels had loosed when he expired, and dried excrement stuck to his thighs. This was not uncommon, but she found her hands unsteady and her armpits damp as she scrubbed it away. Behind her, Colm was setting out supplies on a card table brought up from the parlor. Every clink and clumsy clatter sent a shudder down her spine. She'd not felt this nervous since that day in the morgue and had the sense that just as much was riding on her performance now.

More bruising covered the young man's torso, and the back of his skull was cracked. Lucky the blow had come there and not to the front of the head, where it might have caved in his sphenoid or temporal bone. That required much more work than a broken nose and, even with several layers of molded wax and makeup, never looked quite natural.

She took a wad of cotton from the dressing case and carefully packed it into the back of the mouth. With more cotton in hand, she lifted the sheet covering the loins and rolled the body slightly to its side. Before she could continue, a hand grabbed her shoulder and flung her backward. She stumbled into the edge of the cooling table, her head striking the sharp edge of the window casing. Blood trickled down her scalp. The margins of her vision darkened.

"Great God! What is this?" Colonel Randolph shouted, amplifying the pain in Effie's head. He raised his hand to strike her.

Her insides clenched, but she did not cower or raise her arms in defense. A voice, familiar but unplaceable, rumbled in her mind. *No cryin' now, you hear? You's gotta be brave.*

Before the blow fell, Mr. Whitmark stepped between them. "We must plug the orifices lest they leak. It's a standard part of the process. She meant no disrespect."

Colonel Randolph slowly lowered his hand.

"It's been a long night for you. Perhaps you'd like to—"

"I'm staying here." Colonel Randolph straightened his waistcoat and returned to the corner, his bloodshot eyes never softening.

Mr. Whitmark rubbed his knuckles again and swallowed what she expected was a sigh. "Continue, Effie."

She took a moment to be sure her balance wouldn't fail her and then continued with her work. Her hands no longer trembled, her skin, if anything, felt more clammy than hot. She'd done this before, worked beneath the shadow of violence. Not this type of work and not in any years recent, but she recognized this fear-tempered concentration as surely as that rumbling voice.

She shaved the young man, placed eye-caps on his eyes and closed the lids, sewed his lips together, and swabbed his skin with embalming fluid. *No cryin' now, you hear?* The calming timbre of the voice reminded her of Samson. But the words belonged to someone else.

She thought back to her first summer in Indiana. The hot, sticky air. The hum of insects rising as the sun set over the prairie. She sat on the edge of the porch, swinging her legs over the ledge, polishing her buttons with a scrap of flannel from Mrs. Kinyon's sewing basket.

"Something's wrong with that child, John," she heard the woman say from the kitchen. "Yesterday, she stepped on a nail and didn't cry a peep! Never in all my days have I seen a girl so . . . so dispassionate."

"You speak as if that's a bad thing," the captain had said.

"You've gone cold as a corpse if you think it ain't."

The tingling fume of chemicals brought Effie back to the present. That voice must have predated her time with the Kinyons. Why else wouldn't she have cried? Likely predated the War too. But before that . . . there was nothing.

She wrung the embalming fluid from her rag and stepped aside as Mr. Whitmark and Colm moved the body to the cooling table. Then Mr. Whitmark dismissed Colm back to the shop. Effie, however, he bid stay.

"All I'm going to do now is make a small incision in his neck that we might access his artery and inject the fluid," Mr. Whitmark explained. A few beads of sweat sat at the edge of his hairline, ready to trickle down his brow. "The blood's mostly clotted, but the incision still might weep a bit."

"Just get on with it," Colonel Randolph said.

Mr. Whitmark bent over the body and examined the neck, probing the soft flesh several times with his finger to locate the artery. "Scalpel, Effie."

She handed him the blade. His hand jerked slightly, went still, then jerked again. This was not the tremor of fear, though the pitch of his voice and flush of his skin suggested he too was addled by Colonel Randolph's presence. It wasn't the quiver of too much coffee or kola nuts, though he overimbibed in both now in place of the bottle. She'd seen his hand twitch like this before when lighting a match or straightening the skirt of a casket. She'd seen evidence of it as well in the account books, his clear, straight script trailing off into a string of illegible letters. She'd thought it just a symptom of his drying out, along with the sickness and sleeplessness and headaches he'd complained of, but such effects should have tapered by now.

He wiped the sweat from his forehead. Bent down. Probed the skin. Hesitated. "Damn it, Effie. You're blocking my light."

She moved to the far side of the card table, though her shadow hadn't been anywhere near his field of work. At least this way she obstructed Colonel Randolph's view. If Mr. Whitmark's hand slipped, it might go unnoticed.

He brought the blade close to the skin. Too high. An incision there would be hard to conceal, even with a wide neckcloth. But Effie dare not say so. As if he'd read her thoughts, he moved his hand down, but then too far to the right, where he'd more likely nick the windpipe than expose the artery. Another jerk of his hand. He drew a long breath in through his nose and resettled his hand. Instead of one smooth cut, he made several superficial slashes, but at least he'd found the right location and soon the carotid lay uncovered.

"Aneurysm needle," he said.

She passed him the small, hooked instrument. After three bumbling attempts, he managed to work the hook around the slippery vessel and elevate it above the surrounding tissue. Effie's head throbbed. Dried blood had matted in her hair and likely stained her bonnet. She was little more than a circus ape here, fetching him supplies, moving hither and thither at his command, standing idle while he did work she could more aptly and quickly perform. She'd sealed away her memories as a slave, balled up and buried them long ago, before she'd been an adult and conscious of the doing. But it must have felt like this—threatening and demeaning.

The pain in her head wasn't Mr. Whitmark's fault, she reminded herself. He wasn't the one who'd flung her against the wall. In the months since her arrival, he'd never once touched her. But then, neither had Captain Kinyon, and he'd wounded her just the same.

Once the tubing had been connected to the hand pump and from there to the reservoir of embalming fluid, Mr. Whitmark began the injection. He wiped his brow again in between squeezes and leaned back in the chair Effie had brought for him. "This part will take a while, William. An hour. Maybe two. Why don't you at least change out of your evening clothes and take something to eat."

"How do I know you're not going to slice him open while I'm gone and take his heart or liver?"

This time Mr. Whitmark didn't bother to hide his sigh. "I've already told you, embalming doesn't require the removal of any organs. That's a myth. A vestige from the days when they used to evacuate the body cavity and fill it with sawdust for preservation."

Colonel Randolph didn't move, but Effie could tell from the way he leaned against the wall and blinked slowly that he was tired.

"I'll come fetch you before we dress him, and you can inspect the body yourself," Mr. Whitmark said. "You'll see no cut marks or incisions besides the one I made here at the neck. You have my word."

"Your word's no good in this house," Colonel Randolph said. "But I have the assurance of your brother. His word I'll take. Find me in my study when you finish. If I see any other markings when I inspect his body, by God, I'll . . ." But he didn't finish, only stamped from the room.

As soon as Colonel Randolph's footfalls faded down the hallway, Mr. Whitmark passed the injection pump to Effie. He flexed and splayed his fingers several times like he was working out a cramp and then slumped into a nearby armchair.

Effie readjusted the catheter so later, as the pressure increased, the fluid would not leak out around the sides. For several minutes, only the rhythmic wheezing of the rubber bulb sounded in the room.

What if she squeezed a little faster? A little harder. Faster. Harder. Faster. Harder. Until the tiny blood vessels in the young man's face burst and the skin beneath his eyes, around his nose, across his cheekbones became even more ravaged and discolored than before. A common side effect of the injection, she'd tell Colonel Randolph. Unavoidable really. Serve him right for the way he'd manhandled her.

But Mr. Whitmark would know. She glanced over at him—elbows resting on his knees, face buried in his hands, a sudden twitch of the pinkie—and kept her rhythm slow and smooth. "Who is this Mr. Randolph?"

Mr. Whitmark didn't answer. Didn't even move. Then he groaned, raked his fingers through his hair, and sat up. "He's a cotton merchant. A lauded officer from the War."

Effie pursed her lips and gave a quiet *hmm*.

"The irony is inescapable, ay? You'd hardly know we won the War." He looked at her and grimaced. "Sorry. I don't mean to say . . . I suppose for you the outcome is more . . . pronounced."

Yes, though perhaps less than he thought. Especially today.

"At least we preserved the Union," he said, with little gusto.

"You called Mr. Randolph William. Were you friends?"

He stood and came over to the body. "I was at this boy's christening."

"And that other man—he's the brother you spoke of?"

"James, yes. He and William fought together under General Hood." Mr. Whitmark reached toward the dead man's face, as if to brush a stray eyelash from his cheek or smooth an errant lock of hair, but stopped midway and instead clasped his hands behind his back. "You can fix his nose, can't you?"

"Yes."

"And the bruising?"

"Some of it will fade on its own. The rest I'll hide with complexion powder."

"Not too much. Mustn't have him looking like a Mary."

Effie scowled. If he were going to badger her like this, she wished he'd just leave too. By now, hadn't she proved her skill? She laid aside the hand pump and refilled the fluid reservoir, careful not to spill any of the liquid or splash it upon her skin. The bloom of chemical scent into the air made her eyes water. Still, she preferred it to the rancid perfume smell of before.

"How much fluid have we injected?" Mr. Whitmark asked.

"A pint and three quarters."

"Good, good. Not much more now. Don't overdo it."

Effie clamped her teeth down on the sides of her tongue. She'd already estimated the amount of fluid they would need based on the size and condition of the body. She knew, down to the half-teaspoon, how much each bottle of fluid held, how much it took to fill the rubber tubing, how much each compression of the bulb forced into the body. But these calculations were just a guide. Ultimately, Effie went by feel. She knew the exact force her final squeezes would require, the exact strength each finger must exert.

Mr. Whitmark returned to the armchair but did not sit down. His idle fingers picked at the lace tidy thrown over the top of the chair. Was it that he had known the young man that made him so restless and overbearing? He hardly seemed on amicable terms with the family. She thought back to what Colm had said about Mr. Whitmark having enough to do in defending his name. "This Mr. Randolph is important, isn't he?"

"All our clients are important."

Effie fixed him with a hard stare.

"A good word at the Pickwick Club could go a long way." He sighed and sank back into the chair. "Let's just get the boy fixed up and worry about the rest later."

Effie turned back to the body. A long way toward what? She'd heard that name before, the Pickwick Club, something Tom had said to Samson in relation to the White League. Had she not been so transfixed with the way Samson was flipping one of the wooden nickels tossed out by the paraders over and under his knuckles she might have remembered just what he'd said. But Samson had lovely hands, his long, straight fingers as agile as they were strong. She thought again how he'd tucked her cold hand in the crook of his arm and for a moment she was transported from this dark, smelly room back onto the street, where the sun shone and music played and Samson walked beside her.

The reprieve was short-lived. Pressure built with each squeeze of the bulb, and she readied herself for the final pumps. She had yet to inject the abdomen and cranial cavity, yet to suture the wound, yet to rebuild the nose. Clearly this man had been out yesterday with the crowds. Had he been one of the men who accosted her with flour? Or one of those revelers with soot on his face acting the part of the foolish Negro?

Mr. Whitmark's hand on her shoulder made her start.

"Is it done?"

She gave a final, measured squeeze. "Yes."

"I'm sorry if . . . did he hurt you?"

He was referring to Colonel Randolph, right? Not the man with the knapsack of flour, not Captain Kinyon, not the master whose face she couldn't recall? Anyway, it didn't matter. Like her dry eyes in the face of pain, the lie was ready on her tongue. "No."

CHAPTER 11

"Are you sure this boot is going to work?" Adeline said from behind the dressing screen. A country vista of graceful trees and wooly hills decorated the panels. But the paint was cracked, peeling at the corners, and the fluffy white clouds yellow with age.

"It will work," Effie said, though strictly speaking that was more hypothesis than fact. The boot was far too small to test herself.

After a splash of water and clink of porcelain, Adeline came around the screen in her chemise and corset. She sat on the chaise at the foot of her bed and pulled on her stockings. Then she turned sideways and said over her shoulder to Effie, "Tighten my laces, won't you, *chère*?"

Effie grimaced. She'd come expecting to hand over the boots at the front door and be gone. The Adeline she'd seen at Charity Hospital—so tender and selfless—did not drive from her mind the other Adeline she knew—vain and condescending—and Effie had no intention of wasting an afternoon with such a woman. But Adeline had insisted Effie stay while she try on the boots. Why that required a complete change of her toilette bewildered Effie.

Now, Adeline gave a soft but pointed *ahem*. Effie sighed. After standing idle in this cavernous room of tired, mismatched furniture for near half an hour, what was a minute or two more? She sat beside her on the chaise, horsehair poking her through the frayed upholstery. She set down the boots and untied the knot at the bottom of Adeline's corset.

After Mrs. Kinyon had showed her how to pull tight her own laces and reach all the buttons at the back of a dress, Effie couldn't remember ever having dressed or undressed in front of another person. Adeline, however, was entirely nonchalant. Likely she'd never been without her maid or mother close at hand to tie her off or fluff her bustle. Not until of late. And judging from the crooked laces and haphazard knot, she wasn't very good at dressing alone.

Effie rethreaded the bottom eyelets and synched the laces. "How's that?"

"Tighter."

"You ought to have greater consideration for the health of your organs. When your diaphragm can't fully contract—"

"Don't be a ninny. Tighter!"

She tugged until Adeline let out a little gasp, then tied a double bow.

Adeline smoothed her hands down her nipped waist and took a few shallow breaths. "*Parfait*. Now let's try these boots."

"You should feel a small protuberance beneath your left heel. That operates the lever," Effie said, as Adeline slipped them on. "When you press down, the level triggers the hammer inside the heel to strike."

She waited.

No sound.

"Are you pressing down?"

"Yes."

"Harder."

Still silence.

Effie slid off the chaise and knelt beside her. "Rock your foot back so all your weight's on the heel."

"People will see my leg move."

"Not unless you mean to wear your skirts about your waist."

Adeline huffed but did as bidden. A loud knocking sound rang through the room. "*Mon Dieu!* It's brilliant." She clapped and stood. "Positively—" The boot heel sounded again as she took a step and her gleeful expression deflated. "*Merde*. How am I supposed to walk?"

Effie frowned too. She'd worried that might happen. "You'll have to keep as much weight off your heel as possible."

Adeline paced the length of the room—gait lurching and toes turned inward—until she managed to keep the boot quiet. "Voilà!"

Effie pressed a hand to her lips, but couldn't contain her laughter. "What?"

"You're shambling about like a maimed pigeon."

"You think you could do better?" Adeline bent and started to unlace the boots as if to give Effie a try.

"No, I can't," Effie said, still laughing. "They don't fit."

Adeline raised her chin. "Well, I'd rather shamble like a bird than clomp about with big feet like . . . like *un éléphant.*"

Though Effie had been teased about her big feet countless times as a girl, Adeline's words didn't sting. Instead, they only made her laugh harder. Soon Adeline was laughing too. They laughed until Effie's eyes watered and her stomach muscles cramped.

"Just walk on the balls of your feet—both feet—and you should be fine," Effie said when she'd recovered herself.

A few more turns about the room, and Adeline's gait evened out.

"If you're satisfied, I'll be going—"

Adeline cut her off with a flap of her hand. "I want to try it in full costume to be sure you can still hear it beneath my skirts."

"I'm sure it will be plenty loud." But the bout of laughter had weakened Effie's resolve, and she watched from the chaise as Adeline retrieved her petticoat and crinolette from the wide oak wardrobe and laid them out on the bed. Next she pulled out the same dress of purple silk taffeta and black velvet she'd worn the night Effie first met her.

"Why don't you find real employment instead of this spirit medium ruse?"

Adeline threw the skirt on overhead, swimming through the folds of fabric until it fell into place atop her underskirts. "*Bon Dieu!* I'm not that desperate."

One glance about the room and Effie knew that was a lie. The furniture had the look of money—the large half-canopy bed of richly carved walnut, the lacquered writing desk with gold-painted trim, the marble-topped dressing table and oval-shaped mirror—but none of it matched or seemed entirely suited to the space, as if it had been scavenged from other rooms and carelessly flung together. The Oriental rug at Effie's feet was so worn the threads appeared translucent.

The floral-print wallpaper had faded to a ubiquitous dull beige. Even the mosquito netting tied back beside the bed bore the scars of numerous stitchings.

"It's just a lark, these sittings, anyway," Adeline said, buttoning her bodice. "A way to pass the time."

Effie watched her struggle with the last two buttons before brushing her hand away and fastening them herself. "I'm not one of your simpering friends. You needn't lie to me."

Adeline turned around. Her gaze, hitherto flighty, fixed on Effie with intensity. "No, I suppose not."

"Then why not take up work elsewhere? As a seamstress perhaps or—"

"*Ma chère,* women of my set do not work. One could never overcome the stigma." She walked to her dressing table, the boot knocking with the first step—a sound that made them both jump and then chuckle—but quiet thereafter.

"What do you mean to do, then? Play the medium forever?"

"Of course not. I mean to marry. Speaking of which, have you seen your Mr. Grier lately?"

"Mr. *Greene,* Samson." Effie concentrated on keeping her voice even, despite her fluttering insides. "I saw him Tuesday."

Adeline sank onto the velvet tuffet beside her dressing table and waved Effie over to the nearby chair. "Do tell."

Really she ought to go. It was clear from Adeline's misstep that the knocking device could be well heard despite the shroud of her skirts. But then, what harm was there in staying a minute or two more?

She sat and pondered where to begin. Her encounter with Samson had seemed so momentous, yet so little had actually transpired between them.

"I bought a new dress like you advised."

"*Ça alors!* Why aren't you wearing it? What color is it?"

"Lavender."

"And the style?"

"I don't know. The style that was in the shop window."

"Describe it to me."

Effie sighed, regretting she'd brought up the dress at all, but did her best to explain it.

"Hmm . . . *ça va*," Adeline said when she'd finished. "But really, you must take me with you next time. I know all the best shops."

Effie doubted she could afford the shops Adeline frequented, and the idea of having her fuss over the type of lace, length of the train, or number of flounces seemed pure torture. "After I dressed, I met up with some of the club members on Canal Street to watch the parade."

"And Mr. . . . . Greene was there?"

"Not straightaway." The memory of those men with their flour and lime bullied to the forefront of her thoughts. She shuddered and pushed it back. "But he arrived soon after and we watched the procession together."

"And?"

She debated whether to skip the part about them entering the parade with the banner. Her conversation with Colm had made her wary, and Adeline had showed no interest in politics. Yet once Effie began describing the event—taking hold of the corner of the banner, being swept up with the others into the current of the parade—she found herself compelled to continue. Samson's shoulder brushing against hers. His radiant smile. The noise from the crowd. The shock when that first piece of rind struck her cheek. Her surge of fear at the sight of the police and their billy clubs. The awe Samson's indignation stirred inside her. The stab of sorrow she endured at their parting.

Adeline listened with greater intent than Effie expected. But in the end, she frowned and turned back to her dressing table. "You didn't do what I instructed."

"What?"

"Our conversation. About *l'opéra*."

"I don't think it really applies to the club—"

"It applies everywhere." She untied the ribbon securing her braid and unplaited her hair. "Who's the prima donna?"

"Mrs. Carrière, I suppose."

"And the mezzo?" Adeline ran her fingers through her glossy hair, then divided it into sections and followed with a wide-toothed comb, starting at the tips and working her way up.

Once or twice during the War, Mr. Kinyon had tried to comb her hair but quickly gave up and cropped it down to her skull the way it had been when she'd arrived at the camp. Mrs. Kinyon was not as merciful. She tried a boar's-hair brush, but that only made Effie's hair frizz like the head of a thistle. Next came the comb, a narrow-toothed silver affair that she raked through Effie's curls until Effie thought her scalp might peel off with each pass. "Do you always take such pains with your hair?"

"*Bien sûr,* don't you?"

Effie gave a quick shake of her head, skirting the reflection of Adeline's gaze in the dressing table mirror.

"*Mon Dieu.* No wonder your hair's such a fright. Here, turn around. I'll show—"

"No need." Effie leaned away, but Adeline paid her no heed. She rose from her vanity, comb in hand, and circled around Effie's chair. A quick tug at the bow fastened beneath her chin, and her bonnet was off, flung aside like a soiled rag.

"Really, I must go. I've a—"

"Hush. I know good and well you haven't anyplace to be." She plucked the pins from Effie's bun, tilted her head back, and gave a long *hmm.*

Effie flinched at the feel of the comb's metal teeth on her scalp. But Adeline's touch was surprisingly gentle. Not at all how Mrs. Kinyon had attacked her hair.

"You ought to soften it up with oil and let it grow out some," Adeline said. "In any case, it's not so altogether bad you need hide it under that bonnet like you do." She worked the comb through to the ends. "Quite a rich color, really. If you only . . ."

Adeline prattled on about the latest updos, and Effie closed her eyes. The soft tug of the comb lulled her unease. The sounds of the house fell away—the *ticktock* of the grandfather clock down the hall, the whine of rusty shutters beyond the open window. Even Adeline's voice became soft and muffled.

Effie had wondered when she first arrived North with Captain Kinyon what it would have been like had his daughter been alive. She'd imagined them playing together in the yard, whispering late into the night, plaiting each other's hair . . . But no. That was a child's delusion. A fantasy borne of the loneliness she'd not yet learned to shoulder. Even had Annabelle lived, they'd not have been as sisters.

A shiver worked down her spine. Effie opened her eyes.

"Hold still, I'm almost done." Adeline twisted and pinned the final section of her hair. "Voilà!"

Effie fingered the intricate chignon at the back of her head. She swiveled toward the mirror and eyed her reflection. How billowy and elegant her hair lay. Utterly impractical for an undertaker's assistant, and yet she couldn't look away.

"*Si belle!*" said a voice from the far side of the room. In the mirror's reflection, Effie saw Adeline's mother propped against the doorjamb.

"Mamm, I thought you were sleeping." Adeline hurried over to her, the boot heel ringing with each step.

Mrs. Mercier flinched at the noise. "*Quel est ce bruit?*"

"*Rien,* Mamm. Now back to bed."

"*Non. Mo ne suis pas fatigue.*" She batted away Adeline's shepherding arm and strode into the room.

Effie stood and offered her the chair.

"*Merci, mon chou.*" The woman took hold of the back of the chair and eased herself gracefully down. She seemed far more lucid than their first meeting.

Adeline dragged a wicker rocker across the room for Effie, then flopped back onto her tuffet, with a perturbed but resigned expression. "English, Mamm. Remember?"

"*Ah, oui, ton amie Américaine.* Forgive me."

Amie. From the Latin *amicus.* Friend. Effie thought to correct her—she and Adeline were only . . . business partners. But perhaps that would be too difficult to explain. Besides, Mrs. Mercier likely didn't know of Adeline's self-professed talents as a spirit medium.

"Effie was just telling me about a gentleman she fancies," Adeline said, returning to her own hair. Effie caught her eye in the mirror and glared.

"Oh, *un homme.*" Mrs. Mercier smiled. Her teeth were small and nearly straight, the perfect complement to her full pink lips. "Tell me about your gentleman. What does he do?"

"He's in the state legislature."

"Mmm."

Effie gloried in her approval. He wasn't really *her* gentleman, and she hadn't any hand in his political success. But, as so oft now happened, her feelings disobeyed logic.

"What's his family name?"

"Greene."

She turned to Adeline. "Do we know any Greenes?"

"*Non,* Mamm. He's an American. A freedman."

Mrs. Mercier's expression puckered at the word *freedman.* "They let those types in the legislature? *Ma foi!*"

Effie squirmed and the rocker pitched backward until her feet were nearly level with her head. The old wood creaked and whined.

"Of course they do, Mamm."

"Could be worse, I suppose. And one can't be too picky these days." This last comment, Effie saw as she pulled herself forward and the chair rocked back to an upright position, was directed toward Adeline. "Two proposals my daughter's turned down. Did she tell you? Two!"

Adeline set down her comb with a loud clap.

"Two suitable gentlemen with both family and profession—"

"You didn't think so at the time."

"I didn't think you'd take so long to find another. In my day, Effie, before this dreadful war—"

"She doesn't want to hear about the good old days, Mother."

"*Mais oui,* she does. Don't you, Effie?"

Both women's gazes pressed against her. Before she could mutter an apology and insist upon leaving, Mrs. Mercier launched into her tale.

The world she described had more in common with the moon than Effie's own. Her mother had been the lifelong mistress of a white cotton broker when such arrangements were commonplace. Before, Mrs. Mercier was quick to add, the Americans came and all those Haitian refugees and the whole business became quite tawdry. Her father died when she was a young girl, but left them well situated with a handsome cottage on Royal Street and provisions of $600 a year. She spoke of lavish parties, dances, and nights at the theater.

Adeline, who'd made a show of not listening when her mother first began, stilled. She rested her chin in her palm and gazed at the marble tabletop, as if she could see the figures of her mother's story on its shiny surface.

"I was such a beauty in my day," Mrs. Mercier said. "Known throughout the city—from Esplanade to Canal."

It took little imagination to picture her so. Illness had whittled her down to bone and sapped the luster from her skin, but otherwise she remained a model of perfect proportions and striking symmetry, the ideal composite of her biracial pedigree. Effie, in her blackness, in her largeness, in her directness was indeed alien to this world.

When Mrs. Mercier spoke of meeting her husband, Adeline busied herself again, rummaging through the dressing table drawers, pulling out headscarves and necklaces and little pots of cream and rouge. His great-grandfather had purchased his freedom when New Orleans was still a French colony. His father had fought alongside other free men of color under General Jackson in 1815. He had family—which Effie now understood to mean a prestigious Creole lineage—and a lucrative profession as a land speculator.

There were more tales of picnics and soirées, of summering at the lake and of trips abroad. Adeline wound a purple scarf about her head as her mother spoke, tying the two ends together in a large knot just above her forehead. She had her mother's delicate features and pleasing symmetry, but her dark, restless eyes she must owe to her father.

Effie thought of her own features and wondered if her broad nose and sharp cheekbones came from her mother or her father. Had they both been tall like she, big boned, and square shouldered? She wondered for a moment if, despite her own plainness, her mother too had been beautiful. Just as quickly she banished the thought. Beauty was a curse for a slave. Perhaps that was her mother's ultimate gift to her.

Adeline, seemingly displeased with her tignon, unwrapped the scarf and started anew. Her hands trembled as they worked, and her eyes had taken on a glossy sheen.

"Come here, *mon coeur*," her mother said, interrupting the story. "I'll do it for you."

Mon coeur. Had Effie's mother said such things to her too? Growing up she'd kept a tight rein on such curiosity. What good would it do to wonder? She forbid herself to ruminate on the dark eyes she sometimes saw in her dreams, the soft humming that came to her in moments of silence.

Adeline scooted her tuffet in front of her mother's chair and sat still while her mother smoothed her hair and set to work winding the scarf. The sight of them weakened Effie's resolve. She swam back through her fragments of memory, desperate for something—a touch, a kiss, a smile—but there were only those eyes and soft humming.

"I suppose *c'est la fin*," Mrs. Mercier said, snaring Effie's attention again. "The War came and voilà. Here we are."

"Where's your husband now?"

Mrs. Mercier looked out the window and signed. "St. Louis Cemetery, I'm afraid."

"The War?"

"*Non,* a few years after."

"I'm sorry."

"That's what you're trained to say." Adeline swiveled back to her vanity and swiped at her cheeks with a feathery puff. Tears cut through the newly laid powder. "*I'm sorry.* As if you could possibly know our loss."

It was true. Effie had muttered those words a thousand times. Soft, respectful, but void of any real feeling. *Keep your distance.*

"Did your family lose their fortune?" Adeline continued. "Watch their stature slip away as freemen poured into the city?"

"*Tais-toi,* Adeline! Where are your manners?" Mrs. Mercier said. "We're doing just fine. Only yesterday *ton frère* was telling me about a new buyer in Montpellier."

Adeline bit down on her lip so hard the flesh blanched around her teeth. "Damned War. Would that it had never happened."

Effie stood with such force the rocker skidded over the rug, teetering back and forth behind her. "And what of us freedmen? Would that we were still slaves?" Adeline and her mother turned to her aghast, but Effie didn't wait for either to reply. "I don't have memories of parties and dances to call up before the War. I have scant memory of my early years at all. But I know that damned War saved me."

"Effie, I—"

But Effie turned and stomped to the door, unable to explain the sudden churning of her viscera and tightness of her skin. She stopped at the doorway and managed to mutter before leaving, "How ungrateful you are. Would that I had memories of a mother or father at all."

CHAPTER 12

Effie drew a pail of water from the cistern and set about cleaning her instruments. The morning's case should have been an easy one, a slight woman taken with childbed fever and her stillborn daughter.

When the dead suffered neither gross trauma nor the decrepitness of age, embalming fluid suffused into the vasculature and tissues with ease, as if it were the natural replacement of life's blood. The skin was less prone to discoloration, the limbs easier to mold into a restful pose. But as she nestled the cold, stone-like baby in the crook of her mother's arm for the viewing, a bur snagged inside her. Sharp, painful, unshakable. Just as it had when she'd watched Adeline with her mother.

Jealousy?

No. Only a fool envied the dead. Yet how else to explain this feeling or her sudden outburst in Adeline's bedroom?

She dried her scalpel and flushed clean water through her syringe pump. A brick held the back door of the shop ajar, letting in the fitful breeze, and from inside Effie heard voices. Colm's nasal brogue. But also that of a woman. A client perhaps? A paramour? Leave it to Colm to conflate the two.

She stowed her embalming cabinet and dressing case in the storeroom alongside the packets of chemicals, jars of premixed fluid, and spare drapery. Colm's voice still sounded from the front showroom, a continuous stream of muffled babble, more husky and bombastic than normal.

"Not everyone has the constitution for it, mind you. Just think what society would be without men of my sort to look after our beloved departed," Colm was saying as she entered to update the ledger. Effie almost laughed. As if he did anything but lug supplies and drive the hearse. He lounged against one of the display caskets with feigned ease, his posture stiff, his pale skin flushed crimson.

"*Mais bien sûr!* How fortunate there are men like you, Mr. McLeary."

Effie recognized Adeline's voice even before she spied her beside the decorative plumes and large stone urn near the front window.

Her insides clenched and she stepped back, hoping to retreat unnoticed. For the past two days, she'd replayed Adeline's words through her mind. Never had she met someone so callous and entitled, so petty and insufferable. Yet Adeline's pain at her father's death—so vivid in her dark eyes—mirrored something in Effie. An aching she could not name or place. An emotional residue coating the void where memories of her own family ought to have been. The Kinyons had filled that void like cotton gauze packed into a wound. A lifesaving remedy perhaps, but painful and apt to fester.

Better now that the void was open to air and could at last scar over. That is, if she could avoid Adeline, whose presence burned like alcohol on the yet tender flesh.

It was too late to slip away, though. Adeline turned in her direction and smiled. "Effie! It's about time." When Effie said nothing, she continued. "Your boss here was telling me all about your noble little profession."

"He's not my boss." She turned to Colm, who'd righted himself and straightened the lace shroud his elbow had dragged askew atop the casket. "I finished my work at the Franklin house. Mr. Whitmark is undoubtedly waiting on you and your iron constitution to move the parlor furniture for tomorrow's service."

He scowled at her. "I couldn't very well leave your—er—Miss Mercier here alone, now could I?" He turned back to Adeline and bowed slightly before heading out the back. It wasn't lost on Effie that he couldn't envision a world where someone like Adeline— dressed smartly in a bouffant skirt and jacket bodice of grenadine silk, her hair sleek in a low-lying chignon—and Effie with her plain work dress and simple bun were on familiar terms. Effie couldn't either. For all her longing to impress Samson, she knew her and Adeline's arrangement was futile.

"How'd you find me?"

"There are fewer undertakers in the city than you think," Adeline said, sweeping her hand over the fuzzy tops of the ostrich plumes. "Fewer still with a Negress in employment. Why you might be the only one between here and Charleston."

"There was a problem with the boot heel I take it."

"No, it worked fine. Better than fine, really. *À la perfection.* You should have seen their faces!" She turned from the plumes, came a step closer, and then stopped. Her gaze brushed the floor and her fingers twined together. "No, I came for, well, because . . . perhaps I spoke a touch too bluntly before and wanted to make amends."

An apology? Women like Adeline didn't *make amends* with women like Effie. Not in her experience.

"You were a bit ungracious yourself," Adeline said after a few moments of silence, her eyes still skittish. "Speaking so harshly and then running off like that."

"It was the truth."

"Mamm was quite upset."

"Are you here because of her?"

"I just thought, well, I had an idea. You said you don't know who or where your kin are. Maybe they're looking for you."

Surely this was a trick. Surely she wanted something in return. "What do you mean?"

"The Freedmen's Bureau used to get all kinds of letters from people searching for lost family. The papers even printed a few." She cocked her head. "You must have wondered."

Effie searched her eyes for the glint of guile. Her lips for Madame Desâmes's sinister smile. But the Adeline before her was the same benevolent woman she'd seen at Charity Hospital. "The Freedmen's Bureau is gone."

"Their records aren't. They're stored away in the statehouse somewhere, and I know a fellow who can help us find them. Come on."

Effie hesitated. She had wondered. As much as she'd tried not to in the eleven years since the War's end, that quiet ache, that longing had never gone away. When fleeing Indiana, she might have gone anywhere. New York. Philadelphia. Even London or Paris after saving a few more coins. But she'd come here. South. To New Orleans.

Unconscious acts of the soul, one theorist she'd read described such phenomena. At the time, Effie had been skeptical. Was skeptical still. But she ventured a nod at Adeline and fished the shop key from her pocket.

She followed Adeline along the busy streets downriver. As they walked, Adeline peppered her with questions about her childhood, to which Effie could only answer, "I don't know, I don't remember."

Adeline frowned. They waited for the streetcar to pass, then crossed Royal Street and headed down St. Louis. "What do you remember, then?"

Her first fully formed memory began with smoke wafting through the early-morning mist of a swamp. Mud caked her tattered clothes, and insect bites welted her skin. She followed the smell through the ferns and palm fronds and drooping moss to a break in the trees. Triangles of stretched cloth sprawled across the patch of high land while men in blue trousers and dirty undershirts squatted before cook fires. The scent of roasting coffee beans and boiled meat mixed with that of the smoke. Despite the snarls of her long-empty stomach, fear of these men kept her hidden in the undergrowth.

One man sauntered over and relieved himself only inches from where she crouched. She kept perfectly still, holding her breath until her windpipe spasmed for need of air. Urine splattered onto her neck and cheek. When he buttoned his trousers and turned to go, Effie thought herself safe, but a nettlesome ibis honked from the waterways behind her. The man spun back around. His eyes, still crusted with sleep, swept the bayou. He took a step forward, his scuffed boot flattening the grass beside her. He gazed out another moment, then yawned and threw his arms up in a stretch.

"There's a darkie right there by your feet, Joss," a voice said.

In trying so hard to keep still, Effie hadn't noticed the other man approach.

The man called Joss hollered and leaped back while the other heehawed like a mule, drawing the attention of several others. Joss dragged her from the underbrush. "What you doin' here, boy?"

When she didn't reply, he shook her and asked again. His fingers circled so tight about her arm she thought her bone might snap.

"I's lookin' fo de Yankees."

"Where you come from? How long you been watching me?"

"I's lookin' fo de Yankees."

He pulled her up so that her tiptoes barely brushed the ground. "You a spy for the Rebs?"

"I's lookin'—"

"You say that one more time and I'll—"

"Let him go," one of the men in the gathering crowd said, his voice quiet but commanding. "He's just a frightened boy."

Joss released her arm and stalked away. Many of the others followed. The quiet-talking one, a man not so young as the others but not so old that his bones had begun to bend or his hair lose its color, told her she'd found the Yankees. Every cell in her body sang with relief. She didn't know just who or what the Yankees were, but she'd been told to run, run until she saw a gathering of men in blue—not gray, that was important—and to say the very line she'd just delivered. Then she'd be safe.

The man, whose calm hazel eyes reminded her of honeycomb, took her to his campfire and gave her water and food. "My name is Lieutenant Kinyon," he'd said as she scarfed down the watery stew and rock-hard bread. "You're safe here with me."

Now, with sunlight winking through the wrought-iron railings of the overhead balconies, Effie relayed the memory to Adeline.

"*Mon Dieu,*" Adeline said, then fell silent a moment. "They thought you were a boy? How old were you?"

Effie shrugged. "Seven. Maybe eight. Captain Kinyon realized I was a girl after a few days, but he thought it best not to make a show of it. So I kept my hair cropped and wore trousers through the War."

She gave Effie that familiar, disapproving look. "That explains a lot. But seven, that's quite old for one's earliest memory. You remember nothing before that?"

"Just bits and pieces. Nothing anchored to a specific time and place."

"Like what?"

They stopped for a moment and let a band of schoolchildren hustle past. "A decrepit shed, running my fingers along a brick wall in some shadowed room. A man's voice. A woman's humming. A pair of—" Effie loosened the knot of her bonnet.

"Go on."

"A pair of eyes. A dead person's eyes." She could see them even now, wide pupils outlined in a thin ring of brown, dull and hazy as if covered by a scrim.

"Dead? How do you know they were . . . *mais bien sûr,* your work." Adeline looked away toward the street, her lips and cheeks newly pale, and Effie wondered if she regretted her questions. A lacquered carriage rolled passed. A policeman on his bay. A wagon piled high with tightly baled cotton. When she turned back, Effie was surprised by the steadiness of her gaze. "That's it? You don't even remember who told you what to say when you reached the Union camp?"

Effie shook her head.

"However is that possible?"

"Schopenhauer believed loss of memory stemmed from the inability of one's intellect to assimilate an event due to opposition from the will." She thought it best not to add he believed this the root of madness.

"Intellect and will?" Adeline gave a dismissive flip of the hand. "Whatever the cause, they must be in there somewhere."

The statehouse, a four-story affair crowned with a dome, spanned almost an entire block. A rust-speckled balcony wrapped around the building, casting shade on the rows of French windows beneath. As they passed through the columned entrance, Effie couldn't help but wonder whether they'd see Samson somewhere inside. She fiddled with her bonnet and gave her skirt a quick shake. A short vestibule led into a grand rotunda aglow with afternoon sunshine from the skylights high above.

"This used to be the most fashionable hotel this side of Canal Street. Mamm said they threw the most wonderful balls here before the War. Can you imagine?"

Effie could not. Aside from a few Reform Society functions, she'd never danced. Still, the look in Adeline's eye—one of such wonder and longing—made even Effie wistful. What would it be like to feel Samson's hand upon her back, his breath upon her cheek? To hear his melodious voice in her ear above the music as he led her around the dance floor? Her blood sparked at the thought as if each tiny cell had been laced with gunpowder. She shook her head to dislodge the fantasy and stymie the conflagration in her veins, pleasant as it was.

Adeline sighed. *"Quel dommage.* Now they've turned the beautiful ballrooms into Senate chambers and the like. All that political humbug."

Effie clutched the worn marble balustrade as they climbed a curved stairway to the second floor. At the far end of a narrow hallway, they arrived at an office. Adeline knocked and a handsome young mulatto answered.

"Adeline, *chérie, quelle surprise."* He took her hand and kissed it. *"Tu es belle comme toujours. Ça va?"*

Adeline looked down and smiled. She'd increased the rate at which she blinked and surreptitiously bit her bottom lip so that it flushed pink. Her friend, meanwhile, had straightened his posture and pinned back his shoulders. His eyes never left Adeline's face.

Effie watched enthralled. She'd seen behavior like this before, but never paid it much mind. Often people's movements were awkward, rigid, their speech riddled with "ums" and "aahs." But Adeline was a master. She said something in French about the man's cravat. They both laughed. Then she playfully adjusted the silk tie as if it had been askew, her hand lingering on his chest a moment afterward. More laughter. Adeline's gaze was teasing, bold then retreating, like a cat pawing at a cornered mouse before sinking in her teeth.

"François," she said, stepping back to include Effie in their repartee. "May I introduce Miss Effie Jones. She's the reason for my little visit today."

He turned as if seeing Effie for the first time and extended his hand. "Miss Jones."

She shook it, both relieved and slightly offended he'd not tried to kiss her hand as he'd done with Adeline's. "Pleasure to meet you, Mr. . . ."

"Rey, but do call me François. My what a strong handshake you have."

Heat rushed to the tips of Effie's ears. "A necessity of my profession. I'm—"

Adeline gave a shrill laugh and nudged Effie in the ribs with her elbow. "We could spend all day on pleasantries, but we really haven't the time. I told Miss Jones here you could help us. We're looking for the old Freedmen's Bureau records."

"I believe they're being kept up on the fourth floor, but I'm afraid they're rather in a jumble. You could put in a request with the file clerk and—"

She tugged playfully at his cravat again. "I'm sure we can manage ourselves. All we're after are the accounts of missing kinfolk. We'll put everything in right order when we're done."

He ran a hand over his closely cropped hair.

"*S'il te plaît, François. Pour moi.*" She smiled and cocked her head, displaying the smooth skin and graceful line of her neck.

"All right. Come on."

He led them up two more flights of stairs, down another hallway, and unlocked a room the size of two streetcars lined side by side. Effie and Adeline grimaced at each other, then waded inside. The air was hot and reeked of mildew. A lone window illuminated the room. Dust motes drifted through the narrow beam of light peeking between the moth-eaten curtains. Otherwise the room was dark.

"I don't think the gas works up here," François said. "Let me see if I can find a lantern." He left down the hall.

Effie followed the weak glimmer of light, knocking into stacks of boxes and tripping over crates on her way to the window. She flung back the curtains and lifted the sash. A light breeze drifted in, pleasantly cool against the sheen of sweat that had already built on her skin. "That's better."

"Much," Adeline said. "Now, where to begin."

Receptacles of all shapes and sizes crowded the room—chests and paperboard boxes, burlap sacks and driftwood crates. Adeline peered into an open box with rolled-up sheaves of papers jutting out like stalks of corn. As she sifted through the rolls, a trio of moths flew up into her face. She yelped and batted them away. From the far corner, somewhere amid the jumble, a rat squeaked and scampered away.

Adeline's complexion turned ashen.

"You don't have to do this," Effie said. "I can carry on from here alone."

"Nonsense." She took a deep breath, then removed her hat and gloves. "I said I'd help and that's what I mean to do."

François returned with an oil lamp.

"All these boxes are from the Freedmen's Bureau?" Effie asked.

He looked around and nodded. He recommended they start in the corner by the window, though he didn't offer any logic in support of this advice, and begged off, promising to come check on them once he'd finished his bookkeeping for the day. He flashed Adeline a smile that seemed to suggest, despite his initial hesitation, he was game for any conspiracy to which she was party.

"Are you lovers?" Effie asked when he'd gone.

"*Mon Dieu,* what a question! You really must try for more tact."

"Fine. Is your mutual interest in each other of the romantic or corporeal variety?"

"Hardly an improvement." Amusement played beneath her words, undermining the glower Adeline had set upon her face. "*Mais, non.* We're nothing of the sort."

"Is it his family name or his income?"

Adeline pulled the lid off a nearby box. "Both, if you must know."

"Then why all the . . . all the—"

"Flirting? That's how you get a man to do what you want, of course." She pulled out a stack of letters. "I hope you were paying attention. No doubt you could use a little flirting in your interactions with Monsieur Samson."

"But I don't want anything from him."

"Of course you do! His heart."

Effie hadn't a reply. She'd never considered love in those terms before, as if it were a game of chess—attack, pin, check—all in the hopes of getting the other player to expose his king. Or in this case, his heart.

She crouched down and opened one of the chests. Its hinges creaked, and stale air assaulted her nose. When she looked down at the mess of papers and ledgers, thoughts of Samson drifted from her mind.

Could the answers to her past really be in one of these containers? Until that moment, she'd not realized the crushing weight hope had brought to bear on her. Her lungs struggled to expand. Her hand trembled as she reached for the top sheet of paper.

But the paper was only a personnel record, listing staff names, hire date, salary, and military rank when applicable. The next several pages were more of the same. She sifted through marriage records, land applications, internment rolls from the Freedmen's Cemetery. She picked through a crate filled with maps of the surrounding parishes.

She too removed her bonnet and gloves, and pulled forward another box. "Anything?"

Adeline shook her head. "You sure you're from around these parts? Not Alabama or the Carolinas?"

"Captain Kinyon said I found my way to camp the very morning they fought the rebels at Georgia Landing, just outside of Labadieville. Considering my age and the terrain, I'd estimate a travel radius of no more than twenty miles."

"Labadieville . . . that's Assumption Parish, *n'est-ce pas?*"

Effie nodded. She'd looked it up once on a map.

"Do you remember the year?"

"Sixty-two. Captain Kinyon said they'd just started up the Mississippi with orders from General Butler to secure all the cotton and sugar plantations there."

"Ah, Le Bête. Careful whom you say his name to around these parts."

They set back to their work. The lovely breeze stolen in through the window weakened, and Effie's skin again became sticky with perspiration. She unbuttoned her collar and fanned herself with a stack of bounty claims. Adeline removed her jacket—a rather bold move should François suddenly return. The shirt beneath, plain white cotton embroidered at the collar and cuffs, bore the marks of age. Pale yellow stains circled the armpits. In a few places, the fibers had worn so thin the ribs of her corset were visible. Effie's undershirt was in little better repair, but she found it hard not to pity Adeline and forgive the crassness of her comments that day in the bedroom. She too knew what it was to want something lost. Or perhaps they were both after something they'd heard tell of but never really known.

"I think I've found something." Adeline held up a notebook. "The front page is titled 'Register of Missing and Lost Persons.'"

Effie squeezed onto the small trunk where Adeline sat. Three columns divided each of the notebook's pages. In the first was recorded the name of the lost or missing person. The next column contained a description of their last known location. A few of these entries were quite specific. *Mr. Silas Marrs's plantation, Donaldsonville, Louisiana, 1858.* Others gave only the city, parish, or state. Some offered even less. *Sold downriver, 1855.* The final column listed the inquirer's name and residence.

Though she knew it anatomically impossible, Effie felt the frantic contraction of her heart halfway up her esophagus. She scooted so close to Adeline their shoulders were overlapping and took hold of one edge of the notebook. Her eyes leaped from name to name to name. She reached to turn the page, but Adeline batted her hand away. "*Espère!* I'm not finished reading yet."

The seconds were agony as she waited. Several names on the next page snagged her gaze: *Ella, Elie, Edney, Eveline*. She moved the letters around in her mind like pieces of a shattered cup, as if in rearranging them, they might come to spell *Effie* or *Euphemia*.

Too soon they came to the last page. After a quick scan of the names, she rent the notebook from Adeline's hand and flipped back to the beginning. Surely they'd just overlooked it. Surely her name was there. Misspelled perhaps or on first pass illegible. But, no. Nothing.

She tossed the notebook into an open box.

"It's just one register, Effie. There's probably a dozen more in the room." Adeline nudged her lightly with her shoulder. Effie nodded once, her skull a weight on her neck.

"And I'll thank you not to sit right on top of me next time and hurry me through. I'm perfectly capable of reading a list of names." Adeline bumped her again. Effie let herself be pushed to the far edge of the little chest, offering only a weak nudge in return.

"You can do better than that," Adeline said, giving her a playful shove.

Had Effie been foolish to come here? To let this hope awaken inside her?

Another little shove from Adeline.

Hadn't she survived all those years in Indiana not knowing? Hadn't that been a better way to live?

Another nudge.

The dust seemed to have multiplied in the air, the smell of moldy paper and rat urine sharpened. Her undergarments clung sticky to her skin. Yet she also caught the whiff of Adeline's vetiver eau de perfume. A breeze once again fluttered the moth-ravaged curtains. She didn't wish herself back in Indiana, not for all the comfort and stability in the world.

Her bottom was hanging off the edge of the chest now, her balance teetering. She planted her feet and pushed back. Her torso met

with Adeline's. Shoulder to shoulder. Hip to hip. For all their petticoats, bustles, and flounces, they came together with surprisingly
little padding. She must have caught Adeline unaware, for Adeline
slid clear across the chest, wobbled on the edge a moment, then fell
to the floor with a thud.

"Great goodness, I'm sorry!" Effie said, kneeling beside her. But
laughter drowned her words.

Effie laughed too. It started as an uneasy chuckle, halting puffs
of breath with just a whisper of sound. But the sight of Adeline on
the floor beside her—fine jacket cast aside, shirt soaked through
with sweat, limbs planted around her like a crab—bolstered Effie's
laughter. It spread down her throat and through her lungs, becoming
louder and more robust. It infected her diaphragm until her entire rib
cage shook. In an attempt to catch her breath, Effie snorted, and she
and Adeline laughed anew.

Her stomach muscles ached when the last of their giggles petered
out. She wiped her eyes and tucked the flyaway hairs back into her
bun. Without saying anything they returned to the papers and note-
books and ledgers. The shaft of sunlight through the window moved
like the hand of a clock across the room, growing long and narrow.

In one box, sandwiched between financial records from the orphan asylum and a roster of destitute and discharged soldiers at the
freedman's hospital, she found a stack of letters and a few newspaper
clippings pertaining to the lost and missing. The first letter read:

> *I wish to inquire for my brother Joseph and sister*
> *Patience, whom I left in Louisiana in 1854, near as I*
> *can remember. At the time of my sale, brother belonged*
> *to Wm. Hines of Cross Bayou. Patience and I belonged*
> *to Jeffery Jackson. Any information about them will be*
> *thankfully received. Address me at Aberdeen, Miss.*

Each letter and clipping read much the same: *I wish to inquire for*
my mother, my brother, my daughter, my uncle, my sister, my father-
in-law, my kinfolk, my people . . .

Effie's name wasn't in any of the letters. Nothing about a girl last
seen in Assumption or neighboring St. James Parish in 1862. Even
so, Effie took comfort from the letters and newspaper ads. She was

not alone in her search. Surely by now some of these people had reunited. She arranged the envelopes and newsprint in a neat stack and tied them together with a ribbon from her bonnet. This way they would stand out for the next person who came looking.

"What about your last name Jones?" Adeline asked a few minutes later. She'd found another Register of Missing and Lost Persons and pointed to a name, *Elijah Jones*. "Could he have been a brother? Iberville is only a few parishes away from Assumption."

Elijah. She rolled the name around in her head, then said it aloud to feel the shape of it on her tongue. "I don't think so. Family names weren't common before the War. Not among slaves."

"How did you come by Jones, then?"

"I picked it myself. Mrs. Kinyon, the captain's wife, said plain Euphemia wouldn't suit. I must be 'Miss someone.' So I thought on it and chose the name Jones."

"Why didn't you take their surname, Kinyon?"

"I was their ward, not their daughter." Mrs. Kinyon had made that distinction clear. So too had the captain, in the end. Not in word but in action. True, he'd saved her life. Saved her from ending up on one of those orphan asylum rolls. Yet a daughter enjoyed affections beyond charity. A daughter was not an experiment in racial aptitude or a badge of virtue. "They already had a daughter—dead before the War—and weren't in want of another."

"Oh." Adeline eyed her with a shrewd expression, one that made her feel as if she did indeed have spirit powers and could stare into Effie's soul. Thankfully, she asked nothing more about the Kinyons. "But Jones, it must have some significance or else you wouldn't have picked it. Could it have been your master's surname?"

A common enough practice, but Effie didn't think so. When she picked the name, but a few months after the War's end, she hadn't any memory of her former master or life before the camp.

With so little to go on, the impossibility of their task grew more apparent. They wrote down the contact information of the woman who'd inquired after Elijah Jones, but Effie had little hope in the prospect. Each new box or crate or chest they sifted through, each new register void of her name, further dampened her hope. They huddled close to the lamp now, the sun long since lost behind the surrounding buildings, and evening quickly approaching.

"Bon Dieu, look at this," Adeline said, holding a thick stack of papers, their edges just beginning to yellow. Her voice trembled.

Effie read the heading on the top sheet of paper. *Murders and Outrages Reported to Bureau Headquarters, July 1865–February 1867.* Below was a succinct tally of the offenses:

Freedmen killed by whites—70

Freedmen murdered—unknown perpetrators—6

Freedmen shot at, whipped, stabbed, beaten &c—210

Freedmen murdered by Freedmen—2

Whites murdered by Freedmen—1

The subsequent pages gave a brief synopsis of each case. Drownings, hangings, rapes, shootings, assaults, lashings. One victim, described simply as a "freed boy," had been dragged for three miles with a rope about his neck. In no instance, the report read, had a white man been punished for these offenses.

She and Adeline said nothing as they read through the stories. After several minutes, Adeline flung the papers back into their box. Her glassy eyes glinted in the lamplight. She grabbed her jacket, fumbling with buttons as she tried to fasten it closed. "It's late. We should have left hours ago."

Effie agreed. The heat and dust and stink were enough now to make her retch. She tidied the papers, closed the lid, grabbed the lantern, and followed Adeline from the room, leaving the stories to regather dust.

CHAPTER 13

‗‗‗⇒•⇐‗‗‗

Effie stared out the streetcar window. Dust speckled the glass and the casement rattled in its frame. The other riders, Sunday regulars like herself, no longer paid her any mind, despite her being the only colored person in the car. Those cars they passed heading the opposite direction were filled with colored women, maids and cooks and nannies heading uptown after their Sunday morning off. She spied their faces, almost like a reflection, as they peered out their windows at the monstrous homes and manicured gardens.

Two new passengers clambered aboard her train, white suburbanites heading downriver to comfort a sick friend or pay an overdue visit to some less-distinguished relations. The man pursed his lips as he searched out a seat for his wife. All the seats were filled. His gaze settled on Effie and his expression screwed into a glower. Effie didn't move, despite the contempt flung from his eyes.

She disembarked at her regular stop. Clouds drifted through the sky like bolls of cotton. She still mistrusted the March warmth and carried along her coat, as if at any moment the snow and wind and ice of Indiana might find her here. The weight of it slung over her forearm comforted her. In the three days since she and Adeline had visited the statehouse, she'd become like a fishing boat teetering in the wake of a mighty steamboat. She no longer belonged to the North. To Captain Kinyon and the life she'd cultivated in his shadow. But the South, New Orleans, seemed at once to embrace her and push her away. Without the anchor of kin or memory, she drifted unmoored, reliant on the river's mercy.

The parlor was empty when she arrived back at Mrs. Neale's. A gentle cross breeze wound through the house, carrying with it the scent of stewing leeks and cabbage from the kitchen out back. She retrieved her writing implements from her room and brought them down to the parlor, as its south-facing window offered better light. With any luck, she'd finish her letter before the other women returned from whatever post-church activities they were attending and descended upon the parlor like a flock of nattering pigeons.

Age dulled the lacquer finish on Mrs. Neale's writing desk. But its legs were sturdy and, save for a few nicks and scratches, the tabletop smooth. Effie dipped her pen in ink and wrote the date and address. Her hand wavered then. She set down the pen so ink would not dribble onto the expanse of blank paper. Damn her dithering. Yet one more sign of her weakening constitution. Either she had words to print or she did not. Her two prior attempts at this letter had ended as kindling in yesterevening's fire. She couldn't afford to waste more paper.

In truth, it wasn't a problem of words. What if her letter went unanswered? Or worse, what if Elijah Jones was her kin, but wanted nothing to do with her? She shouldn't have let Adeline drag her to the statehouse in the first place. She'd slept far better when she hadn't been concerned about a family she couldn't recall.

Best get it over and done with, she decided. Adeline would undoubtedly pester her about it otherwise.

Mrs. Sally Baker
Opelousas, La.

Dear Madame:
I had occasion recently to review the report you
made some years back to the Bureau of Refugees,
Freedmen and Abandoned Lands regarding one Elijah
Jones. I am writing to inquire whether you were able
to locate said individual. I myself am in pursuit of
information regarding family connections last seen
before the War. I have few particulars, but as I share
Mr. Jones's surname—

Effie stopped at the *clickety-clack* of approaching footfalls. Meg and Harriet entered the parlor. They paused in the doorway, Harriet glaring, Meg offering a timid smile, then sat down on a couch across the room and began chatting about the bonnets they'd seen in a shop window on Canal Street. Three other boarders followed a minute or two later, dragging over chairs and stools to form a closed-off ring.

Normally, Effie was good at tuning out conversation. But today their voices tugged at her ear—not what they said, rather the general cacophony of it. The wave-like rise and fall of their pitch and volume. The pauses and sputtering and interruptions. The tangle of two or three voices all speaking at once. She tried three times to finish the line she'd begun before their intrusion, but though her hand sat at the ready, her thoughts refused to settle. Something about their conversation reminded her of what Adeline had said about the opera. She set down her pen and picked up the letter as if to read what she'd written, but instead peeked over the top at their circle.

At first glance, she saw what she'd always seen: that tiresome social ritual of endless yapping peculiar to the female sex. But upon closer examination, she realized far more was happening. Each woman sat with her body angled toward Harriet. They laughed when she laughed, nodded when she spoke. At one point in the conversation, she shifted her weight from one side to the other, moving her right ankle from in front of her left to behind it. Over the next few minutes, each of the other women recrossed their ankles in the same way.

Effie sat fascinated, like the time she'd crouched beside an anthill and watched the little red insects scurry this way and that, each independent yet very much under the sway of the collective. Eventually, they'd crawled up her leg and bitten her through her stockings. Here in the parlor, however, nothing dissuaded her attention. No one interrupted or contradicted what Harriet said. Except for Meg, who cloaked her disagreement between statements of praise with surprising stealth and skill. Perhaps she was smarter than Effie had given her credit for.

Clearly Harriet played the role of prima donna. Meg, the mezzo. The other women were the chorus. Effie smiled. The analogy hadn't made sense when considering the ladies of the ward club. But here it fit. Perfectly. More than that, she saw how much was at play besides the exchange of trite opinions and ideas, now saw why her straightforward approach to these situations had failed. Adeline would be so impressed with her revelation.

"What is you smilin' on about?" Harriet said. "You got your ear up in our conversation?"

It took Effie a moment to realize Harriet was addressing her. "I'm . . ." She stopped. Before she would simply have announced the truth. *I'm smiling because I've deciphered the behaviors you employ to exert your standing within the group.* But Harriet would likely find such a statement pert. "I was just thinking about . . . the opera."

"You've been to the opera?" one of the women asked.

Effie hesitated. This business of thinking through one's speech, of anticipating and correcting for others' reactions wasn't easy work. In the end, she decided the truth would satisfy. "No."

Harriet raised her chin and gave a *humph*. The women returned to their conversation and Effie to her letter, their words and interjections and giggles no longer a distraction.

The burst of satisfaction that had brought forth her smile faded as soon as she picked up her pen. *Elijah Jones*. He couldn't be her kin. A waste of ink and postage, that's all this was. And yet every corpuscle of her body hummed at the idea of a brother, an uncle, a father.

> . . . *but as I share Mr. Jones's surname I thought it prudent to investigate a possible connection. I was taken up by the Yankee army at Georgia Landing, Assumption Parish, October 1862. How far I traveled to get there I can only speculate. White folks call me Euphemia, but I prefer Effie and likely went by both when Mr. Elijah or his kin would have known me. My age is twenty-one years, give or take a year or two. I have no further details to offer. I thank you in advance for any information you or Mr. Jones can supply. Address me at 1730 Thalia St, New Orleans, La.*
>   *Yours, Most Respectfully,*
>
>   *Effie Jones*

She set down her pen and dabbed the wet ink with blotting paper. Her palms were sweaty, and the muscles of her thumb and index finger sore from too tight a grip on the pen. The impulse to crumple the letter or tear it into tiny pieces played through her like a shiver. Then there'd be no waiting. No hoping. No inevitable despair. She picked up the sheet and pulled it taut between her hands.

"Your letters sho are pretty."

Effie looked up. The other women had left the room save for Meg, who now stood beside her. She laid the paper back upon the desk and hid her hands in her lap as if she'd been caught in some mischievous act.

"How'd you learn to make such fine markings?"

"My warden taught me. During the War."

"Bet you practiced a lot."

Effie remembered the hot afternoons she'd spent beside the hospital tent, the camp listless, guns silent save for the errant misfire, both sides dallying and posturing and angling for better position. She'd clear a patch of ground and trace the letters of the alphabet—A to Z—in the dirt. When she finished, she'd smooth over the dirt and begin again. By days' end, the fingers of both hands were worn to blisters.

Later, in Indiana, she'd stay up late into the night, studying German, Latin, anatomy by moonlight, so in the morning she could impress the captain with what she'd learned—*Gib mir bitte einen Keks* or *plus sucus, si vis*—and catch his approving grin, or even a word of praise.

"It took several years to become proficient."

Meg frowned. "Golly, Effie. You sho is smart." She eyed the letter as if it weren't plain foolscap paper, but hundred-dollar banknotes stitched together.

"One needn't be smart to learn to read and write."

"I could never do it."

"Of course you could." Effie folded the paper into a small square and stuffed it in the envelope. Seeing in it now as Meg saw it, each pen stroke a tiny miracle, she lamented the ink and paper she'd wasted the night before and resolved, despite her apprehension, to send the letter on. Meg watched over her shoulder as she addressed the envelope and screwed closed the lid of her inkpot.

The supper bell sounded, but Meg hovered as Effie gathered up her supplies, for once without words.

Finally she said, "Would you . . . that is, if you ain't too busy, learn me to read and write too?"

"It's not a simple undertaking—"

"I promise I'll practice. Every night. However long it takes."

Effie opened her mouth, then shut it again. She hadn't the time, materials, or disposition for such an onerous task. Meg held silent, the raw longing in her gaze something Effie knew all too well.

"Very well. We'll begin after supper."

CHAPTER 14

Effie found herself looking over her shoulder as she headed to the club meeting. The busy streets bustled with freedmen and immigrants, yokels and Chinamen. They carried laundry, pushed street carts, lugged vegetables, led mules, puffed tobacco, strummed banjos, and plucked mandolins. Why would anyone notice a lone colored woman amid such a ruckus?

Still, her skin prickled with the weight of imaginary stares. The man leaning against the lamppost thumbing through a crumpled newspaper wasn't reading, but tracking her. The shopkeeper brushing his stoop was using his broom as a pretense to spy which street she turned down next.

She blamed Colm for this paranoia, for infecting her with cock-eyed conspiracies. These men didn't give a lick about her goings-on. Neither did Mr. Whitmark. He was likely active in a Republican club in his own ward. No harm in her attending one too.

And that's all she aimed to do. Sit, listen, observe. No more stitching or banner holding. She'd come to see Samson, nothing more.

She slipped in beneath the bullet-riddled sign just as the meeting commenced. Mrs. Carrière and Jonah made room for her on their bench three rows from the back. Tom waved an ink-stained hand at her from across the room. In the front row sat Samson, his back straight and broad shoulders square. How easy her eyes found him now, despite the dozens of bodies between them, as if the shape and curve of his profile had been tattooed onto her cornea, the same way his voice had imprinted on her eardrum.

Nearly two weeks had passed since she'd seen him last. Twelve days, six and a half hours, to be precise. What had he done to fill those hours—all 294 of them? In her spare hours, when she'd taken up a book or sat on the balcony and polished the buttons in her old tobacco box, she imagined him engaged in similar or complementary pursuits, perhaps writing a letter or playing a game of chess. But what if his life were totally different? What if he were married, had a family?

The thought made her queasy. She sat up as tall as she could to get a better look at him through the crowd.

It was not as if a married man wore a ring the way his wife might. He didn't change his style of dress or hair. She thought back to all the men she'd embalmed—married men, single men, widowed men. Surely there was some difference between them. Cleaner clothes perhaps. A little more flesh about the ribs. Married men died less often of blood poisoning and disease. But this was purely anecdotal. Still, she strained to see whether Samson's shirt was newly cleaned and pressed, how robust he looked compared to those around him.

The evidence was equivocal.

"Have you been all right since your encounter with those despicable men on Mardi Gras?" Mrs. Carrière whispered, patting Effie's hand.

Effie took a moment to reorder her thoughts. How flighty and soft-minded she must seem these days. "Yes . . . er . . . fine. Thank you."

"We were worried about you when you didn't show for last week's meeting."

Last week . . . she'd wanted to come but . . . ah, yes, the tanner on Magazine Street. Consumption. "I was called to a—" She stopped. Adeline's sharp *ahem* sounded in her mind as clearly as if she were seated beside her. "I was held up with my employer."

Mrs. Carrière gave a thoughtful nod. "I suppose God and his angels don't keep regular hours, do they?"

Samson got up and gave a summary of the week's legislative happenings. She tucked certain words and phrases away in her memory to relish later—his clever turns of alliteration like, *The Negro needn't be told his place, he must needs take it;* his folksy idioms like, *Debating them Democrats is like eatin' soup with a fork;* his charming mispronunciations like *posthumous* with a hard *t*. Twice she was sure he spied her in the crowd and smiled. Twice paralyzing her once-dependable heart.

She leaned close to Mrs. Carrière, but held back the question on her tongue. *Is Mr. Greene married?* Adeline never said or asked anything so straightforward. Neither did her housemates. Instead she whispered, "Does Mr. Greene ever bring a wife to the club meetings?"

"No."

This was exactly why Effie avoided such vague questions. Mrs. Carrière's answer didn't affirm he had a wife but didn't rule out the possibility either.

"What about on other occasions?"

"No."

Effie pursed her lips. This was futile. "But . . . what I mean to say is . . . is Mr. Greene married?"

Though Mrs. Carrière's gaze never flickered from the podium, her lips tottered between a smile and frown. "I don't believe he is, no."

Effie's entire body lightened, as if her bones were hollow like a bird's and she might flit to the cobwebby rafters above.

"I'd caution you against—" Mrs. Carrière continued, only to be interrupted by the not-so-quiet voice of little Jonah.

"We pray on the rosary every Sunday that he finds a wife. Him and Tom and—"

Mrs. Carrière shushed him, a blush deepening the color of her cheeks.

Effie hadn't realized he'd heard the discussion, and her own cheeks warmed.

"Not for my own sake, I assure you," Mrs. Carrière said, turning the thin gold band on her finger. "For the Party's. Samson would be far more likely to get that Senate seat he's after if he settles down a bit."

Effie nodded and they both returned their attention to the front.

Before he sat down, Samson enquired of the club whether they had any concerns they wished him to take back to the statehouse. Several men raised their hands. The first, a light-skinned Negro with a Creole sway to his speech, recounted being turned away by the usher at the Academy of Music unless he agreed to sit in the colored section. Another man spoke of being refused service at a saloon near the levee.

Samson listened to each complaint, his richly hued eyes never leaving the speaker. He nodded in support, asked questions, and promised to investigate.

Mrs. Carrière took the podium next. She passed around a rusty tin can to collect alms for the orphan asylum. Coins clanked and rattled as the tin made its way through the crowd.

"We'll be hosting a baking sale at next month's opening baseball game to raise money for the Negro Veterans Aid Society," she said, her gaze panning the audience. "Please encourage your wives and daughters to attend and contribute."

Effie dropped her eyes and pretended to be sifting through her purse for a coin, though she already had one in her palm for the can. Her baking was worse than her sewing.

"Finally," Mrs. Carrière said. "I hope we can renew our club's discussion on the issue of suffrage for us ladies before the summer holiday."

Chuckles burst from the crowd.

"Here she goes again," someone muttered.

The club president rose and shepherded Mrs. Carrière away from the podium. "I . . . ah . . . once we get some of these more pressing matters off the docket, we'll see what we can do."

Mrs. Carrière's lips pulled together and her eyes hardened, but she said no more. Her head remained high as she strode to her seat, dauntless and dignified despite being silenced.

"Women voting?" a man seated behind Effie said. "Where's the sense in that?"

"Now, if that's all the committee reports we have this—"

Effie stood and spoke over the president. "There are one hundred colored women of voting age in this city for every sixty-five men." Those seated in front of her swiveled around to look at her. She was used to stares, but never had so many eyes fixed on her at once. She snaked a hand into her skirt pocket and clasped the brass button she'd stowed there this morning. Her thumb worked the raised outline of a star as she gathered her courage to continue. "It seems only logical that enfranchising such a group would suit your aims more than it would hinder them. What could be more pressing than that?"

"Where'd you get them numbers?" a man near the front asked.

"Sound made up to me," another said.

"The 1875 Metropolitan Census Report. It ran in the *Picayune* just last month. Surely men such as yourselves have read it."

She'd not meant to seem—what had Adeline called her?— haughty, but judging from the grumbling rising around her, she had.

Samson stood and cleared his throat. "I, for one, favor the *Republican* over the *Picayune*." Several people laughed. The tension strangling the room slackened. "Your point is well taken, Miss Jones, but you mustn't put too much faith in a Democratic rag like that."

Effie remained standing even after everyone had turned back around and the president continued with his closing remarks. Samson's gaze had once again stirred mutiny among her emotions. How kind his voice had been. How warm his eyes. She jogged her head and sat. Kind and warm, yes, but also how wrong in his assessment. The *Picayune* hadn't commissioned the census, only reported on its findings. Likely the other papers had as well. Surely he knew that. Yet he'd discredited her before the group anyway.

The tin can at last reached her. She withdrew her hand from her pocket and dropped in her dime. A dull clank sounded as it struck the other coins. Rust and metal drowned out the other smells in the room. She could almost taste them on her tongue. She passed the can and returned her hand to the comfort of her button. In a matter of moments, she'd gone from feeling overjoyed at his notice of her—he'd once again proven he knew her name, after all—to feeling wounded by his casual rebuke. Was this what love was like? A tizzy of feelings as disjointed as they were intense?

She noticed then that those around her had stood. Men were donning their caps and derby hats, women their shawls. Effie hurried to her feet and grabbed her coat. The better part of her itched for the door, but she couldn't let things rest where they'd fallen. Either Samson believed her a fool or a trifle. She aimed to disabuse him of both notions.

Mrs. Carrière intercepted her before she'd taken but a few steps. "*Merci,* Miss Jones. It's good to have another suffragist in the group."

"I'm not really—"

"Lordy, Marie, why'd you go and bring up that voting nonsense again?" the club president said, coming up beside them with Tom.

"It's not nonsense and you know it."

Tom wagged his head, though a smile played on his lips. "And now you got Miss Effie here raisin' sand too."

"I only meant to point out the demographic advantage women might bring to the ballot box," Effie said. She glanced over Mrs. Carrière's shoulder toward the front of the room. Samson was still there talking with the mulatto who'd been booted from the Academy of Music. He clapped the man on the back and then shook his hand. The man walked away, and Samson was alone.

Effie tried to shimmy around Tom and the president to get to Samson before he left, but Mrs. Carrière hooked Effie's arm into the crook of her elbow. "The vote for women is just as important as the vote for Negroes."

The president laughed. "You're forgetting white women will be voting too, then."

"For shame!" Mrs. Carrière said.

"You ain't never been a slave. Them missuses could be just as nasty as their husbands," Tom said. "More so when the mood struck 'em. Ain't that right, Miss Jones?"

Effie released Sampson from her sights and cocked her head in Tom's direction. His dark eyes regarded her evenly, as if he'd long ago seen beneath her skin and examined her heart. "Am I wrong?"

She thought of the white woman who'd yanked her from the steps, scattering the newly shelled beans from her bowl. "No."

She held Tom's gaze a moment longer before remembering Samson. He'd gathered up his hat and gloves and strode toward the back of the hall. Before Effie could extricate her arm from Mrs. Carrière's and follow, a group of men grabbed him and drew him into their conversation circle. At least he hadn't made it to the door. One of the men said something that made the others laugh. Samson smiled widely, bearing his handsome teeth and pink gums. The skin about his eyes crinkled and his nostrils flared. She wished she stood close enough to absorb the sound of his laughter.

A tug on her arm drew her attention back. Her head turned first, her eyes following only when they could strain no further in their sockets. The club president had wandered off, but both Tom and Mrs. Carrière stared expectantly at her.

"Ah . . . sorry . . . did you say something?"

Mrs. Carrière glanced at Samson and frowned. "What will you be bringing to the baking sale?"

The baking sale . . . ? Oh, yes. Next month at the baseball game. "I don't cook."

"Like you don't sew?"

"I'm sure whatever you bake will taste mighty fine," Tom said. "How about somethin' you learned up North?"

Effie started to say she hadn't learned to bake anything, but that wasn't entirely true. Mrs. Kinyon had labored for years to teach her to cook. Anytime Effie was not off with the captain seeing to the dead or out in the barn mixing chemicals, Mrs. Kinyon dragged her into the kitchen to help with supper. It took no great skill to peel potatoes or churn butter or sift flour. But Effie struggled with the imprecision of baking and cooking. How much was a pinch of salt? Her pinch would measure different than Mrs. Kinyon's, whose would differ from Mrs. Harris's down the road. And which cup did she use to measure out flour or sugar? The tin cup she drank from at supper? The porcelain teacup Mrs. Kinyon kept high up in the cupboard? The small glass cup the captain hid in the study alongside his whiskey? Once, when Mrs. Kinyon had asked her to add half a pound of butter to the cake batter, Effie ran to the barn to fetch her scale. When Mrs. Kinyon saw her weighing out the butter she about swooned.

"What in the Good Lord's name are you doing, Euphemia? You use that filthy thing on the dead."

"No, ma'am. We use it to weigh the arsenic and mercury for our preserving fluid."

Mrs. Kinyon huffed, removed the slab of butter from the scale, and cut off a chunk. "This is a half-pound. It's not something you measure, it's something you just know. Take mind for next time."

But when Mrs. Kinyon turned her back to see to the stove, Effie snuck the chunk onto the scale. Three-eighths a pound, not half.

It hadn't mattered, though, for there weren't many "next times" after that. Mrs. Kinyon relegated her to peeling and churning and sifting. An arrangement that had suited them both.

Across the room, Samson tipped his hat to the men and backed free of their circle, snapping Effie's attention back into focus. "Will Mr. Greene be playing?"

Mrs. Carrière pursed her lips. "I believe he's on the team. Isn't he, Tom?"

Tom let the tip of his cane fall to the floor and cast his eyes downward before nodding.

"I suppose I can think of something," Effie said, her gaze returning to Samson. "Will you excuse me?"

After a faint sigh, Mrs. Carrière released her.

A few quick steps and Effie was at Samson's side. He smelled again of bitter orange and rosemary. His collar was clean but not newly pressed, evidence he hadn't a wife. "Mr. Greene, a word if you've a moment."

"Miss Jones." He bowed from the shoulders and pulled off his hat. "We missed you at our last meeting. I feared our little adventure at Mardi Gras might have proved too much for you."

His charm and the knowledge that he too had noticed her absence momentarily stupefied her. With some trouble, she continued. "I've a stronger constitution than you think."

"Indeed." He smiled, and she had to look away lest he further waylay her intentions.

"About the census. I think you'll find it was—" She stopped. A drumming sounded from outside on the street, its measured rhythm immediately familiar.

"Company halt," a voice called. The drumming stopped.

"Company about-face. Company present arms."

"What the devil?" Samson said, stomping toward the nearest window. Effie followed. At least a dozen club members remained in the hall, but all had fallen silent.

Through the dirty glass, Effie saw a group of about twenty-five white men arranged in two lines out on the street. They stood at attention facing the clubhouse, rifles in their arms. Most of the men looked to be in their early twenties, too young to have fought in the War. A few, though, including the commander, were older and wore their Rebel grays.

"Company shoulder arms," one of the older men acting as drill commander said. Each man in the group dropped his arms to his side, one hand cupping the butt of his gun.

Though Samson stood beside her gaping out the window, Effie could no longer smell his shaving soap. Instead the memory of cook fires, gun smoke, and putrefying flesh awakened in her nose. She heard the drill commander's words in her mind even before he said them.

"Company load in ten times. Load!"

At the next command, *handle cartridge,* the men reached into the cartridge boxes slung about their waists, but didn't withdraw any ammunition.

Samson turned from the window. "Damn White Leaguers!" He stomped to an upturned crate, where a newly extinguished oil lamp sat, smoke still drifting up the glass chimney.

The drill continued.

"Tear cartridge!"

Samson kicked the crate with such force it cartwheeled across the room, the lamp shattering on the ground.

Effie startled at the sound. Kerosene mixed with the phantom war smells choking her throat while the din outside continued.

"Charge cartridge!"

"It's okay, everyone," Tom said, lurching away from a nearby window with his cane. "It's just a drill."

His words did little to ease the panic inside the hall. Mrs. Carrière held Jonah fast to her side, as if she might shield him with her skirts. The group of men Samson had been speaking to before Effie stood still as scarecrows on a windless night.

"Draw rammer!"

Tom walked over to Samson, the thud of his peg and cane atop the floorboards the only sounds from within.

"Ram cartridge!"

He whispered something lost to Effie beneath the outside noise.

"Return rammer!"

"We can't let them intimidate us like this," Samson replied. "We have to—"

"Cast about!"

He moved toward the door, but Tom put out a hand and stepped in front of him. More whispers.

"Prime!"

Samson dragged a hand over his hair and nodded.

"Shoulder arms!"

"All right, everyone, let's exit through the back," Tom said, his voice calm and steady. "I'm sure they don't mean any trouble, but best not give them opportunity."

"Company ready!"

Effie turned back to the window.

"Aim."

The distant glow of lamplight cast strange shadows on the men's faces. A narrowed eye, a snarled lip—their obscured expressions formed a patchwork of focus and aggression. She knew they hadn't actually loaded their rifles. Even so, she flinched at the command to fire, her heart floundering and muscles knotting in anticipation of a spray of bullets. In the blink of silence that followed, her hands snaked across her stomach, up her sternum, and to the hollow of her neck. No holes or seeping blood. Foolish to think there would be, yet she trembled with relief.

One man among the ranks, whose beard had not quite the fullness of a man's, seemed to stare right at her. His trousers hung several inches too short for his lanky frame, exposing frayed bootlaces and slouched socks. Mismatched fabric patched the elbows of his jacket. Likely he was a common laborer. A dockhand, perhaps, or a grocer's assistant.

What could he see of her through the unwashed window, backlit as she was in the feeble light of the remaining lanterns? What but the outline of her stout shoulders and bonnet-capped head? She could be anyone to him. Had he focused on her silhouette when aiming, or off to the side so that his imaginary bullet would splinter the wooden window casement instead of her skull?

She shuddered and turned away. Samson hadn't moved from where he stood amid the shattered glass and spilled kerosene while Tom shepherded the others toward the back of the hall. Effie bent down and gathered up the shards.

"Miss Jones, please," Samson said, his voice heavy with fatigue. "I, we . . . we'll worry about that another day."

She didn't look up, but plucked more glass from the floor, depositing it in a pouch she'd formed from the fabric of her skirt. Then she stood and marched to the front door. Anger coursed alongside her fear. She opened the door and stepped onto the small landing.

"Recover arms," the drill commander said, but her sudden appearance snagged the attention of many of the men. They stood gaping, their rigid posture going slack.

She met the eye of the young man with the ill-fitting trousers. Here, without the grimy window to obscure her, his gaze was skittish. She flapped her skirt, sending a spray of glass tinkling to the ground. A few of the men jerked at the sound. Had their guns truly been at the ready, they might well have shot. As it was, their expressions darkened. Her bravado faltered. Another flap of her skirt and she turned around, retreating into the clubhouse.

"What the deuce, Miss Jones!" Samson said, pulling her away from the doorway as soon as she reentered and jamming the door shut behind her. "You can't go out there."

He'd woken from whatever stupor he'd been in just moments before, his eyes once again alert, his voice urgent, his grip about her upper arm so tight it might well leave a mark.

"Just because they're only drilling don't mean they're harmless," he said.

"The glass. I couldn't well leave it in a mess on the floor." It sounded less rational than it had felt at the time.

He hurried her to the far end of the room, through a door, and down a short dark hallway to the back exit. "This ain't the North. They whip niggers here. Beat them. Knife them. Shoot them. Rape—"

"I am not a nigger."

Samson stopped. He rattled his head. "No, I'm sorry."

They were outside on a narrow side street now, the cool, humid air prickling her skin.

"Indeed you're not." He regarded her with that nonplussed expression she so often met, as if she had a third nostril or insect antennae sprouting from her head. "Confounding, that's for sure, but there's something to you. . . ."

She tried to free her arm from his grasp. The weight of the night's events finally struck her, and she hadn't the strength for such scrutiny.

His grip held, tightened even for a moment, before loosening just enough to allow blood flow to her hand. His gaze changed too. Sharpened. No longer curious but hungry in its intensity.

The surrounding brick buildings seemed to pull in around them, the dark sky a twinkling canvas above their heads. The White Leaguers had resumed their marching, but the clap of their boots and bang of their drum was all but drowned out by the whoosh of her pulse.

"I'm sorry if my comment about the *Picayune* and that census report offended you," he said, stepping closer.

Effie held his stare, determined not to let him derail her thoughts. "You can't discount the report as biased when—"

His lips silenced her. His delicious scent blotted out the stench of the street. He paused, his flaring nostrils drinking in all the air between them, leaving Effie dizzy as he kissed her again. Who knew asphyxiation brought with it such bliss?

Abruptly, he pulled away and released her arm. The night's chill shocked her senses. The sour smell of rotten food and urine stung her nose. She winced at the sudden cacophony in her ears—the drilling White Leaguers, the screeching crickets, the scampering rats on the tile rooftops above. And something else. The thud of wood and footfalls atop the uneven pavers. Tom.

"I saw Mrs. Carrière off along with—" He stopped and glanced between her and Samson.

Effie shuffled back a step and tried for a placid expression, steadying her breath and locking her eyes forward.

"Miss Jones tarried to pick up the glass from the lantern I so carelessly knocked over," Samson said, his smooth voice betraying nothing. "She's had quite a fright from these buckras tonight. Can you see her home, Tom?"

Her gaze broke free and flickered to Samson. The cool comportment she so struggled to achieve sat easily upon his face.

"I needn't an escort," she managed, despite the sudden dryness of her tongue.

"Please, Miss Jones. It would be my pleasure." Tom offered her his arm.

She hesitated, hoping Samson would change his mind and insist he be the man to walk beside her.

He did not.

"Thank you, Mr. Button," she said at last.

"Tom."

"Tom." She accepted his arm and they started off. The smoothness of his gait surprised her. So too did his speed and the surety of his muscles. Were it not for the slight rock of his body and knock of his peg and cane against the stone, she'd not know he'd lost a leg.

"Night," he said over his shoulder to Samson.

"Good night," Samson called from behind them.

Effie said nothing.

CHAPTER 15

─────⊱◈⊰─────

"Got yourself a feller, do ya now?"

Effie froze at Colm's words, her scalpel flat against the whetstone. Had he followed her to the club meeting last night? Been among the White Leaguers drilling in the street? No. Surely she would have seen him. And he'd certainly not been there on that side street when . . . no, no more thoughts of that kiss.

She turned around. Colm was leaning against the doorjamb of the storeroom. His long legs and broad torso all but blocked the exit, caging her in the small room. She squeezed the cool metal handle of the scalpel and took a step back, her bustle flattening against the lip of the workbench. Then she noticed the folded square of paper clasped in his hand. "Did that arrive for me?"

"Maybe," he said, flipping it round in his fingers to hide the writing on the front.

Who would send a note to her here? Her mind immediately turned to Samson. An apology for not walking her home? A request to meet her again? Her free hand rose to her mouth unbidden, her fingers skating across her lips.

"Ha! I knew it," Colm said.

Effie dropped her hand and glared at him. The note couldn't be from Samson. He didn't know what she did, let alone where her employer kept shop. The greater part of her, however, ignored such logic and she snatched at the letter. Colm whisked it from reach, holding it high above his head.

"What's his name?"

"I haven't got a fellow. Now give it here."

"Maybe I'll just read for myself." He raised his other hand and began unfolding the paper.

Her hand tightened around the scalpel. "Don't you dare."

"Share-eh Effie, un-eh pet-it-eh fet-eh—"

She stomped on his toes with her boot heel. He cried out and his arms slackened. She grabbed the letter with one hand and held out the blade with the other, lest he try to take it back.

"Sheesh, I was just joshing with ya." He balanced on one foot and rubbed his toes through his balding leather boots.

"Haven't you the wagon to oil?"

He lingered a moment more in the doorway, boxing her in. Sweat slickened her palm around the metal handle and the air grew stuffy. When at last he lumbered off she set down the scalpel and finished unfolding the letter.

Chère *Effie,*

Une petite fête demain soir. *Wear your purple dress.*

—*Adeline*

Another lesson. She tucked the note into her apron pocket and returned to the whetstone. With each scrape of the blade across the stone she chided herself: for goading Colm, for the excitement she'd allowed herself to feel at the prospect—however dim—that Samson might have written her, for getting herself into this ridiculous situation where her Sunday evening plans now included *une petite fête.*

She made the mistake that evening of mentioning the fête to Meg during their reading lesson, who then announced it excitedly to the other women in the parlor. Much brouhaha ensued—squeals and snickers, questions and speculation—derailing their lesson completely and making Effie dread the coming event all the more. Who was hosting the party? Would there be music and dancing? What would she wear? How would she style her hair?

To this last point, Meg offered her a small bottle of elixir before they finally all parted for bed. "You simply gotta try this. My friend Peggy used it fo her weddin' and her hair done shine like satin."

Haddy's Oxidizing Ox Marrow, Hair Straightener. Beneath the name was the silhouette of a woman with an aquiline nose, diminutive lips, and long, sleek hair. Effie frowned. "This is bunkum. Ox marrow isn't an oxidizing agent." She tried to hand back the bottle, but Meg wouldn't take it.

"Peggy swears by it. Trust me. I can help, if you like. Ain't easy to manage on your own."

Effie declined. In her room, she sat on the bed and read the back label: *Get rid of snarly, ugly, kinky hair with just one use.* She unscrewed the lid and inhaled. Citrus blossoms and chemicals. Barium dioxide perhaps?

The next afternoon she lined the tin basin in the bathing room with a linen sheet and filled it with several buckets of water from the cistern. Her skin prickled from the cold shock as she clambered in and sat down. She lathered the soap and scrubbed her skin, starting with her arms, neck, and shoulders, then working her way down until she reached the crevices of her toes. She doused her hair and likewise scrubbed her scalp.

When she finished, Effie lingered in the sudsy water, watching the tiny soap bubbles skate atop the surface until one by one they burst. Her fingers brushed over her stomach and up to her breasts, dancing over her tented nipples. More than one man had groped and pinched her—in church while others bowed their head in prayer, on a crowded streetcar when she reached for a handrail, in that awful memory she'd recalled on Mardi Gras. Each time her stomach folded in on itself and her muscles turned to rocks.

But what would it be like if it were a man she desired, a man whose touch she craved? She'd read a few of the dime novels Mrs. Kinyon secreted beneath the spools of thread and scraps of fabric in her sewing basket. Enough to know that some women, in the right moment, with the right man, enjoyed such a touch. She imagined the fingers atop her skin were Samson's, not her own, and decided she too might be such a woman.

After toweling off and draining the tub into the gutter that led out to the street, Effie returned to her room and picked up the bottle of hair elixir. Likely it would do nothing for her curls, but at worst her hair would smell of citrus blossoms. Following the instructions printed in tiny lettering on the back, she set her iron heating on the coal stove, then worked the elixir into her hair from root to tip. Her scalp tingled.

Lay hair out flat and iron Haddy's serum into hair, the next step read.

Just how the deuce was she supposed to accomplish that? Pulled taut her hair extended little more than a hand's width from her head. She cleared her bedside table and moved it closer to the stove, covering the top with a towel to keep the iron from scorching the wood. Then she knelt and leaned her head against the table. With one hand pulling a section of hair as straight as possible, her other groped for the iron, blistering her pinkie on the stove before she found the handle.

The tingling across her scalp was more of a sting now, growing in intensity the longer she dallied. The iron sizzled when it touched her hair. She did her best to drag it over the strands in a smooth, continuous motion. In the brief moments when the iron was stilled atop her hair, the smell of blossoms and chemicals turned to that of singed animal hide.

She quickly finished with that section and set the iron back on the stove. The hair she'd ironed was still hot, but smooth and impossibly straight.

Buoyed by this success, she repositioned her head beside the table and grabbed another section of hair. Never mind that her knees ached and her scalp no longer tingled or stung but positively burned. To have hair like Adeline's or the woman's on the label she could bear a little discomfort.

She straightened another section, starting closer to the roots, then reheated the iron. But the hair closest to her scalp remained coarse and kinky. That wouldn't do. With the next section, she brought the iron as close to her scalp as she dared.

It took a moment for her brain to register the pain. Then she flung the iron and clapped her hand to her head, closing her lips around a scream. She doused her head with water from her pitcher before snatching the iron from where it had fallen and returning it to its rest on the stove.

The rug alongside her bed bore the singed imprint of the iron. Lucky it hadn't caught fire. She probed her scalp and winced. The skin was bald and blistered from the iron's scorching heat. Clumps of burnt hair caught in her fingers.

She sat on the edge of her bed and fought the urge to crawl under the sheets and close her eyes. Water dripped from the ends of her hair, the sections she'd managed to straighten already screwing back into curls. She hadn't time to finish, let alone start all over again.

Small cracks zigzagged across the plaster wall opposite her bed. Other women in the house decorated their walls with magazine cutouts and cross-stitch samplers, postcards and tintypes, beads and crosses. Hers were completely bare.

She imagined throwing the bottle of hair elixir against the naked plaster. Imagined the shattering of glass. The blooming of citrus and chemicals in the air. The oozing of brown serum down the wall. Her hands tightened into fists, itching for the bottle.

Perhaps she shouldn't have refused Meg's help. Perhaps she shouldn't have tried at all. Foolish to think a few drops of goopy elixir could transform her into someone beautiful.

She willed her eyes from the wall and her legs to stand. She fastened the tapes of her crinolette about her waist, donned her skirt, and buttoned her bodice. It had taken her several brushings and washings, but the dirt and lime from Mardi Gras were all but gone. Gingerly, she combed back her hair and pinned it in a simple bun, then tied on her bonnet, and forced herself to away.

A hired coach waited in Adeline's carriageway when Effie arrived.

"You're late," Adeline said as way of greeting. Her eyes roved Effie's body, as if she expected her to have grown a third arm in the days they'd been apart.

"Your note didn't specify a time."

"*Non?*" She waved a finger for Effie to spin around. Effie frowned but complied. "Haven't you anything besides that bonnet? Un chapeau, perhaps?"

"No."

"Hardly à la mode. And your chignon—"

"Make one more comment about my hair and I'm leaving."

"I was only going to suggest—"

Effie turned and stomped past the carriage toward the street.

"All right, *d'accord.*" Adeline caught her by the arm. "I'm sorry. You look, well, quite lovely really. That shade of lavender suits you."

For once, Adeline's voice was free of artifice, and Effie allowed herself to be steered toward the coach.

"You look lovely too."

And Adeline did. Her skirt of sleek blue silk fell in beautiful flounces from her sleek bodice. Her hair, smooth as the woman's on the bottle of elixir, sat in a crown of braids atop her head with thick ringlets cascading down her back. Even if Effie had succeeded in straightening her hair, she never could have managed such an updo. As it was, her scalp still ached and molted strands of singed hair.

Inside the carriage, Adeline fidgeted with the strings of her reticule, twining them this way and that about her fingers.

"Where are we going and why are you nervous?" Effie meant to sound conversational, but her words came out sharp, accusatory, a betrayal of her own nerves.

"Here, let's at least take off this ghastly bonnet. We're going to a party, not a quilting bee." Before Effie could protest, Adeline untied the strings of her bonnet and tugged it from her head.

Effie quickly patted and smoothed her hair, making sure the bald spot was covered. "You didn't answer my question."

"I'm not nervous, simply excited." Adeline plucked one of the pearl-studded combs from her updo and stuck it in Effie's hair just above her bun. "Voilà."

Effie fingered the smooth pearls and silver filigree. The weight of it tugged on her hair, sharpening the pain of her blistered skin. But never in her life had she worn something so . . . fine. It wasn't just that she hadn't the money. Such ornaments were meant for pretty girls. White girls. Or so she'd thought until she met Adeline.

Effie turned away and looked out the window. Gas lamps twinkled above the sidewalks. Palm fronds and sweeping banana leaves spilled over courtyard walls. She blinked in rapid succession to sweep the dampness from her eyes. Beside her came the rasp of Adeline's purse strings again.

"If you're nervous I'll embarrass you, you shouldn't have invited me."

"*Ma foi,* Effie. Of course that's not the cause. But best not mention what you do or talk too much in general, I suppose. Just nod and laugh. That's your lesson for tonight. Nod and laugh."

"And if no one says anything amusing?"

"You fake it, *bien sûr.* Men love to feel clever."

She turned back to her. "Is that it, then? A man?"

The corners of her lips turned upward. "There is a gentleman I'm keen to make acquaintances with tonight."

"What's his name?"

"Monsieur Chauvet."

The carriage dropped them at a two-story townhouse set back from the banquette on Esplanade Avenue. It was a warm night and guests had spilled out onto the lower gallery, lounging on cushioned benches or leaning against the grand fluted columns. They all seemed to know Adeline, several of the gentlemen hastening down the steps to meet her street side. Effie could scarcely rise from one curtsy before the next introduction began.

Inside came the din of French, violins, and clinking glassware. Cigar smoke curled through the double parlor. Portraits and watercolor landscapes in thick, gilded frames adorned the walls. Gasoliers with frosted shades hung from the ceiling. Effie hovered at Adeline's side through more introductions, clinging to the words and phrases she'd memorized and no longer needed to filter through Latin. She nodded whenever Adeline did and choked out a few fake laughs.

Otherwise her attention wandered. The elaborate molding, the bright carpet, the polished furniture all reminded her of the colonel's house across town in the American Garden District. But the feeling here was entirely different—jovial and intimate. Even without the shadow of death, she doubted that home ever shed its aloofness. And of course, nearly every face here was black. A few were darker than she, but most a shade of deep yellow, some so light they could pass as white.

Adeline flitted about the room, never lingering with one group too long. She thrust a flute of bubbling liquid into Effie's hand and laughed when Effie puckered at the taste.

"First time trying champagne?" a man standing nearby said in English. "I take it you're a freedwoman?"

Effie nodded, the warm, bubbling sensation in her stomach strangely pleasant. She took another sip.

"*Ma foi,* Monsieur Rousseve," Adeline said. "You shouldn't embarrass her with such a comment."

He bowed to Effie. "Apologies, ma'amselle."

"It's all right. I'm not ashamed."

"Nor should you be," he said. "You mustn't listen to those Creoles who call your kind churlish and backward."

"I didn't know they did. But then, my French is *pas bon.* Should they express such sentiments in English, Latin, or German, I'd have words for them in return."

"My what a vixen you have here, Adeline!" he said with a smile. "You ought to run for office. We could use someone like you."

"You're a legislator?" she said, ignoring Adeline's pointed stare. "Do you know Mr. Greene?"

"Samson, of course. Quite the firebrand too. Is he a friend of yours?"

The room, already warm and humid, grew positively sultry. "An acquaintance, yes. Is he here?"

"No, I'm afraid not. Though I dare say he'd love all the beautiful women here tonight. Present company included, of course." Mr. Rousseve smiled at Adeline, rested his elbow on the black marble mantel beside him, and swirled his drink. "No, this is not really Samson's set. Too much *vin* and *français,* I should think. He's an American, through and through."

Effie's jaw tightened. "We're all Americans, sir."

He laughed.

Before she could rejoin with a more pointed rebuke, Adeline looped a hand about Effie's elbow and squeezed. "*Mais oui, nous sommes tous Américains.* Oh look, there's Mademoiselle Detiège. What a lovely gown. How nice it plays with her dark eyes. I simply must tell her so. Won't you excuse us, Monsieur Rousseve?"

"Of course." He bowed his head to Adeline, then turned to Effie. "You should stop by the Republican Office sometime, Miss . . ."

"Jones."

"Miss Jones. 94 Camp Street. We can always use an Eliza such as yourself."

Adeline kept hold of her elbow as they strode across the parlor toward Miss Detiège. "Nod and laugh—it's the simplest thing. You'd think a woman with your brains could grasp that."

"I didn't say anything untoward."

"You were about to, I could tell." She took Effie's near-finished glass of champagne and swapped it for a full one from a passing waiter. "Here, next time you have the urge to speak, take a sip instead."

Adeline chatted briefly with Miss Detiège, whom Effie remembered from the sewing circle. Her dress was indeed lovely, and Effie ventured it safe to say so.

"Oh, do you think so?" she replied, followed by a tiresome accounting of the fabric and style.

Effie took note not to compliment anyone else's gown lest she be subject to the same drivel. Adeline seemed equally uninterested. Her gaze flickered several times to a newly arrived man at the far end of the room. "Charlotte, *ma chère,*" she said, talking right over Miss Detiège. "Keep an eye on Effie, won't you? The room's so stuffy, I simply must sit down."

Before Effie could protest or Miss Detiège reply, Adeline sashayed off in the direction of the man. Instead of going to where he stood, she seated herself on a nearby couch and took up conversation with someone else entirely. Her eyes, however, continued to wander to the man and she sat angled ever so slightly toward him.

"That's Monsieur Chauvet," Miss Detiège whispered. "Of course she'd set her sights on him."

He wasn't a particularly handsome man. Rather stout, with beady eyes and a balding head. "Why?"

"He's just returned from Marseille. Was gone nearly a decade. He's a commission merchant. His family's been back and forth from France since early days."

Money and a good family name—everything Adeline wanted.

"Of course, Adeline won't be the only woman after him. I've an understanding with Monsieur Delille, otherwise even I might venture . . ."

Effie nodded but no longer listened. She watched Adeline pull a fan from her reticule and fling it open with a snap of her wrist. The sound drew the attention of Mr. Chauvet, who eyed Adeline as he carried on his conversation with a group of gentlemen. Effie suspected that had been Adeline's intent, for she feigned a sudden raptness in her own party's dialogue. The heat and humidity that dulled the eyes of others in the room, that melted their wax makeup and frazzled their hair, seemed only to enhance Adeline's beauty. Her chest flushed pink. Her skin glistened in the gaslight. A minute later Mr. Chauvet departed his circle and came to stand before Adeline. He bowed and gestured to the seat beside her on the couch.

The flash of a smile and he was seated beside her. An exchange of words. He tugged on his cravat and smoothed his mustache. She laughed and nodded and played with her fan, snapping it closed and trailing the tip along her neck and collarbone. More words, nodding, and laughter. A quick whisper in her ear.

Effie turned away and picked her way through the crowd outside to the gallery. She'd hoped to catch a breeze, but the air was just as still and heavy. She'd long since finished her champagne and felt strangely off balance. The lull of violins from inside blurred with that of the crickets in the yard.

How easy it had been for Adeline to lure Mr. Chauvet to her side. It wasn't just her beauty, for the room was filled with lovely women. Effie pulled the comb from her hair and turned it over in her palm, watching the lamplight reflect off the silver. She ought to feel lucky then to have so skilled a teacher. But whereas Latin and anatomy had been easy to learn, this skill, this talent of Adeline's still seemed utterly beyond Effie's grasp.

She leaned against the cast-iron railing and looked out into the night, trying to imagine herself seated on that parlor couch with Samson beside her. Nod and laugh. She could do that instead of talking about politics or embalming, couldn't she? And she best get a fan like Adeline's, one she could snap open and closed instead of the palm leaf fan she'd bought off a street vendor.

She rubbed the pearl comb against her skirt to buff away the sweat and oil from her hands. Captain and Mrs. Kinyon wouldn't approve of all this: the finery, the gaiety, the spirits. Certainly not on a Sunday evening.

The Kinyons were not poor but frugal, their puritanical tendencies reinforced each week from the pulpit. They were strict, staid, but not overly stern. No talk of death or embalming was allowed at the supper table. No reading until daily chores were done. No chemicals inside the house. No anatomy textbooks left open in the parlor, lest one of Mrs. Kinyon's friends glance upon the pages and suffer a fright.

There were other rules too, unspoken rules Effie learned by observation. No drinking, except in secret. No dancing, except at formal events. No laughing, except the occasional polite chuckle. No talking about Annabelle.

Effie started to tuck the comb into her purse but stopped and slipped it back in her hair. She needn't please anyone but herself anymore.

"Effie, *ma foi,* there you are."

She turned around at the sound of Adeline's voice. Mr. Chauvet was with her, dabbing the sweat from his brow with a silk hankie. He looked older than Effie had guessed from afar, perhaps twice their age, but his face was kind.

Adeline rapped her on the wrist with her closed fan as if Effie were a wayward child. "I looked all through the parlor for you."

"I needed some air."

"Not a good night for it, I'm afraid," Mr. Chauvet said. "By my recollection, late March was never this hot."

"You've been away too long, then," Adeline said, turning her fan on him and tapping him on the chest.

"Indeed I have."

Without looking in her direction, Adeline said, "Effie, allow me to introduce Monsieur Chauvet. Monsieur Chauvet, Miss Effie Jones."

"*Enchanté,* mademoiselle." He bowed low.

"Pleased to meet you."

"Forgive me, but your accent. Are you from the North?"

"Miss Jones was born here but raised up North after the War," Adeline said. "Illinois, was it?"

"Indiana."

"Indiana. By white folks, no less. Poor Miss Jones's an orphan, see."

Poor Miss Jones's an orphan? The words had the shock and sting of a hornet's bite. Heat flamed up her neck and into her cheeks.

"*Quel dommage,*" he said. "What a pity. Between slavery and the War there's not a life left unmarred. My condolences, Miss Jones."

Effie didn't want his condolences, his pity. Hadn't she gotten enough of that up North? Must it come now from her own people?

Then again, looking over their expensive clothes and high yellow skin, maybe they weren't her people at all.

"I . . ." Anger choked her. Or was it shame? Effie couldn't make head or tales of what she felt, only that she didn't want to be here. "Could you . . . I need a drink."

"Of course, mademoiselle." He bowed again. "I'll get us all something to wet our throats."

As soon as his back was turned, Effie hurried down the gallery steps.

"Where are you going?" Adeline asked.

Effie spun around. "Is that why you brought me here tonight? To parade me around as your charity case?"

"*Mais non.* I only—"

"That's how you see me, though. How everyone in there sees me. An Eliza, a hapless freedwoman, an orphan."

"Monsieur Rousseve merely mistook your name." She flapped her hand. "Eliza, Effie, they sound nearly the same."

"And I'm sure he mistook Mr. Greene for Uncle Tom, and that dark-skinned waiter in there for Sambo."

Adeline dropped her gaze to the white-painted steps. "Oh."

"I've had enough of our little arrangement. It was madness from the start." She turned and marched toward the street. The effects of the champagne had worn away, but still her step felt shaky.

"I'm nervous, all right? Scared stupid. My mother's sick. My brother's a drunk and a gambler. We haven't nearly any money left at all."

Effie stopped just before reaching the banquette but didn't turn around. There was a tremble in Adeline's voice, a rawness she'd not heard before.

"*Tonnerre!* I had to sell my father's watch just to afford the hansom tonight."

With the warm, numbing sensation of the alcohol gone, the burn on Effie's scalp had begun to throb again. She wanted nothing more than her quiet little room and lumpy bed. But she turned back to the grand house. Adeline had sunk onto the steps, skirts crumpled around her, head leaning against the baluster.

"I could have paid the coachman," Effie said.

"Invite you to come and then ask you to pay the cab?" She

straightened, and her voice steadied. "I still have my dignity, even if I haven't anything else. Besides, you haven't money either."

"I've more than you it seems." She sat down on the far edge of the steps, yet undecided if she'd forgiven Adeline the insult, but too tired to stand. She patted her head and hissed at the pain. Where was Mr. Chauvet with their drinks?

"What's wrong?" Adeline asked. "You've touched that same spot on your head at least a dozen times tonight."

"I burned my scalp."

Adeline scooted over and parted Effie's hair. Despite her light touch, Effie winced.

"*Mon Dieu!* However did it happen?"

"An iron. I thought to straighten my hair."

"By yourself?"

Effie shrugged.

"I recant what I said earlier. You haven't any brains at all to try something like that on your own. Lucky for you I've got the perfect thing for it at home."

"One of your potions?"

"They're not all humbug. I'll have you know my *grand-mère* was a renowned healer in her day."

Footfalls sounded behind them on the gallery. "Apologies, mes-dames. Monsieur Dumas insisted upon showing me his wine cellar."

Adeline rose as gracefully as an egret and brushed off her skirt. In the time it took to flick open her fan, she'd recast her forlorn expression into one of blithe serenity. Effie had more the gait of a loon upon rising and managed only to soften her frown.

He handed them both a glass of wine. "A claret. Of a good year."

They toasted and drank. Effie gagged on the tart, earthy flavor, but took another sip in lieu of having to speak or smile.

Presently several others joined them on the gallery—two gentle-men, plus three more women Effie remembered from the sewing circle. Among them was Béatrice, the soubrette.

She embraced Adeline and said loud enough for all to hear, "So good to see you, *ma belle*. I didn't think you'd make it tonight."

"Why ever not?"

"Well, you know, the cost of these parties does add up."

Effie balked. That was the sort of thing she might say, but in a matter-of-fact, observational way. She might even do a quick calculation —tallying and averaging all the little expenditures—to elucidate her point. But that was not Béatrice's intent. The only thing she wished to elucidate was Adeline's unfortunate financial position.

Adeline, however, seemed unfazed. "Indeed, one must be judicious in all things. But how I would have hated to miss Monsieur Chauvet's homecoming."

"Lucky for me you did not," he said, clinking his glass to hers and taking a long pull of wine.

From there the conversation wound to staider topics. The wine proved less a medicament than the champagne, adding weight to Effie's arms and legs and eyelids, but not touching the ache of her scalp. She'd given up her pitiful attempts at laughter and found herself nodding at random bits of chatter when all other heads were still.

The night had taken full command of the sky now, black and starlit in all directions. Mrs. Neale had likely nodded off in the parlor, her housemates long since lumbered up to their rooms. How Effie envied them.

Her attention returned to the conversation in time to hear Mr. Chauvet remark that his old tailor had moved North, and he'd not yet found a suitable replacement. Miss Detiège, who'd since joined them on the gallery, replied, "Why don't you just hire Adeline. She's quite the seamstress." She giggled as she said this, wagging her glass in Adeline's direction. Good thing it was empty or wine would have spilled all over her moiré silk Parisian dress. Effie wished in fact it had.

"Indeed," said another of Adeline's friends from the sewing circle. "You manage to make last season's gowns look positively à la mode."

The lovely blush drained from Adeline's cheeks. "I don't know what you're talking about, I'm sure. Though I'd be happy to recommend you a good tailor, Monsieur Chauvet. The one my father used is still in business down on Chartres Street, I do believe."

He smiled, though with less ease than before. "*Merci.* I'll . . . ah . . . call on him."

Effie looked down at her drink. The claret trembled against the glass. "You make it sound as if it's bad to have a skill. A talent beyond just standing on display and nattering."

"We can't all be a working girl like you," Béatrice said. "Why, there wouldn't be enough corpses to go around."

All the women but Effie and Adeline laughed. The men furrowed their brows and tugged at their shirtsleeves.

"I provide a needed service. I may have been born a slave, but I'm freer now than any of you." Effie set her glass on the banister for fear she might shatter it. "I was at your little tea and saw all your handiwork. I think you're jealous because Miss Mercier sews better than all of you put together."

Adeline put a hand on Effie's arm. "Now, now, I'm sure—"

"Speaking of our little tea, as your friend so quaintly put it, Adeline, you're behind on your membership dues, two months I believe," Béatrice said, languidly fanning herself as if they were talking of nothing more than pickled oysters or spice cake. "I'd hate for you to be dismissed from *Les Jeunes Amis.*"

Adeline dropped her hand. Lamplight glimmered in her wet eyes.

"Surely thirty dollars isn't too much for someone like you."

"Now see here," Mr. Chauvet said. "If we're squabbling over a mere thirty dollars, I can certainly advance the money."

His words wiped the last vestige of serenity from Adeline's face. "*Non. Merci, mais non.* It just slipped my mind. Mamm's been sick and I—"

"She's got the money right here," Effie said, fumbling with her purse strings. She stilled her hand, reached in, and pulled out all her bills. A month's worth of wages. She thrust them at Béatrice. "Take it. You wanted it badly enough to debase the conversation. Take it!"

Béatrice evaded her stare, but snapped closed her fan and took the money. "You're dolling out Adeline's allowance now?"

"No, she'd lent me the money for . . . for a . . ." Effie stumbled to find purchase on a lie. The night's labors had drained her empty. "A new chin supporter."

"*Comment?*" someone said.

"Pardon, a what?" Mr. Chauvet asked.

"A chin supporter. To hold the jaw closed should surgeon's silk prove insufficient." She looked from one aghast face to the next. "I dare say you wouldn't want the deceased's mouth gaping open. Hardly—how do you Creoles say it?—*comme il faut.*"

The group stood in such silence the bells of St. Louis could be heard tolling in the distance.

"*Ma foi,* is that the hour?" Adeline said in a voice too thick for the weary smile she wore. "I best call for our carriage."

"Allow me, mesdames," Mr. Chauvet said. He strode into the house, returning a moment later with their shawls and escorting them down to the street. Adeline perked at his attention, waving adieu to her friends without a backward glance. He helped them both into the hansom when it arrived and kissed Adeline's hand in parting.

"*Bon Dieu,* Effie. A chin supporter? Could you think of anything else ghastlier to say?" Adeline said as the carriage pulled away. But then she laughed, and Effie too. Her first real laugh of the evening. Adeline pulled her close, cradling her in a sideways embrace. Effie, far too tired to resist, lay her cheek upon Adeline's shoulder.

"Poor *chère.* How your head must hurt. I've got just the ointment." Effie closed her eyes.

"I'll pay you back, you know. Every cent of it. Madame Desâmes has two spirit sittings next week. And my brother means to sell some of our land holdings in Metairie."

Effie nodded without lifting her head and enjoyed the gentle rock of the carriage as it rambled down the lane.

CHAPTER 16

W ind tugged at the crepe bunting and velvet coffin skirts draped over the clotheslines in the courtyard. It fluttered the hem of Effie's skirt and whipped strands of hair about her face. Dust billowed as she brushed the fabric, stinging her eyes and gathering at the corners of her lips. At least a year's worth, maybe more, for who knew the last time anyone had bothered to clean them. She doubted Mr. Whitmark had even noticed the dingy state of these draperies, and Colm wouldn't deign to do any such "women's work."

The clatter of horse hooves and iron-rimmed wheels in the carriageway startled her. Both the wagon and the hearse sat parked in the carriage house behind her. Clients never entered this way, and the shop wasn't due for any deliveries.

A hard-top buggy with painted side panels and a plush upholstered seat rocked to a stop before the loggia. Mr. Whitmark's brother stepped down and tied his horse to a metal ring drilled into the brick sidewall. A folded newspaper was tucked beneath his arm.

Hitherto, Effie had not gotten so long a gander at the man. He had the same deep-set eyes and cleft chin as Mr. Whitmark, the same broad shoulders and imposing height. But the brother's chest tapered to a narrow, almost effeminate waist. Wax tamed his bushy eyebrows, and though he couldn't be more than a few years Mr. Whitmark's junior, his dark hair hadn't a fleck of gray. The most pronounced difference, however, was his step, quick and resounding, where Mr. Whitmark scuffed and shambled.

He didn't inquire of Effie whether Mr. Whitmark was in, bid her good day, or remark about the tempestuous weather. But he did tip his hat to her before entering the shop's back door. A few moments later the door swung open.

"Listen for customers, Effie," Mr. Whitmark said, propping the door open with a brick. "I'm going upstairs a moment." His brother followed him up the curving loggia steps. From the upstairs gallery, Mr. Whitmark called down, "Boil us some coffee too."

Effie frowned. He might at least have said *please*. In the kitchen, she set a kettle of water on the stove and tossed a handful of coffee beans and chicory into the grinder. Would that he had hired a maid instead of that lout Colm.

While the grounds and water boiled, she returned to the shop with an arm's load of velvet from the line and set about arranging the newly brushed skirts around the caskets. Mr. Whitmark had been affable enough this morning when she'd arrived, bade her good morning with a grin, whistled about the shop, complimented her on the fine job she'd done with yesterday's apoplexy case. But just as at that grand house in the Garden District, his brother and other men of his ilk seemed to sour Mr. Whitmark's disposition.

The kettle's whistle called her from the shop. In her haste, she stepped in a pile of dung the horse had left at the mouth of the carriageway. Drat! Nothing today had gone her way. Though Adeline's ointment had indeed helped her burned scalp, the blisters had begun to scab and flake, making her hair appear infested with nits. Worse still, the letter she'd sent inquiring after Elijah Jones had returned to her this morning, undeliverable and unclaimed.

She sat down and scraped the warm dung from her boot while the kettle shrieked from the nearby kitchen. Evidently, Mr. Whitmark could hear it too for he called from the upstairs window, "Effie, the coffee," as if she might be deaf, tempting her to add a bit of the boot scum to the kettle before bringing it up.

Her conscience got the better of her, though. In the kitchen, she arranged the coffee on a tray along with the sugar bowl and creamer, then stalked across the courtyard, more careful of her footing this time, and up the stairs.

"Damn it, James. You think I don't read the papers?" Mr. Whitmark said, loud enough for Effie to hear from the steps. She paused on the mezzanine landing and listened.

"I didn't know how your Republican rag might spin it," James said.

"Spin it? You think the danger here is lost on us?"

"Them. Lost on *them*. You've got to start distancing yourself from this."

A chair scraped across the floor.

"Us, them, the point is I'm not blind to what's going on. I know the resolve of the North is . . . wavering."

"Wavering? Those mangy radicals who seduced you to their cause have all but abandoned you. And it won't just be wayward Negroes the Ku Klux comes after."

Mr. Whitmark laughed, a hard, bitter sound that prickled Effie's skin. "You talk like they're not one and the same—the Klan, your little White League, the Democrats."

"Now you're just spouting Kellogg rhetoric." James's voice was calm, almost paternal. "You saw how the League behaved back when we took the statehouse. No unnecessary violence. And the Democratic ticket has pledged to uphold all the lawful rights granted the Negro after the War."

In the quiet that followed, Effie heard a soft rattle. The tray in her arms was shaking. She hurried up the remaining steps and slipped quietly into the parlor. Mr. Whitmark was standing by the far window, staring out at the street below. If he'd heard her enter, he made no show of it. She set the tray down on the lip of the tea table near where James sat, keeping her gaze downcast for fear that he might read from her face that she'd been listening. With one hand steadying the tray, she gathered up the newspapers cluttering the table.

GRANT PARISH CASE DECISION SUSTAINED, one of the front-page headlines read. For a moment Effie stood paralyzed. She'd heard talk of the Supreme Court's pending decision at the club meetings, remembered reading about the bloodshed at Grant Parish when she was yet living in Indiana. How enraged Samson would be at the news. And Mrs. Carrière, hadn't someone said her husband was among those killed?

She jogged her head and slid the tray to the center of the table.

"Leave those," James said. When she looked up at him, he pointed with his chin at the papers she'd cleared from the table.

She set the papers on the side table, wishing she'd managed to read beyond the first few lines, and backed out of the room.

"Thank you for the coffee," James said.

At this, Mr. Whitmark turned around. He looked at her, but his gaze was diffuse, as if she were a specter and he could see right through her to the wall. "Yes, thank you, Effie."

She heard the clink of coffee cups as she descended the stairs. Then James spoke again. "Listen, Georgie, now more than ever you've got to be reasonable. Carpetbagger rule is coming to an end. The South belongs to the South again."

Mr. Whitmark only harrumphed. She imagined him rubbing his knuckles and looking wistfully to the card table, where his bottles once stood.

His brother continued. "You don't have to be excluded from that. Colonel Randolph mightily appreciated the care you took with his son. He might even be willing to support your nomination to the club. Think of what that would do for the shop."

"Business is going fine."

"This isn't just about your business, but your life. It's not too late to marry, settle down. You work with the dead, know what a difference it is to have family left to mourn. Do you really want to meet your end alone?"

Another pause, and Mr. Whitmark said, "I was a colonel too, you know. Funny how he can still wear the rank and I've got to slink around and hope no one remembers."

Effie left the remainder of the black fabric flapping in the courtyard and hurried down the street until she found a newsboy. The *New Orleans Republican*'s summation of the Grant Parish decision was unimpassioned and succinct. She read the entire article standing on the street corner in the span of a minute. A quick rifle through the pages revealed nothing more. She dropped the paper onto the newsboy's stack and drifted back to the shop.

She returned just as James descended the stairs. She tried to read in the clap of his footfalls whether he'd been successful in swaying Mr. Whitmark's loyalties. Not a triumphant clap, she decided, but not a defeated one either.

Effie resumed her brushing. She hurried from one cloth to the next, ignoring the dust that settled on her skin and eyelashes, anxious to be done and go . . . go where? The other women at Mrs. Neale's would not have heard the news nor understand what she relayed. Effie wasn't sure she fully grasped its significance. But it had been significant, for why else would Mr. Whitmark's brother have come? She might go to Adeline, but likely her friend—if that's what they were now—wouldn't care. No, she must see Samson.

The Republican Office at 94 Camp Street was a three-story stone affair with arched windows and carved molding. She wasn't sure if Samson or any of the others from the ward club would be here, but the halls of the statehouse were empty and she hadn't any idea where else to look. Several young colored men lingered outside. A few of them smiled and doffed their hats as she climbed the stairs to the entry. Others, lost in conversation, didn't look up. Words like scoundrels, abuse, injustice flew between them.

The vast foyer was a hive of activity, boot heels clapping on the stone floor, voices pinging from the mosaic walls and high vaulted ceiling. A printing press hummed from some far-off workroom. Effie stepped to the side and scanned the faces for one she knew. Men of every sort were here—old and young, black, white, and every shade in between. The office doors on either side of the foyer stood open with men crowded about the jams. Boys, as young as five or six, scampered about delivering telegrams, letters, and parcels, paper-wrapped sandwiches, tins of steaming gumbo, even bottles of whiskey.

Gaggles of men barely old enough to vote had overtaken the benches lined about the room, some sitting, some standing, some with their muddy boots propped upon the wooden bench tops. None she recognized, however. They blustered and argued, smacking their caps in their palms or throwing up their arms. When their eyes lit upon her, they quieted and straightened. More smiles.

Effie checked that her bonnet hadn't fallen askew or that she hadn't spilled sodden coffee grounds down the front of her dress, then credited their curiosity to the paucity of women about. Indeed, she realized, almost none. Two white women—schoolteachers judging from their chalk-dusted skirts and ink-stained fingers—stood at a small reception desk in the corner, speaking with an attendant. A white-haired negress lumbered up the steps at the far end of the room. That was all.

Effie half thought to follow the old woman, half thought to flee. The crowd, the din, the stares harried her already tender nerves. Then an arm coiled about her own.

"Oh, Effie, *est-ce vrai?* Is it true? What have you heard?"

It took Effie a moment to recognize Mrs. Carrière, so altered she appeared. A black bonnet restrained her frazzled hair; the bow at her neck hung loose and lopsided. Her eyes, ever shrewd and steady, fidgeted in their sockets like a madwoman's.

"I . . . er . . . just got here. I don't know anything other than what was reported in the paper."

Effie tried to gently extricate her arm, but Mrs. Carrière's grip held fast. She tugged Effie toward the stairs. Her other hand was clasped about Jonah's, dragging him along too. When he looked up at Effie, his little face was grave.

Upstairs, Mrs. Carrière hurried them to a large meeting room. Tall, multipaned windows lined two of the walls, their sashes raised high to invite a breeze. The outside air, however, did not oblige, and the room was stifling, redolent of sweat and charged with anger.

Several men crowded around a long table. Jonah wiggled free of Mrs. Carrière's grasp and slipped into the horde. Most of the men at the table were white, though she did spy Mr. Rousseve and a few other light-skinned Creoles seated among them. Those pressed together at the periphery were black.

Effie stood on her tiptoes, searching for Samson. She heard his sonorous voice before spotting him at the far end of the table, standing in a narrow gap between chairs. "We ought to be down at the jailhouse protesting the release of these murderers."

Several of those standing clapped and hurrahed at his comment.

"So we can have a repeat here of what happened at Colfax?" one of the seated men said. Murmurs followed. A few nods.

Mrs. Carrière's grip tightened about Effie's arm. Her face had the sallow undertone of the dead. Effie scanned the room for someplace to sit her down—a bench, a couch, a chair. But there was hardly room to stand let alone a spare seat. Perhaps the wide lip of the windowsill would suit, so long as Effie kept hold of her, lest she faint and fall backward to the street below. Fresh air would certainly do her good. Effie charted a path through the bodies to the nearest window, but then found herself tugged in the opposite direction. Mrs. Carrière bullied them through the crowd until they stood right behind those seated.

"So it's true? They're releasing those murderous devils?" she said over the mutterings. "*Mon Dieu!* Hundreds dead and they walk free?"

The room quieted. Those seated at the table turned to look at her. Just as quickly they looked away—down at their manicured hands, pressed trousers, and polished shoes. Even Samson took sudden notice of the floor.

After a silence as stifling as the heat, Mr. Rousseve said, "*Mo chagren,* Marie. I'm sorry."

Mrs. Carrière swallowed. She clenched her jaw and blinked back the tears building in her eyes. Again Effie searched out the nearest window, but the body beside her was steady, unwavering.

"So what now?" Mrs. Carrière managed after a moment.

"That's what we're here to determine," the man at the head of the table said. He was a thin, soft-spoken man, with hooded eyes and a broad nose. She'd not seen him at Adeline's petite fête, but likely he was of the same set, a *gens de couleur.* Unlike Mr. Rousseve, however, who oozed self-importance, this man bore a cordial disposition, solemn but warm. "It's clear we cannot rely upon the Federal courts for justice. The state has sole purview of crimes committed by her citizens now."

"What's to stop the White Leaguers from runnin' out the rightfully elected sheriffs and putting in men of their own, ones who don't care a grain about the Negro and won't arrest nobody?" someone in the crowd asked.

"They're already doing that in East Baton Rouge," Samson said. "The sheriff, the parish judge, the tax collector were all forced to flee under threat of violence."

"And in Feliciana," said another man.

"And St. Helena!" came a voice across the room.

"Governor Kellogg"—the man at the head of the table raised

his voice to be heard above the rising din—"Governor Kellogg has drafted a letter to address the recent disorder in East Baton Rouge."

Samson snorted. "It'll take more than words to stop these buckras."

"*And* he authorized a posse comitatus should they not reinstate the officers and prosecute those responsible for their removal."

"They had an entire militia in Grant Parish! Little good it did them," Samson said.

Effie glanced askew at Mrs. Carrière and saw her flinch at the mention of the massacre. Her slender arm remained intertwined with Effie's like a beanstalk about a pole.

Several men among the crowd harrumphed in agreement. Others gave a stomp, sending a tremor through the floorboards that traveled from the soles of Effie's feet clear to the top of her head.

"We can't change what happened at Colfax," came a familiar steady voice. "And it looks like we won't have the satisfaction of justice no time soon. But we can work to stop future bloodshed."

A few more grunts and stomps. Effie saw Tom moving forward through the crowd. Little Jonah hung about his neck, as if to get a better view of the events. Once they were front and center, Jonah climbed down and plopped cross-legged beside him on the floor.

"Marie and all them who lost beloveds that day have our deepest and lasting sympathy." Tom bowed slightly in their direction, and Mrs. Carrière nodded back. "But we gotta fight not with weapons, but with the vote." He banged his cane atop the floor. "That's the only way we can get officers of the law who'll be sympathetic to our cause."

"Hear, hear!" several men rejoined. Even Effie found her head bobbing in agreement.

"What good is it to elect such men if we haven't the power to enforce their rule?" Samson said, the fire and earnestness in his voice swaying Effie as surely as Tom's logic. His eyes met hers for the flash of a moment, sending a flush through her body as delicious and unnerving as Sunday's champagne.

"That's what we have the Federal Army for," Tom said.

Mr. Rousseve lit a cigar. "*Oui,* but we can't rely on them forever."

"Hell! We can't rely on them at all," Samson said, eliciting a short but loud round of laughter.

"*Ça alors*. I can't do this," Mrs. Carrière whispered as her body sagged against Effie. These men didn't seem any closer to a decision than when they'd first arrived.

Effie looked at Samson, willing the thrill of one more glance, but his attention stayed with those at the table. She turned back to Mrs. Carrière. "Let me take you home."

They shuffled through the crowd and out of the room. While the cool hallway air invigorated Effie, Mrs. Carrière's step remained sluggish, her hold about Effie's arm fierce. She led Mrs. Carrière down the stairs, across the busy foyer, and out to the street. Evening shadows shaded the road, creeping up the brick facades of the buildings opposite them. She steered Mrs. Carrière upriver and they walked in silence.

They'd shuffled along three blocks before Mrs. Carrière raised her head and stopped. She looked right, left, right, then back over her shoulder. "*Non,* this isn't right. We've gone the wrong way."

"Don't you live in ward two?"

She shook her head. "Faubourg Marigny."

Effie bit down on her tongue and turned them around the way they'd come. "Where in the Marigny?"

"Umm . . . Rue Dauphine. Two blocks beyond Esplanade."

They walked again without speaking, arm in arm, Effie navigating them through the waves of workers heading home from the business district. Mrs. Carrière scuffed along like a yarn doll, her slight form offering no direction or resistance.

"Why don't you attend club meetings in your own ward?" Effie asked when they'd made it across bustling Canal Street. For once it was a relief to be in the French Quarter, no one elbowing past in a hurry.

"I did live in ward two, for a time."

"On account of your husband?" Today, of all days, Effie ought to take Adeline's advice and keep quiet, but the question slipped out before she could check it.

"*Oui.*" Mrs. Carrière raised her head, her gaze passing over Effie and fixing upon some distant spot above the slate roofs and stucco chimneys. Her eyes, though red-rimmed and bloodshot, were dry. Thankfully they remained so, despite Effie's question. "We met not far from here. On Chartres. His master hired him out as a stonecutter. He was one of the best in the city, his services in such demand that—"

"He was a slave? But you—"

"No, I wasn't. And the law strictly forbade association between us free people and those yet in bondage." Her lips wobbled, almost reaching a smile. "We didn't care, though. Youth predisposed us to recklessness, I suppose. And love . . . well, love turns even the best of us on our heads."

Effie stumbled over an uneven row of pavers. Why wasn't any part of this cursed city flat? Mrs. Carrière trod on smoothly, for a moment baring Effie's weight instead of the other way around.

"We married in secret and saved to buy his freedom. But even when we had enough, his master—*ce bâtard*—refused."

The vinegar in her voice saved Effie from having to work out the translation. "What did you do?"

"We made plans to flee North, but the War saved us the trouble."

The War. Hadn't it changed everything? And yet seemingly so little.

"What was your husband doing in Grant Parish?"

"He had a few friends who settled there after the War. Went as soon as he heard about the trouble. Not to fight but to help work out a compromise. Both parties claimed to have won the sheriff's seat in the election and Samuel thought . . . well, he'd always been an optimist. But things had progressed too far by the time he arrived and . . ." She freed her arm from Effie's and sobbed into her hands.

Dusk had fallen and lamps were being lit. Enough twilight remained, however, to see the dispassionate stares of passersby, heading to the theater or gambling house or dance hall. Effie stood a moment, dumbfounded as to what to do. She'd never been good in the face of such overwhelming emotion. The dead, after all, gave up nothing. The living, the mourning, that was always Captain Kinyon's or Mr. Whitmark's charge.

She glanced around and pulled Mrs. Carrière to the lee of an open carriageway.

"*Bon Dieu,* Effie. He burned alive in that courthouse! And the men responsible wiggle free from punishment." She clawed about in her purse, then gave up and wiped her nose on her sleeve before Effie could offer her hankie. "God may have his vengeance when they die, but what of me? Don't we deserve some small measure of earthly justice for all they've done to us?"

Effie swallowed, unable to reply. All she could think to do was run, to pull free of Mrs. Carrière and flee into the night. Her calves twitched at the ready. Her brain charted the fastest course back to her dark, quiet room. But her overlarge feet remained planted. She raised her arms, not pushing Mrs. Carrière away, but drawing her close, until her wet cheek rested against Effie's breast.

They stood this way for several minutes, night deepening around them. Effie had no answers to her pleas for justice. No lies to spin about how fate would be righted in the end. All Effie had to offer was her stillness, her steadfast arms and sturdy legs. But it seemed enough.

Eventually, Mrs. Carrière's sobs dwindled to a few errant tears. She straightened, took hold of Effie's arm, and they started off again for the Marigny.

Mrs. Carrière's home was a stucco cottage with two French doors, each elevated a step above the banquette. Lamplight caught the gleam of its freshly painted shutters.

"This was my parents' home. I returned after . . ." She didn't finish and started on the lock of the rightmost door. Just as it whispered opened she dropped her purse and spun around. "*Mon Dieu!* I've forgotten Jonah."

She hurried back in the direction they'd come, shaking her head and crying anew, leaving her door open and purse on the step. "*Tellement stupide! Mo suis horrible.*"

Effie ran after her. "I'm sure he's all right. I saw him with Tom. They're probably still together."

"How could I leave him there? He's all I have." She wavered as if she might faint. Her eyes had that look of madness again.

"I'll fetch him home straightaway." She steered Mrs. Carrière back to her cottage, despite her protests.

With the sidewalks less crowded now and only herself to mind, Effie made good time back to the Republican Office. The windows on the second story were dark, however, as were most on the ground level too. She tried the brass handles on the double-door entry and found them both locked. She knocked, but no answer.

Now what? She sat down on the steps, untied her bonnet, and used it to dab the sweat from her face. Damn this city's humidity. Could nothing today go right for her?

She tied her bonnet back atop her head and willed her legs to stand. How wonderful her bed would feel right now. A basin of cool water for her feet. A slather of Adeline's burn ointment. But she couldn't return home. Not yet. Not until she'd found Jonah. She rapped on the lighted windows one by one until at last one creaked open. A balding white man with silver-rimmed spectacles popped his head out.

"Excuse me, sir. I'm looking for Tom Button. A Negro with a peg leg. He's perhaps seventy inches in height, mid-length hair, dark eyes, solid—"

"Yes, yes, I know Tom. He's not here, I'm afraid." He started to shut the sash.

"But he was here earlier, upstairs with a crowd of men, discussing the Grant Parish ruling."

"You his wife?"

Effie frowned at the irrelevance of his questioning, even as a flush lit beneath her skin. "No, I only wish to—"

"They're at Ruggy's Saloon, the lot of them I expect."

Yet more slogging across town. She sighed, but thanked the man and followed his directions to a row of dingy-looking buildings fronting the levee. Fog had rolled in off the river, dampening the glow of the streetlamps. Music and laughter and ruckus spilled from the open windows. Effie clutched her purse strings and stayed wide of the men stumbling from one establishment to the next. She read the creaky shingles swaying above the doors until she saw RUGGYS— no apostrophe—in chipped green lettering. Before opening the door, she peered in through the window.

The saloon was nicer on the inside than it appeared from without. A polished cedar bar ran the length of one side with matching leather-topped stools and a long brass footrest crowded with boots. Booths with plushly upholstered benches lined the opposite wall. But it was at the center of the saloon, where several sets of tables and chairs sat clustered, that she saw the men from the Republican Office. Mr. Rousseve balanced on the back legs of his chair, his feet stretched out before him and his hands laced behind his head. The soft-spoken man sat upright beside him, sipping lager from a mug. She recognized several of the white men from earlier too, one playing with the corner of his graying mustache, another undressed to his shirtsleeves.

A few of the men standing around the far-most table sauntered off to the bar with empty glasses. In their wake, she saw Samson. He too had shucked his jacket and loosened his tie. His shirtsleeves were rolled back to his elbows, exposing his forearms. Each muscle showed beneath his dark skin—*flexor carpi ulnaris, extensor digitorum, extensor carpi radialis longus, brachioradialis*—as clear as in her anatomy texts.

A woman sauntered to the table, one of only two in the saloon. Her low-cut dress hugged her bosom, accentuating her tawny brown skin and ample cleavage. She leaned across the table and plucked a pickle from the plate of food in the center. The men's conversation seemed to stall. Their eyes followed the line of her long bare arm from her manicured fingers to her full lips as she placed the pickle in her mouth. Samson's gaze lingered the longest, his head cocked in her direction long after she sauntered off and the men resumed their discussion.

Effie watched, though it pained her, so consumed she didn't hear the footfalls until the man's hand was already about her waist, his sour breath hot on her cheek. "Hello there, pretty."

His touch bristled her skin. His roving hand groped between her legs. She jerked upright and jammed her elbow into the man's gut. He wobbled, unsteady with drink. She turned around and pushed him from the banquette. A pile of manure cushioned his fall to the street.

Her relief at being free lasted only a second before her fear redoubled. The man was white. And a gentleman.

He sat there, either too stunned or too drunk to stand. Effie hurried into the saloon and prayed he wouldn't follow.

The din petered to a murmur when she entered. Heads turned. Brows furrowed. The piano tune slowed. Then, just as quickly, all resumed as it was. Men went back to their conversations. Glasses clanked. The piano's tempo rallied. Effie listened for the door to open behind her. Listened for some outcry from the street. Nothing.

Someone touched her elbow. She jumped.

"*Chérie,* whatever are you doing here?" Mr. Rousseve said to her.

"I . . . I . . ."

"Come, have a drink. You don't look well."

"No, I—"

"Miss Jones," Tom's voice cut across hers. "What are you doing here?" He took her other arm.

"I asked her the same question."

And then Samson: "Miss Jones, you're hardly the person I'd expect to walk in a saloon at this hour."

The words piled one atop the other in her fear-addled brain, and she couldn't reply. They seated her at a nearby table, Tom and Samson pulling up chairs beside her, Mr. Rousseve fetching her whiskey from the bar. It left a trail of fire down her gullet and shocked her to her senses. "I came looking for Jonah. Is he here?"

Tom nodded to the corner booth, where Jonah lay curled asleep on the bench. Effie made to rise, but all three men put a hand out to stop her. "I've got to get him back to Mrs. Carrière. She's beside herself with worry."

Samson laughed. The sound warmed her insides as sure as the whiskey. "And you mean to walk him back? By yourself? At this hour?" He stared straight into her eyes and her thoughts once again muddled. Surely on account of the whiskey.

"Night doesn't frighten me, Mr. Greene," she said, even as her gaze flickered back to the door.

"No, I suspect nothing does, Miss Jones. I just can't decide if it's bravery or damned foolishness."

"*Le courage, bien sûr,*" Mr. Rousseve said. Effie turned and smiled at him, though in truth she'd forgotten he was even there.

"Life takes a measure of both, I suspect," Tom said.

Before Effie could rejoin, a rustling noise drew near, snaring the men's attention. The woman she'd seen through the window approached, her magenta-colored dress a riot of lace and flounces, her hair a sleek crown of curls, her skin smelling of jasmine blossoms.

"Aren't one of you gentlemen going to offer me your chair?" she asked. Then to Samson, she said, "Or perhaps your lap."

Effie would gladly give up her chair, provided the woman find another table to sit at. Better yet, another saloon.

"Here," Tom said, the legs of his chair scraping over the floorboards as he stood.

"Thank you, *cher*. Though I hate to impose upon a cripple," she said, not hesitating to sit.

Effie took another sip of whiskey, then set her glass down with a thud. "He gets around just fine without your pity."

"Not pity, no. Concern." She scooted her chair closer to Samson, who'd not for one moment returned his eyes to Effie. "I've concern for all the brave men who fought in the War."

The smell of the woman's perfume roiled the liquor in Effie's stomach. If she could hear the insincerity in this woman's voice, surely Samson could as well. But he listened on enrapt.

"I bet you've a few war stories to tell. A scar or two beneath this shirt." She tickled her finger along his bare forearm, along the contours of muscle Effie had admired from the window.

Effie took another bitter pull of whiskey and stood. She'd rather take her chances that the man outside had left than watch this. "I've got to get Jonah home."

But the whiskey proved stronger than the champagne and wine she'd drunk on Sunday, turning the floor to a rolling bog beneath her feet. She clutched the lip of the table and drew in a long breath of perfume-soured air.

"Miss Jones," Samson said, standing, his gaze favoring her once again. "Are you sure you wouldn't like to settle yourself a bit more?"

"I'll walk you and Jonah home," Tom said.

Effie knew she should be grateful for such an offer, but found herself wishing yet again another man had made it.

"Take my horse," Mr. Rousseve said, and it was settled. Tom clomped off to rouse Jonah. Mr. Rousseve left to untie his horse from the bollard out front. Samson stood long enough to bid her goodbye, then returned to his seat beside the woman.

Outside, the air had turned cold and the fog thickened. Thankfully, there was no sign of the man she'd pushed into the gutter.

"I don't think this is what the Party big bugs had in mind when they suggested Mr. Greene might make a more promising senator if he found himself a wife," Mr. Rousseve said, readying his horse. He chuckled and handed Tom the reins.

"No, I dare say not," Tom replied dryly.

Effie glanced back through the saloon window as Tom helped her into the saddle behind Jonah. She watched the woman in her fancy magenta dress scoot closer to Samson. Watched him lean in and say something that made the woman laugh. Watched her move closer still and whisper in his ear. She watched his hand come to rest on her thigh, satin bunching beneath his fingers as he gave a quick squeeze. At this, Effie could watch no more and turned her gaze upon the darkness.

CHAPTER 17

E̶ffie jabbed the iron poker at the flaming logs. The cook fire didn't need tending, but it gave her an excuse to hide her face from Adeline.

"Brood all you want, but I can tell something's wrong."

"Nothing's wrong," Effie said, setting aside the poker. "I'm tired is all." She stirred the pot of sand hanging from the crane above the fire, working the wood spoon round and round through the granules, preferring the flame's heat to Adeline's interrogation. The image of Samson's hand about that woman's leg wouldn't leave her mind, the way her lips brushed his skin when she whispered in his ear. She pulled a hankie from her pocket and mopped the sweat from her forehead.

For two sleepless nights and two overlong days, she'd thought of nothing else. No, that wasn't true. The letter too. *Unclaimed—Return to Sender.*

Wasn't that the story of her life? She never should have gone to the statehouse with Adeline. Never should have rifled through those boxes. Never should have allowed such hope into her life.

"The sand requires constant stirring? Are you sure this is worth it?" Adeline asked from across the kitchen.

"Yes. No. I mean . . ." She stopped stirring and set down the spoon. After taking a moment to becalm her expression, she turned around. "No, the sand doesn't require constant stirring. And yes, this will be worth it. Hand me my bag."

Adeline's incredulous stare only deepened when Effie unwrapped the round, flat-bottomed flask she'd purchased that morning at the pharmacy.

"What's this for?" Adeline picked up the flask by its long neck and peered through the glass as if she'd never seen such a container. Perhaps she hadn't. Most young girls, Effie reminded herself, played with dolls, not beakers and flasks and laboratory tubes.

"Careful, it's fragile. Now pay attention."

Adeline leaned in, plopping her elbows down on the kitchen table and cradling her chin in her hands. "And people say you're not pleasant and charming. I can't imagine why."

"You're the only one who says that."

"Well, they're thinking it."

Effie frowned, but couldn't argue. She pulled a bottle of olive oil from her bag along with a small pouch of waxy yellow powder. "Six to one, that's all you have to remember." She measured out two spoonfuls of powder into the flask followed by twelve of the oil, then swirled it together. After it had sufficiently mixed, she set down the flask and heaved the pot of sand from the fire onto a cast-iron trivet set atop the table.

"Now we add the sand?"

Effie about laughed. It was perfectly obvious the sand—

"I hope you don't eye your beau that way."

"What way?"

"With that *haven't-you-a-single-wit?* expression. I told you, *les hommes* like to feel smart, not inferior."

Heat radiated from the pot. The fire crackled at her back. Effie dabbed her forehead again. Why ever would Adeline have cause to know the uses of a sand bath? "I'm sorry. I'm not myself today."

"You are yourself. *Mais encore pire.* Good thing at least one of us is of *bonne humeur* today. Go on."

Effie gave the flask a final swirl, then nestled it into the sand so only its narrow glass neck protruded. "The sand affords a gentler, even heating." She placed the pot back on the crane and swung it over the fire.

"How long must we wait?"

"Half an hour."

They moved out to the courtyard and sat on the lip of the crumbling fountain. Effie took off her bonnet and flapped the cool air toward her face.

"How's your burn?"

"Better."

"See? I told you that ointment would work."

The garden that fringed the yard had grown bushy since last she'd seen it. Weeds crowded the budding perennials. Thorny rose canes twisted this way and that, the first of their blooms just beginning to unfurl. It was a welcome respite from the bustling streets just beyond the walls. The entangled scents of wisteria and sweetshrub smelled far better than the dirty bath water and horse piss in the gutters.

"Is Mr. Chauvet the cause of your *bonne humeur*?"

Adeline smiled. "Maybe."

"Then maybe you have no need for this latest trick of mine, after all," Effie said, making a great show of retying her bonnet as if she were about leave.

"Let's not be too hasty, *chère*. I need more than a few days to cast my spell."

Did she mean that literally or figuratively? Likely both, Effie decided. "Have you seen him again since the party?"

"He may have called once or twice."

Effie scowled. "I'm not one of your *Jeunes Amis,* remember?"

"Béatrice did behave deplorably Sunday. Bringing up money like that. At *une fête* no less. Not at all—"

"I know, not at all *comme il faut,*" Effie said, waving her hand. Though in truth it was nice for once not to be the one who'd broken etiquette. "Mr. Chauvet . . ."

"Oh, *oui.* Monsieur Chauvet called Monday. Sooner than I expected, really. I thought perhaps Tuesday, but he took a drink in the parlor while I freshened up my hair and . . ."

Effie listened. Distractedly at first. She didn't care the style of dress Adeline had changed into, the particulars of Mr. Chauvet's waistcoat, or how gentlemanly he sipped his tea. In little time, however, she found herself drawn in, her worries over Samson and the letter receding from her mind. The excitement in Adeline's voice was contagious. At some point she took hold of Effie's hand, squeezing every time she said Mr. Chauvet's name. Instead of pulling away, Effie leaned in.

"Do you love him, then?"

Adeline drew back her hand. "*Ma foi!* Before becoming reacquainted Sunday, I hadn't seen Monsieur Chauvet since I was a child. Five days is hardly time enough to fall in love."

"I loved Mr. Greene the moment I heard his voice in Tivoli Circle." It sounded foolish spoken aloud, and saying his name rekindled the pain of the last two days. Nevertheless, it was true.

"We can't all live some fabled romance, Effie."

It didn't feel like a storybook tale, except perhaps the part in *Aschenputtel* when the ravens plucked out the stepsisters' eyes. That was how it had felt watching Samson with that woman. Effie shook her head and turned her thoughts back to Adeline and Mr. Chauvet. "But you could love him? In time."

Adeline shrugged.

"Right. A good income and a good name. That's all you're after."

"You make it sound so mercenary."

They sat a moment in silence.

"Has it been half an hour yet?" Adeline asked.

"No."

More silence. A lizard skittered up the far wall. The leaves of the magnolia tree fluttered in a limp breeze. Beside her, Adeline shifted and fidgeted, crossing and uncrossing her ankles, picking at her cuticles. The heady excitement they'd shared bled away.

A pigeon landed on the head of the cherub at the center of the fountain, cooing once before Adeline shooed it away. "You don't know what it's like. The indignity of poverty. It's one thing never to have had money. Something else entirely to have had it and then lost it."

True, Effie didn't know about money. Not French silk and crystal stemware kind of money. The Kinyons were well off, but not at all wealthy. Here, on her own in New Orleans, she had enough to get by. Enough to build a small savings. Enough to feel lucky when she passed the street-side beggars and prostitutes. But then, what did Adeline know of poverty?

"Have you ever been back-of-town? Deep back-of-town where

sewage mixes with swamp water in the streets? Where entire families live in shanties smaller than your parlor and draw water from drainage canals? That's poverty."

Adeline closed her eyes and pressed her lips together. A long breath whistled in and out of her nose. "I'm not like you, Effie. I'm not smart like you or strong like you." Her voice cracked with a sob. "I don't have any skills besides table-rapping and . . . and flirting."

Effie looked down at her hands. Perhaps she'd been too harsh. Again. "That's not true. You're good at . . . making burn ointments."

Adeline laughed in between sobs.

"And you're far better at making conversation than I am. At not saying the wrong things."

"Hardly a feat."

"And your sewing. You could open your own dress shop if you wanted. The only thing I can sew is . . . well, you see my point."

Adeline wiped her cheeks and stared up at the second-story windows of her grand house. "I've got Mamm to think of. And my chucklehead brother. Monsieur Chauvet can take care of us all."

What could Effie say to this? She had no family, after all. No one to worry after. No one to constrain her ambitions or affections. She ran a hand over her dress pocket, feeling the raised outline of a button, and beside it, the returned letter. Stupid she should carry the letter still. It had no use now but as a taper for her bedside candle. "I think our admixture is done heating."

She stood and started toward the kitchen.

Adeline grabbed her hand. "You must think me perfectly wretched."

But she didn't. That was the trouble. Yes, Adeline was vain and flippant and conniving. She was also vibrant, generous, and tender. Effie wished she didn't find her company so altogether tolerable. Wished she didn't care whether Adeline wasted her life on a man she didn't love.

How had their arrangement gotten so . . . messy?

She tugged Adeline up without answering. The fire in the kitchen hearth had dwindled to a few smoldering logs. She covered her hand with her apron and pulled the flask from the sand.

"It looks the same," Adeline said.

"Nonsense." Effie held the flask up to the sunlight streaming in through the open door. "The phosphorus has dissolved into the oil."

"And?"

Effie stoppered the flask with a piece of cork. "Close the door and shutters."

Adeline did as bidden. The room went dark, save for the crackling embers in the hearth and a faint, greenish light emanating from the liquid in the flask.

"*Mon Dieu!* It's glowing." She crossed herself and whispered a prayer.

"It's only the phosphorus reacting with the air in the bottle."

Adeline's green-lit face remained wary. She reached a trembling hand toward the light, then shrank back.

Effie unstoppered the bottle. She poured a few drops of the liquid onto her palms, rubbed them together, then held them up. They shone milky green in the darkness. "See. It doesn't hurt. I thought this might impress your sitters. You could say it's the spirits working through you or some such nonsense. Or keep it in the bottle and use it as a divining lamp of some sort."

"How did you . . ."

"I read about the luminescent properties of phosphorus years ago. But it wasn't until a few nights ago when I saw a firefly blinking outside my window that I thought there might be application . . . well . . . beyond the purely scientific." No need to mention *why* she'd been awake in the dark hours of the night, gazing listlessly out the window. How, through her bleary, sleep-starved eyes the bug's light appeared strangely spectral.

Adeline pushed wide the shutters and opened the door. Her expression was that of the marble angels in the St. Louis cemetery—somber and reflective. She stared unblinkingly at the bottle, then accosted Effie with a hug. "It's genius! Madame Desâmes will be the envy of every medium in the city."

Effie extricated herself from Adeline's embrace and looked around for her bag. "Keep this corked and stored someplace dark. Let me know if you run out of phosphorus powder. Better I get it from the pharmacist than you. He's used to my . . . unusual requests." She found her bag slouched beside the cupboard and started for the door, but Adeline blocked her path. She looped an arm through Effie's. "I hope you don't presume to be leaving, *chère*. We're celebrating with a glass of sherry."

"Celebrating what?"

"*Ma foi,* you Americans are so blue. Monsieur Chauvet, your little admixture, *rien du tout*. And then you're going to tell me why you're so dreadfully glum today."

CHAPTER 18

The deeper she and Adeline ventured into the Quarter, the more Effie's misgivings stirred. The street pavers grew worn and cracked, the houses smaller. Blood-red brick showed beneath the crumbling stucco. They stopped before a small cottage with faded blue shutters. Leafy tendrils sprouted between the clay shingles like stray whiskers. Not for the first time that afternoon, Effie chided herself for agreeing to such a foolish errand.

She blamed the sherry Adeline had insisted they drink two days before. Even with the liquor's aid, Effie couldn't bring herself to talk about Samson and that woman. Instead, she blamed all her glumness on the returned letter she'd written inquiring after Elijah Jones. Adeline, it seemed, had taken on the search for her lost kin as a secondary project, an addendum to their agreement, and suggested they visit a woman she knew, a healer with experience dislodging old memories.

By then, the sherry must have taken effect, for Effie agreed to see this woman before learning just what sort of healer she was—a Voodoo queen.

Now, Adeline knocked on the cottage door. After several moments a woman about Mrs. Carrière's age opened the door. Effie wasn't sure what she'd expected—wild hair, bare breasts, animal bone jewelry—but this woman had none of these. She wore a blue tignon, dangling gold earrings, and simple cotton dress, not unlike many in the Quarter. Adeline said something in French Effie was too distracted to make out. The woman replied in thick Creole patois and let them in.

Cracklings glowed in the hearth, and sunlight slipped in through gaps in the vertical shutter boards. Otherwise the room was dark. The woman motioned to a worn velvet sofa that creaked when Effie and Adeline sat down.

As Effie's eyes adjusted to the low light, she noticed a large clay statue of the Virgin Mary on a table in the corner. Finely woven lace covered the table, and two tin frames leaned against the base of the statue, each holding a watercolor drawing of a saint. One, having wings and armor, Effie guessed to be the angel Michael. The other, a robed figure holding a set of keys, she didn't recognize.

"Those represent the spirits Blanc Dani and Papa Limba," Adeline whispered. She pointed to a wooden carving of a snake curled into a circle with the tip of its tale inside its mouth that stood next to the drawings. "Le Grand Zombi."

The queen lit the four white candles surrounding the statue and another on a round tea table she pulled before the sofa. A few more words of patois and Adeline opened the large linen handbag she'd brought today in place of her dainty silk reticule. First, she withdrew a pint of rum and handed it to the woman. Then a boiled egg and sugar-dusted roll wrapped in cloth. The queen placed the food on the table beneath the statue. The rum she poured into a clay cup.

"Offerings," Adeline whispered.

"To whom?" Effie said, and then, seeing Adeline's scowl, more quietly, "The Virgin Mary?"

"The spirits."

And just how were these incorporeal beings supposed to ingest an egg? Even if they had a digestive tract, wouldn't the egg slip right through, like a hand through fog? Effie knew better than to ask these questions and tried not to let her derision show on her face. But another scowl from Adeline told her she wasn't succeeding.

She turned her attention back to the woman, who dipped her fingers in the rum and splashed a few droplets on the statue table. The candle flames hissed and sputtered. She turned to Effie and Adeline and sprinkled them with rum as well.

Effie flinched as the liquor peppered her face and dress. "What in—"

"It's a blessing," Adeline said, resting her hand on Effie's forearm, as if sensing her urge to leave.

The woman left the cup beside the other offerings and sat down opposite them in a wicker-backed chair. She leveled her brown eyes on Effie and said in heavily accented English, "Why are you here?"

Effie turned to Adeline. Hadn't she already explained the nature of their visit? What had the two of them been saying if not—

"I want to hear it explained from you," the woman said.

"Well, I . . ." Effie shifted, the sofa creaking beneath her. "I'd like help remembering."

"Remembering what?"

"My childhood. My life before the War."

The queen pulled a small pouch from her pocket along with a shortened palm stem, frayed like a brush at the end. She wetted the bristled tip in her mouth and dipped it in the pouch. More spirit offerings? Then Effie caught the sweet, nutty smell of tobacco. Snuff. The woman rubbed the dark powder onto her gums before fixing her gaze on Effie again. "Perchance you disremember for a reason. Perchance you ought let that which is dead stay dead."

Effie glanced at the shuttered windows. How nice a cool cross breeze would feel right now. A stirring of this damp, pungent air. Why must it be so dark anyway? Was that some requisite put forth by the spirits? Likely this woman preferred the dark for the same reason Madame Desâmes did: to better confuse and manipulate her patrons. Effie straightened. *Let the dead stay dead.* She could almost laugh. No one knew the dead better than she.

"It's the living I'm concerned with. My kin. I'd like to remember so I can locate them."

The woman stared at her a moment and then nodded. "How old are you at your earliest remembrance?"

"About seven."

"Seven? *Mo Djé.*" She made a *tsk-tsk* sound with her tongue. "And you remember nothing before that?"

A bead of sweat trickled down the back of Effie's neck, causing a brief shudder. "Are all these candles really necessary?"

"They're for your protection."

"From what?"

"Evil."

Beside her, Adeline nodded, her face grave, as if she really believed in this nonsense. Effie wiped her neck. Why weren't the other two sweating? A lifetime of exposure to the city's cursed heat and humidity no doubt had inoculated them.

Adeline squeezed Effie's arm. "Tell her."

If for no other reason than to get this whole silly ordeal over with, Effie did. She told the Voodoo queen of her memory of the shed, of the brick wall, and even of those eyes. The woman bobbed her head as she listened, her gold earrings swaying, now and then catching a glint from the surrounding flames. Her silence held even after Effie finished, stretching on for several moments. Then she said, "Open your mouth."

Her mouth? Surely Effie had misunderstood on account of her accent.

"She wants you to open your mouth," Adeline whispered, nodding even as Effie flashed her an *are-you-mad?* look.

Effie closed her eyes in a protracted blink, then let her jaw fall open.

The woman stood and lifted Effie's chin so she faced the ceiling. "Wider."

Effie parted her teeth farther, but apparently not far enough, for the woman stuck her fingers in Effie's mouth and pried open her jaw. Her skin tasted of rum and tobacco.

She ought to have bit down on those fingers. Ought to have pushed the woman away and left. She wasn't chattel to be inspected, a slave upon the block. Yet when the woman removed her hand, Effie held still, chin up, mouth gaping. She looked past the woman's pinched face and dangling earrings at the cobwebs hanging in the corners, at the ceiling's cracked and soot-stained plaster, trying to ignore a rising sense of dread.

At last, the woman stepped away and spoke in patois to Adeline.

"She thinks you've been fixed by a curse," Adeline said. "That you swallowed some bad gris-gris as a girl and that it's still there, that it burned a hole inside of you and all your memories fell in."

Effie closed her mouth. What a ridiculous explanation. That it bore a resemblance to her own likening of the affliction—a grave of sorts deep inside her where she'd balled up and buried all those dark memories—was pure coincidence. Of no greater mathematical significance than rolling snake eyes in a game of dice.

After another string of patois, Adeline said, "She says for two dollars she can make a special gris-gris to uncross you and your memories will return."

Two dollars! For some bogus charm? She might as well drink sugar-sweetened cat piss.

The queen stood waiting, hands on her hips. "Well?"

"It is why we came, *chère*."

Effie shook her head and loosened her purse strings. She just wanted to be gone from this place. Her hand shook as she fished for the coins. Likely just the heat. Or the stale air. She paid the woman two silver dollars, hoping it took little more than some grinding of herbs to concoct this gris-gris.

The coins clanked in the woman's pocket as she strode to the statue and held up her arms. She chanted more patois gibberish. Something about Papa Limba and a door. She finished with the words *ainsi soit-il*, which Adeline echoed, crossing herself.

The woman then busied herself about the room, rifling through baskets, drawers, and crannies until her arms overflowed with jars and pouches and assorted flotsam. Effie's hands refused to still until she caged them between her knees. She felt strangely unmoored, as if she were at once in the room and somewhere else entirely. Her jaw began to ache and tingle. She realized she'd clamped her mouth shut, molar to molar, after the woman had finished her inspection and held it that way still.

Overly tired, overly hot, overly vexed by all this tomfoolery— all logical explanations for her disquiet. It had nothing to do with this woman and her Voodoo. Effie forced her attention on the odds and ends the queen set out on the tea table between them and set to identifying each, first in English, then Latin. Dried fig leaves. *Ficus carica*. Juniper berries. *Junipera*.

She'd taught herself the game as a child. Played it when her own screams woke her from a nightmare, or when the ground shook with artillery fire, or when the mention of her name set the Kinyons to quarreling. First, it was just her letters: *a, b, c . . . z, y, x . . .* Then simple words and their spelling. When that no longer proved sufficient distraction, she added Latin or German. Eventually her mind would still, her heart slow, her panic settle.

But not today. Mandrake root. *Mandragoras*. Feather. *Pluma*. Too many of the items Effie couldn't name. Were those salt granules or sugar? Crushed shell or pulverized bone? Was that a jar of beeswax or beef tallow?

A sharp pain rent her concentration. The woman had plucked a mess of hairs from Effie's head. "Ouch!" She rubbed her scalp and glared at the woman. "I could have done that myself, thank you."

The queen ignored her, mixing the hair in with the bits of roots, berries, and leaves. She opened the jar of whitish salve and scooped out a gob.

Effie's stomach heaved. Her pulse bounded. It was tallow, not beeswax. She stood, knocking the tea table and nearly toppling it. Leaves and granules scattered. The candle atop the table sputtered out. "*Fi donc!*" someone said. Adeline? The Voodoo queen? The trader?

More words. Effie dry heaved again. She could no longer smell the candle smoke, rum, or tobacco. Only tallow . . . Like the stench of suet the trader slathered in her hair . . . She didn't like the way it made the back of her neck greasy . . . Didn't like the way the men poked and pinched and prodded when they came.

Effie squeezed her eyes shut. Rattled her head. A hand about her arm made her flinch. But she was supposed to stay still. Stand up straight. Be gay and lively. She'd get the paddle for sure tonight. When asked tomorrow about the welts and blisters: skeeter bites, she knew to say. Don't you cry when he's a'wallopin' you, Joncsy had told her in his rumbling baritone. Don't you give him dat satisfaction. And she wouldn't. He'd be right proud of her, Jonesy.

Wait, where was Jonesy?

She opened her eyes and looked around the dark room.

Jonesy?

The Virgin Mary gazed at her from the far corner, candlelight flickering across her pale, mournful face. The weak light of late afternoon stole through chinks in the shutters. The cracklings in the hearth popped. The stale air once again smelled of cheap rum and tobacco. Jonesy wasn't here. Of course not.

But Effie knew where she could find him.

* * *

She stood before the high brick wall that she'd stumbled upon Christmas Eve. The sudden dread, the phantom smells and ghostly sounds, the strange familiarity that had accosted her that day all made sense now.

The first blush of sunset showed above the westerly rooftops. Shadows encroached upon the street. A coffee shop stood only a few buildings down at the corner, the scent of roasting beans mixing with that of manure and pigs. In the opposite direction an upholstery shop and cotton brokerage.

Had they been here a decade and a half ago when this building with its high brick wall hadn't been a stockyard? What had people thought as they passed by? Men in their top hats and suit coats after a drink and a leisurely smoke, women with their parasols and hoop skirts out to survey the latest fabrics. She remembered the wooden sign above the main door—white with black lettering, though at the time she couldn't read the words. From within she'd heard its hinges squeak like a rusty wagon wheel when harried by the wind. So they must have known—those passersby—what business was conducted behind these high walls.

She crossed the street to the break in the wall and clambered over the picket fence, heedless of those out for a late-Sunday stroll. A few of the pigs grunted and lumbered up to her, sniffing her skirt with their mud-covered snouts. Most, however, ignored her. They lay about the yard, rooted at the empty troughs, or plodded aimlessly along the walls.

At first, Effie couldn't move, her legs so wobbly she could barely stand. More memories came back to her. Not just snatches but entire days and weeks. As she had before, she reached out and ran her finger along the gully of mortar between the bricks. Hours she'd spent like this, circling the pen, tracing her finger along the wall. Waiting.

She took a deep breath and continued farther into the pen. A trestle table had stood there in the corner, where traders took their dinner while she and the other slaves ate squatting over the hard-packed dirt. Bacon, cornbread slathered in butter and dipped in milk. Eat up, you scrawny pickaninny, they'd told her. And eat she did. Except when one of dem older boys stole her plate behind the trader's back. Then she went to bed hungry, same as before. Till Jonesy came, leastways, and put a stop to dem boys.

When Effie closed her eyes, she could picture him, slumped against the wall across the yard. Shoulders like an ox. Nose just like one too. The breath in and out of those wide nostrils could be heard clear across the pen. Eyes nearly as black as his skin. Mean nigger eyes, the traders said, and told him to keep 'em turned to the floor when buyers came around. They were scared of him, the traders, though they tried not to show it. Everyone was. Especially Effie, seeing as he was big enough to swallow her whole without bothering to chew, if he'd had a mind to.

Effie picked her way among the pigs toward the back of the pen. To the left was the door to the showroom. Despite standing in the shade with the day's heat waning, she began to sweat. Not a light dappling of moisture across her upper lip, but full droplets on her brow and temples.

The first day she'd crossed that threshold, the splendor of the room struck her dumb. Papered walls, ornate molding, finished floors so shiny she could see her reflection. Candles hung suspended from the ceiling surrounded by huge raindrops of cut glass. Not many days later, clouds had darkened the sky, and the candles, at last, were lit. But by then Effie no longer noticed the wallpaper or shiny floor or glass raindrops, only the men parading about, asking her questions, and pinching her chest in search of breast buds.

The male slaves were lined up on one side of the room, the girls along the other. They stood tallest to shortest, Jonesy at one end of the room, Effie clear across at the other. She wasn't supposed to look at him or anyone, except the buyers and traders, and only when they asked her a question. But she did look at Jonesy, whenever she could sneak a stare.

At first, she looked out of sheer awe. Later, to see which buyers took an interest in him that she might try to impress them too. More than once, Jonesy caught her gaping at him. He glared at her at first, the way he glared at everyone. Effie didn't glare back, nor did she look away. They were wrong, the traders. He didn't have mean eyes.

She blotted her brow on her sleeve and turned from the door. A short way down stood a rusty steel water basin for the pigs. Back then, the traders had used that ground to set up their screens. Only twice they'd taken her there. She remembered a small tear in one of the linen panels and the shame she felt when, at the buyer's behest, the trader made her remove her clothes. Could the other slaves, those left milling in the yard because they didn't suit any of the buyers' fancy, see her nakedness through the tear?

Effie shivered. Her stomach heaved again. She'd been too young to know why a man might want to see her without her dress, and far too young that any man, save the most deviant, would make such a request. If there were a God, he'd been with her those days, for whatever attributes tickled those men's perversion, she didn't possess.

"What the . . . excuse me, miss. You can't be in here."

Effie looked over at the sound of the voice. Across the yard, opposite the showroom, rose the outbuildings. A man stood on the second-story gallery, leaning over the balustrade. "Don't know how you wandered in here, but you best wander your way right back out."

The rooms behind him used to have bars crisscrossing the windows. They'd slept in there, on the dirty unfinished floor, sometimes ten to a room. Did the doors still lock only from without?

"You deaf? I said get!"

The sharpness of his tone jolted her back to the present. But she wasn't finished here, wasn't finished remembering. "I ain't—am not disturbing anything here, sir." She looked at the row of rooms beneath him. Kitchen, storage shed, more sleeping quarters. The bars were gone here too. She noticed for the first time the mud and pig shit caked over her boots and hem. The sky above had that final shade of pale blue before bruising over into night.

All the slaves had looked forward to this time of day—buyers gone, dinner cooking, traders preoccupied with their ledgers and logs.

"I don't care what you're doing or not doing. If you don't get, I'll fetch the police."

Effie looked up again. She couldn't think with him talking. Something else lay buried in these walls. Something else she was supposed to remember. Who had brought her here? To whom had she been sold? And what had become of Jonesy?

CHAPTER 19

Her jail cell stank of urine. Cockroaches skittered across the stone floor. The room was too dark for her to see them unless they wandered into the small pool of light that spilled through the barred window of her cell door. Or that was cast by the moonlight through another barred opening high up in the wall. But she could hear them, the cockroaches, a constant patter of frenzied legs and dragging exoskeletons.

She wrapped her arms around herself and wished she'd had the presence of mind to bring a shawl. Then again, she'd not left Mrs. Neale's—however many hours ago that was—expecting to pass the night in jail.

Perhaps she ought to have listened to the man when he told her to leave the stockyard. She'd believed him when he said he'd fetch the police, but at the time, that hadn't seemed important. A few more minutes, that's all she needed to fully remember. A chance to stand in the far corner and see the entire space laid out before her—the door that led to the traders' office through which she'd first entered the yard after being sold by her master; the wooden cistern tucked around the corner where they drew water to drink and bathe; the outbuilding where they changed each morning from their rags into suits and calico dresses for show, where the traders polished their faces with oil and slicked their hair with tallow, where she first saw the tangle of scars on Jonesy's back, a briar patch of raised flesh, when he pulled off his shirt to change; the heavy oak door at the back, still rigged with iron locks, leading out to the alley. She'd exited only once through that door, she and Jonesy and four or five others of the season's dregs, coffled together, bound for whatever new hell awaited them.

Beyond that door, Effie remembered little. A few flashes of sound, of sight, of smell, but nothing concrete. Nothing from which she could glean where they'd gone or the name of their new master. Maybe if the man at the stockyard hadn't accosted her before getting the police, grabbing her from behind and binding her with rope as if she were some wayward sow, maybe then she would have remembered more. She leaned back against the cold plaster wall of the cell. The crude stool beneath her creaked and wobbled.

No, likely not. She'd remembered all she could from the place. Her life before, her life after had been locked out as surely as she'd been locked in. What, then, did she have to show for the day? Two dollars gone to some Voodoo queen. The memory of this Jonesy—a man not her kin. Charges of vagrancy and trespassing, which might well cost her her livelihood once Mr. Whitmark found out. And a desire to scrub her skin raw. Not from the mud and pig shit clinging to her boots and skirts and stockings, but from those hands. All those men's hands.

What she wouldn't give for a bar of soap and pitcher of water! Hot, cold, it didn't matter. If only she could likewise scrub her mind. She was done with this. Looking for her past. She'd tell Adeline straightaway. No more of these little excursions. Damn her anyway for meddling. Adeline just wanted to assuage her guilt—she who had a mother and a brother and had never been a slave.

Footfalls sounded in the hallway. Likely the police had rounded up another ruffian from the streets. A prostitute from down by the levee. A drunk passed out in the rail yard. But as the *click-clack* grew louder, she realized it came from only a single set of feet. A set of feet that stopped right before her door.

Effie sat forward and straightened. Dawn was hours off yet, the sliver of sky visible through her window lit only by the moon and stars. So whoever it was, they had not come to usher her before a judge for her arraignment, nor to toss another ne'er-do-well into her cell.

She readied her voice to scream. Surely those in the surrounding cells would hear. The other officers in the guardroom. But what could her fellow prisoners do if the man at the door attacked her? And the officers? Likely they'd grown deaf to such screams.

A key rattled in the lock. Strange how this was now familiar—the tiny, foul-smelling room, the barred windows, the click of rusty pins and springs, the foreboding. The door swung outward. The man before her, a tall, square-shouldered mulatto, said nothing but motioned for her to exit. Effie hesitated, but as he stepped back and glanced over his shoulder, his face caught the lamplight. She recognized him not only as the guard who'd taken down her name and led her to her cell earlier that evening, but from somewhere else as well.

He closed the cell door quietly behind her and, after another furtive look toward the guardroom, nodded down the hall in the opposite direction. They passed several cells before the hallway curved into darkness. The man grabbed a lamp off the wall and stepped around her, illuminating another short stretch of hallway, three descending steps, and a heavy wooden door. Effie's hands went cold. Her feet shuffled her around the bend. She hesitated again at the top of the stairs, but he waved her down, a look of urgency in his eyes, and handed her the oil lamp.

"Hold this," he whispered, and flipped through several keys bound together on an iron ring. Despite her stranglehold on the handle, the lamp quivered, the yellow flame hissing and sputtering. He looked up from the keys and laid his hand over hers around the handle. "I'm Hiram. I've seen you at the club meetings. I've called someone to take you home."

He let go of her hand and returned to sorting through the keys. Effie replayed what he'd said through her mind. Yes, that was where she recognized him from. He sat a few rows from the front. Always made a point of talking to Samson and Tom afterward, and kissing Mrs. Carrière on the cheek before he left.

He fitted the key into the lock. When it wouldn't turn, he tried another.

"But the charges . . ."

"I didn't record your name, Miss Jones. You were never here."

"I broke the law." The whine of unoiled hinges sounded over her words. If he'd heard what she'd said, he made no show of it. A rush of cool air entered through the open door. Beyond it lay a dark side street, the sound of crickets, the smell of damp stone and day-old vegetable scraps. Freedom. She thought to repeat herself. She had in fact been trespassing, but it seemed a small turn of justice that after so many closed and locked doors, here, at last, was one open.

"Thank you, Mr. . . ."

"Elliott. Hiram Elliott." He took the lamp from her and smiled.

Footsteps hurried down the street toward them. Effie shrank from the threshold, but Mr. Elliott stepped out unconcerned and greeted the newcomer. "Samson." The sound of clapping hands. "She's right here."

For a moment, returning to her bleak, stinky cell seemed preferable to meeting Samson like this. Filth soddened her dress. Dust had dried with her sweat, making sandpaper of her skin. She hadn't the energy to laugh, smile, nod, to use any of Adeline's little tricks. And that woman from the saloon. The remembrance still made her sick.

Effie's arms fell limp to her sides. Only a perfect fool would think of such things at a time like this. But after all that had happened today—or yesterday—whatever day it was, dabbling in Voodoo gris-gris, breaking into a private yard, inviting arrest, she could hardly claim to be anything but a perfect fool.

Had Samson not taken her elbow and shepherded her into the street, she might have lingered forever there in the doorway. He brushed a strand of hair from her face and held firm to her arm. "Miss Jones, are you all right?"

She managed a nod.

"A bit shaken, I think," Mr. Elliott said.

Samson thanked him and bid him good night, then hurried her down the street. They didn't speak until several blocks later when they'd reached the levee. Strange how quiet it was now, how still. A line of steamboats slumbered along the dock. Farther downriver the masts of fishing smacks and schooners bobbed and swayed against the black horizon. Her lungs welcomed the crisp air, expanding fully against her ribs for the first time in hours. It smelled of earth and river weeds here, of the tar-coated canvas draping the sugar barrels stacked about the dock.

The waxing moon hung pregnant above them, its light glinting off the water. Hadn't it just risen when she clambered into the police cart? "What time is it?"

Samson patted his waistcoat pocket. "I hadn't the presence of mind to bring my watch. A few hours before dawn, I'd venture."

She noticed the stubble on his cheeks, the white crust at the corner of his eyes, the mismatch of his coat and trousers. "They woke you, then?"

"I'd only just gone to bed."

"I'm sorry."

"Sleep's not so important."

"On the contrary, necropsy done on the brains of mice after extended—" She stopped when she saw his smile. He was joking of course. Hadn't wanted her to feel bad about the trouble she'd caused tonight. How different he seemed now than he had only a few short nights ago at the saloon. How attentive and caring. Just as he had the afternoon of Mardi Gras, the night of the ward meeting when they were alone in the alley. Her brain, perhaps suffering the same affliction as those mice, struggled to reconcile his behavior. Her heart, however, readily dismissed the contradiction, surrendering to his kindness without struggle at all.

"Miss Jones—"

"Effie."

"Effie." He stopped walking and faced her. "Sergeant Elliott's man said you'd been arrested for trespassing and vagrancy. You needn't tell me what happened, but is everything all right?"

She opened her mouth to speak, but couldn't tame her thoughts into words. Her newly unlocked memories remained raw and jumbled. Something else silenced her as well. Not some high-order reasoning, but a base and visceral feeling she couldn't quite name. Her eyes retreated to the river. The moon's pale reflection undulated like a ghost upon its surface.

Shame. That was the feeling.

Not because her hair and clothes were a mess. Not because she stank of pig excrement. Not because she'd been arrested and jailed.

She'd been a slave, subject to all its indignities. Her past was no longer an abstraction but a reality she could taste and smell and remember.

Samson coaxed her to walking again. "I was arrested once. No twice, I think. Just after the War. The usual charges. Vagrancy, impudence, swearing. They'd have arrested a black man just for breathin' if they could in those days."

Effie knew about the Black Codes, how hard the Southern Democrats had tried to clip the wings of Emancipation. It wasn't a fair comparison. "I deserved to be arrested. I was trespassing."

"Whoever you were trespassing on could have just asked you to leave."

"He did. Several times. I ignored him."

Samson laughed—a rich sound she drank through her ears like pure honey. "Now see, that don't surprise me one bit."

"You were a soldier during the War, weren't you?"

"Yes, ma'am. Seventy-fifth U.S. Colored Infantry."

"And before that?" Effie knew the answer. She'd gleaned it from his speeches. From the stories other people told of him. She could hear it in his voice too, those country words and phrases and pronunciations that broke through his polished vernacular when he was particularly impassioned. From their first encounter in Tivoli Circle, she'd known it. But she wanted to hear him say it.

He steered her among towering piles of baled cotton awaiting passage on tomorrow's ships and sat down on one of the shorter stacks. Effie sat beside him, her feet swinging just above the ground.

"I was a slave. A field hand. Up north a ways." He pulled a wisp of cotton from a tear in the burlap and worked it between his fingers until it became a knotted ball. "I picked more of this shit than God had tears." He threw the pea-sized ball onto the ground. "Sometimes I think I can still feel the fibers in my nose, my ears, wet and stringy on my tongue like they used to would get during pickin' time."

Effie had the urge to reach out and touch him. His forearm, perhaps. His hands, now clasped and lolling between his knees. His rounded shoulders. Not in a romantic way, but as a tether of sorts. An anchor.

A breeze rolled across the river, sending a tremor across the water's surface and scattering the reflected moonlight. The canvases stretched atop the nearby sugar barrels flapped and rippled.

"The stockyard I was arrested at had been a slave pen." Her words came without conscious thought to voice them. She glanced askew at Samson. His heavily lashed eyes regarded her intently, his expression one of earnest curiosity. Had she really thought he'd look down on her for a past over which she had no control? For a past they shared? Still, she looked away before continuing. "I didn't remember until yesterday, but I'd been there as a girl. I mean, I was sold there."

Another sideways glance. He sat as before, his entire attention upon her, and it was impossible not to give over to it. She told him everything then. A rush of words flying from her mouth like expelled poison. She told him how she'd emerged from the swamps into the Union camp without memory of whence she'd come. She told him of Captain Kinyon and her time in Indiana. She told him of her work as an embalmer and even at this, he didn't flinch.

Never had she given such a complete and uncensored accounting of her life. The telling undressed her. Or so it felt. A shoe, a glove, a hat at first. Mundane stories of life in the camp or the journey North after the War. Then came the buttons trailing down her blouse, the ties of her skirt, her stockings. Here her voice wavered. Were it not for his steady gaze she'd have abandoned the telling. The why of her leaving Indiana, only that she withheld. And when she'd circled back to the present, to the Voodoo queen and the stockyard and awful memories it triggered, she could almost feel the river's cool breeze trailing over her naked body.

In turn, Samson told her more of his days on the cotton plantation. He too was an orphan, his mother dying of childbed fever only days after his birth. His father sold off a few months later to pay his master's gambling debts. The other women in the slave quarters took turns caring for him, though. He learned early he had a gift for storytelling, and became a vagabond of sorts, roaming among the slave cabins, spinning a yarn for any who asked in exchange for a turnip from their garden or a leg of rabbit from their stew.

He shrugged out of his jacket and leaned back against the surrounding bales of cotton as he spoke, his hands laced beneath his head, eyes turned heavenward. Effie eased back too, painting his words into a moving picture in her mind. He was easy to imagine thus— dapper, even as a boy; precocious; seducing those around him with his wit and melodious voice.

It wasn't until the War he'd learned to read and write. Said he wasn't all that good at it even now. Not like Tom. Certainly, not like her.

Effie turned onto her side, reclined as she was against the soft bales, and propped her head up with her hand. Only a narrow expanse of cool night air separated them. "There are far fewer orators than there are ready pens to transcribe their words."

"That's kind of you to say, considering you were teaching others to read and write by War's end."

"I'm not being kind. I'm being truthful."

He smiled at her. "That's what I like about you, Effie. I reckon it impossible for you not to say the truth."

She lay back and stared up at the sky. The moon had dipped toward the horizon, but the dawn had not yet broken at the opposite edge of the sky. The air was still now, heavy with that river smell, and for the first time that night, Effie felt its chill. "I was wrong to look into the past."

"How can you say that?"

"I'm no closer today to finding my kin than I was yesterday. Yet now I have all these, these . . . disquieting memories dulling my attention."

Samson rolled toward her onto his side. "That's not true at all. There are records of those sales. Who bought you. Who sold you to those traders in the first place. It was law to record such things."

"Really?" In her excitement, she flopped to her side to face him, shrinking the space between them to but a hair's breadth. For a moment her brain idled and muscles froze. The surrounding cotton bales concealed them from any who might pass. Not that she'd seen or heard anyone since their arrival. She wiggled back a few inches. They were still far too close for any claims of propriety, but at least he needn't vie with her greedy lungs for air.

He brought a hand to her face, tucking a frazzled strand of hair behind her ear. But then his fingers lingered, dragging lazily over the curve of her jaw and down her neck. "Really. Tom could help you. He's good with records and bookkeeping, and all those kinds of things."

Her lips parted, but she couldn't speak and settled for a nod. His fingers flirted with the collar of her shirt, tracing the edge of the fabric, then dipping beneath.

"You could even look into what happened to your friend Jonesy."

The name jolted her from her pleasant stupor. Jonesy.

"None of the buyers wanted him," she said and then, after a moment, "Me either." She explained the lash marks on his back and how, despite Jonesy's size and strength, as soon as a prospective buyer saw them, he'd back away, mumble something about vice of character, say he wasn't interested in no bad Negroes. Effie they'd called queer, touched, dull.

He rolled away from her and she feared what she'd said—that she too had been unwanted—was too much.

But he didn't sit up or make to leave. Instead, his hands worked the buttons of his waistcoat, tugged his shirttails free of his trousers, and then pulled both up and over his head. "They'd have called me a bad Negro too, then."

Several thin scars streaked across his back. Not like the gnarled mess that had marked Jonesy's, but painful to behold nonetheless. She reached out, this time without hesitation, and traced the dark raised lines with her fingertips. Water rimmed her eyes. Her hand shook with hatred for the vile scourge who'd inflicted these lashes. She reached the small of his back, where the scars tapered into smooth, warm skin and started over again at the top, as if her fingers could somehow erase what had been done to him.

She sniffed to staunch her running nose and he turned back to her, cradling her face in his palms. "It's behind us now. It doesn't define us the way it still defines them."

His voice trembled with that same passion she'd fallen in love with back in Tivoli Circle, and when his lips found hers she let them guide her through a kiss. And then another. Harder than the first, flattening their mouths together and open, his tongue flicking inside her. For once, her rational self disengaged, and she was all emotion and sensation. His fingers loosening the top buttons of her shirt. His hand working beneath her chemise and corset to find her breasts.

She felt his other hand grasping at her skirts, pulling them upward. Over her calves, her knees, her thighs. Her senses surfaced a moment, just to glance between the bales and be sure they were alone. Then she surrendered fully, throwing her head back, inviting his lips upon her neck. He worked his hips between her legs. The sketches of human anatomy she'd studied flitted at the edge of her consciousness. How clinical they'd seemed. How void of any—

A sharp pain rent her from her musing. She winced and tried to reposition herself beneath his weight. Samson slowed a moment but did not withdraw. He kissed her again and breathed her name. The pain dulled, and she returned his embrace.

CHAPTER 20

The home on Josephine Street that Mr. Whitmark had dispatched her to reminded Effie of Adeline's. It was lovely on the outside, with a wide front gallery and fluted Greek columns. A crepe myrtle flanked one side of the cottage with reddish-green shoots and small, glossy leaves just beginning to sprout from its pruned-back branches. Winter's detritus had been raked from the yard, the flowerbeds and rose bushes groomed for spring. But the interior told a different story. Worn carpets, faded wallpaper, sparsely appointed rooms.

"Shall I set a fire for you?" the woman who'd let Effie in and led her back to the bedroom asked.

With the shutters closed to morning sunlight, it was cold in this part of the house. She glanced at the fireplace. A fine layer of dust dulled the cast-iron screen. But no soot. Likely this woman and her dead husband hadn't spared coal for this room all winter. All the more kind of her to offer.

"No, thank you. It's best to keep the room cool until we're done with the . . . er . . . process."

The woman nodded, her gray eyes flickering to the bed and then back to Effie. "Can I get you some tea? Coffee? Louisa down the street brought over biscuits. I think I have a jar of last year's—"

"I'm fine." In truth, a cup of coffee sounded divine after the few short hours of sleep Effie had gotten, but she never ate or drank while embalming. Captain Kinyon had told her once of a man who'd mistaken a jar of injection fluid for a glass of water and nearly died. She'd not believed him, the captain, when he'd told her the story. How could one be so distracted as to drink embalming fluid? Surely the sharp smell of chemicals would have alerted him. But in those days, she had only her work, her studies, a worry or two over whether Mrs. Kinyon would drag her to the church pie sale or quilting bee. Nothing to truly divide her attention.

Her current state of mind, however, gave credence to the story. She'd not even remembered to tie her boots this morning until she'd nearly tripped over her laces hurrying down the stairs.

"You just let me know if you need something." The woman's gaze wandered back to the bed. Her fragile smile tottered. "I didn't know if I should"—she nodded to a wooden leg propped against the far wall—"you know, put it on. He hated for anyone to see him without it."

"I'll reattach it at the end."

"Of course, of course." She looked around the room, clasped and unclasped her hands, then, at last, shuffled out, reminding Effie there were coffee and biscuits in the kitchen.

Effie shut the door behind her. She leaned back against the smooth wood and closed her eyes a moment. The woman's violet-scented perfume lingered in the air, mixed with the smell of camphor and a body just beginning to turn.

Though Mr. Elliott had assured her he'd not recorded her name in the jail's logbook last night, Effie had feared somehow Mr. Whitmark had gotten word of her arrest. Her hands had quivered such that it took her three tries to unlock the shop's carriage gate. What a relief when Mr. Whitmark bade her good morning, chirk and lively as if it were Christmas Day. He asked nothing of her bloodshot eyes nor her unpolished boots nor her mismatched gloves, but directed her here, to this kindly woman's house, and said he'd follow presently.

She opened her eyes and set to work. She was tired, yes, but altogether glad to have something to occupy her hands and mind. Something solitary and familiar.

Without even pulling back the coverlet, she could see the body of this man had been made gaunt and shrunken by some drawn-out illness. Malaria, perhaps. Consumption. His bewhiskered cheeks

sagged. His collarbones all but jutted through his skin. Upon undressing and washing him, she found his arms bruised from where
he'd been bled.

As promised, Mr. Whitmark arrived at the house shortly thereafter. He helped her lift the body onto the cooling table, though it was
so light and emaciated she likely could have moved it herself.

"Did you know this man?" she asked, when he lingered, staring
down at the body. His once-cheerful expression had gone wan.

He shook his head and she realized it was not the man's face Mr.
Whitmark was gazing at, but his missing leg.

"At Stones River we were camped so close to the enemy line, I
could hear the screams of the Rebs across the field under the saw at
the same time I was operating on our Union boys. Seemed between
us there'd been enough feet and arms and legs to damn the Mississippi."

Effie too remembered the screams. The piles of bloodied limbs.
The endless flies buzzing and circling.

"And what for?" he continued. "To die like this, wasted and im-
poverished?"

She ought to have said nothing. Kept her tongue still and gone
about her work. Or else muttered something banal about preserving
the great Union his forefathers had created. Instead she said, "That
every drop of blood drawn with the lash be paid by another drawn
with the sword."

He cocked his head toward her and blinked, as if only just realizing she was there beside him. Then his eyes narrowed.

Her gaze retreated to the scuffed floorboards. "Lincoln, sir."

"I know damn well who said it, Effie." He grabbed her embalming cabinet from beside the cooling table and thrust it into her arms.
"I don't pay you to quote dead men at me. I pay you to work."

Her jaw tightened, but she said nothing as he clomped from the
room.

It took her four tries to elevate the artery from the cut she made
in the underside of the dead man's arm. Another two to cannulate
the flimsy vessel. Hypovolemia—that was the cause of her troubles.
It had nothing to do with her scattered thoughts or clammy fingers.

Mr. Whitmark hadn't been the same since his brother's visit the
week before. No, further back than that. Since the day they were

called to that palatial Garden District house after Mardi Gras. True, business was up. She welcomed the extra money. He was sober and eating more now than just kola nuts. And hadn't it been good to see him smile? Not that wistful half smile he'd worn on occasion those first months after she came. But a true smile, one she imagined had graced his face often before the War.

Yet Effie rather missed the aimless drunk he'd been on her arrival. Apathy was easy to navigate. This moodiness—happy one minute, glowering the next—was far more treacherous terrain.

She could hear him now through the thin wall separating this room from the parlor. His voice came low, even, and professionally somber. He spoke of casket options, pallbearers, and plumage. Of hymns and bible verses for the service. Of the advantages of crepe bunting over flowers.

Perhaps she'd spoken out of turn. No need to lecture a man who'd fought against his countrymen, against his very brother, that the Union cause would triumph. Hadn't Samson said something about that in a club meeting once? About holding fast to their allies?

Samson. Not six hours ago he'd been kissing her, stroking her skin. She wasn't naive to what they'd done. More than once Mrs. Kinyon had lectured her on the virtues of chastity, on the shame and ruin that awaited girls who gave in to lust. Swarthy as she was, but a few generations removed from those heathens in Africa, Effie was particularly susceptible. Or so the lecture went.

But she was not penitent or ashamed as Mrs. Kinyon forewarned. She didn't feel spoiled or dirty. No, not like she had when those men in the slave pen had touched her. She wished rather Mrs. Kinyon had told her something useful, cautioned her about the initial pain, the blood, the stickiness afterward.

Her dress, her petticoat, her crinolette, her chemise had all ridden up and bunched uncomfortably beneath her. The cotton bale's burlap covering had chafed the exposed skin between her gartered stockings and corset. Mosquitos had bitten her thighs.

She'd felt so vulnerable at first. Bare to the world. Unable to move, to disentangle herself, to scarcely breathe for his weight upon her. But then in the throes of it all—the pain, the chafing, that feeling of suffocation—she'd looked up into his face. His eyes were scrunched shut, his lips parted. Beads of sweat glistened at his hairline. He was at once entirely apart from her, lost in his own sensations, and entirely hers. Just as bare and vulnerable as she and utterly beholden. The dock could have sprung to life at that moment, steamboats blaring their horns, stevedores rolling sugar barrels up the gangplanks, merchants barking orders in a dozen different languages, and Samson would not have flinched. She'd wrapped her legs around him then, enmeshed her fingers in his hair, urging him closer, deeper that he might stay lost in her forever.

A steamboat did sound just then. A sharp, high-pitched whistle. No, not a steamboat. A kettle. She heard the woman of the house pad from the adjacent parlor, over the threadbare runner in the hallway, and into the kitchen. Effie rattled her head and looked down at her work. Her hand had stilled on the injection pump, blood-tinged fluid backing up into the tubing. Her first impulse was to squeeze the bulb harder and faster to make up the lost time. Mr. Whitmark's mood would only sour further if he found her dawdling. But embalming couldn't be rushed. And this man looked ravaged enough without his capillaries bursting into bruises across his skin.

The clank of china in the parlor told her Mr. Whitmark was yet engaged anyway. Her stomach rumbled as she thought of the warm tea and jam-covered biscuits he and the woman were likely enjoying. She thought she caught a whiff from beneath the door—nutty, sweet, and rich. But that was probably just her scattered mind again. When she inhaled a second time she smelled only muriatic acid, arsenic, and chemical salts.

She was glad for the sharp odor. It kept her tethered to the present. For a moment she'd slipped back to the slave pen, to those early days before Jonesy had come and the other children—a dozen inches taller and years older—had stolen her food. How her stomach had grumbled then.

But the smell of the embalming fluid had saved her from falling back fully into the memory. The whoosh of the injection syringe. The muted voices of Mr. Whitmark and the woman sounding through the wall.

Effie inclined her ear toward the sound. She didn't care what type of casket the woman chose, how many black plumes she ordered, whether Father Girardy from St. Alphonsus or Reverend Chase from

Christ Church would perform the service. But she'd never finish her work if her thoughts kept drifting.

"Did you know my Matthew?" the woman asked. And then, after a short pause, "Before the War?"

They couldn't possibly have become acquainted *after* the War. The woman's tone, though not unkind, said as much. Before the War, perhaps. When decent men would still receive Mr. Whitmark, invited him into their studies to drink bourbon and smoke cigars. Before he'd turned scalawag and sided with Yanks. Before her husband lost first his leg, then his fortune. Before the world turned topsy-turvy on them all.

How Mr. Whitmark's past stalked him. A decade gone and still relentless. It wasn't just vagrants defacing his shop, or Ku Kluxers disparaging his trade, but even goodly women talking around the subject like it were unfit to be spoken of plainly.

"Only by reputation," he said. "I believe he and my older brother were at university together."

"Ah, yes. I was sorry when I heard he'd been lost at Vicksburg."

Effie scooted her stool as close to the wall as the embalming tubing would allow. She'd not known he'd had an older brother too. On which side of the Vicksburg line had he stood and fallen?

"Matthew was there too, you know. That's when he lost his leg."

Silence followed. The sound of pouring liquid. The clink of a spoon against porcelain. More silence.

"We had such high hopes at the outset of the War. To be free of Northern tyranny. To continue on with our beloved way of life. And to come back to this . . ." Her voice diminished into sobs.

Effie imagined Mr. Whitmark shifting in his chair and longingly eyeing the parlor door while he reached into his suit pocket for a hankie.

"You can't imagine the humiliation my husband endured, Mr. Whitmark. And not him alone. All our men returning home. Though they'd never right admit it."

A few sniffles sounded through the wall, followed by a dainty honk of the nose. Humiliation? What did these men know of humiliation? They'd not been poked and fondled, bidden to step lively and act the genial slave while on display. Effie stopped her work. She didn't trust her fingers not to strangle the pump. And Mr. Whitmark. What of his humiliation? To come home the victor but be treated as the vanquished.

"All those rights they'd fought and bled to protect—gone! One illegitimate government after the next. Taxed to the very brink of poverty." The woman blew her nose again. "I'm sorry Mr. Whitmark, I know you're a Republican, but I just can't abide what our beloved South has become. It killed him. Just as sure as the illness. It killed him, Mr. Whitmark. A man must be able to hold high his head."

More sobs.

"Every time he strapped on that dratted leg, it was a reminder of what he'd lost. What we've all lost."

Effie looked at the man on her cooling table. Even with that wooden prosthetic, he must have hobbled when he walked. He'd likely not passed a single black man on the street without the niggling reminder of his folly and defeat. She started up with the injection again, the slow, rhythmic squeeze of the pump, the steady course of fluid. Judging from the pressure and resistance, his veins were nearly filled.

But Tom had lost a leg too and managed to hold his head aloft. He'd been born and raised as chattel and yet had dignity. Effie pitied the woman her sorrow, the loss of the man she'd loved. But though she managed to keep the flow and force of the injection even, she could not pity this man.

She'd finished the injection and was tying off the artery when the woman's tearful diatribe ended, and Mr. Whitmark spoke. For all his moodiness and disorganization, his shaky hand and mediocre skill, his talent for undertaking showed in these moments. He could lay a banquet of the most unpalatable things—death and loss and all their costly accoutrements—as if it were a feast. In similar form, he would disagree with the woman now, defend the Union cause, Republicanism, Emancipation, without seeming the least contrary.

His first words were conciliatory. How awful all that had befallen her husband. So ugly the ravages of war. History would remember all those who bravely fought. He cleared his throat. The low whistle of a sofa cushion taking in air sounded. Floorboards creaked. Effie guessed he'd stood. Perhaps wandered to the window or marble hearth.

"Life certainly isn't as tidy as I supposed in my youth," he said. "This certainly wasn't the future I'd envisioned when I joined up with the Unionists. All these Northern opportunists—vultures, really—and the corruption. But take heart. Change is coming."

Northern opportunists? Had Effie heard him right? Is that what he thought of her? She hastily tied off the final suture, sealing closed the incision she'd made in the man's arm. Still clutching the needle and thread, she pressed her ear against the wall, the peeling lime paint cold and scratchy against her cheek.

"Do you really think so?" the woman asked.

"Look at what happened last fall in Mississippi. A sweeping victory for Democrats in the statehouse. Why, that carpetbagger Governor Ames resigned just last week."

"But you're a Republican, Mr. Whitmark. Surely that doesn't suit your cause."

"I'm a Southerner, ma'am. Beyond that . . . I don't know what I am."

"I must confess, I'd thought not to hire you. Didn't seem right to have an enemy of our cause profit from my husband's death. Not when . . ." She blew her nose again and took a ragged inhale. "But Mr. Randolph said you and your Negress were the best in the city. You came from a good family, after all, and weren't like those other scalawags. He was right."

"Thank you, ma'am." The words came out hoarse, hesitant. Or was that just the muffling effect of the wall? He cleared his throat again. "I best check on my assistant. She ought to be close to finished by now."

Effie hastened from the wall, her heel striking one of the open jars scattered about on the floor. Embalming fluid seeped into the pine floorboards and wicked into the rug, its sharp scent blooming in the air. She rummaged through her dressing case for scraps of muslin to soak up the fluid, tossing pins, collar buttons, shaving soap, a brush, a razor, a comb onto the floor around her. The bedroom door opened just as she covered the spill. She scrambled to her feet, standing over the sodden scraps of cloth so they were hidden beneath the hem of her skirt.

Mr. Whitmark winced and wrinkled his nose. His gray eyes roved the mess of supplies cast about the floor. "Are you finished?"

The conversation he'd had with the woman didn't seem to have upset him. Not her rationalizing or misplaced blame. Not her unintended insults. He just looked tired and impatient.

"I still have to inject the cavity. I . . . er . . . was just looking for my trocar."

"It's there, in your embalming cabinet."

She glanced at the case laid open on the side table, her long metal trocar nestled against the pink velvet backing in plain view.

"Of course. I . . . I thought I'd moved it." She dragged the fluid-soaked rags into a pile with the toe of her boot, trying to keep the rest of her body still.

He frowned and did not move. Was he going to stand there and watch her finish? "Well, get to it. I've orders to place back at the shop."

She turned back to the body, keeping the pile of cloth hidden as she moved. Her gait was awkward. The sound of the cloths a deafening murmur over the floorboards, leaving a damp trail in their wake. "I'll fetch you as soon as I'm finished. It won't be but a few minutes."

He lingered a moment more. Surely he'd seen the spill. She grabbed the trocar and steadied it above the dead man's belly button. Mr. Whitmark had never shouted at her. Never struck her. Never threatened to let go of her service. But this new man, this man who disavowed Republicanism, who lauded a victory won in Mississippi by terror and violence, she didn't know how this man would react to even the smallest mess.

"You've a quarter of an hour. And crack a window. It smells like the dickens in here."

CHAPTER 21

⟹•⟸

"Baseball?"

Effie nodded.

Adeline swished her silk fan to and fro with the same languor as the drooping evening sun. "And a . . . what did you call it?"

"Baking sale. To raise money for our club and the Negro Veterans Aid Society."

"And just what can you bake that anyone would pay money for?"

"I've a recipe for marble cake."

"Whose recipe?"

"My landlady suggested it. I picked up all the necessary components from the market this morning."

Adeline laughed and sipped her lemonade. "Ingredients."

"Components, ingredients, whatever you call them, I have them all."

"Have you ever made a marble cake before? Any cake for that matter?"

Effie pursed her lips and looked out over the courtyard. Yesterday's rainwater had pooled in the derelict fountain. A pair of finches sipped and splashed. Perhaps she ought to have purchased extra eggs and flour for a test run beforehand. But how hard could it be? "Am I to believe you bake?"

"*Mon Dieu,* no. That was always the cook's job. Until . . . well, you know. Now I survive on pain perdu, molasses, and dinner invitations—which have dried up quiet dreadfully on account of the Lenten season. I'll be positively gaunt come Easter Sunday."

"Well, you needn't bake anything. Just come for the baseball match."

"I don't know the first thing about baseball, *chère*." She took another sip of her drink and continued to fan herself.

If it was this hot in April, what must July be like? Effie swigged her lemonade too. It tasted weak and sour but blessedly cool. She didn't know a thing about baseball either. In truth, she'd forgotten all about the match and the baking sale. But yesterday, in the pale predawn light, when Samson had walked her home from the levee, he'd asked her if she were planning to attend. She'd still been befuddled by all that happened in the stockyard, at the jail, atop the cotton bales at the dock, and had walked beside him in silence.

There at the base of Mrs. Neale's steps, with the scent of magnolia and banana shrub heavy in the air, she'd nodded to his question and let him kiss her again, heedless of whomever might be up and at their window.

Now, nothing would keep her from the match nor from making the most delicious marble cake anyone had ever eaten.

"I should like to introduce you to the other club members."

"The club members or your Mr. Greene?"

Effie grabbed her own palm-leaf fan and flapped it before her face, both to cool the heat blooming beneath her skin and to hide the smile that sprang unbidden to her lips at the mention of his name. "He is a club member."

"*Désolé, chère.* But I can't. Monsieur Chauvet is taking me and Mamm on a ride out to Lake Pontchartrain tomorrow after mass. She's feeling better than she has in weeks. I think it's the warm weather. And Monsieur Chauvet's carriage has the loveliest . . ."

Disappointment nettled Effie, though she knew she shouldn't feel so. She was glad for Adeline, after all. The improved health of her mother. The continued attentions of Mr. Chauvet. Glad Adeline had been relieved, not angry, when Effie called to apologize about leaving her behind at the Voodoo queen's house. She'd pulled Effie in off the banquette and embraced her, insisted she stay and take some lemonade with her out back on the second-story gallery.

Perhaps it was that their worlds seemed so separate. Yes, Effie had attended that party with Adeline on Esplanade Avenue. And the sewing circle with her friends from the Jeunes Amis Club. But Effie had stood out on both occasions like iced tea at a wake. And not once had Adeline deigned to step into Effie's world.

They were friends, weren't they? Or had Effie misread the situation as she was so apt to do? More than anything, she wanted to tell Adeline about Samson. About what had transpired between them on the levee. But Adeline had to meet him first. To see his robust, healthy stature, the near-perfect symmetry of his features. To hear his melodious voice. To listen to the thoughtful workings of his mind. Then Adeline would understand how such a man could overwhelm Effie. Overwhelm her objectivity, her reticence, her inhibitions.

She did tell Adeline about the memories unleashed at the stockyard. At first Effie relayed only the most salient facts. The yard had been a slave pen. She'd been sold to a trader. Sold again several weeks after. She wrung all emotion from the words before speaking them and kept a steady gauge of Adeline's expression. Could one who'd never been a slave understand? Or would she treat this as just another piece of gossip batted about over afternoon drinks?

But no, Adeline only listened. Her lips pressed together and did not waver. Not to smile or sneer or frown. Her eyes widened but did not look away. So Effie continued, filling in the outline of her tale with day-to-day details. Emotion slipped into her voice. Her fingers tightened around the handle of her fan until the dried palm fibers splintered off into her skin. She continued even as evening gave way to twilight.

Even after Effie finished, Adeline held silent. She worked the fan from Effie's grasp and refilled her glass with the last of the lemonade. Effie hadn't realized how thirsty she'd become and drank down the entire glass.

"Your name," Adeline finally said. "At least you know where it came from."

Jonesy. He'd protected her in the slave pen. Cared for her like a brother. But there was more to it than that. Something lurking just beyond the edge of her remembrance.

"What now?" Adeline asked.

Effie told her of Samson's suggestion to search the old deeds of sale.

Adeline reached over and held Effie's hand. "*Ma foi,* you must be . . . well, I don't know what you must be feeling."

Effie couldn't name it either. A small prickling of shame remained. But also relief. And hope. Above all a longing to know more—about the master who'd sold her to the slaver in the first place, about the man who'd bought her and where he'd taken her, about Jonesy and why he meant so much to her. And where that shed, those dead eyes, and the humming fit into her past. But all this was too much to stuff into words. Besides, her tongue was tired. She let Adeline hold her hand and watched the sky darken.

"I told you that Voodoo queen would help," Adeline said after a while.

"It hadn't anything to do with her supposed spirits or gris-gris. It was the tallow. The smell of it. And the darkness. And the way she'd pried my mouth open like I was a mule. A collection of sensory stimuli similar enough to what I'd experienced to . . . I don't know . . . jog my memory."

"*Oui,* but the right stimuli, all together. Are you telling me there's no magic in that?" She laughed and Effie did too.

Effie emptied the ash box and stoked the embers from that morning's breakfast fire. The large cast-iron stove set back into the kitchen's hearth was similar enough to the one Mrs. Kinyon had that Effie was certain she could operate it. Still, she regretted now not having paid better attention to the uses of the various dampers, trays, and cubbies.

She cleaned the soot from her hands and studied the recipe. Easy as a wink, Mrs. Neale had promised, and positively delicious.

The recipe looked more complicated now that all the components— *ingredients*—were spread out before her on the kitchen table. Perhaps she ought to have accepted Mrs. Neale's offer to bake the cake for her. But no, that wouldn't do at all. When Samson tasted the cake, she wanted to delight in his praise without having to admit someone else had baked it. She pinned the parchment atop the kitchen table beneath the salt shaker and donned her apron. If she could turn zinc chloride, arsenic, and mercury into embalming fluid, she could turn flour and sugar into cake.

She started by mixing the ingredients for the dark part of the cake—molasses, brown sugar, butter. A tin cup from the cupboard served as her standard unit of measure, along with a soup spoon and a teaspoon. Hardly the sort of standards the National Academy of Sciences would approve of, but she doubted Mrs. Neale would take any kindlier to her bringing a pharmacy scale into the kitchen than Mrs. Kinyon had.

Trouble arose almost at once. The dark part of the cake required seven yolks, the light seven whites. Effie had anticipated the need for two separate bowls right from the start, but she cracked the first egg with too much force. Yolk, whites, and shell all ended up a goopy mess in the bowl. She spent several minutes scooping out bits of shell and broken yolk.

With the next egg she was more careful, calling to mind how Mrs. Kinyon would crack the egg in two, tipping the yolk back and forth between the two halves while letting the whites drip down into the bowl. In all, she managed to cleanly separate four of the yolks from their whites with only a little mixing between the others. Good thing she'd started straightaway after church. Already the baking process was taking longer than anticipated.

Cinnamon, allspice, nutmeg, cream of tartar, soda, flour, and the dark part of the cake was done. Effie started then on the egg whites. *Beat to a stiff froth,* Mrs. Neale had said. Effie stirred until her arm ached. She sat down on a stool and stirred some more. The egg whites turned cloudy and frothed but never achieved a consistency one might call stiff.

She gave up on account of the time and added the sugar, butter, and cream. As she measured out the flour, her nose began to itch. Her hands were far too sticky, however, to fish around in her pocket for her hankie. She'd sifted out her last cup when a sneeze caught her. Flour billowed around her like gun smoke, settling on her blouse, her eyelashes, even her tongue.

Fi donc! She wiped her face on her sleeve, dirtying the fabric further, and cursed again. Already she was running late and now she'd have to change. She gave the mixture a quick stir and grabbed a cake pan from the far shelf. *Pour alternating layers of light and dark into pan, then draw a knife through.*

Effie glowered down at her writing. How deep should each layer be? How many layers in total? Why hadn't she the sense to ask when taking down the instructions? Too late now. Without Mrs. Neale around to clarify, Effie decided on six.

She did her best to pour an even third from each bowl into the cake pan. The dark batter was thick and lumpy, dropping into the pan in clumps. The light proved overly wet, running from the bowl almost like water.

When she'd scraped both bowls clean and drawn a knife through the batter, the contents looked more like mud than marbled cake mix. But a quick lick of the knife gave her hope. Sweet and cinnamony. She opened the oven and tested the heat with her hand as she'd seen Mrs. Kinyon do. Warm like noontime in July, but not hot enough to cook a cake. She put the pan in anyway and closed the dampers to the chimney flue to increase the heat. Mrs. Neale had said to bake for forty minutes. An hour might be better on account of temperature.

As she gathered up the dirty bowls, cups, and spoons, her thoughts strayed to Samson. Had he missed her with the same ferocity she'd missed him in the days they'd been apart? She imagined him turning out his pockets for a second piece of cake. She filled the sink with hot water drawn from the stove and heaped in the sticky dishes.

After they'd made love she could have lain atop those cotton bales forever in perfect contentment. How the stars glimmered, their brilliance no longer dampened by the moon's jealous light. How soothing the steady whisper of his breath beside her. But how quickly quotidian concerns bullied into her head. Her dress, already filthy from the stockyard and jail, now had additional stains to tend. Best get it soaking before the blood had a chance to set. And were those stirring seagulls or voices she heard from farther down the dock? The breeze kicked up again, turning her sweat-kissed skin to gooseflesh.

She'd sat up then and buttoned her blouse. *I've got to get home and ready for work,* had been her excuse. To which Samson had enquired what she did. Had it been horror that flashed across his handsome face when she reminded him she worked as an embalmer? Or merely surprise? Not horror, no. She'd told him the whole of it, from her earliest days in the Union camp fetching water and clean bandages, to her later apprenticeship in Indiana. He understood how she'd come to such an uncommon profession. He must.

Effie worked the soap into a lather and set to scrubbing the bowls and spoons. Horror or no, seeing the lovely cake she'd made would set his mind at ease, prove she could do womanly things too. She pushed her sleeves above her elbows and plunged her hands into the warm water. The scent of soap mingled with that of allspice and molasses. She tried to reel her thoughts back to the present, to focus on the scrubbing and scouring, the feel of the water against her skin, the quiet pop of the soap bubbles. But cleaning dishes demanded far less of her attention than baking had.

She ought to have told Adeline about her night with Samson. Adeline would have instructed her just how to behave at the baseball match to further things along. But there was something oddly delicious about the secret of it. That the night belonged only to her and Samson. She alone knew the feel of his hands—soft yet calloused from his years of toil. His whisperings belonged solely to her ears. His scent—that of shaving soap, and hair balm and sweat and smoke. . . . Smoke?

Effie spun round to the stove. Wisps of smoke curled from behind the oven door and beneath the top covers. When she unlatched the door, a black cloud spilled out into the kitchen and with it a bloom of heat that stung Effie's cheeks. She scrambled about the kitchen, throwing open drawers and cupboards in search of an oven mitt. Nothing but teacups and ladles and knives and skimmers. An apple corer, a pie crimper, a cherry pitter, a spice grater. Oh, hell! She'd have to just use her skirts.

With the fabric bunched about her hands, she reached into the hot oven.

"Lordy, Effie!"

Meg's voice made her stop and turn around.

"You's about to burn a hole clear through your hands. Here." She moseyed from the doorway to the smoking stove, grabbing two thick potholders from pegs beside the flue.

A black crust covered the top of the cake when Meg pulled it out. She dropped the pan on the table and shook out her hands. "Sweet Mary and Joseph! What you doing cookin' at such a heat?"

"Do you think it's ruined?"

"Like perfume in a pisspot, it is."

"What if I just cut off the burnt layer? Underneath should be fine, right? It couldn't have been in the oven for more than twenty minutes."

Meg pursed her lips and grabbed a knife from one of the drawers Effie had flung wide. She chipped away at the charred surface, revealing a dry, crumbly layer beneath. "Puts me more in mind of the hardtack them soldiers done ate during the War than cake."

Even in her distress, Effie couldn't help but smile at so apt a description. She'd lost more than one baby tooth biting into the stuff. "Perhaps the middle is salvageable."

Meg excavated farther, but the center proved nothing but a gooey, brown mess. "What sort of cake were you bakin', anyhow?"

"Marble."

"Don't look much marbled to me. And it didn't rise none either. Did you sift together all the dry ingredients before adding the wet ones?"

Had she? Effie grabbed the instructions. "Mrs. Neale didn't say to do that."

"Probably 'cause she rightly expected you to know." Meg turned back to the stove. "And you've got the dampers all the way closed. No wonder it burned." She shook her head. "You's smart as the dickens, Effie, but ain't got a lick of mother wit."

Nearby church bells chimed noon. Effie had little better than an hour and a half to get to City Park. She grabbed the pan and the knife. Some part of the cake must be edible. She started slowly, the way Meg had done, chipping away layer by brittle layer. Who would eat such rubbish? It wasn't worth a penny! She stabbed the knife through the burnt brick of a cake, striking the tin bottom. Then stabbed again, and again. Samson would think her the worst cook ever if he tasted this. Why, he'd spit it out and laugh. But she couldn't go to the baking sale empty-handed. What would he think of her then? She threw down the knife and upended the pan, shaking in the hopes that what fell out might miraculously resemble a cake.

"Effie, dear . . . Effie!" Meg grabbed hold of the pan and wrenched it from Effie's hands. "It's all right. You can just bake another. I'll help."

"I haven't the time or the compo—ingredients." She bent over, planting her elbows on the table and enmeshing her fingers through her frazzled hair. Who was she fooling anyhow? She couldn't bake. She could barely churn butter. Meg was right, she hadn't any common sense. All those afternoons when Mrs. Kinyon had called her to help in the kitchen—why hadn't she paid attention? She'd thought Mrs. Kinyon did it to punish her, thought the woman believed her suited for naught but domestic drudgery on account of her race and sex. Perhaps instead she'd been trying to help, to teach Effie something truly useful.

"Let's see what you've got left here. Molasses, sugar . . ."

Effie kept her head lowered, staring at the flour-dusted tabletop as Meg listed what odds and ends remained. Allspice, soda, milk.

"Go fetch four eggs from the coop and a lemon from the pantry. We'll borrow a little ginger and some flour—"

"But Mrs. Neale—"

"Mrs. Neale won't mind none. Everyone knows she's a soft spot for you on account of you reading her psalms to her. Stop your moping now and git."

"These ginger cakes are *délicieux,* Miss Effie."

"I . . . um . . ." Effie's gaze broke with Mrs. Carrière's, taking refuge in the adjoining field. The baseball match was under way, the men's trousers rolled to their knees and caps shading their eyes.

"Especially for one who professes not to bake," Mrs. Carrière said with a faint smile as she arranged the wares at their makeshift stand. Her composure had returned since the dreadful day of the Grant Parish case decision. So too, it seemed, had her shrewdness.

"I . . . er . . . a friend helped me. It's her recipe."

"Is that lemon peel I taste?"

Effie nodded. She'd grated it in herself while Meg did practically everything else. She'd bustled out of the house and onto the streetcar with the cakes still hot in their pans. Only then did she realize she'd forgotten to change her dress and remake her hair.

Hopefully the customers lining up at their stand didn't notice. And Samson. Hopefully he wouldn't either when he took a break from the match and came to taste their wares.

She watched him from the corner of her eye while she made change for the customers. A dusty path had been worn into the newly green grass in the shape of a square. Samson loitered around one of the vertices, facing inward toward the man at the middle who tossed the ball at the man farther on with the stick. The sport seemed a lurching one. Fits of action followed by great lulls. Banter was the only constant—hoots and jibes and cheers—lobbed not only between players, but from the spectators as well.

She gathered that after a player struck the ball, he was able to progress around the square, stopping at each vertex, sometimes momentarily, sometimes for several minutes. Great fanfare greeted him once he made it all the way around, though it hardly seemed deserving for such a trivial accomplishment.

Nevertheless, she enjoyed the freedom to stare in Samson's direction. He was so alive. He brought the same passion and animation he displayed speechifying atop that banana box to the field—smiling and laughing one minute, grimacing and hollering the next. He jumped and stomped and clapped and wheeled his arms, though what any of this had to do with the game she wasn't sure.

When Jonah bounded over for a jar of lemonade, Effie offered him a ginger cake in exchange for a more thorough explanation of the sport.

"What'd ya wanna know, Miss Effie?"

"What's the objective?"

"Objective?"

"The goal, the purpose."

He crammed half the cake into his mouth and spoke while chewing. "Ain't you ever seen a baseball match before?"

"Don't talk with your mouth full," Mrs. Carrière said, then to Effie, "Surely they have clubs up North."

"Bet your boots they do!" Jonah said, quickly swallowing. "You've got the St. Louis Blue Stockings, the Chicago Uniques, the Cleveland . . ."

The line of customers had dwindled, and Effie took the opportunity to sit a moment on the grass beside their stand. Jonah plopped down beside her, lemonade sloshing in his jar. The twisted boughs of an oak shaded them from the afternoon sun. He finished the ginger cake with another two bites, licking his fingers clean when Mrs. Carrière turned away to help a customer. "That man there, with the ball, he's the pitcher. He throws the ball for the batsman to hit."

"With his stick."

"It's called a bat, Miss Effie," he said as if the nomenclature ought to be obvious.

"With his bat."

"Then he runs to first base, second if he can, while the others try to field the ball. Sometimes he'll make it all the way around. That's called a home run."

Effie nodded, though it seemed little more sensible than when she'd understood nothing.

"If a fielder catches the ball, that's a hands out. Three hands out and it's the other team's turn to bat."

"They play on teams?"

His frown answered in the affirmative. "Sheesh, you don't know nothin'."

"Hush now, Jonah," Mrs. Carrière said, still tending the stand, but close enough to hear their conversation. "Miss Effie knows a lot of things."

"Like what?"

"I can name every bone in the human body. The muscles, the organs—"

"What's this one?" He pointed at his forearm.

"The lower arm has two bones actually, the ulna and the radius."

"And this?" He jabbed a finger at his thigh.

"The femur."

He yanked off his boot, leaned back, and raised his foot. His big toe peeked through a hole in his sock.

"There are twenty-six bones in the human foot. The navicular bone, the cuboid bone, five metatarsi—"

"*Ma foi,* Jonah," Mrs. Carrière said. "I told you not to wear those socks until I'd had a chance to darn them! And put your boot back on. Miss Effie doesn't want to smell your stinky foot."

He drew his foot to his nose. "It don't—"

Eh! was all Mrs. Carrière had to say for Jonah to pull on his boot. "How come you know so much about bones?"

Effie opened her mouth. Closed it again. Perhaps this was one of those moments it best to smile and nod. Or tell one of those lies Mrs. Kinyon insisted was not really a lie because people needn't know everything about you and death wasn't a topic for polite conversation. But this was hardly teatime in some stuffy parlor. Besides, Jonah was an orphan. Surely he knew about death.

Then again, such a discussion might upset Mrs. Carrière, remind her yet again of her husband. She seemed her usual stoic self today, no tears or hysteria. But best not—

"Miss Effie works for an undertaker. She's an embalmer," Mrs. Carrière said. "Do you know what that is?"

Jonah shook his head. Mrs. Carrière nodded at Effie.

Did she really mean for Effie to explain? No one had ever asked that of her before. Not in earnest. She turned to Jonah, who'd scooted close and gazed up at her. She brushed a spot of flour from her skirt, readjusted her bonnet to shield her eyes from the afternoon sunlight that stole between the fluttering leaves. Suddenly she cared very much if she said the wrong thing or spoke too bluntly.

"When a person dies . . . their body . . . begins to putrefy."

"What does that mean?"

Effie glanced over her shoulder at Mrs. Carrière, who was too busy showing off the different types of pie to be of any help.

"Spoil."

"Like old meat?"

"Precisely. An embalmer's job is to arrest the putrefaction process, that is to say, stop the body from spoiling."

"How?"

Effie shifted. The downy grass felt suddenly hard and prickly. "I inject an admixture of chemicals into one of the main blood vessels and pump it throughout the body so that it can seep into all the tissues."

"You cut them open?"

"A small cut"—she gestured to the underside of her arm below the armpit—"usually right here if I'm able. Otherwise here." She drew her finger down the side of her neck.

His little nose wrinkled and brows pinched together. "Eew. Is there blood?"

"Not much. The blood coagulates . . . er . . . clumps together when the heart stops, so the process isn't all that messy."

"Oh." His shoulders slumped at this.

Had she said too much?

But then he smiled. "What about all the guts inside the belly? What do you do with those?"

Effie couldn't help but smile too. She explained about thoracic injection to preserve the organs and cases where more extreme measures might need to be taken. Jonah all but clambered onto her lap to listen. She'd just begun to describe how the ancient Egyptians used to embalm their dead by pulling out their brains through their noses when Mrs. Carrière cleared her throat. "Perhaps you ought to finish telling Miss Effie about baseball."

By the fifth inning, Effie was a baseball expert. Jonah refilled his lemonade jar and skipped back to the diamond—it wasn't a square after all—and she returned to her duties at the cash box just as a new crowd swelled around the stand. By the seventh inning, they'd sold nearly all their wares, netting $31.16 for the Aid Society. Many of the players had sauntered over between turns at bat for lemonade and a slice of pie. Samson was not one of them.

He'd seen her not long after she'd arrived and smiled, returning her wave with a nod from where he stood at second base. But he didn't come over when his turn in the field was done. Nor after the next turn or the next. His gaze seemed to favor the ball and runners, even the dirt and grass, above her and the bake stand. She wrapped up the last ginger cake for him and stowed it in her basket before it could be sold along with the remaining biscuits, pralines, and the final slice of Mrs. Carrière's apple pie.

When Tom, who'd spent the game between the batsman and the catcher in the role of—what had Jonah called it?—the umpire, called the match, the sun yet shone bright in the westerly sky. Samson's team had won twelve runs to ten and they celebrated with a loud whoop. Samson hugged the pitcher, lifting him clear off the ground. The catcher tossed his gloves into the air. Mr. Elliott, who she'd spied playing left field, hoisted Jonah onto his shoulders and paraded him around. Meanwhile, the spectators, hitherto standing beyond the foul line or seated deep in the outfield, swarmed around them, eager to join in the back-slapping and cheers, and more eager still to collect their winnings from the bookmakers who'd loitered about soliciting bets during the match.

Effie helped Mrs. Carrière pack up the club's banner and dismantle the trestle table they'd used for the baking sale, all the while eyeing Samson. His sweat-shined skin and flushed cheeks reminded her of their lovemaking, and her own cheeks blazed at the thought. Several women milled among the crowd, twirling parasols or batting fans. They smiled and laughed with the players in the coy way she'd seen Adeline do. None was as lovely or skilled as Adeline, but they succeeded in stealing Samson's attention every time he seemed ready to look or move in Effie's direction.

What did they say that made him so readily chuckle? Was it their prettily made hair or colorful Sunday dresses that commanded his attention? One of them, a dark girl with big eyes and a dainty nose, proved so bold as to take his arm while chattering in his ear. Watching this, Effie felt as if someone had slit her open and stirred around her insides in the manner Jonah had assumed she did with the dead.

"Effie."

Mrs. Carrière's voice startled her.

"Are those the last of them?" Mrs. Carrière nodded toward the clutch of sticky lemonade jars in Effie's arms.

"Oh . . . ah . . . yes." She packed the jars into a crate and heaved it onto the waiting cart. Was that strumpet still holding fast to Samson's arm? Still leaning close as if she had some great secret for his ears alone? Effie didn't want to know and yet was desperate to look. Mrs. Carrière, however, stepped between her and the crowd.

"I'm much indebted for your kindness the other night after that meeting at the Republican Office. Seeing me home, returning to fetch Jonah. So I hope you'll take this as it's meant, in a maternal sort of way." She paused, and it was all Effie could do to keep her eyes from straying toward the field. "I've noticed the particular fondness you show toward Mr. Greene."

The mention of his name snared Effie's attention. What had she done to betray her feelings? Surely Mrs. Carrière didn't know they'd been intimate. She couldn't know. That was impossible—well, not in the strictest sense of the word, but entirely improbable. Did she suspect, though?

Effie couldn't think what to say to refute Mrs. Carrière's hypothesis. Even her silence felt incriminating.

"I caution you against such feelings, Effie. Mr. Greene is a good man. A great man. And I'm not so very old as to be blind to his charm and good looks. But some men don't make for suitable husbands and I fear Mr. Greene is one of them."

Temptation proved too great, and she glanced above Mrs. Carrière's head, fighting a surge of panic when she no longer spied Samson or the doe-eyed woman in the crowd. She made to step around, but Mrs. Carrière gently clasped her arm. "*Si tu plaît,* Effie, listen. I've seen other girls, far less . . . delicate than you lose their hearts to him and get nothing but sorrow in return. He doesn't mean to—"

Effie pulled free of her grasp. Delicate? She'd survived three years in a Union camp and worse in that slave pen. She wasn't delicate. And Samson did care for her. He must. Mrs. Carrière hadn't seen the burn in his eyes or felt the urgency of his kiss that night on the levee. "You're right. You're not my mother. So I'd thank you to keep your maternal advice to yourself."

She brushed past her and into the thinning crowd. Tom called her name, but she feigned not to hear. He'd bought three of her ginger cakes and complimented her after each bite, but she couldn't muster even a smile for that now. Mr. Elliott touched her elbow and enquired how she fared. She turned away without reply, frantic now to find Samson.

He must be here still. Surely he'd not have left without so much as a hello and goodbye.

She wound through the crowd again. And again. And again.

He had left. He was gone.

She sat down on a bench a little way off and shoved the entire ginger cake she'd saved for him into her mouth. She chewed and swallowed without tasting. Then she took the streetcar back into town, disembarking two stops early to retch alongside the tracks.

CHAPTER 22

——⊱•⊰——

Effie awoke to a pinging sound against her window. Had she been dreaming? It called to mind the sound of hail. Another ping, this one so sharp she expected the glass to be cracked when she pulled back the curtain. No crack. No hail either. A gibbous moon shone in the sky above. Below on the street, a flit of movement caught her eye. A man?

Samson.

She half thought to yank the curtain closed and return to bed. After Sunday's game, she'd vowed not to see him again and subject herself to more heartbreak. But even from this distance, she could tell something in his aspect was amiss. She raised the sash and climbed out onto the gallery.

When he saw her, the deep-set furrows bracketing his mouth slackened.

"Effie, thank God, we need your help."

She leaned over the wrought-iron railing and hissed down at him, "Shh! If my landlady catches you here, she'll toss me out."

He came to stand directly beneath her and lowered his voice. "You've got to come straightaway. I'll explain everything on the way." His upturned face looked gray and haggard in the moonlight. His eyes were bloodshot, his chin covered in stubble.

Effie hesitated. What help could he possibly need of her in the middle of the night? Did he think her some trifle? Someone he could bed when he wanted and ignore when he did not? But Samson hadn't come for an amorous liaison. Effie could see that plain in his expression, hear it in the thinness of his voice. "I've got to dress. Wait for me across the street."

"Bring your embalming tools."

Her tools? Whatever for? But then, there could be only one answer. Had something happened to Tom or Jonah? To Mrs. Carrière? Effie's insides shriveled. How rude she'd been at the baseball match when last they'd spoke.

Samson must have read the distress in her expression. "It's no one you know. But please, Effie, hurry."

"I've got my scalpel and pump, but I'll need preserving fluid from the shop."

"Have you a key?"

She did, but what if Mr. Whitmark woke to the rattle of the gate or the pad of her footfalls across the courtyard?

"We'll stop there on the way," he said before she could answer.

Effie crept back through her window and shrugged out of her nightshirt. She'd washed her stockings that evening and hung them over the back of her chair to dry. It mustn't be that late then—eleven o'clock, maybe midnight—for the cotton was yet damp when she tugged them on beneath her dress.

Samson waited for her across the street, shadowed from the flickering streetlights by the wide boughs of an oak tree, pacing and muttering. Tucked into his waistband was a gun. When she told him the location of Whitmark's shop, he took her hand and ran there—not so fast she couldn't keep up, but fast enough her lungs soon strained against the steel ribbing of her corset. Rats squeaked and scampered up drainpipes and across darkened roofs at the sound of her and Samson's feet atop the banquette. Condensation dripped from cottage eves and townhouse balconies. Otherwise the city slept.

On Julia Street just before crossing Magazine, Samson pulled her into the shadowy lee of a doorway as a policeman sauntered past. Flush against the cold wood, she struggled to quiet her ragged breathing. What was Samson about that he needed to carry a gun and hide from the police? His palm was hot and sticky against hers. His temporal vein pulsed quick and steady. Once the officer was gone from sight, Samson tugged her onward.

When they arrived, the new lettering painted in block script across the storefront window shone in the lamplight: GEO. WHITMARK, UNDERTAKER. Behind the glass, the new model caskets and funeral plumes lay in darkness.

Effie glanced down the street in both directions. Empty. She inspected the shuttered French doors and windows on the stories above. Not a glimmer of light between the louvers. Even so, she hesitated. What excuse would she offer should Mr. Whitmark catch her sneaking in—or worse, sneaking out with jars of embalming fluid?

Beside her, Samson shifted his weight from foot to foot and held his pocket watch up to the lamplight. She fished in her skirt pocket for the key to the carriageway gate. It slipped her grasp as she pulled it out and landed with an echoing clank on the brick pavers at her feet. Effie winced. Three times she tried before fitting the key into the hole.

She cracked open the gate and slipped in, Samson behind her.

"Wait here," she whispered. If Mr. Whitmark awoke, her own presence perchance she could explain. But Samson's? Impossible. She tiptoed down the carriageway and across the moonlit courtyard to the storeroom. The windows on this side of the house were naked of their shutters, a few cracked open to catch the night's breeze.

Last week she'd seen Colm tinkering around the shop with an oilcan at Mr. Whitmark's bidding. But the storeroom door screeched as she opened it, a sharp, high-pitched sound loud enough to wake the dead. Of all the hinges that lout could forget to oil. She froze and listened, expecting to hear footfalls from the house, the door onto the gallery opening, a shout or the cocking of a pistol. But no sounds came.

Effie groped her way to the back of the storeroom. She knew the layout well enough to keep from knocking over the cooling board or stubbing her toe on the workbench. When her hands found the cold, smooth jars of fluid she realized she'd forgotten to ask Samson about the body. Was it that of a man or woman? An adult or child? What had been the cause of death? All this had bearing on the amount of embalming fluid she'd need.

She pulled out several jars, rearranging what remained so it wouldn't be immediately obvious any had been taken. Not that Mr. Whitmark would notice. He rarely ventured into the storeroom and still relied on her for most of the accounting. Colm paid little mind to anything. She could clear out the entire room without arousing his curiosity. Even so, best not to invite questions. She packed the jars into a traveling case, padding them with strips of linen to keep the glass from clanking. Cotton, court plaster, wax, eye caps, and a small can of white lead filled the remaining crannies.

The door whined again as she closed it behind her. This time Effie didn't wait to see whether the noise might wake Mr. Whitmark, but skirted the edge of the courtyard, keeping to the shadows until she reached the cover of the carriageway. Safe from view, her jittering pulse slowed but did not steady. Even though she intended to replace the supplies, she felt like a thief.

Samson checked to be sure the street was empty before they locked the gate and set to running again. He carried both the traveling case and her embalming cabinet, but still she struggled to keep up, her skirt and petticoat caging her strides.

Not until they reached the levee did Samson slow. The docks were far busier at this time of night than they'd been when she and Samson had dallied on the cotton stacks in the hours just before dawn. Sailors staggered back from the nearby saloons and gambling dens. Roustabouts crouched together shooting dice. Women, whose brightly colored dresses matched the rouge smeared across their cheeks, sauntered on the arms of men off to dark corners.

Effie slowed and watched one such couple disappear into the berth of a small boat. She felt suddenly dirty. Had her and Samson's encounter been so different? After the way he'd all but scorned her at the baseball match, she wasn't sure. No money had been exchanged. And she loved him, even if his feelings were less true. Yet she couldn't shake her affinity with the woman.

Samson touched her arm. He held both cases in one hand now and looped his free arm about her elbow. Her body reacted with a delicate shiver, her nerves sparking like a lighted wick. Would she ever be immune to his touch?

She pulled free and continued in the direction they'd been going, though still uncertain of their destination.

Large steamers gave way to schooners and tugboats, then to a spattering of skiffs and fishing smacks moored on the pebble-studded shore. She could no longer hear the ruckus from the saloons and dance halls. No longer spied whores and their eager consorts. The slaughterhouses lay just upriver, and the water here carried that familiar stench of death and decay.

A man waved at them from a small rowboat. Samson glanced about, down the winding bend of the levee to the east and then to the west, before hurrying toward the boat. His caution, his silence, his evident agitation gave Effie pause. That part of her still capable of logical assessment warned her against following. But her feet were already picking their way over the rocks behind him.

She recognized the man on the boat from the Republican Office. He helped Samson stow her cases, then clasped his hand with a firm but silent shake. He wore a somber expression much akin to Samson's, one that only deepened when he turned to Effie. "Where's the embalmer you spoke of?"

Samson clambered onto the rowboat. "This is her."

The man frowned. "The body . . . the Regulators did some number on him, Samson. And they're still about. Said they'd whip but good anyone who touched him."

Samson yanked off his hat and wiped the sheen of sweat from his forehead. "Damn it. You might have said."

"I didn't expect you to bring no woman."

Effie stepped onto the boat. "I've worked under worse conditions."

They crossed the river to Algiers and from there traveled by wagon to where the town petered out into swampland. She and Samson sat in the bed. More than once, they'd hidden beneath a dusty canvas at the sound of approaching horses, while the man—Benjamin was his name—made excuses to passersby for his late-night travel.

What had she gotten herself into? Even with Samson close, her body knotted with fear.

"What's going on?" she finally asked when the second band of riders passed.

Samson and Benjamin explained the situation in clipped whispers. A man, a ward comptroller and newly appointed election commissioner, had been murdered after submitting several reports and complaints to Governor Kellogg and the election board. A marauding group of whites, who fashioned themselves Regulators, were to blame, leaving his body to rot in the swamp.

"Why not just retrieve the body and bury it?" she asked.

"That's just what they want, the whole affair to pass away real quiet-like. A midnight burial, or better yet lost to the gators. No body, no fuss."

"Serves double purpose that way," Samson said. "They get to terrorize his family, deny them a proper funeral, make him an example to other colored folks, without it catching the attention of the army or any friends we have left in Washington."

Eventually, they arrived at a small tarpaper shack elevated on rotting wood poles a few feet above the boggy ground. Faded scraps of flannel covered the window holes, and the front door sagged on its hinges.

"This is where he lived?" Effie asked.

"Ain't safe to bring him home," Benjamin said. "Once them Regulators find out the body's gone, you can be sure they'll come a-lookin'."

Samson grabbed her cases, and Benjamin handed her an unlit lantern. "How long you reckon you'll need?"

"I can't say without inspecting the body." She lit the lantern and climbed the worm-eaten steps. Frogs croaked from the nearby waterways, and mosquitos buzzed about her ears. The dead never frightened her, but she found her hand trembling as she reached for the door.

The inside of the shack was bare save for a rusty pail, a length of knotted fishing line, a toppled chair missing several rungs. And the body. It lay atop the unfinished floorboards in the center of the room, bloated with swamp water. Samson, still standing by the wagon, gasped—likely from the smell—but Effie moved farther inside and crouched beside the dead man, holding the lantern aloft.

The man's left orbital socket had been crushed, and the surrounding skin was swollen and discolored. Dried blood had matted in his hair where he'd suffered another blow. His right radial bone was fractured and jutted out a full inch through his skin just above the wrist. She suspected yet more bruising and lacerations lay beneath his torn, wet clothing.

Her comment about having worked under worse conditions now seemed not only glib but inaccurate. Every errant sound from without the shack sent a pulse of fear through her. The men who'd done this, these Regulators, might already be out looking for them. She needn't any imagination to know what they'd do to her and Samson if they found them.

"Well?" Benjamin asked.

The stairs behind her creaked. Samson made a choking sound, then tried to cover it with a cough. When he spoke, his lustrous voice was thin. "Can you help him, Effie?"

She wrangled control of herself and nodded. Though the swampy night air was cold, she shrugged out of her coat and balled it beneath the man's head that gravity might reduce the swelling. Then she stood and faced the men. "I'll need at least four hours, maybe five."

"Best you be gone and across the river before sunup," Benjamin said.

Samson groped in his vest pocket. The brass chain trembled as he opened his watch. "Can you do it in three?"

Effie glanced back at the body. Three hours? Highly improbable. But no use wasting time debating it. She grabbed the rusty bucket and traded it to Samson for her cases. "Water." And then to Benjamin, "A fresh set of clothes."

By the time Samson returned with the water, Effie had already reset the fractured arm and stitched up the skin. The oil lamp cast only a weak glow, but she dared not raise the wick for more light.

Samson laid the pail down beside her, then set to pacing, stopping every few turns to pull the tattered drapes back from the windows and stare into the night.

"I'm going to need your help," she said, as much to silence his footfalls as from true need. "Undress him while I lather the soap."

Samson nodded, but for a moment just stood there, staring down at the body. "I'd thought the War had brought an end to this."

Despair turned his voice into that of a stranger. But what could she say to comfort him that wasn't a lie? "His clothes, Samson."

"Right." He took off his own jacket and cuffed his sleeves before undressing the man.

They washed the body together with nothing but the sound of splashing water and hum of insects to fill the silence. When they'd cleaned away the mud, swamp grass, and dried blood, she tasked Samson to shave the face while she massaged the swelling and sutured the numerous cuts and gashes. The injuries to the man's head required more care: cotton and wax to build up the eye socket and shattered cheekbone, a small incision in the scalp to realign the fractured skull bones.

Samson shrank away as she performed these tasks, sitting in the far corner with his head hung between his drawn-up knees. "How do you do this, Effie?"

"With a basic understanding of the underlying anatomy, it's really not that difficult to—"

"No, I mean, be around death all the time and not . . . not go mad?"

Was that judgment underpinning his words or bewilderment? Either way, the short distance between them—a mere half-dozen feet of weatherworn floorboards—seemed to lengthen. The intimacy they'd shared, the friction of their sweat-slickened skin seemed almost a fantasy.

Sometimes she wondered if she turned her scalpel on herself, if she opened wide her body, what it would look like inside. Would her liver lay to the right, her heart up and to the left, her intestines coiled neatly through her abdomen? Or would there be some physical sign of her sentimental defect, a reason she seemed to see the world differently than everyone else? Perhaps she hadn't organs inside at all. No lungs or spleen. No heart. Only cogs and gears and springs like the inner workings of a clock.

But then, what explained her pride when Meg read an entire paragraph without tripping over a word, her concern when Mrs. Carrière had wept in her arms, her worry that Adeline would settle for Mr. Chauvet and never know love? If she hadn't a heart, what had pained her when Samson left Sunday's baseball match? What pained her still?

"The dead can't hurt you. Only the living can."

"That surgeon, he never should have kept you. War's no place for a girl, a child."

Effie retrieved the jars of embalming fluid from her case. "The smell of this is quite . . . sharp."

He raised his head and regarded her with a queer, glassy-eyed expression, and she had to look away. She feigned attention at connecting the lengths of rubber tubing from jar to syringe and syringe to needle. Her hands were dry and ashy from the soap, the pads of her fingers thick and hardened from years of the same repetitive movements.

Though the incision might show above the collar of whatever shirt Benjamin brought to dress the body, Effie chose the carotid, both for time's sake and to help flush the bruising from the man's face. A sharp intake of breath sounded from the corner when she made the careful cut through skin and fascia.

"It was better than the contraband camps. Or being sent back to whatever plantation I'd run from." She elevated the artery and began the injection. Her back and knees ached from kneeling so long on unforgiving floorboards. Her eyelids tarried shut with each blink. "Anyway, Captain Kinyon didn't do this to me. I was this way when I arrived. He would never have kept me on had I not been so . . . unaffected."

"I'm sorry."

At this, she glanced up and dared meet his eyes again. Sorry for what? Did he mean it in the pitying way? Sorry for the years she'd spent in the surgeon's tent among the dead and dying. For the years of slavery before. Or was it an apology? Sorry for bringing her here amid such danger. Or for leaving the baseball match without taking one bite of the stupid cakes she'd made for him. Perhaps he meant it in the sense of regret. Sorry to have made the acquaintance of one so peculiar, to have kissed her lips, touched her skin, and moved inside her.

Adeline would know which he meant, would be able to read the line of his mouth and subtle tilt of his head. Yet another way Effie was defective. "I—"

The distant howl of dogs silenced her.

"The light, Effie," Samson whispered. "Dampen the light!"

But Effie couldn't move. Every command to her muscles misfired. Even her lungs seemed frozen, suspended mid-exhale. Samson scrambled over and snuffed the lantern.

"It's all right." He scooted up beside her and wrapped an arm around her shoulders, but even that failed to touch her. Another howl and she began to shake. Not a quick twitch or shiver. Not a diminutive tremble. A body-racking shudder. The syringe pump fell from her hand, the resulting clamor disquieting her all the more.

Samson pulled her closer still, caging her against his chest. She could feel the cold steel of the pistol in his waistband, but even this didn't calm her.

"I'm sorry," he said again, but this time her mind could barely latch on to the words, let alone ponder their meaning. He rubbed her arms and stroked her cheek. "They won't find us."

More barking.

Something warm dampened her skirts and spread across her thighs. The smell of urine bloomed in the air. Humiliation rose alongside her terror. She tried to pull away, but Samson's hold didn't slacken, though surely he must have noticed the wetness.

"I never should have dragged you out here. It wasn't fair or right in the slightest."

What was wrong with her? She'd worked beside Captain Kinyon with cannons booming and gun smoke choking the air, the Rebs a half mile away and advancing. She'd survived weeks in that slave pen and who knew what before and after. And this, the howl of dogs across the swamp, incited convulsions and a bodily purge akin to the neurotic fit of a lunatic. If Samson hadn't been repulsed by her before, surely he was now.

She scrunched closed her eyes, tears at the ready should she open them. The self-imposed blackness only agitated her other senses. The savage barking, the loamy smell of the swamp, the cold night air.

Everything else receded.

She was alone.

Panting. Listening. Running.

A root caught her toe. She stumbled forward and splashed into the mud. The footfalls she'd been tracking stopped. She waited for them to start up again, then peeled herself from the ground and scurried after. An arm circled around her waist and a hand clamped over her mouth.

"What the devil you doin' out here, Effie?" Jonesy's resonant voice had an edge of anger.

"I's followin' you."

He shook his head and released her. "Effie."

"You don't want me round no more?"

"That ain't, it's just—"

"What she doin' here?"

The four other men Jonesy had been traveling with had circled back and stood glaring at her.

"Send her back," one whispered.

"She'll slow us down."

"Lead them patrollers right to us."

Jonesy's cross expression held a moment more, then softened. He brushed the mud from her cheek with the pad of this thumb. "I's bringing her along. If you got a problem with dat, you's welcome to go your own way."

The others continued to harrumph, but didn't sass Jonesy further. They walked on together straight through the night. Effie did her best to keep up and didn't complain one peep. When at last her little legs tired, he carried her and still outpaced the other men.

"Where we goin' anyway?" she said, resting her head on his shoulder.

"Someplace better."

She felt the words rumble through his chest as he spoke. Someplace better was fine by her, so long as they were together.

"Effie . . ."

That deep, pleasant rumble.

"Effie!"

She opened her eyes. The walls of the cabin took shape around her, pallid gray in the moonlight. "Someplace better," she whispered, desperate to hold on to the memory, to follow it through to the end.

"What?" Samson said.

It was gone.

The swamps surrounding the cabin had quieted. Her skirts clung damp to her thighs. Death perfumed the air.

"I can do this," she said. "I can finish this." Still shaking, she groped along the dusty floor until she felt the cold metal of her syringe.

"It's all right, Effie. Let it rest. I daren't light the lamp again, anyway."

But she didn't need light. Not for the injection. She fumbled along the tubing until her fingers brushed cool skin. By some miracle, the needle had not been pulled from the artery. At first, she struggled just to close her hand around the pump, but with each squeeze and release the motion grew easier. Her bounding heart slowed. She could do this. Whatever her defects, this she could contribute.

CHAPTER 23

⸻◦⸻

Effie hadn't intended to attend the vigil or the funeral service. Best put that night, with all its humiliations, as far behind her as possible.

Benjamin had arrived back at the tarpaper shack not long before dawn with a fresh set of clothes. By then, Effie had finished the arterial injection, sutured up the wound, and was nearly done filling the thoracic cavity through her long metal trocar. All this she'd done in darkness. Even the gibbous moon had shrank behind the moss-strewn cypress and set. Touch alone guided her.

She'd ridden back to Algiers Point in the bed of the wagon alongside the body, a dusty blanket shrouding it from view. The three of them crowded upfront with the bed seemingly empty would have begged questions. Samson insisted he be the one to ride beside the dead man, but the idea plainly sickened him. Benjamin pointed out it would look more natural for a woman to ride in back and Samson quickly conceded.

Her skirts still damp with urine, Effie hadn't said a word, but climbed into the bed beside the body. It no longer smelled of day-old meat, but faintly of chemicals. Its flesh was cold and hard to the touch.

The sway of the wagon as they started off nearly rocked her tired body to sleep. Her mind, however, would not be lulled. What did it say of her that she could nigh fall asleep beside a corpse? And Samson. Just thinking his name made her head throb. In one night she'd unraveled weeks' worth of effort to fashion herself normal and desirable under his gaze. Even Adeline would concede failure at this point.

But mostly, her thoughts circled around Jonesy. They'd been running away, him and those other men. She knew that somehow, while the rest of the memory remained fuzzy and elusive. The War was on; had they hoped to make it to the Union line? Was that the better place he spoke of? But then, where were they, Jonesy and the others, when she'd stumbled into Captain Kinyon's camp? Where were they now?

Safely across the Mississippi, she, Samson, and Benjamin parted ways, the men with the body to St. Augustine and her home to wash and change before work. She'd walked a short distance along the levee before turning back, just in time to see Samson climb into a new wagon and start off in the opposite direction. The rising sun cast his profile in a jaundiced glow. His cheeks bore a dark shadow of whiskers. His short, coiled hair was in desperate want of oil and a comb. And still he was the handsomest man she knew. The bravest and most committed to his cause. Despite all that had happened, perhaps indeed because of it, she loved him all the fiercer. And it had taken her very last scraps of energy and will to turn away.

For the next two days, New Orleans burned with rumors about the comptroller from the fifteenth ward who'd been murdered. Jacques Guillot. She was glad to learn his name, felt a strange kinship with him. Another break with the captain's rule to maintain her distance.

He'd been trying to protect her, Captain Kinyon, to spare her the heartache death left in its wake. That had been his reasoning, hadn't it? Not simply to engender indifference that she might remain the perfect ward, never demanding affection; the perfect undertaker's assistant, never allowing the messiness of life to interfere with the noble business of death. Either way, he'd failed. She too.

At the Poydras Street market, she heard a fruit seller whisper to a customer that Mr. Guillot had been shot twenty-three times and his body eaten by alligators. The old woman seated in front of Effie on the streetcar told her companion it was the rougarou that done got the body. Harriet informed the other women gathered after supper in the parlor Monsieur Guillot wasn't dead at all but fled to Mexico, and that's why ain't no body been found. Effie bore the gossip in silence, waiting for it to die down, as gossip always did, and allow her to go about forgetting.

She'd taken out her key to lock the carriageway that second evening when she heard a passerby mention Mr. Guillot's name again. This time in connection with a vigil at St. Augustine later that evening. Effie couldn't help herself. She slipped back through the gate and pilfered a few supplies from the storeroom—face powder, black court plaster, and putty darkened with charcoal. She'd started the job, managed the preservation before having to flee with the dawn, but there hadn't been time for cosmetic concerns. If the body was to be on view, she must make it as presentable as possible.

After explaining who she was and why she'd come—first to a prune-faced nun who spoke only French, then to a man with a priest's collar who called himself Père Villeré—she was shown to the sacristy where Mr. Guillot, in a casket of polished walnut, awaited transport to the chapel. When she opened the lid, that pungent, slightly sweet odor of rot wafted upward. It was faint, though, barely noticeable even to her well-trained nose. The incense already being lit in the adjoining hall would soon mask it. With so many contusions to the body, there were bound to be broken vessels, leaving some tissues untouched by her preserving fluid. In truth, Effie was surprised the body did not smell more strongly.

The swelling around his eye had lessened, as had the greenish-purple discoloration. She built the sunken brow bone up with putty, smoothing out the edges until they blended with his marble-hard skin. Then she dusted his entire face with powder. It wasn't quite the right shade—too light for his tawny skin.

Beneath his cravat and collar, wide, unevenly spaced stitches tattooed his neck. Not her best work, but then she'd sewn him up in complete darkness. She concealed them with a strip of black court-plaster just in case his cravat slipped down.

With nothing more to do, she knew she ought to steal away. Already she could hear the hushed voices of those gathering for the vigil. Soon they'd come to move the casket into the chapel. Yet Effie lingered. She fussed with the knot of his cravat, aligned the buttons of his suit just so, licked her palm and smoothed a stray lock of his wavy hair.

Considering the state of the body when she'd arrived at the shack—battered, stiff, and water-logged—she ought to be proud of how well he looked. Instead her nerves were raw. Despite her care to his bruises, her efforts to realign his broken bones, despite the putty and plaster and powder, the violence done to him was inescapable.

"Effie?"

She startled and spun around. Samson stood before her, worrying his hat in his hands. He took a step toward her. "I'd hoped you'd come tonight."

"I didn't come for the vigil, only to ensure the embalming had taken." She shuffled back and sideways, her hip bumping into the casket, her eyes measuring the distance to the door.

"You must stay."

"I'm not . . ." She started to say she wasn't rightly dressed for it, but her black work dress wouldn't allow such a lie. "I'm not Catholic."

"Me neither. Don't matter none."

He reached to take her arm, but she shrank back. How could he want to touch her after that night? He cocked his head and studied her. She felt like an insect on a pinning board beneath his gaze.

"Mr. Guillot's kin would like to say a few words to you, I'm sure. And others. You're a right celebrity."

"Whatever for?"

"For this." He gestured to the body. "For what you did."

Effie frowned and wrung the cords of her purse. "If I'd had a bit more time maybe . . . better lighting . . . The fluid didn't penetrate all his tissues, I'd have to undress him to determine just where, and his orbital bone . . ." Her gaze fell to the floor. She couldn't bear another look at the corpse or Samson. A faded, rust-colored stain showed on the rug. Wine likely, or blood. He moved closer, but she sidestepped his advance, nearly toppling the plume-filled urn beside the casket in her haste.

"Effie"—he raked a hand through his oiled hair—"about the other night."

The incense wafting from the chapel roiled her stomach. Heat flushed beneath her tight collar. She stepped wide around him and hurried to the door. It led to a small interior courtyard. The cool night air was a godsend. Light spilled through the church's stained-glass windows, casting the cracked stone pavers and trembling palm fronds in an anemic glow. Samson followed her, evidently intent on reviving her humiliation. They spoke at the same time.

"You must think me awful—"

"Please, let's not discuss—"

They both stopped. Samson gave a nervous chuckle. Effie bit down on her lip and skirted his gaze.

"Can we sit?" He motioned to a stone bench dappled with pale green moss.

"I've got curfew."

Samson chuckled again, this time full and earnest. "Curfew? On a Saturday? It's not yet seven o'clock." He took her by the hand before she could work out a better lie and tugged her to the bench. "Effie, that night when we . . . at the levee . . . I'm sorry I didn't . . ." He ran his free hand through his hair again then wiped his oil-slickened palm atop his trousers.

It took Effie a moment to shuffle around her thoughts. *That* was the night he wished to speak of? The heat beneath her skin became a burn. She tried to read his expression, a difficult task in the best of lighting, but the slight cock of his head cast his features in shadow. What would Adeline say at such a moment? Again, Effie regretted not confiding in her. "Neither one of us are impervious to nature's imperatives. Mr. Darwin writes in *The Descent of Man* that—"

"Lord! We're not animals, Effie. It wasn't just . . . nature, as you say. But I can see how you might rightly think that how I left things afterward."

Effie looked down at her feet. Her boots were in want of a good polishing, her laces in need of replacing. "I had hoped you might try my ginger cakes. I didn't make them entirely on my own, mind you, but I've since practiced with the oven's dampers and am quite confident—"

He raised her hand to his lips. "You done scared me, Effie Jones. You're too good for me and I know it."

How could he say that? He was a representative in the statehouse, the darling of the Republican Party. Everyone, not only her, coveted his attentions. "That's preposterous."

"See there, that's it. Who else is gonna say something like *pre-*

posterous, or face a band of drilling White Leaguers, or sneak out in the middle of the night to help bring peace to the soul of a man she doesn't even know."

Effie pulled her hand away. "But that night I . . . I don't know what came over me. That howling . . ." Even now, at the mere remembrance of the sound, her pulse sputtered. She let the silence dangle between them a moment that he might call to mind just how unbeseeming her reaction had been. When he didn't stand and leave, she said, "Something's not right with me."

"You sure are different than most womenfolk. Knew that about you straightaway."

Effie looked up at the glowing stained glass seated in the stucco wall opposite them. White saints draped in blue and red tunics stared back at her. Their expressions seemed plaintive and despairing. A piano began to play. "Best get inside or you'll miss the vigil."

He pulled back her hand, but she held steady the gaze of the saints. "Look at me, Effie. You got such pretty eyes."

No one had ever described her that way—not her eyes, or her too-big feet, or too-curly hair. Few people remarked on her at all—save for her unruly tongue—as if she were more a specter than a flesh and blood being.

"I know it's not the proper time for such discussion, but, well, I was hoping you might consider being my wife."

Effie blinked and turned to face him. The piano's slow, strident dirge had swelled to mezzo forte, and surely she'd misheard him. "What?"

"My wife. I wanna marry you, Effie." Her face must have telegraphed her confusion for he hastily followed with, "You don't need to decide straightaway. Think on it some."

Thoughts pinged helter-skelter in her brain. The women from the saloon and baseball match. Mrs. Carrière's warning. "You needn't ask just because we—"

"That ain't it. You're a good woman, Effie. Smart and brave. We care about the same things, come from the same bedeviled past. We make sense together."

They made sense together. A sound-minded assessment. "I see."

"Is that a yes?"

Effie didn't reply. Of course she wanted to marry him. Couldn't remember wanting anything more deeply in her whole life. But something gave her pause. She ought to rejoice that he'd come to so dispassionate a decision. Marriage was far too important a matter to decide based on emotions. Yet however sensible a union between them might be, she wished he'd said simply, I love you.

"I did something to show you how earnest my intentions are." He reached into his vest pocket, pulled out a folded piece of paper, and handed it to her.

Effie let go his hand and unfolded the paper. *Mr. A. P. Saulnier, St. James Parish,* was all that was written.

"What's this?"

"I asked my friend at the records office to look into your sale. He couldn't find a deed for your original sale to that trader on Common Street. But he found the name of the man who bought you afterward, this Mr. Saulnier."

Effie stared at the letters scrawled on the paper.

"He was a sugar planter," Samson continued. "And word is, a real breaker. That don't bode well for your friend Jonesy."

The paper seemed to burn in her hand. Part of her wanted to wad it up and hurl it across the courtyard. Part of her wanted to cry out with joy. Instead she folded it neatly along the crease and tucked it into her purse alongside the too-light face powder and charcoal-colored putty. "Thank you."

"St. James isn't but sixty miles upriver. I already talked to Tom— I hope you don't mind—he's got business out that way for the office. Said we could come along. A visit might spark your memory. And someone about those parts is bound to know something."

Her nausea had returned, faint but unsettling. Did she really want to remember more? If this Mr. Saulnier were a slave breaker, maybe it was better to let that time lie. The dirge was over and the piano silent. A man's voice sounded from the chapel. Though she couldn't make out the words, his sorrow and fury rang clear. Mr. Guillot's brother perhaps. His father. A son. Who would speak of Effie when she joined the dead?

"Yes."

"Yes?"

"I mean, I'm amenable to the idea of traveling with you and Tom to find this Mr. Saulnier."

Samson's smile dampened but didn't break. He glanced down a moment, then back to her eyes. "And my other proposal?"

"I . . . I'll think on it."

Effie attended the funeral the following morning, Samson by her side. They sat toward the rear of the church with Tom and the other Protestants. Mrs. Carrière knelt with her rosary beads in her family's pew near the front. Little Jonah, spick-and-span in his Sunday suit, squirmed beside her. Mr. Elliott, Benjamin, and several others from the ward club and Republican Office were there, standing along the walls and spilling into the aisles when the pews filled. Men and women continued to press in even as the church bell tolled and the music began—freedmen, Creoles, even a few whites.

More than once, heads turned in Effie's direction. Gazes lingered. People she didn't know pointed and whispered. She checked that her hat hadn't fallen askew and all her buttons were fastened.

Perhaps they were staring at Samson. He was a state representative after all and easily the most handsome man in the chapel. But then an old woman in the pew in front of her turned around and reached her wrinkled hand in Effie's direction. Effie hesitated, looking about to be sure the woman hadn't meant to reach for someone else before taking her hand. The woman's skin was thin and fragile as an insect's wing. She squeezed Effie's fingers and gave a solemn nod.

"I told you you're famous now," Samson whispered.

"How does everyone know?"

"Word gets round."

Her stomach tightened. "But Mr. Whitmark, if he finds out I took the embalming fluid without license, the wax and eye caps—"

"No one here gonna say a word to no white man."

Effie shifted on the hard pew. How could he be sure? She'd already replaced the used jars of fluid, filling each with a splash from the remaining stock until they all looked more or less full. Still, she suddenly itched to go back to the storeroom, to double-check each jar, to make sure she hadn't left anything in suspicious order.

Samson took hold of her hand. "When I was a slave back on the plantation, a big ol' buck by the name Gus stole a melon from Massa's garden. No little one either, but the fattest in the whole patch. He and some other fellas ate every bite, down to the rind. Now we was over a hundred slaves on that plantation and every one of us knew about the melon. But when Massa asked, under threat of the lash, mind you, who'd taken it, not one slave said nothing."

She glanced at Tom, seated at Samson's left, for further reassurance. Hitherto he'd seemed engaged in their conversation, listening and nodding, but he'd since turned away. He sat now with great stiffness, his gaze fixed on the distant wall. Was it simple grief, or had something Samson said offended him?

Just before the service began, a handsomely dressed couple squeezed into the third row from the front. A black lace veil obscured the woman's face, but Effie immediately recognized Adeline's graceful carriage.

How did she know the deceased? She'd never made mention of anyone from across the river. Perhaps Mr. Chauvet, seated close beside her, had some acquaintanceship with him. It seemed an odd time to introduce her at last to Samson, but when might their worlds overlap again?

When at last the mass concluded the congregation shuffled forward to the open casket. Many touched the body, laying-on their hands or bending down to kiss the cheek or forehead. The attendants had laid out the casket so the more battered side of Mr. Guillot's face showed away from the crowd. Still, up close they couldn't help but see, a fact made plain in their tight expressions and skittish eyes.

Again Effie felt she'd failed him. She'd seen his wife in the front pew, two small children, and wished she might have left them a better likeness. They ought to have closed the casket. Mr. Whitmark would have advised so. No need to see. But those passing down the side aisle after viewing nodded at her as the old woman had, solemn but appreciative. They'd wanted to see, to bear witness and say goodbye.

Outside, more than a dozen carriages lined the street to travel in the cortege to the cemetery. A brass band wet their reeds and tuned their instruments. A wagon draped in black crepe bunting awaited the casket, with plumes and flowers overflowing the sides.

"Not even your Mr. Whitmark would hire out his hearse when he learned who it was for," Samson whispered. "Thought you said he was a Union man. A Republican."

"He is," Effie said. At least, he had been.

Building gray clouds wrestled with the midday sun, its light by turns bright, then muted. The air was heavy with last night's rain, and insects buzzed above lingering puddles on the uneven road.

As always in a crowd, people seemed to gravitate toward Samson, clapping him on the back and shaking his hand.

"Damn near four hundred people turned out, I reckon," one man said.

Samson turned his gaze to the sea of mourners awaiting the procession. "At least."

"Heard you managed this," another said.

"Only helped where I could." He moved a step closer to Effie and rested his hand on the small of her back. Her lungs floundered a moment before recalling how to expand and contract.

"Others wouldn't dare it," the first man said. "And what's this I hear about a colored undertaker?"

Samson smiled and nodded toward Effie.

"I'll be. And a woman to boot!" The man grabbed her hand, shaking it with such vigor her entire arm wagged. "Didn't right believe it when I heard."

The other man followed suit. And another. Effie tried to smile and not wriggle at the feel of their chapped skin against her own.

Then a white man with a small pad and chewed pencil approached them. "You Representative Greene?"

"I am."

"Bud Langdon with the *Natchez Gazette*."

"They send you all the way down here to cover this here funeral?" one of the men asked him.

"No, actually I was here reporting on yesterday's races, but I saw the crowd on my way to breakfast and thought I'd take a gander." He turned back toward Samson. "They say you're the man to talk to."

"The crowd you see gathered is here to honor the passing of a great man, Mr. Jacques Guillot," Samson paused, eyeing the man's blank pad. "That's G-U-I-L-L-O-T."

"Right," the reporter said, and started writing.

"A rice merchant by trade, father to two little boys, and a stalwart Republican. Appointed just last year comptroller to the fifteenth ward. It was for that, you see, and the color of his skin that a band of

White Leaguers across the river ran him down, beat him dead, and left his body to rot in the swamps."

The man's hand flagged. He took off his hat and mopped his brow.

"That make you uncomfortable, Mr. Langdon?"

"No, it's just"—he glanced at Effie—"perhaps you might leave off some of the unseemlier details."

Samson's nostrils flared and his hand slid from her back to about her waist, pulling her closer. "You think just 'cause she's a woman she's been spared the horrors done our race? The details are important, Mr. Langdon."

The other men around nodded.

"How do you know it wasn't just some accident? Maybe the man—"

"Mr. Guillot."

"Mr. Guillot just fell off his horse and knocked his head."

Samson turned to one of the men. "They bring the casket out yet?"

"Don't think so."

"Perhaps you'd like to go see for yourself. No fall could crush a man's skull like that."

The reporter's pale, freckled skin turned greenish. "No, that's not necessary." He gestured at the crowd. "But why all this . . . pomp."

"Mr. Guillot was well-liked throughout the city," the first man who'd shaken Effie's hand said. "A free man before the War and his pa too. Family's been in New Orleans for generations."

"Yes, but this? You expect me to believe they do this for every well-liked nigg—Negro in these parts?"

"The White Leaguers who killed Mr. Guillot forbade his family, under threat of violence, from going out to retrieve the body," Samson said. "We gather today to honor a great man and to send a message that we will not be intimidated or let murders like this go unnoticed."

"Speaking of that, I heard rumors a local undertaker helped some with the body."

Effie's insides plummeted.

Samson responded without pause, his expression unflapped, his voice steady. "I don't know anything about that. Likely just as you say, a rumor."

Mr. Langdon looked at the other men, who, only minutes before, had been wagging Effie's hand. They shrugged and shook their
heads. "You heard tell of that, Benji?" one asked another.

"Not me? You, Pete?"

"Nah, sir."

Mr. Langdon tucked his pencil behind his ear and started to close
his notebook. "What makes you so sure they mean to intimidate you,
Mr. Greene? Or that the White League was involved at all? Might
just of been a band of renegades."

"Way I see it, they're one in the same," Samson said. "And
look"—he pointed to a group of white men loitering with their rifles
half a block down across the street—"them Leaguers think they can
intimidate us even here."

Mr. Langdon moved the pencil from his ear to his mouth, chomp-
ing absentmindedly as he flipped back open his notebook. "I think
I'll let them speak for themselves," he said around the pencil before
taking it out of his mouth, a string of spittle trailing behind.

"You do that, Mr. Langdon," Samson said. "Good day to you."

Others had spied the white men too, it seemed, for tense shuffling and whispering overcame the crowd. Samson went to check
the progress of the pallbearers, and Effie wound her way among the
restless funeralgoers in search of Adeline. Only a handful of top hats
rose above the sea of flannel caps, slouch hats, and derbies, making Mr. Chauvet easy to find. Adeline stood beside him, her hand
perched on his elbow, her gaze listless.

Her eyes brightened when she saw Effie. "I thought you might be
at this dreary little affair. *Si triste, n'est-ce pas?*"

She flitted from Mr. Chauvet's arm to Effie's, pulling her close.
Vetiver clung to the pleats and flounces of her dress. It calmed Effie
somehow, crowded here among so many strangers, to smell something so familiar. "What are you doing here?" She felt Adeline's
clasp about her arm slacken and added, "I mean, did you know Mr.
Guillot?"

"No, but Monsieur Chauvet knew a cousin"—her eyes cut to Mr.
Chauvet, who'd taken up conversation with another well-dressed
Creole man, then back to Effie—"a brother . . . some such relation
and thought we best come. I'd hoped we might ride out to the lake
after mass. It's so dreadfully swampy today." She plucked a fan from

her reticule and snapped it open. *"Mais malheureusement,* Monsieur Chauvet says we must stay and ride with the cortege."

The air stirred by Adeline's fan swirled across Effie's skin, a welcome reprieve from the stagnant heat. A wellspring of words bubbled inside her—of that awful night in Algiers, of Samson's proposal, of their impending trip to St. James—but she kept them stoppered inside, awaiting . . . awaiting what?

The clouds finally won their battle with the sun and a light rain began to fall. An umbrella or two popped open, but most in the crowd didn't bother. Voices rose to combat the patter.

Mr. Chauvet turned to her and Adeline, his hand lighting on Adeline's back just above the silk rosette crowning her bustle. She stiffened at his touch. *"Bonjour,* Mademoiselle Jones. Always a pleasure to see you, even under tragic circumstances such as these."

He wasn't an unhandsome man, Mr. Chauvet. His eyes, his lips, his nose were all well-proportioned. His skin, though lined across the brow and about the mouth, radiated health. And she trusted the kindness in his words. Under different circumstances, Effie would favor such an acquaintance. But her heart quickened with the impulse to pull Adeline away and flee with her into the crowd. Not away from him, per se, but away from the dreary life she foresaw for them both.

"I hope you've not come alone." His light brown eyes flickered to the White Leaguers still milling nearby. "Won't you share our carriage to the cemetery?"

"Actually, I—"

Samson's voice rose above the din of the crowd. She, Adeline, and Mr. Chauvet all turned toward the sound.

"Thank you, friends, for being here today." Samson stood on the long step of a wagon. Far taller now than any among the gathering, he made an easy target should the White Leaguers raise their Enfields. Effie cringed. Three days ago such a thought would never have entered her mind.

"I've nothing to say that Father Villeré hasn't already said in his eulogy or weren't already spoke last night at the vigil," he continued. "No amount of praise gonna rid you of the sadness you feel like a yoke about your heart. No amount of preaching gonna wash away the rancid taste of injustice heavy upon your tongue. Be we here."

Raindrops fell more steadily now, but not one among the crowd moved to open her umbrella or cover his head with newsprint. Effie glanced askew at Adeline, but couldn't parse out her expression. Her bottom lip pulled away from the top, too slack to be either a smile or a frown. A drop of rain struck her temple, just beyond the scalloped hem of her veil. It rolled down her cheek and dripped from her chin as if she hadn't felt it at all.

"Be we here," Samson repeated, drawing back Effie's attention. "And we're gonna attend this brave soul to his final resting place with the honor and dignity he deserves. Despite the rain. Despite all those who mean to intimidate us. We got to carry on the cause Jacques Guillot died defending."

Samson stepped down from the wagon. The brass band took up song. If any among the crowd had thought of slipping away before the procession began to flee the rain or avoid the White League's notice, none did so now.

"There's quite *un homme*," Mr. Chauvet said. When Adeline, whose gaze yet lingered on the wagon where Samson had stood, gave no reply, he tapped the ferrule of his cane on the pavers. *"N'est-ce pas, chérie?"*

"Hmm?"

"L'homme."

"Oh." Adeline shrugged. "A fair orator, *je suppose.*"

Fair? Had Effie heard her rightly? "You didn't find Mr. Greene's speech stirring?"

"Mr. Greene?" Adeline glanced again at the wagon and then back to Effie. "That's *your* Mr. Greene?"

"You know that man, Mademoiselle Jones?"

Adeline answered before Effie could. *"Oui.* Monsieur Greene is a state representative and a . . . an acquaintance of Effie's."

Effie suddenly wished she accepted Samson's proposal and that she might correct Adeline. Not acquaintance, betrothed. Or, how did they say it in French? *Fiancé.*

But that was just semantics. Hardly worthy of concern today. And she hadn't accepted. Not yet. Rain dripped from the brim of her hat and down the nape of her neck. Effie unpinned her hat, even as the sky continued to drizzle, and shook away the water that had beaded on the woven straw and ribbon rosettes.

"S'il vous plaît, let's to the carriage," Mr. Chauvet said, gesturing

to a handsome coach with dark blue paneling and glass windows. "Perhaps Monsieur Greene would like to ride as well."

"Thank you, but I believe he means to walk with the others from our club."

"And you too, *je suppose*," Adeline said with a disapproving pout. She handed Effie her ferruled umbrella. "Effie's quite the political enthusiast."

"Do you know this undertaker everyone's whispering about?" Mr. Chauvet asked. "A colleague perhaps?"

"It's a mystery to me too," Effie said, giving Adeline's hand a final squeeze before taking her leave of them.

The pallbearers carried the coffin from the church and settled it in the wagon. People clambered into their carriages or took position behind the band to follow on foot. Effie joined Samson and more than a dozen others from the club gathered near the front of the cortege and opened Adeline's umbrella. Jonah grabbed Effie's hand and pulled her in line with him and Mrs. Carrière. He swung between them as they walked, his weight easily borne, his smile a welcome sight amid so many tight-lipped frowns.

She glanced askew at Mrs. Carrière. Her black dress and veil didn't diminish her upright stature, though Effie imagined they were a heavy reminder of her own grief. How dreadfully she'd behaved to her at the baseball match. Right or wrong, Mrs. Carrière's concern was well-meant. And how many people in Effie's life had cared enough for her to muster concern at all?

The band began "Down by the Riverside." Many of those around her took up singing. Over the drum and horn and voices, she said to Mrs. Carrière, "Marie, last Sunday at the park, I—"

"Think nothing of it, *chère*."

The rain had petered to a dribble by the time they reached the cemetery, and just as the casket was laid in the vault the sun broke through the thinning clouds. Light sparkled off the marble and whitewashed stucco surrounding them. Jonah let go of her hand to chase a lizard scampering along the moss-covered eaves of a nearby tomb. The crowd began to thin and carriages rambled away.

Effie again found Mr. Chauvet's top hat towering conspicuously above the other heads and hurried over with Adeline's umbrella. They stood just off the walkway beside a long wall of multi-leveled vaults. Mr. Chauvet talked animatedly with another light-skinned Creole Effie recognized from the petite fête on Esplanade Avenue. Adeline smiled on cue when the men glanced at her, nodded when they nodded, laughed when they laughed, but otherwise kept her gaze lowered, the toe of her polished boot tickling the stem of a fern that had sprouted among the pavers.

Her smile for Effie was far warmer. She plucked the hankie from Mr. Chauvet's pocket and led Effie to a nearby bench, using the square of silk to dry the seat for them.

"Your Mr. Greene is quite self-assured."

She followed Adeline's gaze to where Samson stood at the far end of the row of tombs. "You don't approve?"

"It's just a peculiar quality for a freedman."

"You expect us all to be docile and obsequious?"

"I'd hardly count you among them, *chère.* You've got too much of the North in you."

"What a pair we must seem to you. A carpetbagger and braggart." Effie stood to leave, but Adeline captured her arm.

"*Ma foi,* I didn't mean to work you into a conniption. I'm sure he's perfectly genial. I've only got you in mind when I say such things. Men like him—" She stopped suddenly and looked away, as if newly captivated by the pools of muddy rainwater at their feet.

"There you are, Effie."

She turned at Samson's voice and found herself smiling in the same forced way Adeline had to Mr. Chauvet.

"You about ready to be off? Tom suggested we might stop over at Haverdeens for some . . ." His gaze snagged on Adeline and he doffed his derby. "Mademoiselle."

She'd never heard him attempt French before and the word rang dissonant in her ear, not just for his imperfect pronunciation, but the throaty way he said it. Adeline stood, her lips pursed, her brown eyes raking over him before settling conspicuously elsewhere. The ensuing silence pained Effie. Not until Samson coughed lightly did she remember herself enough to make introductions.

"Miss Mercier, this is Mr. Greene."

"A pleasure," Samson said.

"Likewise."

Their clipped words hardly made a dent in the silence. What had

Mrs. Kinyon said all those years ago before she'd given up schooling Effie in the social graces? Something about smoothing over an awkward introduction with pleasant facts about the respective parties. "Miss Mercier is an excellent seamstress."

"Oh?"

"I dabble a bit when the mood suits me." Adeline tossed her head, her lace veil fluttering outward, then settling back around her face. "You know, to pass the time."

"I'm afraid I don't know. I've had little time in my life to . . . dabble."

Adeline rejoined with a shrug.

Effie fought the urge to stomp on Adeline's shiny boot tips for all the help she was being and fished for something else to say. "Mr. Greene's a representative at the statehouse."

"Indeed?"

"Got my eye on the Senate come November."

Adeline perked at this. "Is that right?"

"Yes, ma'am. Maybe one day the Custom House or Lieutenant Governor should the Party and the Good Lord see fit."

She smiled, but not in a way that gave Effie any calm. "And pray tell, Mr. Greene, which of those, the Good Lord or the Republican Party, do you hold in greater esteem?"

"The Lord, of course."

"And yourself?"

He frowned. "Myself?"

"*Oui.* Where do you rank yourself among those three?"

"I should never conflate myself with either, miss."

"Really?"

Effie laughed, loud and thin, a sound not unlike the braying of a mule. They both looked at her as if she might be choking or taken with hysteria. Thankfully, Mr. Chauvet stepped over, eager to know Samson and compliment him on his impromptu oration back at St. Augustine.

Effie shuffled beside Adeline and did step on her toes. Not with any great force, but enough to draw her attention and a penitent gaze.

"Please be nice," she whispered as the men continued to talk. "For me."

Adeline pursed her lips, stared at Samson, and said nothing.

CHAPTER 24

———⟫◦⟪———

Effie had just arrived at the shop when she heard the clop of hooves down the carriageway. Mr. Whitmark walked beside their shabby cart mule and began hitching him to the wagon. "Fetch your embalming cabinet and some fluid," he called to her across the courtyard.

The sky was still streaked red with the dawn, and it surprised her he was up so early. Colm, who usually readied the mule and wagon, hadn't even arrived yet. But she let her questions lie and did as bidden.

They sat in silence as the wagon lumbered down Canal Street toward the river. The streetcar rumbled past, its squeaking wheels sending a prickle down her spine. Something about Mr. Whitmark was off this morning, more than his early awakening. He sat overly rigid, his hands tight about the reins. He stayed the mule in front of the crumbling stucco building she remembered from her first day in New Orleans: the morgue.

Her breakfast of coffee and biscuits stirred in her stomach. Was this another test of some sort? Mr. Whitmark clambered down and tied the mule to a rusted hitching post. "Come on."

He heaved open one of the great, vertical board doors leading to the ground level. It swung wide on groaning hinges and slammed against the adjoining wall. Mr. Whitmark straightened his suit coat and entered, leaving Effie to juggle the dressing case, embalming cabinet, and case of fluid on her own. She shimmied the door closed behind her with her foot as the supplies teetered in her arms. After the morning's brightness, her eyes struggled to adjust to the dim.

The inner doors leading beyond the anteroom in which they waited were closed, but the yellow glow of oil lamps shown beneath. Mr. Whitmark rapped. The same portly coroner she remembered from months before answered. He stood in the jamb, wiping his hands on his trousers, and glanced over his shoulder into the morgue.

"What's this about, Lafitte?" Mr. Whitmark asked. "Your missive said it was urgent."

"Ah . . ." Another backward glance. "*Désolé,* George," he whispered, and stepped aside, revealing a cluster of men within.

Mr. Whitmark's raspy breathing faltered. One foot slid backward over the gritty tile floor.

"Colonel Whitmark, at last," a man said from within. "Won't you join us? We've a case we hoped you might help us with."

In the shadowy light of the anteroom, Mr. Whitmark's skin seemed to gray. The corners of his compressed lips twitched. But he squared his shoulders and entered.

The coroner waved her in too, as if in some hurry to shut them in. Her muscles refused the command. She didn't recognize these men, but they looked little different from the men she'd seen parading in front of the clubhouse or those lingering with their rifles at yesterday's funeral. Young men, antsy and cocksure.

One of them looked at her. "You too, girlie. Boss man might be needin' that there equipment."

Mr. Whitmark turned and nodded at her. She slunk inside, jumping when the coroner closed the door behind her.

The men were clumped shoulder-to-shoulder around an examining table. A pair of feet jutted over the table's edge, stiff with rigor mortis, the pink soles scraped and dirt-stained. As Mr. Whitmark approached, the men parted to reveal the full length of the table and the body upon it.

Effie's arms went slack, the supplies tumbling from her grasp. One of the jars of embalming fluid shattered, choking the air with chemicals. Others rolled helter-skelter around the room.

"Darkies," one of the men said, wagging his head. He pinned one of the bottles beneath the mud-encrusted sole of his boot and rolled it back in her direction. The sound of it atop the dusty, blood-splattered tile stripped her nerves raw. She crouched down to collect the mess at her feet—rubber tubing, cotton packing, spools of thread—stuffing it haphazardly into the cases. She did this all by feel, groping along the ground, her gaze ensnared by the grizzly site on the table.

The body of the man laid out before them had been beaten like Mr. Guillot's, the face bruised and swollen beyond recognition. A red stain darkened the man's trousers about the loins where Effie guessed they'd hacked away his manhood. Where it wasn't bruised over, his black skin had turned pallid from blood loss. His limbs twisted at odd angles—broken, then frozen with death.

Her mind, slow to register anything beyond shock, awakened suddenly. Samson? Samson! . . . But no, the body was too thin, muscles wan, bones protruding beneath the skin. This man was likely a vagabond, some poor soul new to the city in search of work. A stab of shame followed on the heels of her relief. It wasn't Samson, but surely this man was dear to someone too.

A sudden prick of pain drew her attention away from the body to her hand. What started as a faint sting quickly became a fierce burning. She'd sliced the pad of her finger on a shard of broken glass wet with embalming fluid. She wiped her finger on her skirt, heedless of the stain, then milked yet more blood from the wound to flush out the searing chemicals.

"What's the meaning of all this? Who is this man? Why have you called me here?" Mr. Whitmark's eyes—skittish of the body— undermined the authority he'd mustered in his voice. His complexion colored from gray to green.

The tallest of the men spoke up. He had the sharp nose and prominent chin of men in newspaper advertisements. "Seeing as you helped out that last Negro across the river, we thought you'd like to fix this one up too."

"I haven't any idea what you're talking about."

"One of them light-skinned coons workin' under Kellogg. Comptroller he called himself."

Mr. Whitmark took a step back, glass crunching beneath his boot heel. "I still don't know whom you mean. I haven't been across the river to Algiers in years. They've got their own undertakers there."

"Yep," another of the men said, using the tip of his pocket knife to clean between his teeth. "We asked them too. Say they don't know nothin' neither."

"Difference is, them's good men, loyal to the South. God-fearing Democrats, the lot of 'em," the tall man said. The others nodded as he spoke. "You's a scalawag."

Even as she listened, as her finger throbbed and the smell of the morgue settled in her nostrils, Effie's mind snagged on what Adeline had said about the opera all those weeks—no, months—ago. This man, the tall handsome one, was the primo uomo. Adeline had said her little lesson didn't apply to men, but the subtle fawning of the others, the deference, the hierarchy all seemed to fit.

Effie finished picking up the scattered supplies and shuffled away from the table until her back hit the wall. The plaster was cold and rough through the thinning weave of her dress. The men took little note of her, their attention trained on Mr. Whitmark, but she knew that could change and fast.

"I don't see what bearing it has on today. The War was said and done a decade ago when you boys were still in diaper cloths." He turned to leave, but several of the men broke line and circled around him, blocking the exit.

The tall man, the primo uomo, grabbed the scruff of Mr. Whitmark's jacket and dragged him back to the table, pinning him cheek-to-cheek with the battered corpse. "Take a good look, Colonel, and tell me how you don't remember nothin'."

Mr. Whitmark struggled free of the man's hold. He staggered back several paces, then yanked a hankie from his pocket and wiped his cheek. "Are you mad?" He turned to the coroner. "Lafitte, go fetch the police."

But Mr. Lafitte didn't move.

"We ain't done nothin' wrong," the tall man said. He walked over and looped an arm over Mr. Whitmark's shoulders. "We's just askin' a few questions and havin' a little fun."

Mr. Whitmark shrugged him off and gestured toward the body. "You call this butchery fun?"

The other men moved in closer, blocking any further retreat. "See, I knew he was a Negro lover," the primo uomo said.

They corralled him like a stray cow back to the table.

"I'm curious how you done it. Fixed up that other blacky all perdy like."

"I told you, I don't know what or whom you're talking about." Mr. Whitmark's voice had gone thin. Despite the cool air, sweat shined across his skin.

Effie inched along the wall toward the door. Five minutes at a run and she'd be at the French Market and in easy shouting range of any number of police.

"How's about you show us on this here hawbuck."

Mr. Whitmark shook his head while the young men shouted their assent. One pulled a half-empty bottle of liquor from his shabby top-coat and took a long swig. He passed the bottle and the rest of the men drank too. They backslapped and hooted as if they'd pulled up a seat at a minstrel show. The man beside Mr. Whitmark offered him the bottle. He eyed the liquor an overlong moment, then batted the bottle away.

Effie watched, counting the steps yet to the door. Eight in her estimation.

Seven.

Six.

"You need a knife?" The tooth-picker offered up his blade to Mr. Whitmark, pointy end first.

"Nah, nah," another said. "Them embalmers got special tools."

Effie froze just as the men's gazes turned on her. The last three steps to the door seemed now like a mile. She daren't take them. She daren't even breathe.

"Well," the tall man said to her. "Bring your boss man his tools."

She locked eyes with Mr. Whitmark. He looked tired, as if his fear had burnt so hot he had nothing left to feed it. "Bring me my scalpel, Effie."

In her earlier haste to pick up everything from the floor, she'd mislaid the scalpel, and fished through the cases with the men's stares heavy upon her. At last, she found it at the very bottom of the dressing case beneath wads of rumpled linen and the granite shaving cup. She handed it to Mr. Whitmark.

Heavy bruising and rope burn about the man's throat prevented Mr. Whitmark from dissecting the carotid. Was that how they'd finished the man off? Hanging him from a tree or dragging him behind a horse until he suffocated? Effie pulled her shawl higher about her neck, as if the thin fabric might somehow prevent the same from happening to her.

Sooner or later these men would tire of watching Mr. Whitmark. Sooner, judging by the scant liquor remaining in their bottle. Then what? Would they turn their violence on her and Mr. Whitmark too?

Mr. Whitmark inspected both arms before choosing the left axillary. Sweat dripped from his brow onto the body, and his hand wobbled like a loose wagon wheel. He nicked the skin several times before managing a cut, ragged and too shallow so that he had to draw the scalpel through the tissue several more times before revealing the artery.

"Why ain't there no blood?" one of the men asked.

"It's stagnant and clotted," Mr. Whitmark said, laying aside the scalpel. Effie was ready with forceps. He mopped his face with his shirt sleeve before taking them.

With no blood to sate them, the men grew restless, shifting and fidgeting. They finished off the last of the liquor and tossed the bottle to the floor. Mr. Whitmark jumped at the sound. He tried several times to elevate the vessel, but each time the artery slipped his shaky grasp.

"Stop your dithering and get on with it," the man with the pocket knife said, jabbing an elbow into Mr. Whitmark's side. "Elsewise we'll try it out on you."

Mr. Whitmark glared at the man, then drew a long, whistling inhale, and tried again. By now his hands were slick with sweat and the pale lymph fluid that had begun to weep from the incision. He grasped the artery, but the forceps slipped from his hand before he could raise it above the skin.

"You's a right lousy undertaker, seems to me," one among them said, garnering a host of chuckles. "Don't nobody call on him when I done knock over."

More chuckles. Effie gulped down a breath to steady her nerves and said, "He sho is a lousy undertaker."

The men's laughter faltered and every gaze—including Mr. Whitmark's—turned upon her.

She caught the primo uomo's eye before looking hastily down to her feet, a newly remembered trick from her days in the slave pen. "Well, you've seen him. Too much drink. Can't hold them tools steady but for nothin'." She peeked up again to be sure the tall man's attention was still on her. "Not them forceps, not the scalpel, not no needle for sho."

"What you gettin' at, girl?" the primo uomo said.

"It just"—she shifted her weight and rasped her boot back and forth across the tile in feigned uncertainty—"just, no way he could'a embalmed that Mr. Guillot. Ain't got the skill. I been at the funeral and seen the incision." She gestured to her neck. "Straight as a ruler. And just as neat too. Sewed up real nice like."

Another glance up revealed a spattering of confusion across the men's faces. Mr. Whitmark too seemed befuddled, torn between wounded pride and dawning comprehension.

"Hold out your hand, Colonel," the primo uomo said.

Mr. Whitmark did as instructed. His hand trembled as she knew it would, not with an affected tremor, or even the quake of fear, but with the jerky twitch of an invalid.

The men looked from one to another with uncertain expressions, as if they'd never considered Mr. Whitmark mightn't have been involved. One scratched at his overgrown sideburns. The man with the knife set to work again on his teeth. Their liveliness was waning. Likely the men had devoted all night to this escapade—shoring up their courage with cheap whiskey, trolling the back-of-town streets for a suitable victim, bribing or bullying the coroner to comply with their plan and send for Mr. Whitmark.

Still playing docile, Effie strained her eyes upward to regard the primo uomo without raising her head. She only needed to convince him. He too looked tired, sagging shoulders and twitching eyelids. "How you still in business with a shake like that?"

"I cover them messy sutures with court plaster and powder," Effie said before Mr. Whitmark could open his mouth and incriminate her. "But anyone with any know-how can still tell."

"You sure got a lippy wench here," primo uomo said.

"Indeed," Mr. Whitmark replied.

"You got an alibi for Wednesday last?"

Mr. Whitmark's shoulders straightened. "You might have started with that question instead of wasting my time with this charade. Wednesday was the Gerhing funeral, wasn't it, Effie?"

"Yes, sir."

"And that evening I was out late at the theater. You might ask my brother." He yanked the watch from his pocket. "You'll find him lunching at the Pickwick Club in a few hours."

At the mention of this, the men stiffened.

The primo uomo glanced between Mr. Whitmark, Effie, and the body, his jaw tight and eyes narrowed. Seconds piled one atop the next, adding to the already heavy silence.

At last, he said, "Let's go, boys. I'm tuckered." He picked up the scalpel and rammed it like a stake into the wooden examination table. "Keep your nigger-lovin' nose outta trouble now, ya hear?"

Not until the men had left did Effie draw a full breath. It couldn't be more than nine o'clock, though it had seemed like they'd been possums in a wolf's jaw for hours. A handy stool and she would have collapsed. But then, best not tarry should men think to return and resume their sport. She reached for the upright handle of the scalpel. Before she could pry it free from the bloodstained wood, a hand circled around her arm and yanked her back.

"You ever do anything like that again, I'll not only sack you but see that you haven't enough fingers to ever work again," Mr. Whitmark said, spittle flying from his lips onto her cheek. He muscled her against the wall. The rough plaster bit into the nape of her neck.

Effie blinked and tried to focus. Hadn't she just saved his life? "It was the only thing I could think of to call them off."

"Not that. Your little act is the only reason I'm not firing you here and now." His grip tightened. "You think I don't know you embalmed that body?"

"I . . . I . . ."

"Who else could have done it? Did you stop and think how word of this could destroy us? The shop? All the progress I've made?"

"We can get by without such clients."

"Look around you! Who do you think runs this city? It's not that band of carpetbaggers and Negroes dithering about at the statehouse. Besides, I'm done getting by. I don't know what kind of radical nonsense you're involved in. But it stops. Today." He released her and staggered back, bracing his hands on his knees as his chest heaved.

Effie swallowed, anger burning like bile in her throat. Only eleven years on from the War, and freedom and dignity were radical nonsense now? She wanted to remind him that he himself had fought for such nonsense.

She wanted to remind him too that her personal affairs were none of his concern. She was his assistant, not his property. But she remained silent, watching him wrest control of his ragged breath and twitchy limbs. When he righted himself, his gray eyes were hard as whetstone. How dissimilar he'd become from the broken man she'd stood beside in this very morgue last December.

He tugged again on his suit coat. It was too small for him now, constrained about the shoulders, pulling at the waist. Indeed, that tremor was the only vestige of the sickly man he'd been. Two months ago, she'd say outright he looked a bumpkin and needed a new coat. Now, she daren't speak at all.

"You're lucky those men were too sapheaded to connect you with all this."

The thought had surfaced after she'd mentioned her attendance at the funeral. Might the men figure her involvement? But no. In their puny minds, a Negro couldn't manage such things, and certainly not a woman.

Mr. Whitmark gestured to the haphazardly packed cases beside the table. "Take this mess back to the shop and get it set right. I'm going for some air."

He started toward the door, stopped, and glanced over his shoulder at her. For the flicker of a moment, his stony regard cracked. His incisors pulled at the corner of his lips. The set of shoulders slackened. He opened his mouth—to apologize for the bruises he'd left on her arm? To thank her for saving their lives?—but he closed it just as quickly and stamped from the morgue.

The coroner had gone too, perhaps upstairs, perhaps at last to fetch the police, leaving her alone in the cold, dank, ill-lit room. She pulled a bar of soap and several washing cloths from one of the cases. She didn't dare embalm the man on the examination table, but she'd not leave him dirtied and bloody either.

CHAPTER 25

"You forgive me that I can't come with you?" Samson asked, handing her traveling bag to Tom, who loaded it along with his own onto
the steamboat. "I'll send my regrets to Mr. Chauvet this very minute
and jump on the boat with you."

Effie shook her head, uncertain she could keep the disappointment from her voice were she to speak. The trip to St. James Parish had been his idea, after all. But Samson was right not to come.
It would be bad form not to accept the invitation to Mr. Chauvet's
party after he'd sponsored Samson's membership in the Louisiana
Progressive Club. With the club's backing, Samson's bid for state
Senate was as sure as April rain.

"You look after her," he said to Tom, then pulled Effie close and
kissed her. She felt both thrilled and a touch embarrassed at such a
public display, especially in front of Tom, who frowned toward the
river.

"Good luck up there," Samson said. He'd released her lips, but kept
a snug hold about her waist. "And don't let any of those swampers
charm your heart away, you hear?"

Effie managed a laugh, her first in weeks it seemed, ever since
Mr. Whitmark and the morgue. Her diaphragm was stiff with the
effort. "I won't."

"And you'll think on my proposal?"

"I will."

Samson waved to her from the dock as the boat pulled away, then disappeared into the blur of the crowd. Despite the warm day, Effie reached about her shoulders, only to remember she'd packed away her shawl.

She and Tom sat portside near the stern wheel amid the seed bags, farming tools, and barrels of rum going upriver. Tom knew one of the roustabouts who'd taken them aboard without fee, provided they keep to the lower decks. Effie unwrapped a bundle of cornbread Mrs. Neale had sent, and Tom opened a can of pickled herrings. They shared the luncheon treats between them and stared out at the silty water rippling in the boat's wake.

"Heard you got in a spot of trouble with your boss after the funeral," Tom said, spitting out a bone and tossing it in the river.

Spot of trouble. An ill-fitting description, but she had no desire to correct him and relive the events at the morgue in the telling. "He's trying to distance himself from his position during the War."

"Outrun his reputation as a scalawag, you mean?"

"Yes, so he's . . . wary of political matters."

Tom stopped eating and turned to her. "Effie, why you defending him? Way I heard it, he slammed you into a wall and threatened to cut off your fingers if you done such nonsense again."

"He . . . I . . . We're all just trying to get by."

"We's free now, Effie. Don't need to take that from no one no more."

"Embalming is all I'm good at."

"That ain't true. You the smartest gal I know. You could be a nurse, a teacher, even start up your own undertakin' business."

"Tom, you're plumb crazy if you think that would ever work. Not even up North would they take to that."

"So you just work for the coloreds."

"Plenty of them would still object on account of my sex."

"Something else, then."

She'd never considered work beyond the dead. The idea tarried in her brain, an unexpected but not altogether unwelcome stranger.

Tom drew her attention back with a gentle nudge and handed her the last herring. "How'd you manage these four days away without getting your boss's dander up, then?"

"He's at the lake this week, fixing up his mother's summer house." She didn't tell him of all the chores he'd left for her at the shop, how she'd been up past midnight the last two nights sweeping and scrubbing.

"Must be nice, taking the summer by the lake." He leaned back against a stack of seed sacks, resting his head on his interlaced hands. "You ain't been here for a summer spell yet, have you? Some treat you're in for."

"I lived through the Indiana winters. I'm sure I can endure the New Orleans summers."

Tom laughed. "Don't know about that."

His laughter drifted into silence and they sat quietly for several minutes. The sway of the boat and warm, river-scented air soothed her nerves. She tucked her legs beneath her and rested her head atop a small wooden keg. She let go of the foreboding that had followed her from the docks and tried not to think about what lay ahead. A heron called from the shore. Dragonflies hummed overhead, their spindly bodies iridescent in the sunlight.

"You remember the first time it really hit you that you weren't a slave no more?" Tom asked.

Effie raised her head but didn't answer.

"Me, was a few years on in the War. The company chaplain been teaching us to read and write. When there weren't no trenches to be dug or lumber to be cut. I was mustered in for pay and instead of signing an *X,* I spelled out my full name, Thomas Button."

"You didn't feel it when you first enlisted?"

"Nah. Your rifle, see, they can take from you. Hell, if you was captured and not killed they could send you right back to the cotton fields. Even a leg they can take from you. But this"—he tapped his temple—"ain't no taking away what's in here."

Effie considered his reply. She too had learned to read during the War, but didn't remember feeling materially different at any one point during the process.

Then it struck her. There had been a moment. A line, a fracture, that proverbial point of no return she'd traversed by no one's hand but her own.

She told him about the Kinyons and the daughter they'd had before the War. "I never flattered myself that they held for me the same affection. But I did replace her, in some measured way. Slept in her bed, played with her dolls, wore out her dresses."

Mrs. Kinyon had never thought of Effie as a daughter. But Mr. Kinyon had. Or so she'd thought. And though she'd never called him papa, he'd been idol, savior, and father to her all in one. How eager she'd been to impress and please him, to prove herself worthy of any affection he might spare. She kept her distance, studied tirelessly, endured the cold nose and slobbery tongue of his mangy dog Otis.

Again Effie groped about her shoulders for her shawl, ruing the decision to pack it away. "I hadn't a family back here. None that I knew of, none I remembered. Peculiar as our situation was—the captain and missus and I—I suppose I thought . . ." Effie stopped, surprised how her throat constricted around the words.

"Thought you'd found a new family," Tom finished for her.

Effie nodded. But fascination, not paternal affection, motivated the captain. Effie realized that now. Realized how he too saw her as an oddity, a museum curiosity more than a girl. Astounding intellect! Unmatched skill! Impervious to the labile emotions and fragile sensitivities so common to her sex.

"One evening a man came to dinner, a well-known naturalist from Philadelphia. I didn't know his niche of study, but hoped we might talk of botany or ornithology. I'd recently read Mr. Audubon's *Birds of America* and hoped—" Effie stopped again. She was shirking the subject and would soon bore Tom dead.

She turned and faced him. "Are you acquainted with the field of craniometry?"

He shook his head.

"It's the examination of the skull and facial features, measurements of the cranial circumference, facial height, nasal breadth, and the like. Scientists use it to explore variation within and betwixt species."

"You mean, like animals?"

"People too. It's used to buttress claims of Negro inferiority, hayseed theories that the races developed from different origins instead of a single ancestral species. Polygenism, they call it."

Tom's expression darkened, his eyebrows bunching and his full lips cinching together.

"Neither the captain nor I favored that theory. But this naturalist from Philadelphia did. He was one of the foremost proponents of such . . . rubbish." Effie stared beyond the river at the foliage-entangled shore. Cypress trees and ferns and marsh grass. Creeping vines and drooping moss. She drew her knees up to her chest, wishing as she had then to disappear like vapor into air. "Captain Kinyon brought this man to our—*his* home, that he might measure and examine me."

At the time, Effie hadn't been able to explain her dread, didn't remember her days in the slave pen, the daily indignity of being poked and prodded. She declined the examination, but Captain Kinyon pressed her. Think what a contribution she'd be making to science. It wouldn't hurt a bit. The man had come hundreds of miles for this, after all.

A father would have noticed her fear—the frantic push and pull of her breath, the sweat aglint on her forehead—but Captain Kinyon had not.

"I thought you said the captain didn't believe in this polygenism," Tom said.

"He didn't. He thought I was the perfect specimen to disprove the theory."

"Specimen?"

Effie kept her gaze trained on the river's shoreline. Not even Samson or Adeline knew of this sliver of her life. After all, if Captain Kinyon, the man who'd saved her from the War and raised her up since she was small, saw her in that light, a mere specimen to be studied, surely others would too.

"I did as he bid and let that man . . . measure me." She took a deep breath to fill the sudden stab of emptiness. "Eleven years—since the first day in camp—I'd done as the captain bid, thinking . . . thinking that's what love looked like. But that night, as that vile scientist tinkered about with his tools, that was the moment. I sat there and I knew. I'd never do as Captain Kinyon bid me again."

After the examination, she'd lain awake, recalling the cold pinch of the man's caliper against her skull, the flutter of his measuring tape, the pads of his probing fingers across her cheekbones, down her spine, and other places of no relation to craniometry at all. She'd disgorged her dinner into the chamber pot many times over and couldn't bring her quaking limbs to heel. Before dawn, she'd packed her trunk, her traveling bag, her embalming cabinet, and was gone.

Tom touched her hand. She peeked at him without turning her

head. "You must think me foolish for leaving after so trivial an offense."

Neither his hand nor his gaze retreated. "It ain't trivial, Effie. Not at all. You're a woman, not some specimen."

The emptiness inside her lessened. She turned to him and did her best to smile. "Thank you."

Tom returned her wan smile. He picked up the empty herring tin, tossed it up and down in his palm a few times, then chucked it into the water. It floated a moment atop the waves, then sank below the surface. "We're going to be all right, living through what we've done. You'll see."

Effie longed to believe him.

Several hours into the afternoon, the boat stopped at a small dock affronting a wide swath of sugarcane fields to unload cargo. Effie and Tom disembarked and headed down a narrow dirt road paralleling the river. The sugarcane stalks reached thigh height, the neat rows in which they were planted blurring to a sea of green as they stretched to the distant tree line. Between the far trees, Effie could just make out the shingled roof and dormer windows of a monstrous plantation house.

"Is that—"

"No, the Saulnier place is the next tract upriver. But likely some of the old field hands sharecrop these parts too. We'll find a place we can bed down for the night and see what folks can tell us."

Inland from the river, beyond the rows of sugarcane lay a spattering of clapboard shanties raised on pillars a few feet above the muddy ground. Rust streaked the tin roofs a bloody red. A spattering of children played with sticks and rag dolls in the shanties' lengthening shadows, but anyone big enough to hold a pail or hoe bustled about fetching water or tending the gardens.

Tom introduced himself to an old woman hanging out the day's wash. Her filmy eyes narrowed slightly when he mentioned he was from the Republican Office. Not here to stir up any trouble, he assured her, only to see how things were faring in these parts and if the Party might be able to help.

Effie had worried without Samson they'd struggle to make headway with these people. He was the great speechifier, after all. And

with that smile, he hardly needed words. It struck her now, however, how well-suited Tom was for this work. He'd removed his faded
slouch hat before addressing the woman, exposing his shaggy hair.
Samson's hair, trimmed short and slicked to the side with oil—à la
mode in the city—would seem ostentatious here. Tom had brought
his wood-whittled crutch instead of his brass-tipped cane to better
navigate the uneven terrain and this too seemed fitting. The woman
eyed his cotton suit—tidy and well-tailored, but not at all foppish—
his stump leg and travel-worn boot. He too had a handsome smile,
Effie realized, broad and earnest.

The woman nodded, then looked at Effie. "This your wife?"

"No, ma'am." Tom looked down, the dark coloring of his cheeks
deepening. "This is Effie. She was sold to Mr. Saulnier during the
War. Worked his land a spell before escaping. We were hoping someone about these parts might remember her and them other slaves
brought up from the city with her."

Effie extended her hand. The old woman grasped it with surprising strength and pulled her close. Her free hand patted the planes of
Effie's face, the dip and swell of her cheekbones, the rise of her nose
and the slope of her jaw. "You couldn't have been but a babe then."

"Seven, according to the bill of sale."

"Weren't supposed to sell ones that young. Not that it ever stopped
'em." The woman sighed. "Effie. We got several here about this
bayou who done slaved for Mr. Saulnier. Several more a little farther
on who still work that land. I'll see who I can rustle up."

Effie helped her hang the last of the washing while Tom passed
out candied pecans to an ever-swelling crowd of children. By suppertime they had a bowl of rice and crawfish in their hands, and a
worn couch and a bedroll in the front room of the woman's home on
which to sleep. Word had spread of their arrival and people gathered
around, dust-covered and sweaty from the day's labors.

Effie sat on the woman's front porch, her bustle tucked beneath
her, legs dangling over the side. The moss-speckled wood creaked
beneath her weight. Tom stood beside her, shaking hands and repeat-
ing his introduction. Then he listened. Those in the crowd were ten-
tative at first, crossing their arms and glancing over their shoulders.
But once the first spoke, others quickly chimed in.

The men talked of heavy debts and diminishing wages. They

wanted their own land, but rarely had a dollar to squirrel away. They wanted their wives out of the fields. A colored school for their children.

"There isn't a school here?" Effie asked.

"Nearest school's twenty miles yonder in Thibodaux," one of the men said.

"Don't take no colored children anyhow," said another.

Tom flashed a wistful smile. "New Orleans is likely the only place in the whole South with integrated schools, and the White League's made such a hullabaloo about it, I doubt they'll last long."

Mention of the White League brought forth a slew of new complaints. Armed Regulators roaming about with lynching rope conspicuously hitched to their saddles. Crops plundered. Threats of whippings, beatings, and worse against anyone who voted the Republican ticket in the coming election.

"My boss wants me to sign some Loyalty Certificate, saying I promise to vote Democratic," one among the crowd said. "Scared if I don't, he'll fire me. Or worse."

"A colored man from Lafourche Crossing was kilt just last month."

"The Smiths down by Chevreuil Bayou was run off their farm."

Anger wrestled with the fear in their voices. Mr. Guillot's body, stiff and swollen, bullied into her mind. The vagabond from the morgue.

She stood and walked away from the crowd. The last rivulets of sunset pooled at the far horizon. Frogs croaked from the nearby waterways. Emotion bloated inside her, pressing at the underside of her skin. Would that she had her trocar and could drive it into her gut to relieve this pressure.

The old woman—Maddie was her name—came up and handed her a burning cattail. "Keeps the skeeters away."

The smell was familiar to Effie, not only the woody fragrance of the smoke but the earthy scent around her. The moss-draped oaks, the still water of the nearby swamp, the blooming spider lilies. The reminiscence hit her not as it had at the slave pen, sharp and sudden, but with the almost sleepy awareness of one coming to from a dream. She breathed in deep and let the scent fill her lungs, hoping to fill the familiar surroundings with concrete memories. Nothing.

A fleck of hot ash flitted onto her hand, burning her skin. She snuffed out the cattail and retreated to bed.

In the morning, Tom borrowed a bony old mare—the only horse anyone in town owned—and traveled to meet with men from the neighboring communities. Several people remarked how well he road despite his missing leg. Effie had grown so used to his smooth gait and nonchalant demeanor she'd all but forgotten the injury. She was glad not to be going with him. Last night's disquiet had only just begun to deflate, and any more talk of politics might start it building again. Besides, she had her own affairs to attend. No sooner had she and Maddie finished scrubbing the breakfast pans than an old man arrived in a dilapidated box cart.

"This here's Joe Watkins," Maddie said. "He born at the Saulnier place and worked there till Emancipation. He'll take you around, see if anyone who came up with you still here."

Effie shook his hand and clambered into the cart beside him. The wheels squeaked with each rotation and the loose-fitting side boards rumbled, but they managed a conversation over the din. He asked many of the same questions Maddie had yesterday—when Effie had come to the Saulnier place, how old she'd been, how many slaves had been in the coffle with her up from New Orleans—then sat quietly a moment with her answers.

"Don't reckon I remember ya, but them War years were funny about the plantation."

She stared out at the threads of mist still tangled about the underbrush and tried to swallow her disappointment. "I came up with a man. Jonesy he was called. Young, early twenties maybe."

"Jonesy . . . big feller, right?"

Effie nodded with such vigor her bonnet slipped down over her eyes.

"Yeah, I 'member him, I think."

"Is he still here?"

"Hmmm . . . Jonesy." He took a swill from the water jug beside him and smacked his lips several times. "Nah, don't think so. But we ask Lula. She ought be about today."

"What about Mr. Saulnier? Would he remember?"

"He done passed a few years back. Lost both his boys in the War. Just him and the missus till he died. She done sold what she could and moved back to be closer to her kinfolk. Charleston, I think."

Another disappointment. She tried not to let it rattle her, made a point of keeping her shoulders from slumping and forced a smile when Mr. Watkins looked over.

They passed over a narrow bridge as creaky and weather-bleached as the wagon, then through a patchwork of forest and fallow fields. She wiped the stickiness from her brow and tried to conjure specific memories to hang upon the familiar landscape. Soon they were back in the company of rows of sugarcane. Dark figures dotted the fields, backs bent over the green leaves, clothes wet through with perspiration.

"Not much different than before the War. Plantin', growin', cuttin', millin'—we's busy all year round," Mr. Watkins said. "Mean work it is. When they's ready for harvest, them canes be taller than your head."

He asked for the second time how old she'd been when Massa Saulnier bought her. Seven, she yelled over the wagon's rattle.

"You seem like a strong girl. Bet you was out in the field with the rest of us."

Like the forests and smell the night before, his description of work in the cane fields stirred nothing more than a vague recollection. Her past was all around her, yet still beyond her reach.

Effie jumped from the wagon without bothering to ask Mr. Watkins to slow the mule. Soft red dirt cushioned her landing. She walked into the field, letting her hand trail over the thin ribbed leaves that drooped from the canes. The lower leaves, just starting to brown, rasped against her skirt. She closed her eyes and let the sun's warmth sink into her skin. The air hung still, trapping the dampness and buzz of insects like a sleeve around her.

Yes, she'd been here, at work in the fields. She remembered the way the leaves' pointy tips had pricked her bare forearms. She remembered the rustling sound that heralded those rare but heavenly breezes. Snatches of those days bombarded her then: flicking away the dried mud from her skin after hours of weeding, waddling along the rows with a heavy water bucket and ladle, lumbering toward the wagon with an armload of newly cut canes.

But something wasn't right. She ungartered her stockings and flung them off along with her boots. The soil was cool and silky beneath her soles. It swallowed her feet when she stepped and squished between her toes. Phantom sounds rose around her—voices lifted in song, knives hacking against cane, a whip cracking somewhere in the distance.

Despite the sun's heat, Effie shivered. She listened, straining to hear that rumbling baritone above the others. Yes, there it was. Jonesy.

When she climbed back into the box cart, Mr. Watkins asked no questions, but urged the mule onward. They reached the heart of the plantation and he pointed out the brick sugar works building and several rows of weather-rotted slave cabins. Effie tried to dredge from these a more continuous stream of memory, but again only flashes came, nothing that linked to her life before the slave pen. Her mind, it seemed, had born the ravages of time no better than these untended cabins, worm-eaten and rusted. Foolish to have thought she could raise intact something so long interred.

The vast plantation house had fared little better than the cabins. Faded white paint peeled from the grand colonnades. Vines swallowed half the facade.

"Some feller in St. Louis owns it now," Mr. Watkins said. "This and about near all the land. Sho did shine back in the day."

He seemed almost wistful, and strangely the neglect and decay roused a similar pang in Effie. Not for her former master, nor the sons who'd died in the War. Not for the house or the cabins or the crumbling sugar works. But for the connections forged and broken here, now weathered to dust. At least some testament to it should remain. Even the chains and shackles would someday rust and crumble. Then who could say it happened at all?

"What about this Miss Lula?" she asked, fearing Mr. Watkins too had lost himself in the past. "Might we still talk to her?"

They found Miss Lula with her lunch pail sitting with a group of other field workers in the shade of an oak tree. They all knew Mr. Watkins and greeted him warmly, dragging over a stump for him to sit on and pushing chunks of cornbread and cold chicken into his hands. They offered food to Effie too, but she declined. Her stomach hadn't stilled since leaving New Orleans.

"You 'member a young buck that come in the War years, name a Johnny?" Mr. Watkins asked Lula.

"Jonesy," Effie said.

Lula bit off a hunk of biscuit and chewed for some time. "Yeah, I remember him." She turned to Effie. "You some kin of his?"

"No, a . . . friend. We came up in the same coffle from New Orleans."

Lula cocked her head and stared. "I'll be! Little Effie. You sho did grow up big and fancy. What you doin' back?"

"I'm trying to piece together my life before the War. Jonesy and I were together in New Orleans before Mr. Saulnier bought us. I'm hoping he might know something."

"Why you talk all funny like?" one of the other laborers asked.

She spun the shortest explanation she could, eager to return to the topic of Jonesy and wary of spawning more questions, leaving out all mention of what Adeline termed her *unfortunate occupation*.

"But about Jonesy," she said when they were satisfied. "Does he yet live in these parts? I'd so like to see him again."

Lula flashed a curious expression, then shook her head slowly. "No one seen him since you's all run off. We thought since neither of you was brought back by them patrollers that you made it to safety together."

Effie tried to wind back from her recollection of hiding in the grass at the edge of the Union camp to when she'd been with Jonesy in the swamp. He'd carried her as they fled, his arms tight around her, his heart thumping steadily in her ear, and then . . . nothing. She squeezed her eyes closed and tried to envision it. Only muted daylight shone behind her lids.

"Real shame about all that," Lula said. "Some of them other boys weren't so lucky."

"What do you mean?"

"Massa had them two who the patrollers brought back covered in hot tar and nailed to the fence. Kept 'em there even after they was dead so no one else would think of runnin' off to join the Yanks."

Effie was grateful she hadn't eaten. Bile burned in her throat and rose the longer she listened. Had she slowed them down after all? Had they been right to want to leave her behind? She looked at the ground between her feet. A fat millipede scampered between the tufts of grass and burrowed into the red soil. "When I followed them into the swamps that night . . ." Her voice caught. "I didn't know they were running away."

Lula shook the biscuit crumbs from her skirt. "You always was on Jonesy like a wart on a frog. At his heels every morning on the way out to the field, beside him every night by the fire, gobblin' up everything he don't eat, though your cabin be clear across the yard."

"You talk like I was a stray."

"You was!" She balled up her lunch cloth and tossed it into her pail. "Queer little thing, as I remember."

Effie stood. She wished she were back on the boat bound for New Orleans. A mosquito landed on the back of her neck. She slapped it dead and wiped the smear of blood off on her skirt. "That's all you know?"

"Don't take no offense. All orphans is strays. And Jonesy didn't seem to mind much . . . 'cept . . ."

"Except what?"

"Well, only one of you's here."

CHAPTER 26

Effie carried Lula's words with her the rest of that day and through the next. They sat with her on the steamboat as they chugged back to New Orleans a day early. Tom said it was because he'd made it round to all the settlements and towns and best get back to update the big bugs on the goings-on here. But Effie knew they'd left on account of her. She'd not managed a smile, not even a fake one, since returning from the old Saulnier plantation.

Only one of you's here.

Just because he'd not made it to the Union line with her didn't mean Jonesy was dead. They'd gotten separated was all. By that time of the War, the Yanks held much of southern Louisiana. Maybe he ended up at a different camp. Or stowed away on a boat and made it downriver to New Orleans.

She would search the War records. The enlistment rolls, pension applications, contraband camp filings. Adeline or Samson would know how to get such documents. His name was bound to turn up.

Tom offered to walk her home when their steamer docked at the levee, but Effie declined with a flat no. It struck her only after they departed she ought to have added thank you. Instead of heading up Poydras toward Mrs. Neale's, she took Canal, then Royal Street into the Quarter. The streets were still crowded, despite summer's quickening, thick with the smell of hot pepper and roses.

She started toward Adeline's house, but then realized it was Sunday, the day of Mr. Chauvet's fête. Samson would be there too. Not an hour had passed in St. James that her thoughts didn't circle back to him. She found him in the fields, laboring as she had done all those years ago. She found him in the lengthening shadows of the slave cabins, where he too must have hidden from the sweltering heat and sun. She heard the echo of his voice in the sharecroppers' woeful tales.

But with her wind-snarled hair and travel-rumpled dress, Effie was hardly fit to call at Mr. Chauvet's. Her feet slowed, and she thought to turn around. Best return to the boardinghouse and wash the St. James mud from between her toes, the stench of river and burning cattails from her skin, and set about polishing her buttons to quiet her mind.

But what of this pressure, threatening like the noxious effluviums of the dead, to bust her from within? Three days gone and only a spattering of new memories to show for it. Nothing that connected her to kin. Only Jonesy. Who'd not been seen or heard from since they'd run away into the swamps.

Had Lula been right? Had Effie been nothing more than a stray to him? Like a wart on a frog. Had she been the reason the patrollers found them?

Effie kept walking, farther into the Quarter. Her arms ached from carrying her travel bag, but she did not slow. Adeline had mentioned St. Phillip Street when speaking of Mr. Chauvet, and she headed there in hopes of finding his house.

She wouldn't trespass beyond the foyer or tarry long. Wouldn't ruin the fête with her dour mood and drab attire. She and Adeline could speak in the carriageway, the kitchen, out on the street. Effie didn't care. She only needed Adeline to tell her Jonesy wasn't dead. To reassure her they would find his name on some ledger or roll, even as they'd failed to do with her kin.

Then Adeline would fetch Samson for her and he'd walk her home. How foolish she'd been to dither over his proposal. Would that she were already his wife and needn't part with him on Mrs. Neale's steps and pass night's hours alone.

The afternoon sunlight was waning when she reached St. Phillip Street. Several stately townhouses lined the road. She asked a flower peddler if she knew which residence belonged to a Monsieur Chauvet. The girl, a dark-skinned Creole with dirt-stained palms, shrugged and shook her head.

"He's hosting a party. You might have seen a line of carriages earlier."

The girl pointed to a wide, three-story home down the way. Effie bought a gardenia bloom from the girl for her trouble and threaded the stem through one of the buttonholes of her jacket. A small improvement to her tired appearance. And certainly to the smell of burning coal and river weed and mud that clung to the fibers of her dress.

Two homes the size of Mrs. Neale's could fit within the residence the peddler had directed her to. White molding crowned the brick facade with a wrought-iron balcony stretching the width of the second-story. More molding and a fanlight window capped the front door.

Voices sounded from within. Laughter. Clanking glasses and the strings of a mandolin. Effie hesitated, wishing herself across town in the quiet of her small room, but desperate to see Adeline and Samson.

A servant in a crisp, tailored suit answered when she knocked. He eyed her like she were a fishmonger trying to sell last week's catch, and bid her wait—not within the chandelier-lit hallway, but on the steps—while he gave Mr. Chauvet her name.

Effie smoothed the flyaway hairs about her temples and adjusted the gardenia at her breast. Through the half-opened door, she could see into the parlor, where several guests lingered by an unlit fireplace carved of dark green marble. Others sat on velvet-upholstered chairs and at a small, polished-oak tea table.

The servant returned, and with him Mr. Chauvet.

"Mademoiselle Jones, such a pleasure to see you again." He didn't scowl over her dress and frazzled hair the way his servant had, but took her arm and ushered her in. "But you're meant to be in St. James, *n'est-ce pas?*"

He nodded to her travel bag and his servant reached to take it, but Effie waved him off. "I don't mean to stay. My apologies for intruding at all. Our trip ended early and I'd hoped to speak with Adeline a moment."

Mr. Chauvet held fast her arm, despite surely noticing the dust rubbing off onto his sleeve. "She'll be delighted to see you. She's always her best self around you. But you must come in, at least for a moment, and have some champagne and hors d'oeuvres."

Reluctantly, Effie laid her bag beside the lacquered hall table and strode with him into the parlor. Looks of curiosity and surprise flickered over the faces of his guests. A frown, a knit brow, a puckered mouth. But none let their smiles lapse for long.

"I hope it wasn't some misfortune that cut short your trip," Mr. Chauvet said, handing her a flute of champagne from a passing tray. "You look rather upset."

"No, only tired."

They passed from one room of the double parlor to the next. Silky red drapery festooned the windows, and plush carpet cushioned her step. The stark contrast to the modest cabins in St. James, where flannel rags covered the windows and spiders crawled through gaps in the unfinished floorboards, made Effie dizzy.

The champagne didn't help. Nor her dizziness nor this unshakable feeling of guilt.

"Adeline was here but a moment ago." He looked around the room and through the French doors into the sunlit loggia. "Perhaps out back in the gardens."

A waiter passed bearing a silver tray with clam fritters and tiny beefsteak pies. Mr. Chauvet grabbed a fritter and Effie did likewise to be polite. She tasted parsley and nutmeg and the slightest sweetness of cream. The rich food churned in her empty stomach.

"Your friend Mr. Greene is here too," Mr. Chauvet said, leading her toward the garden. "Having some political set-to with Monsieur Rousseve in the study, I believe. It was providence making his acquaintance at the cemetery, if one might say such a thing without being indelicate—"

The clank of shattering stoneware from somewhere within the bowels of the house stopped them in the loggia. A toppled vase in the parlor, perhaps. The urn in the hallway.

"Soirées," he said, shaking his head.

"You don't enjoy them?"

"*Sincèrement,* I'd just as soon a quiet afternoon in my study." He let go her arm. "Excuse me just a moment, mademoiselle."

Effie liked him all the better for his answer. If Adeline must marry for name and money, Mr. Chauvet was a worthy choice. Kind and frank as he'd been, Effie itched to be gone from this place as soon as she'd seen Adeline.

She wandered through the garden. Save for staff bustling to and fro from the kitchen, the courtyard was empty. She wound her way back through the loggia and parlor, leaving her half-drunk glass of champagne among several empty flutes on the marble-topped tea table. A waiter passed with more food, but though the aroma wafting from his tray made her stomach rumble, she'd settle for cold ham from Mrs. Neale's larder.

Across the wide center hall was the study. Bookshelves lined the walls. A fat, polished desk with legs curved like S's sat to one side. Cigar smoke curled through the air. Several men lounged within, but no Samson. He and Mr. Rousseve must have taken their discussion elsewhere.

At the far end of the center hall curved a staircase. Effie hesitated, then ascended the steps. The noise of the party diminished as she climbed, the music and the banter, the footfalls and clatter. She walked down another hallway to a door leading to the front balcony. Light, colored pink from the sunset, spilled in through the flanking windows.

For the first time since arriving, Effie relaxed enough to draw breath into the bottom lobes of her lungs. Gardenia perfumed the inhale, heavy and fragrant, though the edges of the petals had already begun to brown.

She'd passed several rooms on her way to the windows, all quiet and closed. Adeline wasn't up here, but Effie lingered a moment more in the rosy light to bolster her nerves for another pass through the parlor before giving up and going home.

Then, from one of the rooms, Effie heard laughter, soft and tremulous, a timid intrusion into the silence. She followed the sound to a door, not fully closed as she'd thought at first pass, but cracked a hairsbreadth open. More laughter. Familiar now that she was up close. Adeline's.

Effie raised her hand to knock, but another sound, a voice, deep and rich, stayed her knuckles.

"That's all you do? Strike these keys and the corresponding letter is printed on a piece of paper?"

Effie flattened herself against the door and peered through the crack. This room looked similar to the study below. More bookcases, another desk, but this one smaller and more modestly appointed. Mr. Chauvet's private office, perhaps? Adeline and Samson stood side by side gazing at a contraption on the desk. It reminded Effie of a sewing machine, with painted paneling and boxy shape, but a roller sat atop. Samson leaned over and pressed a button, one of many seated at the near end of the machine. A clicking sound and movement atop the roller.

"Bully! That's something," Samson said. "How does it work?"

Adeline shrugged, her expression half as animated as Samson's. "*Je ne sais pas.*"

He took a step closer, turning from the machine to face her. "What's it called again?"

"Typing machine, typewriter, something like that."

"Have you tried it?" He moved behind her then, so close her bustle flattened against his legs, and guided her arm toward the machine.

Adeline gave another weak laugh. "Really, monsieur, I'm sure I can manage on my own." But she didn't wriggle away.

Together, they struck another key. The sound made Effie start.

Adeline turned and batted his chest. "A crackling fire is more impressive."

He moved nearer still. "It might not be *the* most impressive thing in the room, but it's close."

"Oh?" Adeline fluttered her lashes and bit her bottom lip.

Effie's brain struggled to process the disparate evidence presented her. Samson and Adeline disliked the other. Both had made a point of telling her so. He met none of her criteria for a suitable beau. And she hadn't the slightest care for politics and progress—the very things he lived for. But they were standing so close, the pupils of their eyes wide and hungry.

Samson planted his hands on the desktop, caging Adeline between his arms.

Downstairs, the mandolin player started up a new tune. Someone joined on the piano. Effie's knees seemed to have lost all cartilage and wobbled bone upon bone. No amount of rationalizing could change what lay before her.

Samson leaned in and brushed his lips along Adeline's jaw.

"Mr. Greene, please." She hit his chest again, but this time with even less force than before. "Think of Effie."

The sound of her name stopped Effie's heart mid-squeeze.

But not Samson. His lips moved from her jaw to her mouth. For several slurred-together seconds, Adeline stood like a porcelain doll within his embrace, unmoving and rigid. Her eyes strained toward the ceiling and squeezed shut as if she shared in Effie's pain. Then a sigh. Resignation? Desire? Her lips livened and she kissed him back. Effie turned away.

The lush hallway carpet silenced her footfalls. She walked slowly at first, each step a labor. But by the time Effie reached the stairs her feet couldn't move fast enough. She had to get away. Away from the sound of their lips meeting and breath quickening. Away from the sight of their bodies pressed one against the other. Away from that feeling of having been gutted like the bodies of old and filled with sawdust.

At the bottom of the stairs, she nearly collided with Mr. Chauvet.

"Mademoiselle Jones, are you quite well?"

"I . . . I have to go."

"But I haven't yet found Adeline for you. I know she's—"

"Upstairs." Effie swallowed the taste of nutmeg and bile. She grabbed her travel bag from the floor and started toward the door. Before leaving, she turned, squared her shoulders, and looked Mr. Chauvet dead in the eyes. "Upstairs kissing Mr. Greene."

CHAPTER 27

———⟫◆⟪———

Yellow jack arrived with the summer, striking all parts of the city, but paying special favor to the immigrant slums. Barrels of tar and sulfur burned on the street corners to stave off the poison's spread, leaving the air sharp and smoky.

While she pitied jack's jaundiced and emaciated victims, Effie welcomed the deluge of work. She might attend two or three bodies a day, trudging home in the dark, arriving long after supper cooled and the parlor lamps had been dampened. When she did manage to return to Mrs. Neale's before curfew, the other boarders fled to their rooms, afraid the poison had rubbed off upon her. Even Meg, who'd made such progress with her letters, avoided her.

Effie welcomed the estrangement too. Captain Kinyon had been right. Strict detachment was the best policy—with the dead and the living. Had she followed his guidance, she'd yet be whole and well. For as surely as some Union surgeon like Captain Kinyon had sawed away Tom's leg, so too had Samson and Adeline gouged out everything between her breastbone and spine, not even bothering to use a well-sharpened blade.

Both had tried to call upon her. Samson once at Mrs. Neale's. Adeline several times at the shop. But in this at least chance favored Effie and she'd not been around to turn them away. Their calling cards and missives were easy enough to tear or burn, but had she the strength to dismiss them in person? Could she resist Samson's voice and resplendent smile? Could she pull free were Adeline to take her arm?

Sooner or later they would forget her. Perhaps already had. That evening at Mr. Chauvet's fête proved how easily they could cast her from their thoughts. A feat, for all her inadequacies of memory, Effie would never master.

Two weeks passed after her trip to St. James Parish and the arrival of yellow jack before Effie found time to slip away to the pharmacy to replenish their supply of chemicals. Though not yet July, the air was positively swampy. A dappling of sweat beaded on her upper lip as she hurried through the streets. Inside was little better. She fanned herself with her hankie as she waited for the pharmacist to measure out the mercury and arsenic.

Sunshine refracted through the glass show globes displayed in the windows. The water inside was dyed red on account of the epidemic, giving the splintered light a bloody tinge. She browsed the shelves of boxes and bottles—cough elixirs, asthma powder, worm syrup. A leech jar sat on the counter.

She wandered over to an arrangement of perfumed creams and powders. A shiny tin caught her eye. Leaves with swirling, intertwined stems decorated the label, with the words *Crème de Vetiver* printed in the center. Effie brought the tin to her nose. Adeline. She inhaled again.

"*Fini*," the pharmacist said, turning from his pestle and scales. He nodded to the tin in her hand. "That too, ma'amselle? It's a lovely scent."

Effie thrust the cream back on the shelf, then, noticing the upside-down lettering, fumbled to right it. "Just the chemicals."

Outside she could still smell the vetiver and nearly collided with a carriage as she tried to cross the street.

"Watch out, darkie!" the driver yelled. She stepped back onto the banquette and waited for a break in the to-and-fro of carts and buggies. Still that smell, not altogether uncommon here in the Quarter. All the more reason to hurry back across Canal.

"Effie."

She turned reflexively.

Adeline stood in a summer dress of green cotton—likely reincarnated from a previous season as everyone else about town was wearing peach and yellow. And black. "Your friend Colm said I might find you here."

"He's not my friend." Effie brushed past her and hurried along the banquette in the opposite direction she'd intended.

"Effie, wait!" Adeline's shoes clicked atop the bricks behind her, matching Effie's quickening pace.

Another busy street halted her, and she spun around. "What do you want?"

Adeline held her gaze a moment and then looked down. She tugged at the cuffs of her gloves. "I thought we might sit somewhere. Cool off with a soda or some ice cream."

"I haven't time."

"You've not acknowledged any of my calls, returned any of my letters. Did something happen in St. James?"

Close up Adeline looked wan. Her hair was pinned in a simple bun with errant strands feathered about her face. Effie caught herself scrutinizing the hue of her skin and whites of her eyes for jaundice and cursed her relief at seeing none of jack's telltale signs. She crossed the street, heedless of the oncoming wagons, to the opposite banquette. Banana leaves spilled over courtyard walls, and bougainvillea curled down from the overhead galleries. Effie swatted them away. The road she followed petered out beside St. Louis Cathedral into Jackson Square.

She'd not yet shaken Adeline, but the muggy air conspired with her heavy bag to slow her. A crenelated hedge ringed the square and before she could find a break in sculpted foliage, Adeline overtook her.

"*Ma foi,* Effie! What's gotten into you?"

"I've got to get back to work." She tried to move around her, but Adeline sidestepped to block her path.

"You're going the wrong way."

"I know."

"*Chère,* you don't look at all well."

"I could say the same for you."

Adeline flinched and smoothed the flyaway strands of hair back from her face. "Mamm is having one of her spells and I've not—"

"I don't care."

"That's an awful thing to say! Four days in the country and you come back ornery as the devil."

Effie spun around and started back the way she'd come. The *clickety-clack* of Adeline's footfalls again followed.

"Come now, *chère*. Even Samson's worried after you."

The mention of his name hit her like a blow to the ribs. She shambled to a stop but did not turn around.

"He says you've not answered his notes. Haven't come to any of the club meetings. Haven't—"

"Mr. Greene, you mean."

"What?"

"You always called him *my* Mr. Greene before."

"Well, yes, but now that we're acquainted I thought to take the liberty and call—"

"Acquainted?" Effie laughed. "That's a rather ill-fitting description."

"What?"

Effie turned back and closed the space between them, a strange fever overtaking her. "Certainly you're on more intimate terms than that."

"Whatever are you talking about?"

She shouldered her carpet bag and jabbed a finger into Adeline's sternum. "I saw you together at Mr. Chauvet's party."

The flush of exertion faded from Adeline's cheeks. "*Mais,* you were in St. James."

"Was that the first time you snuck off alone as *acquaintances,* or were there times before and I was just too stupid to see?"

Adeline rubbed her chest where Effie had poked her and eyed the passing strangers. "Keep your voice down."

"I should have known better than to trust a charlatan like you."

Adeline opened her mouth to speak. Beneath the narrow brim of her hat, the veins of her forehead bulged. Her hands twitched at her side and Effie took a step back in case she decided to swing. But she did not. She closed her mouth. A sob rocked her shoulders.

Such a scene—here in the most trafficked square in New Orleans—caught Effie off guard. Hadn't she wanted those tears? Wasn't that what she'd tried to provoke? She felt her resolve slipping, but shored it up with the bitter remembrance of the party. Their whispering and laughter. Had Effie been the object of their ridicule? Silly Effie. Strange Effie. Surely she didn't believe a man like Samson could love her, that a woman like Adeline would call her friend.

She slung her heavy bag over the opposite shoulder and started to walk away, but Adeline's voice stopped her.

"I couldn't help myself." Another sob and sniffle. "I know it's wrong, but I wanted to feel what you felt. Love. Passion. You've done nothing these past months but prattle on about how great he is. How handsome, how smart, how brave. I thought for sure you were exaggerating. But then I met him and saw that it was true. I tried to resist. *Ma foi,* I tried!"

Effie's hand squeezed around the strap of her bag. The bottles of mercury rattled inside. Above the leafy treetops of Jackson Square, the pointy masts of schooners docked in the nearby river jabbed at the sky.

"And then Mr. Chauvet. He fancies himself a wire-puller and thought Samson could be just his ticket. After the funeral, we met him over lunch, purely accidental. The men gabbled of politics and the Louisiana Club. *Chère,* I tried to ignore him. I did. His smile, the way he fixes you with his eyes such that you can hardly breathe."

Effie knew all too well the feeling.

"At la fête, when he asked to see Mr. Chauvet's new typewriter, that was the first time we . . . we were alone. I swear on St. Marie."

"The first time." Effie choked on the words, picturing them lying together in bed, the sheets tangled and mattress made lumpy by their lovemaking. She'd not fooled herself into thinking the party had been an aberration, that as soon as their lips parted they'd realized their grave mistake and avowed never to see each other again. But confirmation that their affair had continued, may be continuing still, reopened Effie's wounds.

A couple strode past them. He doffed his hat. She nodded beneath the shade of her parasol. Adeline nodded in return. Neither she nor Effie managed a smile.

"Please, *chère.* You must forgive me. These past weeks have been dreadful." She grabbed Effie's hand and cocooned it between her own.

For a moment time seemed to slip back, taking with it all the heartache of the past weeks. What a comfort it was to hear Adeline's voice again. To feel her soft touch. Smell her perfume.

"Mamm's not risen from bed once. Odette, Béatrice, and the

others have fled the heat and yellow jack. Mr. Chauvet hasn't called
once since his party, busy with business I imagine, but—"

The mention of Mr. Chauvet jolted Effie to the present. She
yanked free of Adeline's grasp. "Of course he hasn't called. Did you
think you'd have this little dalliance with Samson and yet marry Mr.
Chauvet?"

"Well, I—"

"He knows, Adeline. About you and Samson. That's why he's not
returning your calls."

"Nonsense." She straightened and adjusted the tilt of her hat, casting her reddened eyes in shadow. Then she whispered, "I think I can
manage a petite liaison without—"

"I told him, at the party, that you and Samson were upstairs together. I imagine he witnessed your petite liaison himself."

Adeline's jaw slackened. "*Fi donc!* You what? Have you any idea
how this could ruin me?"

"I loved Samson—his name, his modest income, his past—all of
him, and you destroyed that. You destroyed your own life too. I only
helped it along."

Adeline slapped her. The lace gloves she wore blunted the effect,
but Effie still felt the sting. Not only on her cheek but through her entire body. Adeline gasped and recoiled her arm. Her eyes were wide
and penitent. She started to speak, then flattened her lips around the
sound. Her shoulders squared and eyes hardened.

Effie too straightened. Their gazes tangled for the span of several
heartbeats. Then Effie stalked away, half expecting to hear the tap of
Adeline's footfalls again behind her. Horses whinnied in the street.
A steamboat horn bellowed from the river. An infant wailed. But no
sound of Adeline. Gone too was the smell of vetiver, replaced now by
rotting fruit and the lingering tinge of sulfur.

Effie slowed, listening to the church bell toll once for the hour,
then let the crowd sweep her away.

CHAPTER 28

Effie drank her coffee standing, even as it still steamed, not waiting for Mrs. Neale to set out the cream. Upstairs, the other boarders clamored about their rooms, soon to descend for breakfast. She grabbed a biscuit as soon as Mrs. Neale laid out the tray and started toward the door.

"Got some fresh-made marmalade in the kitchen," Mrs. Neale said after her.

Effie only shook her head.

"A letter arrived for you yesterday."

At this, Effie stopped, one hand around the burning biscuit, the other reaching for her umbrella. She waited while Mrs. Neale rummaged through the console table drawer. "That crippled man came by again yesterday. A Creole lady with him. Said he hoped you was well and to remind you about some meeting or other tonight."

"The ward meeting." Effie had no intention of going and wished after eight weeks they'd take her absence for granted.

Mrs. Neale stopped her rummaging and looked at Effie. "I told him you was well, but I reckon he knows, same as I do, that ain't the truth."

"The letter?"

She pulled out several sheets of crumpled paper, old calling cards, a length of dusty twine, before, at last, the letter. "Who you know at the War Bureau?"

Effie plucked the letter from her plump fingers and turned for the door. "Thank you, Mrs. Neale." She didn't bother to add she'd not be back before curfew. Mrs. Neale knew. Though the yellow jack epidemic had begun to taper and soon Effie would need a new excuse.

Outside, she opened her umbrella and hurried across the street before tearing at the seam of the envelope.

> *Dear Miss Jones,*
> *I regret to inform you we have no record of any Negro soldiers enlisted under the given or surname of Jonesy. There are a multitude of soldiers with the surname of Jones, but none mustered in the Louisiana National Guard or Infantry during the timeframe referenced in your letter. Please inquire again with additional limiting criteria.*
> *Sincerely,*
>
> *Lt. Jackson Humphries*
> *Records Division*
> *United States War Department*

Rain pattered against Effie's umbrella, dripping down from its edges. The wind changed and a few drops splattered onto the paper. She watched as the ink ran and words blurred, then crumbled the letter and tossed it into the gutter.

Owing to the rain and early hour, the streets had yet to fill and Effie hardly had to raise her eyes from slickened pavers as her feet carried her to the shop. What now? For the past several weeks she'd done nothing but sleep, eat when food was handy, attend to her job, and search for Jonesy. She'd returned to that stifling room on the top floor of the statehouse and scoured the Freedmen's Bureau records again. His name, like her own, was absent from any of the roll books, letters, and newsprint clippings. She'd written the pension office, the records bureau, even the state penitentiary in Baton Rouge. Where else could she look? It was as if Jonesy were a ghost, a figment contrived by her imagination.

What, then, did that say of her? Besides the misspelled name of a slave girl on a bill of sale and her own corporeal form, what proof was there of her own existence?

When Effie reached the shop, the door was already unlocked and the showroom lamps lit. Fog rimmed the windows, but she could make out Mr. Whitmark and two other gentlemen inside. She entered through the carriageway, stamping the mud from her boots and shaking out her soggy hem. The linen she'd washed and hung the night before drooped sodden from the clothesline stretched across the courtyard. Of course, Mr. Whitmark hadn't the presence of mind to take it down before heading to bed.

She'd trodden light around him since the incident at the morgue, arriving early to perform her chores about the shop before he was up, or waiting until he'd locked the doors and gone to supper before balancing the ledgers and inventorying the supplies. They no longer discussed the dead as they had in the early days—which artery she'd chosen, how much fluid had been needed, what peculiarities made the procedure difficult. Indeed, they hardly spoke at all.

She started for the storeroom when the men's voices inside the shop caught her ear.

"Mr. Ellis will be so pleased," one of the men said. "It's looking to be a tight race and a luncheon is just the sort of thing we need to galvanize support."

"Have you any thoughts on the menu?" the second man said.

"Plan whatever you like. Duck, crab cakes, gumbo. I don't give a deuce. Just have the club send over the invoice." Mr. Whitmark's voice came clipped and thin.

Though she'd stopped attending the ward meetings, Effie still read the papers. Surely they weren't talking about Nathaniel Ellis, the Democratic challenger for statehouse here in ward three.

"Leave all the details to us," the first man said.

There was a shuffle of footfalls and jangle of the front door opening.

"By chance, will your brother be in attendance?" the man asked. "He and Mr. Ellis fought side by side in the Great Struggle, did they not?"

Even from the loggia, Effie could hear Mr. Whitmark's sigh. "I'll be sure to invite him."

Both men thanked him and bade him good day.

She leaned against the stucco wall and watched the rain fall in the courtyard. How had the world turned so topsy-turvy in the eight months since she'd arrived? Mr. Ellis was a known and vocal White League member. He'd written letters to the *Picayune* encouraging hotels and ice-cream parlors and saloons to disregard the civil rights bill and refuse service to Negroes, offering to pay whatever fines the Usurper's government leveed. He called for a return to the days of star cars when the streetcars had been segregated and Negroes could ride only those marked with a star. "Freedmen need a steady, shepherding hand to guide them back to their place," the papers quoted him as saying.

This was the man Mr. Whitmark was helping elect?

"Effie."

His voice gave her a start. She flinched and straightened.

"525 St. Ann Street. Dropsy. I'll send Colm with the cooling board when he arrives."

For the span of several heartbeats, Effie just stood there, her gaze lost in the damp sheets ruffling in the wind. Rain pinged against the pavers and tile roof above. The clouds seemed so low they might suffocate them. Mr. Whitmark cleared his throat. She startled again and nodded.

She was halfway down the carriageway, her hands laden with supplies, the hook of her umbrella wedged in her armpit, when he called to her again. "Effie, boil me some coffee before you go."

Her muscles clenched and she exhaled. Colm, who'd newly arrived, loitered by the gate, finishing his cigarette. He took a drag and shook his head. "You look about as lively as a corpse this morning."

Another exhale. She started to turn back to the kitchen, but his voice stopped her.

"Off with ya." He ground his cigarette into the stucco wall. "I'll fetch his lordship the coffee."

Three days later, Mr. Whitmark dispatched her to yet another dropsy case. She'd stayed busy during the intervening days with two more yellow jack deaths and a woman lost to childbed fever. Her feet ached before even arriving at the small cottage in the Marigny, the soles of her boots already starting to wear thin. She'd passed within a block of Mrs. Carrière's home on her way, and kept her head down lest she spot her among the morning crowd.

Distance, she reminded herself, even as her ears strained to pick out Mrs. Carrière's voice or Jonah's carefree laugh amid the street's banter. She'd spent nearly every day of her remembrance alone— even those days in the company of Captain and Mrs. Kinyon. It ought to be easy to return to such a life. Damn her ears, her wistful heart and weak constitution. Damn herself for ever falling out of practice.

She mounted the whining steps of her destination and rapped lightly on the door. A middle-aged woman answered, her graying hair pulled taut in a low bun. Beneath her sagging, sallow skin, the planes of her face were arrestingly familiar. Sharp jutting chin, peaked nose bridge, tall forehead. Effie found herself gaping, her hands sticky and pulse pounding.

"*Oui?*" the woman said, her voice hard and raspy. Other words, *vilaine négresse* and *diseased as ta mamm,* rang in Effie's mind.

An impatient stamp of the woman's foot jolted Effie to attention. She dropped her gaze.

"Miss Jones, missus—er—ma'am. With Whitmark Undertaking."

The woman humphed and turned back into the house, leaving the door open for Effie to follow. With each step she took through the parlor toward the bedroom, Effie's nerves wound tighter. The house smelled of summer mold and old furniture. Today Colm had arrived before her and draped the mirrors and portraits in black crepe. The arms of the mantel clock sat fixed at twelve to midnight. Nothing out of the ordinary.

Why then did her every muscle itch to run?

Inside the bedroom, she laid out her supplies on the dressing table. Colm had set up the cooling table by the window and moved the body over from the bed. She smoothed back the covers with a shaky hand and turned to regard the body. Disease had ravaged this man before death—bloating his arms and legs into elephantine appendages. His skin was stretched and shiny, his abdomen round as a globe. But it was his face, gaunt and whiskered, she couldn't look away from.

An image flashed before her mind's eye: this very same face, younger and backlit in blinding sunlight. She reached out to the body. Closed the gaping mouth. Peeled back an eyelid to reveal a brown iris. Recoiled.

Yes, this was the same man.

Effie's knees went soft. She shuffled backward and sat on the bed. The stench of this man struck her. Shit and urine and several days' worth of decay. But he had only died last night, and likely hadn't pissed in days on account of the dropsy. Still, the smell was everywhere. In the air. On her skin, her clothes, her hair. She closed her eyes, but not even the blackness brought her calm.

Her mind's vision adjusted to the dark, and though she could feel the lumpy, moss-filled mattress beneath her, she was in a shed. The shed she'd remembered from before. In the light that stole between the wood siding, she saw her mother. Her beautiful, frail mother.

"*Viens-ici,* Effie. Come here." Her trembling hand smoothed down Effie's unbound hair. "*Mon petit oiseau. Mon coeur.*" She gathered Effie up in her gaunt arms and rocked her while she hummed.

Too soon the humming stopped and the memory crept onward. No more light through the siding. Her mother stiff now and sleeping. Too tired to wake and play. How could she sleep with her eyes wide like that?

The glow of sunlight came again, brightest beneath the locked door. Maman sleeping still. Eyes open and fixed on the ceiling. Dull. Hazy.

Effie lay down on the dirt floor beside her. How cold her skin was. How damp and sticky. She pulled her mother's arm around her and said her name over and over that she might wake.

Maman.

Maman.

Maman.

Effie opened her eyes and wrapped her arms around herself. Her entire body shook. In the quiet of this man's bedroom, she could hear the moans and retching that had preceded her mothers' stillness. The tang of vomit and diarrhea stronger now than the scent of death. Effie slipped from the bed onto the carpeted floor. Sweat clung to her forehead, even as her skin prickled with a chill.

All these months of searching for her past, her family, and here it was. Her master stiff upon the cooling table. Her mistress shuffling about in the next room. The memory of her mother in some lightless shack. Sick, dying, dead.

Effie gasped as if her windpipe had narrowed to a thread. She clawed at her collar until the button popped free. It bounced and rolled over the floor, wobbling to a stop beneath the cooling table. Now, at least, she could breathe.

Minutes passed—they must have—though the mantel clock in the parlor remained silent. Effie's chill warmed into a fire. Her muscles hardened. She rose and walked to the dressing table, studying her tools. Instead of picking up the trocar to tap the excess fluid bloating the body, she grabbed her scalpel. She ripped the dead man's thin nightshirt from hem to collar, laying bare his grotesque body. His belly button protruded like a tumor. His manhood hung shriveled between his bulbous legs.

Effie raised her scalpel and slashed at the femoral artery in his inner thigh. No care and little forethought to the cut. The sharp blade sliced easily through his skin, fat, and veins. Milk-white fluid oozed from the tissue. She slashed at him again. And again. Deep, ragged, ugly. The opposite femoral. The inside of his arms and armpits to get the brachial and axillary too. Not one cut but several, eviscerating the arteries.

She remembered now. All of it. The little farm just outside the city. Her mother's sweet voice and gentle touch. Her mournful humming. The shed they slept in at the edge of the yard. Hot in the summer. Frigid in the winter. Too close to the outhouse to escape the flies and smell. Another slave shared the shed, a man as old and twisted as the oak that shaded the yard. But Massa came some nights too and slept beside her mother for a spell.

He and the old slave had been in town when her mother fell ill. Missus was all too happy to lock them in their shed, claiming she feared the pestilence would spread.

"*L'enfant* never cried for help," she'd said when Massa returned from town some three or four days later and unlocked the shed. "How could I have known?"

But why would Effie cry out—a girl no older than four, excused from her dawn-to-dusk chores, in the company of the one person who'd truly loved her?

Effie reached the man's gizzard-like neck and stopped. Milky, blood-tinged fluid slickened her hands and splattered her sleeves. She used his nightshirt as a rag and wiped clean her fingers before making her final cuts. These were steady, careful. She sliced through the skin on either side of his windpipe to reveal his twin carotids. Then she turned the plane of her blade parallel to the artery and cut downward, filleting the vessel in two.

Her hands no longer trembled. Her skin had cooled. The harrowing smells and sounds and sensations had folded back into memory.

She cleaned her blade on the nightshirt and packed it into her embalming cabinet.

Mr. Whitmark would arrive soon to discuss casket and funeral options with her missus. Undoubtedly he'd stop in to check on Effie's progress, sour-faced and silent, as he oft did since the morgue. Best be gone before then.

She grabbed her needle and thread and sewed up the incisions with quick, uneven stitches. His wife had laid out a fresh set of clothes and Effie dressed him, not bothering to align the buttons or straighten his necktie.

Hard to say when Mr. Whitmark would notice she'd not injected any preserving fluid. An astute embalmer would realize right away from the color of the skin and softness of the body. But Mr. Whitmark mightn't notice for hours. If he had Colm straighten the body after they moved it into the parlor, longer still.

Likely tomorrow the smell would alert them. Her missus first, when she awoke.

Effie packed up her embalming cabinet and closed the latch. The other supplies—the fluid and those in the dressing case—technically belonged to Whitmark and she would leave. She also left his button, shined back to its original splendor, resting on the cooling table beside the body. Of all the buttons to have stowed in her pocket that morning, what great portent it should be his.

Before lowering the curtain over the cooling table, she glanced again at the man's gaunt, bewhiskered face. She had his wide-set eyes and chubby earlobes. Her fingers clenched around the velvet. The silk tassels quivered. Would that she could cut those features from his face. Or her own. But she'd already cleaned her scalpel and the idea of unpacking it again seemed more laborious than a day's hard labor.

She let the curtain fall and left the room. Her missus was in the parlor, fussing with the lace chair tidies. Tomorrow, when the smell struck her, she'd send for Mr. Whitmark. He'd try to embalm the body himself and find every vessel spoiled. A sliver of remorse settled between Effie's rib bones for the mess she was leaving him. She wished she might at least explain. But then, the currents carrying them had long since diverged. She could stand before him and scream, and still he'd not hear.

Her missus eyed Effie as she departed without any sign of recognition. But the smell tomorrow—that same smell that must have
wafted from the shed for hours, days even, before Massa came home
and unlocked the door—that she would never forget.

Outside, the midday sun shone down through a tissue of clouds. A
hot breeze swept across the street, stirring the dust and gutter debris.
Her feet carried her with swift, even strides from the cottage. Upriver
two blocks and over another before faltering. She turned down a de-
serted street, taking shelter in the shade of a vine-strangled balcony.

The gravity of what she'd done crept upon her. No undertaker in
town would hire her after this. Mr. Whitmark would see to that. If
he didn't have her arrested. Or worse. But then, he had his reputation
to consider, fledgling as it was. Wouldn't want the scandal in the papers. Likely he'd settle on slander and a few broken bones.

Best stay away from the shop, then, and Mrs. Neale's too, as he
knew where she boarded. But where could she go? With no job and
little savings, who would take her in? Perhaps she had enough for a
steamer ticket back to Indiana, but she'd sooner walk the gangplank
straight into the river.

She slumped against the stucco wall behind her and let her weight
carry her to the ground. The river would be warm this time of year,
the undertow swift. A few stones in her pockets and the weight of her
dress would easily pull her down.

Those were the worst bodies, the ones dredged from the river.
Fish-eaten and waterlogged. Not that anyone would mourn her. She'd
end up like that first body she'd embalmed at the morgue, unclaimed
and decaying.

Her limbs took to shaking again, an uncontrollable shutter she felt
clear to the marrow of her bones. One tear fell. Then another. Then
a veritable torrent. She cried for that man at the morgue, as alone in
death as he'd likely been in life. She cried for her beautiful, ill-used
mother. For Jonesy, lost to her and likely dead. She cried for herself.
For her empty life and broken heart.

Her feet took control again, walking her to a familiar cottage at
the edge of the Marigny. She blew her nose and wiped her eyes before knocking, but her tears returned even before the door creaked
opened. Without a word, Mrs. Carrière embraced her and shepherded
her inside.

CHAPTER 29

For two days Effie didn't move from Mrs. Carrière's haircloth sofa except to trudge to the outhouse. Just when she'd thought her eyes had spent themselves of tears, they'd fill again. It seemed a physiological impossibility that her ducts could expel so much water and the rest of her not shrivel as a result.

On the third day, Mrs. Carrière pulled the crochet blanket off Effie and ushered her outside to bathe. The sunshine stung her eyes, the cool water her skin, but after several minutes of soaking in the basin, her knotted muscles began to unspool. She lathered herself with the violet-scented soap and watched the bubbles glide atop the water's surface, shiny and colorful when they caught the light.

That afternoon she coached Jonah with his jacks. The next day she dredged herself from the sofa to play alongside him.

"I've heard only a few whispers about the Marigny. A blundered embalming, a hasty funeral," Mrs. Carrière said later when Jonah went hunting lizards in the yard. "*C'est tout.* Still, we best be careful. The fewer people who know your whereabouts the better."

Effie agreed. It was hard to muster concern for her own well-being, but she didn't want to endanger Mrs. Carrière and Jonah. "I've got some money saved, back at the boardinghouse. I'll buy a train ticket tonight and—"

"You most certainly will not. You're staying here. With us."

"But—"

Mrs. Carrière flashed her that stern, commanding look she

wielded at club meetings when someone tried to wriggle out of vol-
unteering.

"Thank you. I'll go tonight to fetch my trunk. Alone. After dark,
when the other boarders are asleep. Mrs. Neale stays up late reading.
She'll let me."

"Not alone. Take Tom with you."

Effie shook her head, but in vain.

"He doesn't know anything. But, Effie, *ma chère,* he's worried
mad about you. And, heaven forbid, but you might need some . . .
assistance."

Tom. Effie hadn't seen him since their trip to St. James. She eyed
the sofa, longing to curl up and hide beneath the blanket again. By
right he should hate her, leaving the docks that day so abruptly, re-
fusing his calls. The idea of explaining it all to him—not only of the
man whose body she'd desecrated, but what had come before, Samson and Adeline at the fête, Jonesy and her failed attempts to find
him—made that morning's breakfast rise in her throat.

But he didn't ask any questions. Not when he arrived that evening at the cottage. Not as they serpentined across town, keeping
to lesser-traveled streets and staying wide of the shop. Silence had
always sat easily between them. But tonight it weighed on Effie, stifling as the summer heat.

When they neared the boardinghouse, Tom bid her wait while he
surveyed the road and surrounding buildings. Satisfied no one was
spying on the house or lying in wait for her, he waved her on.

Light shone through the thin drapery shrouding the parlor window. Effie rapped lightly. When Mrs. Neale pulled back the curtain,
her mouth gaped. She hoisted up the sash and pulled Effie into a hug
through the open window.

"Lord, child! We thought you might be dead!"

"Shh," Effie said, enduring her warm embrace a moment before
squirming free. "Is anyone else awake?"

"Just me, finishin' up my psalms." She let them in through the
back door and led the way upstairs, saying nothing as Tom followed,
despite her rule forbidding men in the house. When they reached the
top landing she turned, worrying her prayer book in her hands, and
whispered, "Your boss man been by. Thought you might be hiding
out in your room. Insisted I bring him up."

Effie looked beyond Mrs. Neale to her bedroom. The door hung askew in the jamb, splintered in the middle and sagging from one hinge. She eased the door aside. In the pale glow cast by the flickering hall lamp, the room resembled a detritus clogged canal after a storm. Her trunk gaped open. Her clothes littered the floor. Her books lay scattered, their pages torn and bent, their spines broken. In the far corner, a glint of metal caught her eye. Effie hurried over, her feet snagging on crumbled petticoats and drawers.

Her old tobacco box sat open on its side, buttons scattered around it. Effie fell to her knees and snatched them from the floor. Her shiny sunburst button. Her rifleman's button. The small cavalry cuff button. The pewter one she found at Port Hudson embossed with the letters *US*. But where were the others? She crawled along the floor, tossing aside books and clothing. Dim light and blurry eyes hampered her search. Surely Mr. Whitmark wouldn't have taken any. They were trifles, of no value to anyone but her.

"Effie," Tom said.

She didn't look up. What of her Massachusetts militia button? And the gilded South Carolina state seal button?

Tom eased himself down with his cane to squat beside her. "Effie," he said again, and held out a button.

She gathered it from his palm and wiped her nose on her sleeve. "Thank you."

"How many more are there?"

"Six," she said.

Not until all her buttons had been found did Effie remember what else she'd stowed in the box. She yanked off the lid and flung away the remaining tuffs of cotton.

Gone.

All forty-seven dollars of her savings were gone. So too were the coins from her turned-out purse. She had a few bills yet stashed in the secret pocket of her petticoat, but that was all. Looking about the mess, she felt like a cadaver splayed open in an operating theater, her most private parts displayed for all to see.

Now she was grateful for Tom's silence. Grateful for the way he busied himself with her books as she gathered up her underclothes. He smelled as he had that first day she'd met him, of soap and grease and newsprint—on account of his work at the Republican Office printing press, she now realized. Never mind the reason, though. It was the farthest scent from rosemary and bitter orange shaving soap one could have. For that too she was grateful.

"Suppose I best tell everyone you gone back North," Mrs. Neale said when they'd finished packing and stood on the porch ready to leave.

Effie nodded.

"Meg sure will be sore about it."

Effie's ribs squeezed around her organs at the mention of Meg's name. She opened her trunk and rifled through her physiology manuals and anatomy texts. "Here, give her this." She handed over her well-worn copy of Whitman's *Leaves of Grass*.

Mrs. Neale hugged her again, then said to Tom. "You take care of her now."

He looked down at the weather-bowed steps. Even in the faintly cast streetlight, Effie saw his neck flush a deeper shade of brown. "I mean to, ma'am."

The old woman turned to Effie. "Can't imagine what cause your boss man had thunderin' about like that, but you best lie low for a spell."

"I gave him good cause." Effie grabbed one handle of her trunk and Tom the other. Even now, near penniless, slinking about in the dark, she didn't regret what she'd done.

As summer tapered into fall, Effie remained with Mrs. Carrière, taking on neighbor's laundry and other jobs she could perform closeted in the yard. She didn't ask after Samson and Mrs. Carrière didn't speak of him. The other club members came around and talked with great animation about the coming elections. Effie did her best not to listen, busied herself sorting flyers, stitching banners, fashioning campaign pins, or whatever task was at hand. But words slipped through just the same. Samson's bid for the Senate had fallen through—bad blood with someone at the Louisiana Progressive Club—but he'd likely be reelected to the house. There'd been more deaths in the countryside. More threats and nighttime raids. Even here in the city, Republicans were wary about showing up at the polls.

"Your old boss man's a bona fide Leaguer now, Effie," Tom said one evening. "Saw him chumming with them others over at the Pickwick Club."

Mrs. Carrière shook her head. "Soon we won't have any allies left."

The news didn't surprise Effie but strangely saddened her. How he must hate himself, Mr. Whitmark, ever a traitor to one cause or another. No wonder he'd turned to the bottle. She missed the distraction and sense of purpose embalming had always brought her, yet even with the last of her hard-earned dollars long gone, she was glad to be free of him.

When her attention wound back to the conversation, she found they'd left off Mr. Whitmark and spoke now of a barbecue planned for the Sunday after next in East Feliciana Parish.

"Think you might be up to coming?" Tom asked her. "Reckon you can come out of hiding now, and we sure could use your help settin' up the tables and dishin' out food."

"Two days' journey for a barbecue? Thanks, but no."

"Mrs. Greene won't be there if that's what's troublin' you. On account of her . . . er . . . condition, I expect."

"Mrs. Greene?" Effie asked, choking on the words.

Tom turned to Mrs. Carrière. "You didn't tell her?"

"I was waiting for the right time." Mrs. Carrière cast him a scowl. "Which I dare say wasn't now."

"She's bound to hear tell of it sometime." Tom turned to Effie, reached out as if he might take her hand, then pulled back. "Best you hear it from us."

Effie nodded and waited, though her stomach roiled with what she'd already deduced the news to be.

"Samson married that bright-skinned Creole gal, Amandine, Angeline . . ."

"Adeline," Effie heard herself say.

"That's right. Adeline. About a month back, wouldn't you say, Marie?"

Mrs. Carrière nodded. She strode to her desk and withdrew a letter from the drawer. "She gave me this. Last week at the club meeting. Said something about me being a prima donna and that surely I'd know where you were. I didn't reply. Just took the letter."

A month married? Effie clutched the arm of the sofa until the swaying room stilled. The parlor air was stifling, too hot and bled of oxygen. She recoiled from the folded square of paper when Mrs. Carrière held it out to her. What could Adeline possibly have to say to her? More hateful words about how Effie had ruined her reputation? A gloating description of her and Samson's wedding?

She grasped the letter and crammed it into her pocket. "I'm . . . I think . . . more coffee," she said, grabbing the silver tray from the table. The kettle and empty cream cup rattled as she hurried from the room.

Outside, the cool air needled her sweat-dampened skin. She crossed the courtyard to the kitchen and slammed the tray down on the table. The cup toppled to its side, rolling back and forth as the last drops of cream dribbled out. Her gaze shifted to the stove. A few crackling embers glowed within the firebox. She imagined hurling the letter into the stove's belly and watching it burn. Instead, she tore open the seal.

> Chère *Effie,*
>
> *Samson said you'd returned North, but I doubt he knows any better than that Colm fellow at your shop. Wherever you are, I worry this letter will never find you. Worry you'll tear it into a thousand little pieces before reading it if ever it does make its way to your hand. Can't say I blame you. I know what I did was dreadful,* chère. *Shameful. If I could take back that first kiss and all that came after, I would.*
>
> *I forgive you for telling M. Chauvet about Samson and me. I was cross with you,* bien sûr. *Fuming really, for days. But then loneliness set in. Mamm asked after you and my heart near broke. I meant to make things right between us. I swear. I told Samson we were through. Three weeks I didn't see him. But then I realized,* chère, *I'm carrying his child. What else could we do but marry?*
>
> *I'm scared, Effie. Of Mamm's sickness. Of having this baby. Of what Samson will do when another belle catches his eye.*
>
> *Please call or write.*
>
> Ton Amie,
>
> *Adeline*

Effie stood paralyzed a moment, the words clotting in her brain. She smoothed a hand over her own flat belly, then sank to the floor and wept.

* * *

Mrs. Carrière took to bed with intestinal fever five days before the barbecue. Just a trifling illness, she said, *pas grave,* and insisted upon making the journey. If Effie would just see that Jonah had packed his travel bag and *peut-être* help her pack as well.

Effie refused. She'd seen plenty dead of the disease. Though Mrs. Carrière seemed to be improving with cold sponge baths, quinine, and turpentine oil, two days in a rickety wagon would likely rally the illness and kill her. She argued still—it would crush Jonah not to go; Tom and others depended on her—and tried to rise from bed, only to collapse onto the rug. Effie helped her up, tucked her in, forbid her to rise again. And then, though her own knees threatened to give at the thought of the barbecue, Effie promised to go in her stead.

Two days' travel through rain and mud did nothing to assuage her dread. She couldn't bear to see Samson again, let alone speak to him if he sought her out. She'd mended these last months, but hardly healed. Likely there would always be a scar.

The day of the barbecue, however, dawned bright and clear. A Northern banker and stalwart Republican who'd bought up several hundred acres of land in the parish hosted the festivities. Effie could smell the roasting pigs half a mile out.

When they arrived, she and Tom, with the help of several others from the nearby town, set up trestle tables across the oak-dotted lawn that swept out from the banker's stately home.

Her gaze roved the swelling crowd as she worked. It was irrational to hope Samson wouldn't show. He, along with the local candidate and his Democratic challenger, were the main stump speakers before the feast. But the longer she could go without seeing him, without hearing the siren's call of his voice, the better her fledgling nerves would fare.

Tom came up to her with a glass of lemonade. "Feeling all right?"

"Hmm? Oh . . . fine." She sipped the lemonade in lieu of feigning a smile.

He doffed his slouch hat and wiped his brow. Then, instead of replacing it atop his head, he worried the hat in his hand, folding and scrunching the brim.

"*You* all right?" she asked, as he'd never been one to fidget or dither.

"I . . . it's just . . . I hope you don't mind me saying, you look right pretty today. I think the country air suits you."

Effie narrowed her eyes. Her hair was pinned back in her usual bun and she wore her serviceable navy dress. Likely the new cuffs and collar Mrs. Carrière had embroidered—peach colored to match the rosettes on her bonnet—had caught his attention. "Save your compliments for Marie, she remade the dress for me. I don't—"

"It's not the dress, Effie. Though that's mighty lovely too. It's just . . . you. All of you."

Effie now succumbed to fidgeting, patting her hair, adjusting the ties of her bonnet, smoothing her skirt. That once-elusive smile seized her lips. "Thank you."

She finished her drink and they returned to readying the tables for the barbecue. But somehow, Effie's step felt lighter, her vertebrae straighter, her rib cage less empty.

By the noon hour, hundreds had arrived from the surrounding farms and bayous, infecting the air with cheer. Not even Effie was immune. She helped make space on the tables for all the pies, cornbread, baked sweet potatoes, and seasoned rice people brought to share, and watched the fanfare. Unlike the stodgy Reform Society picnics Captain and Mrs. Kinyon dragged her to, here she watched from within instead of without. Perhaps Tom's compliment had skewed her perception, but when people looked at her she no longer assumed they thought her an oddity, but a regular woman. Perhaps even a pretty one.

Jonah raced over to show her the marble he'd won off another boy. "What d'ya think?" he asked, handing over his prize.

Effie examined the marble—a polished river stone of not quite spherical proportions. Porous and a bit too light for ideal transfer of inertia. She bent down so they were eye level and handed it back. "A fine marble. Take care not to lose it back, now."

Jonah smiled. His two front teeth were all the way in now and he'd lost another incisor.

Effie stood and watched him sprint away. When she turned around, she nearly collided with a man moving in the opposite direction.

"Pardon—"

"Excuse—"

Her vocal cords faltered. Her blood wicked to her core, leaving her stomach heavy and fingers cold.

"Effie!"

Still she couldn't speak. She stumbled a few steps back, knocking into the buffet spread. Her hand landed in a bowl of cooked greens as she tried to steady herself. Bits of onion and soggy leaves squished between her splayed fingers.

Samson smiled, and she longed to die. Right then. Death by unrequited love, humiliation, and collard greens.

He handed her his hankie.

"Mr. Greene," someone called from beside the wooden platform at the center of the lawn, waving him over.

"I . . . er . . . I've got go. I'll find you afterward," he said, his brown eyes lingering on her a moment before he turned to leave.

Effie peeled her hand from the greens and wiped it with Samson's hankie. Grease and leaf juice stained the silky cloth. She brought the hankie to her nose and sniffed. Beneath the smell of ham hock, garlic, and greens was that of his shaving soap. Rosemary and bitter orange. She wadded up the hankie and dropped it to the ground.

The man who'd waved Samson over had taken the platform and called out to the crowd. Voices lowered. He welcomed everyone to the barbecue, said the pigs were near done, but first they'd be treated to some of the best speechifying in all Louisiana. The crowd of onlookers—mostly Negroes, but a spattering of whites too—clapped and cheered.

When the man introduced the first speaker, a tall bearded man from the local Democratic club, the cheers dwindled. A few in the crowd booed and hollered.

"Now, now," the host said. "We're to have a real debate here."

The gathering quieted and the Democrat began his address. Few of his words registered amid the melee of Effie's thoughts. Her sense of normalcy had fled. Her confidence. Her delusions of beauty. Would anyone notice if she wandered away until the speeches were done and barbecue concluded? She charted a path in her mind through the pack of people to a shady spot in the forest where she might hide.

But then, she was tired of hiding. She'd hidden all summer—first in the frantic to-and-fro of her work, then in the tiny confines of Mrs. Carrière's cottage. How exhilarating to stand now in the sunshine! To be among others after so long alone. Instead of sneaking away, she forced her head up and shimmied closer to the platform, training her attention on the speaker. Samson had taken enough from her. She wouldn't give him this day too.

"See what your vote for carpetbaggers has done," the bearded man was saying. "They put heavy liens on ours crops, oblige us to pay taxes, and yet y'all think it strange that we prefer to hire whites, Democrats, to farm our lands. Don't ya see? When white people have plenty, you have plenty."

Effie found his logic laughable. For all Samson's faults, at least he would deliver a sound rebuttal to this man's sapheaded ideas.

"You don't trust those of your race for anything. Not those who manage the clubs, and caucus, and run for office. Admit it! If we can get the government into honest hands, we'll make it a disgrace to plunder the state and swindle her citizens."

Here Effie did laugh, even as her skin burned. Her eyes wandered from the man to the assemblage of onlookers. A mauve hat with feather trim caught her attention, garish among the cottonade bonnets and flannel headscarves most of the women wore. The black hair beneath was smooth and glossy, pinned in fat curls just below the brim. The woman turned slightly, revealing a delicate nose and well-proportioned lips.

For a moment, Effie felt as if she'd breathed in water instead of air. Adeline wasn't meant to be here. What of her condition? Effie craned her neck to see the full profile of Adeline's form. One who knew her less intimately would have missed it—the gentle roundness of her belly hidden beneath the raised waist of her dress.

Effie waited for the rush of envy that had swallowed her that night in Mrs. Carrière's kitchen when she'd read the letter, prepared for the swell of unending tears. Neither came. Instead came relief, akin to what she'd felt upon spying the Union campfires or when she'd stepped off the steamer that first day in New Orleans. It struck Effie how much she'd missed Adeline. How barren her life had become without her.

But the pain of Adeline's betrayal was there too, raw yet and aching. Almost reflexively Effie began balling it up and with it her relief and affection. Tighter, smaller, heedless of what got pulled in with it, until it was so crushed and compact she could bury and forget it.

A tap on her shoulder broke her fixation. "Excuse me, miss. You done dropped this by the picnic tables," a man said, handing her Samson's stained hankie.

"Thank you," she muttered. When he turned away, she crumpled it in her fist. This time she'd take it clear out to the swamps and throw it in the muddy water so it couldn't find its way back to her. But though her hand squeezed tighter, her feet refused to move. Hadn't she done that with the memory of her mother—wadded it up and buried it? With her years as a slave? Did the emptiness feel any better than the pain?

She shook out the hankie, grease-smeared and green as it was, folded it into a neat square, and tucked it into her pocket. A little soap and vinegar and the stains might well fade.

Tepid applause sounded, and she realized the Democrat had finished his oration. Samson nodded to the man as they passed on the platform steps. The man only smirked.

Effie fell in love with him all over again as he began his speech. His confident posture, his lively gestures, his earnest expression. But most of all his voice, smooth and resonant. A voice one felt as much as heard. Effie looked at those around her. Everyone stood as enrapt as she.

Everyone it seemed, save Adeline. Instead of staring up at her husband in admiration, she wandered her gaze about the lawn, shifting, listless, bored.

A twinge of anger surfaced in Effie. And on its heels, sadness. Pity. She let them all course through her, like preserving fluid pumped into an artery, flowing from her largest vessels all the way to her tiniest capillaries. It didn't rid her of the emotions. No more than embalming brought life to the dead. But once felt, their hold on her lessened.

For the first time since returning from St. James, Effie could imagine a future for herself beyond the pain and solitude, a future beyond the dead. Perhaps she would be a teacher, as Tom had suggested, or work alongside a physician. One way or another, she'd find a way to survive. She always had. And this time, she needn't do it alone.

A breeze ruffled the ties of her bonnet, bearing with it the smoky scent of barbecue. She looked again at Adeline, who'd pulled out her fan and used it to swat at the gnats humming overhead. Effie smiled—how ridiculously out of place Adeline was here in the country—and longed to laugh with her about it.

A voice snagged Effie's attention, a man in the crowd calling to Samson. "Get down! You don't belong on that stand any more than you belong in the statehouse."

"Yeah, get down so we can eat," another yelled from a way off.

Those nearest the hecklers shushed them and Samson continued, easily regaining his stride. But then another man standing only a few feet from Effie called out, "You ain't got a lick of sense in that monkey head of yours."

He was a white man, dressed in mismatched coat and pants, a faded slouch hat on his head. When the colored man beside him told him to hush, he spat at the man's feet and shoved him. The colored man shoved back. Samson's voice hummed on in the background. Then the white man reached into his waistband and pulled out a revolver. More weapons were drawn. More pushing.

The roar of a gunshot split Effie's eardrum. Then another from across the lawn.

Samson's voice fell silent.

For a few fleeting seconds, she and everyone around her froze. Then someone screamed. High-pitched and wild. More gunshots. People ran helter-skelter. Effie turned back to the platform. Samson lay sprawled across it, mouth open, eyes fixed. Blood dripped from the platform's edge onto the grass below. Adeline clambered up the stairs and knelt beside him, shrieking.

Effie rushed to them.

"*Mon Dieu, mon Dieu!*" Adeline said, rocking back and forth on her heels. She reached out and lay a hand on his chest, then recoiled, her white glove covered in blood.

Effie felt his neck for a pulse. Nothing. She tried again, wishing for once she didn't know the exact lay of the carotid, the feel of the spongy vessel beneath her fingertips, the telltale stillness of death. Her eyes met Adeline's.

"*Sauve-le!* You can save him, *non*? You must!"

The sound of distant horse hooves drew her attention. Not one set, but many, thundering closer.

"We've got to go," she said. When Adeline didn't respond, Effie shook her by the shoulders. "We've got to leave here. Now."

She'd heard tell at the club meetings of this sort of ruse. White Leaguers, Ku Kluxers, Bulldozers, Regulators, Redeemers—whatever these hateful men called themselves—would stake out Republican gatherings and stir up a "Negro Riot." Under the pretense of protecting themselves and the general citizenry, they'd slaughter all the colored in sight.

"Now!" she said again.

Adeline still didn't rise, but sat weeping beside Samson's body. Effie looped an arm about her waist and started to stand. She'd carry Adeline away if she had to, but then she remembered Jonah.

"Get to one of the wagons or hide in the woods," she said to Adeline, before releasing her and jumping down from the platform.

The lawn was like a riled anthill. Parents scooped up their children and dashed for their wagons and carts. Those who'd come on foot scattered into the surrounding fields and swamps. Some slithered into the crawlspace beneath the banker's house. Then, likely remembering the fire set at Grant Parish, scurried back out, preferring a bullet to being burned alive.

Effie yelled for Jonah until her vocal cords grew swollen. She circled the house. The lawn. Then circled around again before at last finding him huddled between stacks of logs in the woodshed. She gathered him into her arms, both their cheeks wet with tears.

Near the road she found Tom.

"There you are. Thank God!" he said. "Hurry, to the wagon. You can bet more of them buckras on their way."

Effie glanced up and down the road. Carts and buggies rumbled away as fast as their horses and mules could be made go. But in none of them did she see Adeline. "You go on. I'll catch up or meet you back in the city."

"Are you mad?"

She hoisted Jonah into Tom's arms. "I've got to find Adeline."

"I'll look for her, you—"

But Effie had already turned back and was hurrying around the house.

The lawn, only minutes before teeming with people, had emptied. Trampled hats and fans and shawls littered the ground. Two other men, both Negroes, lay dead atop the bloodstained grass. Samson's body remained on the platform, his head lolling over the edge, one arm crossed over his torso, the other stretched out and reaching.

Effie righted his body so he lay atop the platform as if in sleep. She pulled his handkerchief from her pocket and wiped away the thin line of blood trailing from his mouth. The clamor of horse hooves grew. She closed his searching eyes. A final kiss, soft against his cooling lips, and she turned away, leaving him to find Adeline.

No sign of her on the lawn or by the house. Maybe she'd made away on a carriage while Effie was yet searching for Jonah. But then, at the edge of the forest, Effie saw her mauve hat dangling from a low-hanging tree branch.

Just as she reached the tree and plucked free the hat, a posse of mounted white men crested the hill just beyond the house. She hurried deeper into the tangle of trees and brush, squeezing past a thorny greenbrier bush and into the shell of a rotted tree trunk. Her feet sank into the boggy soil. Insects crawled beneath her collar and up her skirts. She crouched. Listened.

Several men dismounted at the edge of the wood. Others galloped off across the field or back to the road. The horse hooves faded and other sounds emerged: boots crunching through the underbrush, dogs barking and sniffing. Just as it had that night in Algiers, the sound injected her with panic. She wrapped her arms around her knees, boring her fingers into her flesh until they met bone. Any shaking and she'd rattle the greenbrier, alerting them to her presence.

The barks and snarls and footfalls drew closer. Then a howl. Her mind drew in on itself, but the dogs were there too. The forest. This one moonlit and swampy. She was no longer crouching but held fast in Jonesy's arms as he loped beside the other runaways.

They heard the dogs before they saw them, barking and splashing through the swamp behind them. Jonesy set her down and pointed in the direction the other men were fleeing. "I'm gonna lead them away. You git along with the others. I'll find you. Run till you see the men in blue. Not gray. Blue. You tell 'em you's lookin' for de Yankees. Say it, Effie."

The thinness of his voice frightened her, but she repeated what he said. "I's lookin' fo de Yankees."

"Good, now git."

Effie didn't move.

"Go!"

She started to cry. Jonesy glanced over his shoulder, then crouched down in front of her and wiped the tears from her cheeks. "No cryin' now, you hear? You's gotta be brave. Just like in the slave yard. Run, now. Run!" He gave her a gentle shove and took off in the opposite direction. A few steps and she turned around, watching him disappear, his bare feet splashing loudly through the swamp, drawing away the dogs.

Effie ran but never found the other runaways. And without Jonesy, she didn't know how to find the someplace better he'd spoken of either. But dawn came and with it campfire smoke and the men in blue.

Now, even with the bloodhounds sniffing and growling only a few yards away, Effie realized she'd found that someplace better after all. Not with the Union army. Not with Captain and Mrs. Kinyon. But here, with Tom and Mrs. Carrière and Jonah.

Another howl. Effie held her breath. The sounds grew closer.

And Adeline. She was part of that someplace better too. Effie had to find her.

"Hey!" someone called from deeper in the woods. "Found footprints headin' this way!"

The clop of the men's boots drifted off in the direction of the voice. The dogs followed. Effie waited through several minutes of silence before standing and peeking about. Her muscles were stiff and her skin bug-bitten. Afternoon sunlight shone in the distance at the edge of the forest. The faint scent of barbecue and gun smoke laced the air.

She picked her way free of the briar bush and trudged into the woods.

Hours passed. The patchwork of sky visible through the canopy drained of color and then began to darken. With dusk coming, she soon ought to turn back. Once it got fully dark, the dogs would have an even greater advantage, and though she hadn't encountered anyone else, she'd heard plenty of screams and gunshots in the distance.

Blisters rubbed at the back of her heels. Her dress was mud-soaked and torn. Crickets screeched. An owl hooted. Possums skittered in the branches above.

Then she heard what sounded like the cry of a cat. Bobcats lived in these parts, she'd been told. Larger, fiercer cats in other reaches of the South. Could one have wandered here? Effie slowly started to backtrack from the sound, her skin prickling and limbs cold. The cry came again, followed by a grumble and rustling. Not a cat's call at all. A woman's muffled scream.

Effie gathered her courage and tiptoed toward the ruckus. Through the trees she spied Adeline on the ground, her mouth gagged with a dirty rag. A white man loomed above her on his knees. He worked free his belt while Adeline struggled beneath him. She clawed at her gag, loosening it, and screamed again. The man laughed. "Call out all you like. Ain't no one gonna hear or do two licks about it if they do."

She yanked off her bloodstained gloves and bared her nails, dragging them down his forearms and slashing at his chest. He turned his belt on her then, lashing her face before she could shield it with her arms. The thwack of leather against skin made Effie's every muscle bunch and tremble.

He struck Adeline again, this time low, across the stomach. When she moved her arms to protect her belly, he whipped the belt across her neck and chest.

Effie had scant recollection of grabbing the gnarled log or creeping closer toward them, but before he could raise the belt for a fourth lash, she bashed him in the back of the head. He fell forward on top of Adeline, who squirmed from beneath him and out of arm's reach.

When the man started to push himself up, Effie took aim for his temple and swung again.

This time, the crack of bone rang loud through the trees. He fell onto his side, motionless, blood trickling from his nose and down the side of his head. A mat of his greasy blond hair stuck to the log. Effie dropped it to the ground, her hands rattling.

"We've got to go," she whispered.

Adeline didn't move. Her eyes were glassy and fixed, her lips mouthing something without the benefit of sound. Effie crouched in front of her and smoothed down her wild hair. A welt had risen across her cheek, and the collar of her dress was torn. "We've got to go."

Adeline looked at Effie with a vacant stare, then down at her hands. Several of her nails had broken off and bled. Dirt caked her skin. She wiped her hands on her skirt, then rubbed them together, frantic and twisting, as if she meant to chafe off her very skin.

Effie tried to still her, but Adeline's hands worked free, turning now to the gag that hung about her neck. She tugged and twisted at the dirty cotton to no avail. *"Dégage-moi! Dégage-moi!"*

"Shh!" Effie reached behind Adeline's neck and untied the gag. "There. You're safe. You're free."

Adeline slung the gag away as if it were a cottonmouth. When she turned back to Effie, the madness in her eyes had begun to settle. They stared at each other a moment. Tears built on Adeline's lashes. Effie's too. The last time they had spoken—that afternoon in Jackson Square—seemed like an apparition, a storyline from someone else's life.

"I'm sorry. I wrote you to—"

Effie pulled Adeline into her arms before she could finish the words. They held each other as if the winds of a hurricane blew.

A gunshot, far in the distance, startled them both, Effie to her senses, Adeline to a frozen panic. The man Effie had killed lay cooling beside them. Night's blackness had overtaken the sky.

Effie gently loosed herself from Adeline's clutches and stood. "Give me your hands, *chère*. We're going to find our way out of here. Someplace safe and better."

EPILOGUE

—➤•◄—

Effie dipped her rag in the sudsy water and wiped the blood, fluid, and sticky whiteness from the limbs. She washed the face and stomach and behind the ears. The hair was dense and matted, but sprang into short, soft curls once wetted down and cleaned.

"*Fe vit,* Effie," Mrs. Carrière said, coming up behind her.

Effie frowned. She *was* hurrying. Bathing a body was far easier with the dead than the living. She tried to wash between the tiny toes, but he kicked and wiggled. She tried to clean his palms, but he kept his chunky fingers closed in tight fists.

Mrs. Carrière put her knuckle in Samson Jr.'s mouth and he suckled. "See, he's hungry. Let's bring him to Maman."

"Almost done." At last, she tickled opened his hand, but he closed it just as quickly, trapping the tip of her finger. His grip was strong, his golden-brown skin soft and warm. He stopped his squirming and stared at her, his dark eyes wide, his little fingers never loosening. Effie laid aside her rag and let him hold on a few moments longer.

The midwife had just finished packing up her supplies when Effie brought the baby back to Adeline. "Spandy-clean and ready to nurse again."

Adeline flashed a tired smile. "Thank you, *chère*."

The midwife said something to Adeline in thick Creole patois that Effie—yet too enraptured with baby Samson—didn't bother to understand. Only when Adeline snickered did Effie become curious.

"She said you've a steady hand and stout constitution."

"Some faint at the first sight of blood or birthing fluid," the midwife said in accented English. "You've a talent for it."

A look from Adeline, and Effie refrained from commenting how embalming the dead and delivering babies wasn't all that different. Both required a sound understanding of human anatomy, a patient and unflappable disposition, a—

"You might consider helping me at some of my other deliveries," the woman said at the door.

"Yes, I'll think on it."

When the midwife left, Effie fussed about the room, opening the shutters for a spot of light, balling up the soiled linen to be washed, freshening Adeline's tea.

"You don't have to stay," Adeline said. "I venture your Tom and *les autres hommes* are itching for news."

Effie sat beside her on the bed, fluffing the pillows and smoothing the quilt, hoping Adeline didn't notice the pink flush that surely colored her ears. "They can itch a moment longer."

"Mamm and Madame Carrière are here." Adeline glanced at Samson Jr. Her smile turned wistful. She swallowed and said with forced levity, "We'll be fine."

Effie felt the pang too. His eyes were the same shade his father's had been, just as clear and arresting. He pursed his little mouth into an O, chasing back her tears. Effie kissed them both. "I know we will."

AUTHOR'S NOTE

In writing my first novel, *Between Earth and Sky,* learning about the experiences of my husband's family compelled me to explore the mistreatment of Native Americans during the boarding-school era. Similar stories of injustice drew me to Reconstruction. No people strove more valiantly or suffered more greatly than African Americans in this era. I didn't want to come at this truth indirectly, but to immerse myself and the reader in their lives. There's hubris in believing I, a white woman, could capture that experience, but also faith in our shared humanity. I hope it is the latter that shines through.

The characters in *The Undertaker's Assistant* are all fictitious, but the backdrop of their lives is based on real experiences and events. Numerous black officeholders served in state legislatures throughout the South during this era. Men like Caesar Antoine and Oscar J. Dunn rose to become lieutenant governors. P. B. S. Pinchback became the first African American governor in the United States in 1872. Others, like Hiram Revels, Blanche Bruce, and Robert B. Elliott, made it all the way to Washington.

The violence and intimidation depicted in the story are based on historical fact as well. White "redeemers" terrorized black men and women throughout the South in a systematic campaign to erode their newly won liberties. The 1873 Colfax Massacre in Grant Parish was one of the largest mass killings in U.S. history. The events of the final chapter are patterned after a barbecue-turned-bloodbath that occurred in Clinton, Mississippi, in 1875.

Not even Mardi Gras was immune from the political strife and terror of the day. The parade floats Effie and her friends witnessed are amalgamated from several well-documented Carnival parades of that era.

To those readers keen to explore Reconstruction further, I recommend the following: *Reconstruction: America's Unfinished Revolution,* by Eric Foner; *Been in the Storm So Long: The Aftermath of Slavery,* by Leon F. Litwack; *Chained to the Land: Voices from Cotton & Cane Plantations,* edited by Lynette Ater Tanner; *Redemption: The Last Battle of the Civil War,* by Nicholas Lemann; *The Portable Nineteenth-Century African American Women Writers,* edited by Hollis Robbins and Henry Louis Gates, Jr.; *Race and Reunion: The Civil War in American Memory,* by David W. Blight; *The Souls of Black Folk,* by W. E. B. Du Bois.

And these brilliant works of fiction: *Red River,* by Lalita Tademy and *Beloved,* by Toni Morrison.

ACKNOWLEDGMENTS

Many people helped bear this book from the first flickering story idea to the finished product. My thanks go out to all of them. In particular:

Jenny Ballif, April Khaito, Angelina Hill, Wendy Randall, and Tonya Todd—my early readers who pushed for more from the story. More heart. More nuance. More direction. All in fewer words.

My agent, Michael Carr, and my editor, John Scognamiglio, who gave me the freedom to follow wherever the story led, then helped me strengthen and sharpen it.

Paula Reedy, Lulu Martinez, Kristine Mills, and the entire team at Kensington, who transformed a simple Word document into this beautiful book and helped bring it to the world.

The staff at the Williams Research Center in New Orleans and Amistad Research Center at Tulane University, whose vast collections of primary source material brought me closer to Effie's voice. Thank you for your commitment to preserving our history.

Fran Lipowitz, my friend and former teacher, who corrected my rusty French. *Merci!* Any errors are my own.

My family. I'm ever so grateful for your love and support!

And Steven. Always Steven, who challenges me to be the best version of myself, while loving me as I am. Thank you.

THE
UNDERTAKER'S
ASSISTANT

Amanda Skenandore

ABOUT THIS GUIDE

The suggested questions are included
to enhance your group's reading of
Amanda Skenandore's
The Undertaker's Assistant!

DISCUSSION QUESTIONS

1. Did the experiences of Effie and her friends align with your assumptions about post–Civil War Reconstruction? If not, in what ways did they differ?

2. Effie spends much of the novel searching for her kin. Though she doesn't find any blood relatives, do you think she's found family in the end?

3. What is it that draws Effie to Samson? Have you ever fallen in love with someone without fully understanding why?

4. Do you think Effie and Adeline's friendship blooms in spite of their differences or because of them? In what ways are they similar?

5. What did you think of the character of Samson? Is he a hero in the story or a villain? Did he ever really love either Effie or Adeline?

6. Effie is confident in her skill as an embalmer, Adeline in her beauty and charm. Were there areas of their lives they seemed more insecure? Did their confidences and insecurities change over the course of the novel?

7. Death in the nineteenth century was a more common and often more intimate occurrence than today. How do our modern customs affect the way we experience death and mourning?

8. Effie remarks that no matter what Mr. Whitmark does he's "ever a traitor to one cause or another." Do you agree? Did you feel pity for him in the end?

9. There are many incidences of betrayal in the novel. Which, if any, surprised you, and which felt the most egregious?

10. What did you think about the character of Jonesy? Are there people in your own life whose imprint far exceeds the time you spent with them?

11. What if the racial equality Samson and Effie fought for had endured beyond Reconstruction? How would today's America be different?

Connect with U s

Visit us online at
KensingtonBooks.com
to read more from your favorite authors, see books
by series, view reading group guides, and more.

Join us on social media

for sneak peeks, chances to win books and prize packs,
and to share your thoughts with other readers.

facebook.com/kensingtonpublishing
twitter.com/kensingtonbooks

Tell us what you think!

To share your thoughts, submit a review,
or sign up for our eNewsletters, please visit:
KensingtonBooks.com/TellUs.